MYSTIC
SKIES

JASON DENZEL

MYSTIC SKIES

TOR

A TOM DOHERTY ASSOCIATES BOOK
NEW YORK

MYSTIC SKIES

Map by Rhys Davies

A Tor Book
Published by Tom Doherty Associates
120 Broadway
New York, NY 10271

www.tor-forge.com

Tor® is a registered trademark of Macmillan Publishing Group, LLC.

Library of Congress Cataloging-in-Publication Data

Names: Denzel, Jason, author.
Title: Mystic skies / Jason Denzel.
Description: First edition. | New York : Tor, 2022. | Series: The Mystic
    trilogy ; 3 | "A Tom Doherty Associates book." |
Identifiers: LCCN 2022019922 (print) | LCCN 2022019923 (ebook) |
    ISBN 9780765382016 (hardcover) | ISBN 9781466885707 (ebook)
Subjects: LCGFT: Fantasy fiction | Novels.
Classification: LCC PS3604.E64 M978 2022 (print) | LCC PS3604.E64
    (ebook) | DDC 813/.6—dc23/eng/20220426
LC record available at https://lccn.loc.gov/2022019922
LC ebook record available at https://lccn.loc.gov/2022019923

Our books may be purchased in bulk for promotional, educational, or business
use. Please contact your local bookseller or the Macmillan Corporate and
Premium Sales Department at 1-800-221-7945, extension 5442, or by email
at MacmillanSpecialMarkets@macmillan.com.

First Edition: 2022

Printed in the United States of America

0 9 8 7 6 5 4 3 2 1

To my mom, Joyce.

For the girl she was,
the mother she became,
and the valiant woman
she's always been.

∞

THE ISLAND OF MOTH

In the vast, unknowable Deep,
　　Where faded memories sleep.
I sailed glorious skies,
　　Unseen by your eyes.
When all fell apart,
　　It shattered my heart.
Lifting my sight,
　　I rose as the light,
And let my voice soar,
　　At last, forevermore.

MYSTIC
SKIES

ONE

THE GARDENER'S DAUGHTERS

On the island of Moth, beneath a gray-clouded sky, Pomella AnDone strolled through her garden with the High Mystic. Despite the early autumn season, the roses were in full bloom, growing beside a dizzying assortment of other flowers. Kelt Apar's garden flourished year-round under Pomella's care, a point she took particular pride in.

High Mystic Yarina sat in her wheeled chair with her hands folded on her lap, while Pomella pushed her along the winding pebbled path. Pomella paused every couple of steps to examine or prune a flower.

"I have high hopes for the lilies this year," Pomella said, making idle chitchat. Yarina, as usual, did not respond. The High Mystic nodded sleepily in her chair, likely not hearing what Pomella said. Yarina's long white hair hung loose, covering her shoulders and the pale blue shawl that hung over her black robes. A thick blanket covered her lap to keep the chill away.

Thunder rumbled overhead, startling Pomella. She caught her thumb on a thorn. "Shite," she muttered, pressing the dab of blood into her own night-black robes.

"I think we're going to have a creek poured on us soon," she said, looking at the roiling clouds. "You can count on Mothic rain like the moon phasing."

The High Mystic moaned, the sound emanated not much more than a wheezing breath. Her eyes remained closed.

"Mistress?" Pomella said, leaning close.

"P-mel," Yarina breathed.

"I'm here," Pomella replied, her voice full of concern. It was the most she'd heard the High Mystic speak in days.

"Is . . . it raining?" Yarina murmured.

"Not yet," Pomella said. "Soon, though. I'll take you inside."

The High Mystic's hand lifted and fell on top of Pomella's. "Stay," she said. Her eyes opened, revealing unfocused, clouded pupils. More than sixty years had passed since their first meeting, but the High Mystic's eyes still saw beyond this world into a deeper reality than what other people perceived.

A sudden tension knotted in Pomella's back as if she'd spent a full afternoon shouldering a heavy load. She had hoped to have a nice stroll, but now a flood of other concerns settled upon her.

Pomella peered over the edge of the garden to examine the wide grass lawn surrounding Kelt Apar's central tower. A pair of black-robed Mystics walked along one of the pebbled paths, while Vlenar chopped wood near the Wall. There were no Hunters in sight, thank the Saints.

Shifting her robes, Pomella knelt beside the High Mystic's rolling chair. She winced. Her knees had long ago ceased to be what they once were, but she still managed to find a reasonably comfortable position.

Yarina reached a bony hand to touch Pomella's hair. Later this fall would mark the High Mystic's one hundred and second year. Pomella sat with as much patience as she could muster as the older woman twirled the deep white strands.

"Still a girl," Yarina said.

Pomella forced a smile, and darted her gaze again toward Oxillian's Wall. Named for its creator, the enormous hedge Wall that surrounded Kelt Apar had stood since Crow Tallin, fifty-four years ago. In more recent years, since the Mystic Accord and the coming of the Hunters, the Wall had been fortified with supplemental walkways and watchtowers.

A pair of leather-clad Hunters walked atop its parapet, their attention focused inward toward the lawn. Even at a distance, the iron tips of their glaives sent a chill down Pomella's spine.

Many of the Hunters stationed at Kelt Apar were out on one of their so-called patrols, but Carn and his cohorts would likely be back soon. Pomella focused again on the High Mystic, trying not to let the Hunters consume her mind.

"Oh, Mistress," she said, "I stopped being a girl a long time ago."

"No," Yarina said. She swallowed, and Pomella saw moisture well at the corners of her eyes. "No titles. We're sisters."

A lump of emotion welled in Pomella's throat. In all their years together, Yarina had never said anything like that.

"The gardener's daughters," Yarina continued. "Remember?"

It seemed like the life of the stars, but Pomella understood what Yarina meant. "Yes," she said. "Lal." They'd shared the same master, and while many years had separated their tutelage with him, in the long view of decades they'd both been his students in their youth. They had both been like his daughters.

"Viv—Vivi—" Yarina tried.

"Vivianna isn't here right now," Pomella said.

"It's . . . time."

The last word trailed off in a breathless whisper, and real fear gripped Pomella. One hundred and two years stretched the potential life-span of all but the most wondrous Mystics. Yarina's eyes moved in slow motion as though she were witnessing a beautiful, wide landscape. Perhaps she was. Pomella recognized what this was and had been long prepared for it. But like many significant moments of life, now that it was here, she felt the challenge of the moment gather before her like an oncoming storm.

"Yarina?" Pomella prompted.

The High Mystic exhaled a tiny breath. Her mouth moved as though she spoke slowly and silently to somebody Pomella could not see.

Wincing slightly at a pain in her creaky knees, Pomella stood. She had to get the High Mystic back to the central tower.

Pomella closed her eyes and Unveiled the Myst. A swirling sensation of life, energy, and supreme awareness filled her. If the world was a painting, then the Myst was both the canvas and the paint, the painter and the brush, as well as the very inspiration for the art. The Myst was the energy of the universe, the breath that coursed through all existence. When Pomella reached out toward the Myst, she really reached for a part of herself. When it blossomed around her, it reaffirmed the truth of their inseparable natures.

"Ena," Pomella whispered, and a heartbeat later her hummingbird gleamed from the sky and alighted onto her outstretched palm. The little fay bird's partially corporeal feet were like twigs of cool water on her skin.

"Tell Mia, Dronas, and Master Kambay to meet us in the tower immediately. Have them prepare the anointment ceremony, including the paintings. Avoid the Hunters and be discreet."

Ena radiated worry but buzzed away, young as ever, over the tall garden flowers toward the cabins where the Mystics lived.

Next, Pomella tapped the air, letting the familiar sound of a silver bell *ting* through the garden.

The ground rumbled and rose beside her. Dirt and stone lifted upward, forming the shape of a towering, bearded man. Roses and sunflowers from the surrounding garden pulled together along with other flowers to dot his body. Polished stones formed his eyes and fallen flower petals made his beard.

"Mistress Pomella," the Green Man, Oxillian, intoned with his familiar, rumbling voice.

His face sank when he saw Yarina sitting peacefully in her rolling chair. "Oh my," he said. "Her heart beats faintly."

"She's dying, Ox."

Oxillian eased himself to one knee and reached a soil-and-stone finger to brush aside a stray strand of hair from the High Mystic's face. "So it has always been, across all the centuries, here in Kelt Apar. What of the ceremony?"

"We'll conduct it shortly. But I need something else from you. Go to the arranged location and prepare what we spoke of," Pomella said. "I will summon you again when it's time."

"Of course, Mistress." He faced Yarina again and bowed low, then took a long step backward. As his foot touched the ground, he merged back into the soil like a swimmer into water. The pebbled walkway restored itself, leaving the garden as it previously appeared. No trace of Oxillian's presence remained.

Pomella allowed herself a brief moment longer to hold Yarina's hand. A lifetime of love and admiration washed over her. The High Mystic had drifted off to sleep again, her chest rising and falling almost imperceptibly.

Light footsteps approached the garden, and if Pomella hadn't been quietly pondering at that moment she would've missed them. For a moment she worried it could be a Hunter, but these footsteps belonged to Vlenar, the old laghart gardener.

The former ranger hobbled forward on his wooden cane, which he carried not because of his crooked back, but because an old injury had rendered his left foot severely twisted. Like all lagharts, Vlenar's scales swirled in thumb-sized repeating triangular patterns across his entire body. His coloring had lightened over the years, having dulled from a deep forest emerald to a paler, stone-washed green. He wore a wide-brimmed straw sun hat that he'd woven to fit his spike-crested head.

His long tongue flicked out repeatedly, tasting the air, when he saw Yarina. Lagharts could sense the world differently than humans.

Vlenar's slitted pupils fixed upon Pomella. "Ssshe isss almost gone," he hissed.

"Yes," Pomella said. "We need to get her into the tower in order to ensure a smooth transition to Vivianna." She eyed the Wall again. One of the Hunters on patrol nudged his companion as he took notice of Pomella and Vlenar standing beside the High Mystic.

"Let's go," she said.

They left the garden together, Pomella wheeling the High Mystic toward the tower. As they walked, motes of glowing light swirled all around them. A swarm of fay geese flew overhead, and silver and gold plants turned to face them.

Above it all, more thunder sounded, and with it came the rain.

They crossed the wide lawn toward the central tower. The torrential rain drenched them, and drummed loudly on the roofs of the nearby cabins. Pomella Unveiled a small barrier above Yarina to keep the High Mystic dry, and extended it to cover herself as well. But with the wind blowing erratically, some rain still fell upon her. She generally didn't mind the feeling of rain on her skin. It kept her alert, present, and connected to the land.

Halfway across the lawn, with her feet frozen, her robes soaked, and her hair streaming with water, Pomella admitted to herself that maybe she'd had enough *connection* to the rain for now. She wished she'd brought her Mystic staff with her, but it had been impractical to carry it and push Yarina's chair at the same time.

It also put the Hunters on edge when the Mystics carried their staves. Although the Mystic Accord did not forbid Mystics from carrying them while they were within Kelt Apar, it had been argued that most Mystics would have no need to carry them if they were simply going about their daily routines.

The rain didn't seem to bother Vlenar, who limped along with his cane as if it were a summer afternoon. His eyes were far away, though, lost in thought.

Motes of silver and golden dust hovered above the grass like fireflies. Long, wispy ribbons of light raced through raindrops, chasing one another and playing to avoid being hit by the falling water. One of those wisps zoomed past Pomella, leaving echoes of faint giggling in its wake. Pomella hardly noticed. The fay were as common as clouds in Kelt Apar.

Without warning, the fay scattered. Some flew back toward the garden while others squiggled into the ground or fled toward the Wall, leaving the rain to fall undisturbed.

Pomella's chest tightened. The commotion had been caused by an approaching trio of leather-clad Hunters. Two were young men in their mid- to late twenties, while the third appeared hardly old enough to shave. The latter had the light skin and blond hair common to people from Moth. The leader, who walked in the middle of the bunch, was also from Moth, at least judging by his flame-red hair that was pulled back in a short tail. The third man had light skin but otherwise-dark features that made Pomella suspect he came from Djain. All three men carried their glaives like walking sticks in perverse mockery of a Mystic staff, only with a curved blade as long as Pomella's forearm sitting atop them. With the men standing this close, a cold and heavy emptiness radiated from the iron across Pomella's senses.

The red-haired Hunter halted Pomella and Vlenar with a raised hand.

"Something wrong, goodmen?" Pomella asked, trying to keep the disdain from her voice.

The dark-haired Hunter, a lanky fellow with a stony expression, circled around Pomella. "What's wrong with her?" he said, nodding toward Yarina.

The red-haired Hunter followed his companion's motion. "She dead or something?"

The teenage Hunter snorted a laugh.

Vlenar's tongue flicked out repeatedly in an agitated fashion.

Pomella knew he was experienced enough to not take their bait. If he lashed out, the whole compound of Hunters would swoop down on them faster than a gang of luck'ns. The Mystics of Moth were free to go about their private business on Kelt Apar's grounds, but any assault on the Hunters—their so-called guardians—was a violation of the Accord.

Her cool glance silenced the boy. "Is it funny seeing a hundred-year-old woman out in the rain? What's your name?"

Blood drained from his face. To Pomella, this boy and indeed all the Hunters were driven by fear in their hearts, beginning with their leader Carn, all the way down to this misguided young man. It was a fear born of living in a changing world. Fear that arose due to a lack of empathetic leadership from the barons, who clung to archaic prejudices. As angry as the Hunters made Pomella, as horrible as they'd been, she knew that they were the result of a world that was floundering after the Change.

A world that she'd created.

"Don't speak to her," growled Red-hair.

Pomella drew herself up taller. "Does the Accord forbid that as well?" She fixed her attention on the young Hunter. "Speak up, boy. Be quick about it. Your name."

So much for keeping her cool. The skulking Hunters always flamed her temper.

"I—um," stammered the young Hunter. He darted his attention between Pomella and his superior. "It's Bandin. Bandin AnStipe."

Pomella's heart wrenched. Her old friend Bethy had married an AnStipe. This boy could be her grandson. Which meant he was also related to Sim.

As always, the thought of her long-lost friend threatened to yank Pomella's heart from her chest. The years had softened the pain to an extent, but some wounds struck too deeply. Some losses could not be forgotten. A hollow in her heart existed now where once there'd only been Sim.

"Bandin. I'm Pomella," she said, tucking those emotions away like she always did. "This woman you skivered at is Mistress Yarina Sineese, High Mystic of Moth."

Finding some spine, Bandin replied, "I know who she is, you old—"

"Furthermore," Pomella interrupted, "she is very much alive and I guarantee that your fathir, mhathir, and grandparents all prayed for her health and blessings."

"They didn't ask her to Change the world," said the red-haired Hunter. "She and the rest of you Mystics meddled too much at Crow Tallin an' now nearly every child is a deformed monster."

Pomella kept her expression neutral. The Change had touched the whole world, beginning with the Mystwood, then spreading across Moth, to the Continent and beyond until the entire world had *shifted*, merging with Fayün, the land of the fay, its mirror twin. That union had brought together two landscapes, two worlds, countless lives—human, laghart, plant, animal, and a wide assortment of fay, as well as their respective cultures. Naturally, it had brought tremendous conflict, and the Accord was just one of the eventual outcomes of those troubles.

It was likely this Hunter's *parents* hadn't been born when Crow Tallin occurred and the Change began. Carn, as well as his enablers and followers, knew nothing of how the Change truly occurred. Devoid of truth, they spewed the conspiracies that now consumed the island.

"Even if you no longer respect her position," Pomella said, gesturing to the High Mystic, "you can show some decency for an old woman." She addressed the teenage boy directly. "You will assist me immediately, Bandin. Vlenar here will escort you to the tower."

Red-hair stepped forward, angling his glaive in the most menacing way possible. "No jagged way he's going with you, *hetch*," he said, emphasizing the vulgar term.

"What are you afraid of, Hunter?" Pomella said. "You're keeping two elders and a limping gardener out in the rain. I require Bandin's assistance and there's no law saying I cannot do that. Now you can glare at me until we're swimming in rain, or you can take your iron sticks and finish your patrol."

The red-haired Hunter glared at her. "We'll report this to Carn."

"I'm certain you will." Pomella glowered, and resumed pushing Yarina toward the tower. "Come along, Bandin, keep up."

As they passed, the dark-haired Hunter shoved a foot out and tripped Vlenar. Agile as ever, Vlenar nearly caught his fall, but his injured foot twisted wrong and he fell into the mud. The two remaining Hunters chuckled and walked away, hardly bothering to look back. Seeing Pomella's glare, Bandin thought better of laughing. He gulped once and lowered his eyes.

Vlenar found his feet before Pomella could offer to help, although she wondered if she would've had the strength by herself to lift him.

"Are you well?" Pomella asked.

The gardener wiped the mud from his coat and replaced his wide-brimmed hat. He nodded in reply but glanced menacingly toward the retreating Hunters.

"What'sss he fffor?" Vlenar said, peering at the young Hunter. His long forked tongue licked the air, tasting the boy's scent.

"We need him for the anointment. Not that any of those dunders considered the possibility," Pomella said with a nod toward the now-distant Hunters. "Bandin here will suffice."

"No way," Bandin said. "I won't be part of your profane rituals!"

"You'll witness history," Pomella said, her tone still sharp. "Take detailed notes because I'm certain Carn will have questions for you afterward. Now hurry up or I'll let Vlenar drag you. Even with his poor foot I doubt he'd have any trouble bundling you over his shoulder."

The boy wilted and grudgingly let Vlenar lead him toward the tower. As they left, two more figures hurried across the lawn toward them. Dronas and Mia were as soaked as Pomella. Mia carried Pomella's staff as well as her own in one hand, and a hooded cloak bundled in the other.

Dronas ran the last handful of steps. The rain splattered on his receding hairline. "We received your message," he said. "Master Kambay is preparing the upper chamber now." He took the cloak from Mia's arms and wrapped it around Pomella. Mia remained half a step behind, silent as ever.

Pomella accepted the cloak, grateful for its thick wool that warmed her chilly bones. It had been a gift from Baroness Elona many years ago, although now Pomella could only wear it atop her black robes. "And the paintings?" she said.

"Ready," he replied.

Dronas was a good man, patient and caring when it came to the older Mystics he tended to, though Pomella often grumbled about being treated as one of those. What he lacked in skill with the Myst he made up for in his kindness and attentiveness. Being an apprentice Mystic, especially in his mid-thirties, was about more than Unveiling the Myst.

"Let's go inside. You're as wet as a fish," Dronas said. He turned toward Yarina. His eyes widened when he saw her sitting peacefully in her chair.

Mia, standing behind Dronas, let out a tiny gasp and placed her fingers over her mouth. Pomella saw realization dawn in her granddaughter's face. Mia had a knack for knowing things before she was told.

Dronas leaned toward Yarina. "Is she—?"

"No," Pomella said. She gently took her Mystic staff from Mia, then placed her hand on the younger woman's shoulder in thanks. Her granddaughter's skin was several shades lighter than her own. The girl's strong Qina heritage stood out prominently with her round face and dark eyes. She'd inherited her mhathir's curly hair, which frizzed in the rain.

"Take the High Mystic into the tower," Pomella said. "I need to speak to Vivianna. Where is she?"

At Dronas's direction, Pomella found her friend in the nearby monument grove. Vivianna stood beside the monument itself in the middle of the circular tree clearing, clutching an old wooden lantern in her hand and using it to peer closely at the names etched into the gray-white surface. The lantern was unlit, yielding no assistance to Vivianna that Pomella could see. Kirane, Vivianna's assistant and companion, stood beside her, holding a parasol over the older woman's head to keep her dry. The grove was better sheltered from the storm than the open lawn, but rainfall still made its way in. Both women wore the thick black robes that the Mystics of Kelt Apar were required to wear by the Accord.

Kirane bowed to Pomella when she saw her but still managed to keep the parasol above Vivianna. "Mistress Pomella," she said. Vivianna continued her examination of the monument, seemingly oblivious to Pomella's arrival.

"Hello, Kirane," Pomella said. "I need to speak to Vivianna in private."

"Is everything all right?"

Pomella sighed. Kirane was a short and humble young woman, not much older than Mia. She'd come to Kelt Apar from a noble family but because of the harsh provisions of the Accord had no master to formally teach her. So instead she'd become a clerical and personal assistant. Her formal upbringing proved to be a boon when it came to handling many of the day-to-day tasks at Kelt Apar, a job that had for many years been Vivianna's.

"I'll explain later," Pomella said. "Wait for us outside the grove. We'll only be a moment."

"Yes, of course, Mistress," she said. "Um . . . could you . . . ?" She held the parasol out to Pomella.

Pomella walked forward with her staff and accepted the parasol with her free hand.

"Thank you," Kirane said, and with another quick bow hustled from the grove, leaving Pomella alone with her lifelong friend.

"Hello, Viv," Pomella began. It had taken Vivianna nearly two decades to warm to that shorter version of her name.

Vivianna turned at last, but it took a moment for recognition to dawn on her face. Her skin was remarkably smooth, despite her age. She'd always been beautiful by anybody's standards. Pomella recognized Kirane's handiwork in Vivianna's nicely up-woven hair. But Vivianna's makeup was ragged and a little smeared. She had always insisted on applying it herself. Like Pomella, she was only a handful of years away from her eightieth year.

"Pomella," Vivianna said. "Where'd you come from? You were as quiet as a flower! Where did Kirane go? She was right here."

"She's waiting nearby," Pomella said. "We'll return to the tower with her in a moment." She gathered herself and silently prayed to the Saints for strength. "We need to talk, Viv. It's about Yarina."

Vivianna straightened her back. "Mistress Yarina is fine."

Pomella hadn't expected that response. "How— What do you mean?"

"You've come to tell me that she's dead. That's why you look so somber. Well, she's not gone. Look at the pillar," Vivianna said, gesturing with the unlit lantern toward the monument. Pomella wondered where her friend had found the rickety lamp. It looked to be at least a decade or two old, its whitewashed wood flaking and its thin glass yellowed with age. Pomella sighed inwardly at the idea of Vivianna using it to apparently try to illuminate the script on the monument.

She peered where Vivianna indicated. The names of the past masters of Kelt Apar were engraved in a neat, tidy script upon the monument's surface. Lal's name was there, along with Joycean, Ghaina, and all those who had come before them.

"I don't see anything different," Pomella said, keeping her voice soft. "And you're right; Yarina isn't gone. Not yet."

"Somebody is spreading rumors then," Vivianna said, her voice full of bitterness. "I think it was Harmona. She's always had a grudge."

At the mention of her estranged daughter, Pomella kept her breathing even. "Harmona's been gone for twenty-five years, Viv. Come, sit down."

With hardly a thought, Pomella Unveiled the Myst to lift a mound of dirt and grass. As it rose, the ground reshaped itself into a small couch wide enough for both of them. Another thought, and the moisture wiped itself away, leaving a dry surface for them to sit on. Pomella seated herself, gently pulling Viviana's hand to encourage her to join her.

Once Vivianna settled and set the lantern aside, Pomella looked her in the eyes. "I'm sorry to burden you with this, but Mistress Yarina is dying. We have to conduct the anointment ceremony today, right now. We may not have much time."

Vivianna stared at her. At first, Pomella could not read her blank expression, but soon her face wilted. "I know," Vivianna whispered. Tears welled at her eyes, and it was that, even more than Yarina's impending passing, that broke Pomella's heart.

"It's time for us to be strong again," Pomella said. "She wants you to do this. Kelt Apar needs you to become High Mystic."

Vivianna looked from her folded hands in her lap to the monument of past masters. "I can feel her," she said. "She's fading, and somehow . . . somehow she's calling me. That's why I'm here, at the monument, isn't it?"

"Perhaps," Pomella replied. "You have a better connection with Yarina than anybody else. I don't doubt that you are feeling a profound stirring of the Myst. It's time to honor your teacher by inheriting the lineage she's passing to you."

They stayed that way for a long minute. The rain tapped on the parasol and ribbons of fay dancers zoomed around them. Vivianna stared at her feet. Finally, she lifted her chin. "OK, then let's go do this. Do the others know?"

"Some of them, yes," Pomella said, carefully. "Mia, Dronas, and Kambay are preparing the ceremony."

Vivianna nodded, looking for a moment like her old, focused self. "What about Tibron?"

At the mention of her husband, a lump formed in Pomella's throat. *Sweet Saints, show mercy*, she prayed silently.

"Viv, Tibron's been dead for twenty years. Remember?" Only confusion played across Vivianna's face. "Remember?" Pomella repeated in a whisper that softly carried her desperation. She felt guilty trying to correct Vivianna because it could further confuse and add to her distress. But when it came to talking about Tibron and Harmona, Pomella needed her to remember.

Vivianna was one of the few people she had left from her earlier life, her closest friend. After Sim vanished during Crow Tallin, and when Harmona left, and then Tibron died, there'd been hardly anybody else left who knew her. But she knew in her heart that in some ways, she'd now lost Viv, too.

It had started nearly three years ago, shortly after the Accord was signed and around the time Mia and Dronas came to Kelt Apar. When Pomella took her granddaughter as an apprentice, Yarina suggested Vivianna take a new one as well. Neither of them had ever taken apprentices before, except for the disaster with Harmona. Thankfully, Mia had been a dream, but Dronas hadn't been as compatible with Vivianna, especially given his lack of natural affinity for the Myst. Perhaps it was Vivianna's perception that she'd failed twice at being a master Mystic, or perhaps it had nothing to do with anything else. But after that, her once incredibly sharp mind began to slip. She forgot to complete daily tasks she'd done for fifty years. She addressed people by the wrong names, or obsessed over the most obscure subjects, such as spending nearly an hour finding the precise weight of leaves to add to Yarina's tea.

A fresh wave of sadness contorted Vivianna's face, but she managed to gather herself, as though that grounded part of her was still there, crawling for control, seeking to bring lucidity to an otherwise-muddled mind.

"Yes, of course," Vivianna said, sniffing back her sorrow. "I'm sorry. My mind slips sometimes these days."

Pomella smiled, but only to mask a deeper sadness. "It's OK. Come."

They stood, and Pomella let the grass-and-dirt couch roll back into the ground. They left the grove, arm in arm. Vivianna's tears had dried up, a distant expression settled upon her face. Pomella wondered what she saw, and what, if anything, she experienced as Yarina approached her death.

"Just a moment," Vivianna suddenly said, turning back toward the monument. "I forgot something."

Pomella opened her mouth to protest, but her friend shuffled back into the grove and retrieved her lantern. She hooked it onto a nearby tree branch.

"There," Vivianna said, and returned her arm to Pomella's.

It wasn't until they were well away from the grove, escorted by Kirane, that it occurred to Pomella that the lantern had been lit when they walked away. She looked back, but other trees blocked her view.

Her curiosity regarding the lantern passed like a dispersing cloud, though. Her greater fear was that Vivianna had most likely already forgotten about the all-important task they were about to undertake.

TWO

THE ANOINTMENT

"She'll be gone soon," Master Kambay said.

Lightning flashed outside the lone window of the central tower's uppermost chamber. Rain rapped at the glass, seeping the room with a damp cold. Pomella settled an extra cloak around Vivianna's shoulders for warmth. The other woman sat cross-legged on a cushion near the center of the room. Yarina rested on a cot beside her.

"I'm ready for this," Vivianna had assured Pomella when they'd first arrived at the chamber. Watching her now, Pomella prayed to the Saints that her friend would have the fortitude to endure this ceremony.

A drop of rain fell beside Vivianna. Pomella peered up at the rafters. The tower's roof had broken apart during Crow Tallin, nearly fifty-five years ago. At Yarina's command, the damage had been repaired but had been fixed in such a way that its broken shape could still be seen, a visual reminder of all that had occurred during those horrific days. The last days before the Change had occurred.

And it was all her fault.

Even now, after so many years had passed since Crow Tallin, few besides Pomella herself knew the secret of *how* the worlds had merged. She'd been the only witness, and she'd been the one to make the choice at the critical moment to reunite the worlds. To this day she didn't fully understand why she'd done it, but she knew with certainty that when she'd been there, floating in the Deep, at the central meeting point of the worlds, the Myst had guided her and the choice had been unmistakably correct, like a musical note sung to perfection. In that timeless moment, there had been no other choice.

Thinking of those events inevitably made Pomella remember Sim. How she wished he were there to help her. Over the years her memory of him had faded. He'd been lost, probably killed, when the Tower of Eternal Starlight vanished at the peak of Crow Tallin. She'd watched as he raced to her, trying to leap through the window that separated them before he and the tower simply vanished. Afterward, she'd spent nearly a decade looking for him, but to no avail.

Mia brushed past Pomella, bringing her back from her reverie. The young woman moved about the room, hastily preparing the final components for the ceremony. Pomella noted that her granddaughter carried a thin candle to light the others. She would've preferred that Mia Unveil the Myst to complete the task, but Mia's relationship with the Myst was different from other Mystics'. Mia herself was notably different from how Pomella had been at that same age in her apprenticeship. Even after three years of instructing her, Pomella was not much further along in understanding the young woman's unusual methods.

Near the window, Kambay consulted a thick tome by the light of a flickering candle. A pair of spectacles rested at the end of his nose. Long braided tendrils of hair with multitudes of painted beads hung from his head. The master Mystic's staff leaned against his shoulder, occasionally slipping until he absent-mindedly caught it. Candlelight played shadows across the black stripes that slanted across his otherwise-brown skin, a common pigmentation of most virga people.

"Vlenar, Dronas, and Kirane," Pomella said. "Please ensure that we're not disturbed. Mia, a hand please, dear."

Mia snuffed her candle and hurried to Pomella's side while the laghart gardener and the other two apprentices left the room. The younger woman took her arm and helped ease her onto a cushion. Mia lingered nearby, but Pomella waved her off. "By the door please," she said.

Mia inclined her head in obedience and moved to stand beside Bandin, the young Hunter posted beside the chamber's lone entrance. She kept her head down and hands folded in front of her. Wearing her black robes and with her dark hair, she seemed to Pomella to blend with the shadows. The Myst stirred around her in its unusual way, splitting and churning, swirling in ways Pomella hadn't witnessed before. She wondered what Mia experienced from moment to moment. Despite her lack of speech, she excelled at listening and at all of the tasks Pomella appointed her.

In sharp contrast to Mia's quiet gloom was Bandin. He shifted from foot to foot with his back to the wall, bleeding nervous energy. Pomella had strictly forbidden him from bringing his glaive into the tower. Without it, he looked more nervous than a cat being dragged to a washtub. He stood as far as he could get from Pomella and Yarina.

"Bandin," Pomella said to him, "you are here because the Mystic Accord requires a witness to what is about to occur. You are charged with watching and reporting to your superior when it is complete. You will not speak during the ceremony. You will not move. You will not interfere. Do you understand?"

The pale-faced boy managed a nod.

"Are you certain you want to do this?" Kambay asked Pomella. Despite the cold, a nervous sweat had already accumulated on

Kambay's receding hairline. A bushy gray beard flared out from his chin.

Pomella looked to Vivianna, whose eyes were closed in meditation.

"We must," Pomella said. "Kelt Apar needs a High Mystic."

Kambay leaned closer to Pomella, speaking only for her benefit. "I mean no disrespect," he said, "but is Vivianna capable enough for this burden? Her impairment could endanger everything."

"We are already in great danger," Pomella said. "If there is no High Mystic, then Baroness Norana will seize these lands and the Mystics of Kelt Apar will become extinct."

"It could be you then," Kambay suggested.

Pomella shook her head. "We spoke of this, Kambay. I'm not Yarina's successor. Even impaired, Vivianna has a far stronger connection to Yarina. This ritual is about more than a ceremonial passing of a title."

"Mistress Yarina knew, or at least had to suspect, that Vivianna was declining," Kambay said. "With so much at stake, I hope her confidence in her chosen successor is well founded."

Old doubts swirled in Pomella's mind. Over the years she'd had her disagreements with Yarina, ranging from the High Mystic's handling of the barons leading to the Accord to her decision to not task Oxillian with tracking criminals who walked on Moth's soil. In these and other debates, Pomella had always pushed Yarina to take more proactive actions in defense of Moth's Mystics. But the more Yarina aged, the more she clung to her ways, and the less of her reasoning she revealed.

"We cannot know the mind of a High Mystic who lives in an enhanced state of presence with the Myst," Pomella said. "Though it may defy the logic we understand, we must continue to trust in her wisdom."

Kambay placed the heavy tome on the table and gingerly closed its pages. He slipped his spectacles off and peered at the framed paintings hanging on the wall. Pomella had insisted they be brought in because tradition dictated it. It was Kelt Apar's collection of portraits of the past masters. What remained of them, anyway. Each was oil upon wood or, more rarely, canvas. One depicted Lal's young stoic face, others showed Joycean and Ghaina's muted strength, while the last shone with Serrabeth's lighthearted beauty despite its age-washed colors. Pomella had wanted a painting commissioned of Yarina years ago, but all hopes of that ended when Crow Tallin and the Accord caused Mystics to become shunned.

"Then let us pray to the past masters to guide Vivianna," Kambay said.

It began, as always, with the breath. Pomella carefully observed both High Mystic Yarina and Vivianna as they inhaled and exhaled. Gradually the two women breathed in restful unison as if they were a single being. The movements were subtle: a slight rise of their chests, and a tiny flare of their nostrils as they exhaled together.

Yarina twitched in her sleep, and Vivianna reacted by moving at the same time, in the same way. Pomella didn't know what either person saw, but judging by the way the energies of the Myst cycled back and forth between them, it was clear that *something* was happening.

Pomella slowed her own breathing, trying to harmonize with them, just in case. It occurred to her that it had often been like this over the years. Yarina had always been the center of Kelt Apar, and Vivianna the chosen successor. Pomella, in contrast, had usually been on her own. Celebrated in the early years for being the Commoner Mystic, known throughout Moth as the Hummingbird, and beloved by people all across the island. Later, in the years following Crow Tallin, Yarina had given Pomella leeway to live her life in a way that was free from the expectations that Vivianna carried. Pomella had married and had a daughter. Most Mystics never married, and it was unheard of for a High Mystic to attach themselves to a spouse or family. Vivianna had never asked for the same privilege, at least, not to Pomella's knowledge. Perhaps, having been born as noblewomen, Vivianna and Yarina both carried the expectations of duty in a way that was different from what Pomella could ever fully understand.

But now, once again, Pomella found herself on the outside of an experience that could not be hers.

Returning to the moment, she focused her awareness onto her breathing. As she did so, she visualized the Myst filling her lungs, infusing her chest and the rest of her body with power. The scent of melted wax, mingling with the tower's wooden beams and stone and mortar, blended in a unique bouquet. With her exhale, she manifested that energy, willing it to take form. After a lifetime of daily practice, this act of Unveiling the Myst was as familiar and easy to her as, well, breathing.

Mia remained still as stone near the chamber door, while Bandin still shifted uncomfortably. At least, his wide-eyed fear had subsided somewhat. If all went well, he'd report to Carn nothing more than that a pair of old women had meditated in front of each other before waking up. Pomella prayed it would be a boring experience for him.

The Myst stirred around Yarina and Vivianna. The energy of the room rumbled. Pomella's arms pebbled as though an unseen chilly wind gusted by. Yarina let out a small moan and Vivianna whispered something that Pomella couldn't hear.

Pomella caught Mia giving her a concerned look.

She shook her head slowly at Mia. They couldn't interrupt. Not now. There was nothing they could do but wait. She could only trust that Yarina knew what she was doing.

In normal times, the High Mystic and their successor would have conducted the ceremony alone. Although Pomella had never witnessed an anointment, she and Kambay had read in the tower's sparse library that it had most commonly been conducted in the Mystwood, near the southern coastline, or atop one of the many nearby peaks in the Ironlow Mountains. Lal had undergone his in the Mystwood, but Yarina had never told Pomella where she'd been anointed.

But with the Mystic Accord now strictly forbidding any Mystics from leaving Kelt Apar without permission, and with Hunters always keeping watchful guard over them, the upper chamber of the tower was the only private location available.

Yarina and Vivianna screamed in unison.

The High Mystic's eyes flared open, wide and cataracted. The screams tore through the chamber, rattling Pomella.

Vivianna's back arched in an agonizing lurch.

"What's happening!" Bandin shouted, his voice cracking.

Pomella scrambled to her feet, but her knees and hips wouldn't have it. She banged her elbow on the floor. Distantly, she was aware of pain shooting up her arm, but she had no time to concern herself with that.

"Get Kambay; go!" she shouted to Mia, who rushed from the room immediately.

The Myst stormed through the room, buffeting Pomella with its invisible strength. The tower itself creaked. Pomella's stomach knotted as the entire tower *shifted*.

Suddenly a stone punched free from the wall, flying across the chamber. It struck the opposite wall in a cloud of dust and debris.

Pomella finally found her feet and hurried to the High Mystic's side. Yarina gulped air as quickly as she could. Her wide, milky eyes found Pomella's.

"Mistress, what's—"

Nearby, Vivianna began to convulse.

"What's happening? What's happening?" screamed Bandin. "Stop it immediately! You're—you're not allowed to do this!"

Pomella ignored the boy. Yarina was speaking, but Pomella couldn't hear. She leaned her ear over the High Mystic's lips.

". . . Changed . . ."

"You have to stop this!" Bandin pleaded.

"What changed?" Pomella asked Yarina.

But Yarina's eyes looked beyond Pomella now. Her body lurched, and a wave of power rippled out from her, surging through Pomella and out of the room.

More stones ripped from the wall and tore across the room.

Using his arms as a shield against the stones, Bandin hurried to Vivianna and gripped her shoulders.

"Don't touch her!" Pomella shouted.

"Stop it!" Bandin yelled into Vivianna's face. "Stop or—"

He cut off as a stone clipped the side of his head. He gasped and staggered back, grabbing the wound. Blood glistened on his hand.

More stones stormed across the room, forcing Pomella to duck. One flew toward her face, but she Unveiled the Myst and vaporized it with a thought.

"Bandin!" she cried.

Snarling, the boy Hunter hoisted a double-fist-sized stone that had previously flown and crashed into the nearby wall. He clutched it in his bloody grip and stormed toward Vivianna with an intent to strike.

The door to the room banged open. Kambay entered, eyes blazing as much as the Myst that swirled around him. He thrust a hand out and Pomella felt the weight of the room shift as he Unveiled the Myst.

The Unveiling shoved Bandin aside, preventing him from smashing the stone on Vivianna's head. Bandin slammed into the chamber wall and collapsed.

A quiet sound, like a whispered gasp, came from Yarina. Pomella looked down at the woman still in her arms.

The High Mystic's eyes dimmed. Her body went limp. Only a wide-eyed expression of fear remained on her dead face.

The agitated energy in the room vanished. A stone tumbled to the floor mid-flight.

Vivianna's screams suddenly ceased with an agonizing choke and she collapsed.

Never, in all her anxious worries, had Pomella imagined this anointment ceremony going so horribly wrong. Yarina was dead. Vivianna lived but was now completely unresponsive to their attempts to wake her.

Bandin's wound was not deep, though it had bled a great deal, terrifying him even more than before. It had been Mia who somehow calmed his nerves when he roused, moments after she, Dronas, and Kirane rushed into the room on Kambay's heels.

Vlenar, who entered the chamber last, knelt beside Yarina and cupped her hand in his own. His long yellowed claws moved gently across the High Mystic's pale flesh. Pomella watched as the old ranger—who had once patrolled and helped defend Kelt Apar and the wider island of Moth—lowered his head beside her hand. Pomella didn't think lagharts could cry—she'd certainly never seen one do so—but she knew Vlenar had known Yarina far longer than she had. The laghart's tongue flicked out, lightly touching Yarina's hand and dragging it across her flesh before retreating and repeating. To some, Pomella knew, such a sight would seem strange, but the lagharts cherished the end of all lives, and had their own ways of honoring the dead.

"By the Saints," Dronas said. "What do we do now?" His hand rested upon Kirane's shoulder. Tears filled both of their eyes. Kirane sat beside Vivianna, stroking the comatose woman's hair and occasionally smoothing her robes.

Grief blanketed Pomella like another darker, heavier cloak than the one she already wore. She longed to fold under its weight, to yield herself to the sorrowful emotions churning inside her. Yarina was gone. The woman who'd changed her life and given her a chance to become something extraordinary.

And now, most terrifying of all, the very lineage of Mystics upon Moth was endangered. By rights, Vivianna was the High Mystic of Moth now. But something had gone wrong during the ceremony and Pomella didn't know what consequences that would bring.

Heavy though the weight of her fears and sorrow, Pomella could not grieve. Not yet. She firmed her grip on her staff and stood, only wobbling a bit.

"Give me your attention," she said to the room. Five pairs of eyes turned to her. Two others remained closed. Bandin listened but kept his gaze looking out the window.

"The next couple of hours are critical. There are eleven other Mystics living here in Kelt Apar, and some, if not most, of them are going to sense the High Mystic's passing in some fashion. When a person as attuned to the Myst as Mistress Yarina dies, the energy of their death can ripple through the Myst like a stone splashing in a pond. The others may already be wondering if something has happened. Master Kambay, your wisdom and comforting grace are needed. Inform them of what's transpired, but they must keep it to themselves. Do you understand?"

Kambay bowed, the beads in his long hair clicking against one another. Dronas rubbed his clean-shaven chin. "Have the Hunters returned from their patrol?" he asked.

"I don't believe so," Pomella said. "But they will soon. I want everyone to be informed by the time they do."

"What happens now?" Dronas said. "Is Mistress Vivianna the new High Mystic? What about the Mothic Accord?"

"Let me worry about the Accord," Pomella said, patting his

shoulder. "Please, just hurry." She wished she were as confident as she sounded.

"Yes, Mistress," Dronas said, and hurried from the chamber to gather the Mystics as Pomella had instructed.

"Kirane," Pomella said, "return to the tower after you meet with the others. We will need you to tend to Vivianna."

"Of course, Mistress," Kirane said.

"What of the High Mystic?" Kambay said, nodding toward Yarina's body, which had been covered with a sheet.

"I will arrange everything," Pomella said, steeling her voice against another surge of sadness.

"Vlenar," Pomella said, and nodded toward Bandin. The ranger understood her silent request, and took the boy by the arm. Bandin glared at the Mystics in the room but let Vlenar escort him out. He would also need to be handled soon.

The others left, but Mia lingered behind, anxious, as if she had a thought bursting to be spoken. Her curly hair fell past her shoulders onto her black robes. She was nineteen now, and Pomella longed to have the luxury of spending these precious days with her granddaughter without the Hunters lurking over their shoulders along with the constant threat of harm or worse.

But those days had not manifested in Pomella's life. Instead, she had to demonstrate strength for Mia and the others.

"Something extraordinary has happened," Pomella said to Mia, her tone of voice belying the sadness growing within her. The memory of Yarina's final, terrified facial expression, wide-eyed and slack-jawed, haunted her mind. She shoved it aside.

"It's a sad day for all of Moth, but rejoice," she said, "for today Mistress Yarina became one with the Myst. Her death is not the end, but rather the beginning of something we can't fully understand yet. She's more present, more aware, more *real*, than she was while her body breathed. It's all right to grieve, but we must also give thanks for her transcendence. With the right mind, you'll find limitless potential with her passing."

Mia studied her. Pomella could see questions and many unspoken thoughts lurking within her.

Mia lowered her eyes, then left the room. As she passed through the door, Pomella heard her whisper something that she could not understand. Times like this demonstrated that the young woman could speak, although she never did so in Pomella's presence. There was far more to Mia than she understood.

With Mia gone, Pomella was left alone in the upper chamber with Yarina's body and an unconscious Vivianna. The painted visages of the past masters stared down at her, and for once, their presence failed to comfort her.

By the Saints, what had she done?

THREE

THE LOST NAME

While Kambay gathered the other Mystics, Pomella met Vlenar at the tower entrance. Night had fallen, yet the rainstorm hadn't slackened. At Pomella's direction, the ranger carried Yarina's cloth-draped body down to the foyer. Even with the additional burden and his limp, he never faltered on the staircase.

Unveiling the Myst to keep the rain off herself, Pomella stepped outside. The rain slashed downward, washing her with cold. She tapped the air with her finger, sounding the silver chimes to summon Oxillian.

Darkness blanketed Kelt Apar. Storm clouds obscured the moon, making the shadows darker, more sinister. Dim lights from the cabin windows and from the more distant Hunter barracks fought against the gloom.

Pomella and Vivianna had known the day would come when Yarina died. They'd made the decision together to not give the Hunters, or their masters, the opportunity or satisfaction of taking the High Mystic's body. So Pomella had made arrangements in secret, and now was the time to see the plan through.

"Come," Pomella said to Vlenar when she felt certain that there were no Hunters around, gesturing for the ranger to bring Yarina's body out of the tower.

Vlenar stepped out with the High Mystic in his arms. His long tail slid over the threshold. Pomella's Unveiling extended to them, keeping them dry.

As they emerged from the tower, the wooden door behind them slammed shut. That seemed strange to Pomella. It was as though the wind had somehow caught it.

"Did you do that?" Pomella asked the ranger.

The laghart shook his head no.

Pomella pushed on the door handle, but it held fast. She frowned. There was no lock on the door.

Settling her staff into the crook of her shoulder, Pomella shouldered the whole door. Beside her, Vlenar's tongue flicked out, betraying his surprise. He generally kept the door in good working order.

"Oh, buggerish," she grumbled to herself, and stepped back. Her fingers found familiar holds on her staff as she Unveiled the Myst, willing it to move the door aside.

But the Myst dissolved like a wave crashing against a boulder, and the door remained still as stone.

A feeling of dread churned in Pomella's gut. With that Unveiling, the door should've opened at her command, even if it was locked, yet something powerful barred her entry.

She peered upward along the length of the tower. The spiraling windows set at regular intervals were all dark save for the upper chamber where Vivianna slept.

Thunder rumbled through the clouds above. Pomella knocked her staff against the door in irritation. "Bah! We'll unjam it later. As soon as Ox—"

She bit her lip. Where *was* Oxillian? Pomella looked around. Had she not rung the little bell to summon him? Perhaps it was just another one of her occasional momentary mental lapses. She swirled the Myst and tapped the air again, noting for certain that the sound radiated out.

But the Green Man did not come.

Vlenar looked at her curiously. His tongue flicked out, betraying either impatience or worry.

"Ena," Pomella said. A light like a lone star twinkled near the cabins, then became her hummingbird, rushing toward her. "Find Oxillian," she said to Ena. With only the slightest hesitation born of surprise, Ena blazed away to find the Green Man.

Pomella gripped her Mystic staff for strength. Despite the cover of darkness, she didn't like standing out here in the rain with the High Mystic's body. The Hunters could come at any moment. She tapped her toe, trying to be patient.

As she waited, she wondered again about Yarina's death. When Lal died fifty-four years ago, his body had dissolved in Pomella's arms, becoming light. Even after all these years, she could still feel the weight of his body falling away, leaving only his robes. But Yarina had not faded as their master had. The feeling of peace that had accompanied Lal's death hadn't washed over Pomella when Yarina died. Perhaps she was wrong in thinking the other Mystics would sense the master's passing. There was still so much she didn't understand.

The familiar rumbling that heralded Oxillian's arrival sounded nearby. He emerged from the ground as a towering figure formed of mud and wet grass, leaving a gaping hole where the materials for his body had been sourced. The flowing mud cycled through his body, generating a sopping, dripping mass of soil musculature and flesh. Even with the rain, the scent of fleshy-churned wet lawn filled Pomella's nostrils.

"Mistress Pomella," the Green Man intoned with his familiar, rumbling voice. "Your hummingbird tells me I missed your summons. Forgive me. What are you doing out at night like this in the rain?"

"Something happened during the anointment ceremony," Pomella said. "Mistress Yarina is . . ."

Oxillian turned to Vlenar and Yarina. He remained standing and, in the darkness, appeared rather menacing. "Curious that I did not sense her passing. Though I feel her added weight upon you, ranger."

Pomella also found that strange. As the conscious, living embodiment of Moth, the Guardian, the ceon'hur, Oxillian had supreme awareness of every living creature and plant upon the island. He had an especially strong connection with Kelt Apar and the High Mystic.

"We can't ponder that right now," Pomella said. "Take her to the arranged location. I will meet you there soon."

"Yes, Mistress."

He knelt and held out his arms, which dripped with mud. Strangely hesitant, Vlenar stepped forward and passed Yarina's body to Oxillian. Wrapped in the white sheet, Yarina stood out starkly against the Guardian's dark form.

Holding her gently, Oxillian stepped backward into the gaping pit that he'd emerged from. His soil wrapped itself around Yarina, consuming her, and pulled her into the ground. Pomella had only seen him do that on rare occasions, and it was stunning to behold every time. She did not fully understand how Yarina's body could be taken into the ground and safely transported to their predetermined destination, but such was the power and mystery of the mighty ceon'hur.

"We could all essscape like ttthat," Vlenar said. His breath puffed from the end of his snout.

Pomella bit her lip. It wasn't the first time she'd considered the idea. One by one, Oxillian could smuggle the Mystics from Kelt Apar to a place of safety. She'd even spoken to Yarina about the idea, back before the High Mystic had begun her final decline. But Yarina had been adamant that she would remain in Kelt Apar. Oxillian's power and influence were limited to Moth. The Hunters would sniff them out eventually, and the barons controlled the ports. Even Baroness Elona, the most sympathetic of the three Mothic barons, denied Mystics access to her ports. Smugglers were punished harshly, and few, if any, wanted to meddle in the affairs of those they deemed to have brought the Change upon them.

The Myst stirred around Pomella, alerting her to a new, approaching presence. A cold tingle shuddered across her skin. Her stomach twisted as though she were about to taste a foul meal.

"I'm afraid we're alone in this," Pomella said to the ranger. "No help is coming."

She turned and readied herself.

"'Tis a bit wet for a midnight stroll," came a gruff voice. The nearby darkness shifted, revealing a tall, lanky figure stepping around from the side of the tower.

Pomella's eyes narrowed at Carn, leader of the Hunters.

He was dressed in bleak attire, brown leathers beneath a black duster coat and a wide-brimmed black hat that curled at its edges. Like his followers, he carried a glaive, but his weapon bore scars and other signs of wear from use. Like its master, the glaive had taken many Mystic lives.

His coat and hat kept most of the rain off him, yet Pomella doubted anything as simple as a thunderstorm ever bothered Carn. His light skin indicated Mothic heritage, and it was as rough and cracked as dry mud. A short, scraggly beard, grown more likely from lack of care than from intentional style, only partially obscured a series of scars crisscrossing his face. His eyes, iron gray, bored into Pomella.

"D'ya need something, *Mistress*?" he asked. His lips curled in a sardonic sneer when he spoke the last word. He glanced at Vlenar and scoffed.

"None of your concern," Pomella said, keeping her voice calm. Carn might frighten most people, but she wouldn't let him intimidate her. He may have the legal right to prevent the Mystics in Kelt Apar from leaving, but he couldn't bully her around.

Carn's dark irises somehow shone in the storm-dark evening. "*Everything* that happens in Kelt Apar is my concern," he said. "Especially the mistreatment of one of my own."

Head down, Bandin emerged from behind the tower. The rain sopped him, adding to his already-dreary posture.

"He was never mistreated," Pomella said. She passed a cool gaze at Bandin, who retreated further into himself.

"That's not his accounting of it," Carn said. "He told me a great deal of interesting things."

Carn seemed to revel in harassing the Mystics, and Pomella in particular. "I dislike when you play your mind games. What do you want, Carn?"

Carn's expression darkened. "I'm not the one playing games, *hetch*. The boy says Yarina is dead. Where is she?"

"High Mystic Yarina passed away this evening. High Mystic Vivianna has replaced her."

"Nobody is replacing anybody without the permission of Baroness ManHinley," Carn said.

"That's not how the Accord works," Pomella countered.

"Where's Vivianna?"

"She's resting in the tower," Pomella said.

Carn peered toward the top of the tower, likely eyeing the now-darkened window, then returned his gaze to Pomella.

"Is that all, Carn? I'd like to return to bed now."

Keeping her chin high, Pomella stepped past the Hunter, but his gloved hand stopped her. She had to resist lashing out with the Myst. Doing so, even in self-defense against a Hunter, could be disastrous.

Carn's wet face leaned close to her ear. He inhaled a long breath through his nose. "You're afraid, *hetch*. I can smell it."

It took every bit of strength Pomella possessed to yank her arm away, and even then, she suspected he may have let her go.

"I've asked you before," Pomella said, keeping her cool, "to not use that vulgar term. Leave me be. You've harassed an old woman enough for one night."

She sensed his crooked smile on her back as she walked away. "The baroness will come soon," Carn said. "There will be an accounting."

A tempest of anger, mixed with a tinge of fear, raged in Pomella's chest like the storm overhead.

When she reached her cabin, she passed through the knee-high gate that enclosed her garden. Peering back toward the tower, she could no longer see Carn. *Good.* Her next actions had to be done delicately.

She paused a moment to catch her breath. It had been a long day. In years past, Lal had instructed her to run Kelt Apar's perimeter and do other exercises for hours. Back then, she had grumbled about the sweat and aching feet afterward, but oh, to have that youthful strength and energy again! Time was relentless in its passing, and now merely walking briskly from the tower to her cabin puffed her out.

She shook her head, clearing her thoughts. Yarina's death had made her nostalgic, but she couldn't linger in those memories. There was work to do.

Slipping around the side of her cabin, she approached her westward-facing fence and Unveiled the Myst. Circling her staff in order to *bend* the wooden pickets, she opened a path through which she could pass. Beyond that boundary, she wove the Myst around her again, pulling more of it from the air and soil and fabric of the universe until it draped around her like a cloak, concealing her from anybody who might be watching her.

Deception had never been her strength, yet she doubted anybody on Moth could Unveil this phenomenon besides her. It came now more easily after years of careful practice.

She walked the short distance to Oxillian's Wall, which loomed high into the darkness. Raised during the days of Crow Tallin by the Green Man at Yarina's command, and later preserved and augmented with iron by decree of the Mothic Accord, it stood as a visual and imposing reminder of the separation the Mystics of Moth were forced to endure.

The presence of the iron in Kelt Apar, once forbidden, now encircled the grounds in mockery. Pomella found a gap in the iron portion of the fence and slid her arm through. She pressed against the hedge and wove the Myst through the bushes. Energy spread from her palm like cold wind coming from the ocean. The nearby iron agitated her skin, but she bared her teeth and ignored the discomfort. With a final energetic *push*, a rounded tunnel appeared in the hedge. Larger it grew until finally there was just enough room for Pomella to carefully duck through.

After willing her stubborn body to cooperate, she hurried down the passage, then released her hold on it, letting the hedge return to its normal shape.

She'd come, again, to the Mystwood. Large swaths of the forest had changed over the years, but the deep portions, like here, south and west of Kelt Apar, were as untouched as ever.

An opening appeared in the clouds above but swiftly vanished, deepening the ominous darkness blanketing the Mystwood. Glowing lantern bugs, no larger than pinpricks, generated the only light. This deep in the Mystwood, in the heart of the island, the trees were ancient and full of secrets. Most of them had existed in the human realm before the Change, but some had come from Fayün as well. The latter appeared like normal trees now, save for their leaves, which shifted from silver to gold depending on the season.

"Ena," Pomella said, and an instant later her hummingbird was there, flying to her open palm. "To the cave, dear."

The little bird latched onto Pomella's finger and *pulled*.

The Mystwood enlarged around her, or, more precisely, she shrank in the blink of an eye, until she was a tiny mote drifting around her hummingbird. Instantly, Ena zoomed away from the Wall, carrying Pomella's infinitesimal form through the darkened forest. They raced through the Mystwood, ribboning over unseen paths.

Pomella materialized beside the western sea. In an instant, her feet touched stone and she returned to her normal size. It took a moment to steady herself with her staff.

Salty winds washed over her. Ena had deposited her near a ledge overlooking a jagged cliff that fell to the sea. Behind her, another cliff rose skyward, and at its summit the Mystwood came to its westernmost edge.

The storm still raged, but Pomella remained dry. Far across the ocean, stretching toward the horizon, great bolts of lightning tore through the storm clouds.

Beside her, a cave mouth yawned wide. A warm, flickering light shone from within.

Inside, she found the familiar cavern that stretched about twenty steps deep and half as many wide. The scent of sandalwood incense, wax, and the ocean wafted around her. The cave also reminded Pomella of a similar, larger cavern near the summit of MagDoon, the tallest mountain on Moth.

Oxillian hunched against the southern wall, his body composed entirely of the same stone that the cave was made of. Plates of hard rock, inked with lines of lighter-colored stone, formed his body that had to crouch to fit beneath the ceiling.

Oxillian lowered his head in a bow. "Mistress Pomella."

"Hello, Ox," Pomella replied. "I trust all is well?"

"Yes. Everything is ready."

Pomella shifted her attention to the back of the cave where

Yarina's body lay beneath a large blanket atop a stone altar. She recognized the smooth angles of the dais as Oxillian's handiwork, something he'd drawn forth from the cavern floor. Four small candles had been lit, two on either side of the High Mystic.

Pomella walked to the back of the cave and leaned her staff against the wall before Unveiling the Myst to lift a small stone stool from the ground beside Yarina. Easing herself onto the seat, she placed a hand on the blanket covering the High Mystic.

"When will you tell the Hunters?" Oxillian said, voicing the very question Pomella had been asking herself.

"They already know," Pomella said. "The baroness will come to Kelt Apar soon. But I need time to think. Did you bring the colored candles?"

"Yes," Oxillian said. He stepped aside revealing a shelf that he'd extruded from the cave wall. Atop it sat five candles, each a different color. Each represented one of the other High Mystic dwellings across the world. Red for Icelance Castle in the baronies of Rardaria. Deep blue for the Gardens of Enduring Light in Keffra. Purple for Shenheyna in Qin, yellow for Iotepa Falls in Djain, and white for Indoltruna in Lavantath, the liberated nation of lagharts. In each home of the High Mystics, a matching set of candles waited, along with a green one representing Kelt Apar to replace their own. When one candle was lit, its matching peers also were illuminated, signaling the High Mystics that their presence was requested.

Pomella Unveiled the Myst with barely a thought, lighting the yellow and white candles. Then she waited.

"Ox," Pomella said after some minutes had passed. "Why didn't you come when I sounded the silver bell?"

Oxillian's stone-polished eyes considered her. "I never heard it," he said. "I only learned afterward that you had summoned me."

"Something strange is happening," Pomella said. "I intend to discover what."

Pomella waited with the patience of the moon until, perhaps half an hour later, the yellow candle flame brightened. The Myst stirred around Pomella, and a fresh scent of pine-tinged air emanated through the cave.

A ghostly apparition materialized near the candle, silver and gold mixed together, depicting a thin, hunched figure.

High Mystic Willwhite was easily a decade, perhaps two, past one hundred years old but hardly appeared a day over ninety. The remains of their white hair were cropped close to their scalp. They had a pale complexion and whisper-thin frame that came with a heavy stoop. Their short staff, no longer than the length of their forearm, hung from their belt on a loop of thread.

Pomella had known Willwhite since those fateful days of Crow Tallin but had only been in their presence a handful of times. The High Mystic's gender was fluid, shifting from woman to man and back again as the moon waxed and waned. Currently they appeared more masculine, although their extreme age made it more challenging to discern a difference. It occurred to Pomella as she watched Willwhite's apparition drift closer to her that at the beginning of human life, and at the end, the difference in genders was less apparent. Like the Myst itself, where all life came from and returned to, there was no separation or contrast between identities. It amazed her that simply by living life, the High Mystic demonstrated a lesson of how everyone was one with the Myst, even if they didn't realize it.

"High Mystic Willwhite," Pomella said, standing and bowing. "I am glad, as always, to see you."

"Pomella, old friend," Willwhite said. "I had not expected you to be the one to light the candle."

The flame upon the white candle flared momentarily and another figure materialized in the cave.

Lean and sinuous, High Mystic Hizrith, a laghart, stepped forward to stand beside Willwhite. Like Vlenar, he had the triple-swirling scale pattern across his body, though the colors were muted by his incorporeal appearance.

Willwhite and Pomella bowed to the newcomer, who returned the gesture along with a flick of his tongue.

"Master Hizrith," Pomella said. "Thank you for attending my summons."

"I came asss sssoon asss my apprenticcce told me of the candle," Hizrith replied. "What can I assissst you withhh?"

A gust of wind howled through the cave like a bird caught indoors, blowing past the candles and threatening to snuff them out.

"Beloved masters," Pomella said, "I regret to tell you that High Mystic Yarina has passed into the Myst."

Hizrth's tongue flicked in and out rapidly in what Pomella assumed was surprise and sadness.

Willwhite nodded their head, a solemn expression coming across their face as they glanced at Yarina's covered body. "She was a great Mystic," they said, "and her passing blesses us all."

"Where isss her apprenticcce, Vivianna, now?" Hizrith asked.

Pomella straightened her spine. "She is incapacitated. This is one of the reasons I needed to speak to you. Something went horribly wrong. During the anointment ritual they both began to scream. The High Mystic died in my arms with a look of surprise and terror I'll never forget. Vivianna has been unconscious ever since."

Hizrith looked at the other unlit colored candles. "Where are the other High Mysticsss? They ssshould know."

"I summoned only the two of you because I've known you the longest," Pomella said. "The others are younger, and, unfortunately, bound far more tightly to the whims of a society that seeks to undo us. They've lived only in the Changed world, and I fear our traditions and way of life ended with their predecessors."

Willwhite's face softened. They let out a long sigh. "How, then, can Hizrith and I help you?"

"I need to know what to do," Pomella said. "With Yarina gone, the lineage of Moth should have passed to Vivianna, but I don't know what failed during the ritual. Can you tell me what is supposed to happen during the anointment?"

"An anointment has many purposes," Willwhite said. "But at its most fundamental level, it is a ritual in which a High Mystic passes the Mystic name of their domain to their successor. In doing so they pass mastery and control of the land. This name is secret, hidden, and generally not a word that can be spoken using human—or laghart—speech. It is the true name of the land that resonates with the domain's very existence. By tradition, the High Mystic passes that name to their successor when the time is right. Kelt Apar and the island of Moth. Shenheyna. Iotepa Falls. The great Gardens of Enduring Light. Indoltruna. Icelance Castle. These are the established domains of High Mystics in our world. Those who know the land's name become its stewards."

A harrowing fear loomed in Pomella's heart. "And what if that name is not passed on?"

"If it is lost," Willwhite said, "then the land will wait for one to come and find it once more."

Pomella placed her hand on her forehead to steady herself and then took a calming breath. "I don't know if Yarina successfully passed the Mystic name of Moth to Vivianna," she said. "At least, I won't know until she wakes up."

"If ssshe wakes," Hizrith said.

Pomella looked at him, wide-eyed.

"Master Hizrith may be right," Willwhite said. "Vivianna may not awaken. The anointment ceremony is not without danger. Did Vivianna have an apprentice?"

"She did, yes, nearly thirty years ago," Pomella said, feeling an old anxiety rise. "My daughter, Harmona. But she had no affinity for the Myst and proved to be a difficult student. She left Kelt

Apar only two years after becoming an apprentice and never returned. She prefers her life of luxury in Qin." The sadness, even now, was difficult to keep from her voice.

"There were no other apprenticesss? Even sssecret oness?" Hizrith asked.

Pomella had come to learn over the years that Mystics, in their strange ways, sometimes saw fit to take a second apprentice when tradition had always dictated that they take only one at a time. Sometimes, in situations like Lal's, the master simply wanted to take on a second student they saw promise in. Other times a master would have a child, which was another taboo, and wanted to train them. Or sometimes there were even more unusual scenarios, such as when a master took a lover and trained them as part of that arrangement.

Regardless of how it occurred, the first apprentice always inherited the master's lineage, while subsequent students taken later in life did not. Pomella was one such apprentice. Lal's first student had been Yarina, and Pomella his second.

"No others," Pomella said. "Yarina had hoped Vivianna would take a second one, a young man named Dronas who lives in Kelt Apar now, but he has even less affinity for the Myst than Harmona did, and nothing was ever formalized. Vivianna and I were very close. She would have told me if there'd been another.

"You think something harmed them during the ceremony?" Pomella said.

"It is a different journey for each person," Willwhite said. "But if the successor is guided by their master, there are rarely problems. But we live in a Changed world now. The Myst is ever evolving, especially in these decades following Crow Tallin."

"Well, whatever happened," Pomella said, "Yarina is gone and Vivianna is incapacitated. Baroness ManHinley has no love of Mystics and she'll use this as an opportunity to end our lineage. Or worse."

A memory, of long ago, flashed to Pomella's mind, of her holding a baby with a scratch on her face. Little tyke Norana, whom Pomella had once rocked in her arms, sweet as a lamb, had grown to become the mastermind behind the Accord.

"It seems then," Willwhite said, "that you may have a considerable crisis in front of you. If the Mothic lineage is broken, then a vacancy will arise. Tell me, since Yarina's death, has Kelt Apar seemed strange?"

"The tower," Pomella said, almost to herself. "It became locked and would not open, even when I Unveiled the Myst." More realization washed over her. She turned to Oxillian. "And Ox, he could no longer hear the call of the silver summoning bell."

"Then it is so. Kelt Apar is without a master," Willwhite said, their grave words echoing through the cave. They looked at Oxillian, who sat silently in the deepest part of the cave, watching them. Ox's stony face betrayed no emotions. "The island's Guardian is untethered. The tower will remain locked until one comes to claim it."

"Have you told othersss of Yarina's passsing?" Hizrith asked.

Pomella nodded slowly, thinking through the situation. "The Hunters know Yarina is gone. Carn, their leader, will tell the baroness immediately, though it will likely take two days for news to reach her in Port Morrush."

"Then the vacancy must be filled," Willwhite said.

A thousand thoughts and emotions tumbled through Pomella, but she stilled them until only determination remained. She voiced the answer she knew in her heart.

"It has to be me," she said.

Willwhite smiled. "There is no other."

Pomella looked from Willwhite to Hizrith, waiting for one of them to say more. Both of their faces remained impassive, as if carved from stone, although Hizrith's long tongue licked the air.

"The Myst," Willwhite said, continuing as they watched these thoughts tumble through her, "works through lives in the most unexpected of ways. You have traveled its depths, Pomella, and abided in its river, knowing how perfect its course always runs. Is it truly a surprise that the Myst would find you, a commoner, and lead you to Kelt Apar, through the fires of Crow Tallin, and now here?"

"I am not special," Pomella said, unable to keep the snap from her voice. "I've been fortunate and had privilege, and by the Saints I'm old enough to have no shame and admit I have talent. But no, High Mystic, I do not believe I am a hero chosen by the Myst to save Moth. I stopped believing in chosen heroes long ago."

The memory of Saint Brigid, and the horror she had turned out to be, would forever be a lesson Pomella would remember.

"Even so," Willwhite said, "Kelt Apar calls for a master. If you do not inherit the lineage, another will. A vacancy in Kelt Apar will attract all those hungry for power. The Iron Mystics. The shadowy Lognics of Veena. Others."

Storm winds from outside shuddered through the cavern. The yellow and white candles holding Willwhite and Hizrith's presence wavered.

"How?" Pomella asked at last.

Willwhite spoke in little more than a whisper. "You must find the Mystic name of the island," they said.

"If it was never passed on, where do I find it?" Pomella asked.

Willwhite glanced at Hizrith, who nodded back to them.

"You must go into the Mystic Skies," Willwhite said. "You have seen and walked them before, I believe, although perhaps you may not have known what they were. There are other worlds besides our own. Worlds of possibility. Parallel realms where what we perceive as time has different meaning. We live on but a single page of a great book, with countless worlds above and below us. Our human world and Fayün were once like adjacent pages, but are now merged. The further you travel into this tome, the stranger the Skies will become.

"Somewhere, in one of those worlds, perhaps on the furthest pages, lies the root of all names, and it is there you must go."

Pomella shook her head. During the days of Crow Tallin, she had indeed experienced some strange visions and seen other worlds, but she'd also been guided by the presence of her master Lal.

"I am an old woman," Pomella said. "I thought my days of adventure were long past."

"Our troubles do not abandon us like our youth," Willwhite said. "I believe you will find, as I have learned, that the greatest challenges and the sweetest triumphs are found in the sunset years of our lives."

The storm and ocean thundered around Pomella as she stood outside the cave. This time, she let the water soak her. Willwhite's and Hizrith's candles had long ago burned down, leaving her alone.

"My massster, *Zurnta* Ehzeeth, once told me," Hizrith had said to her before he left, "that it isss easssiest to enter the Ssskies as the moon isss full."

"On the evening you choose, light my candle at sunset," Willwhite had said, "and I will see you off on your journey."

Together they gave Yarina the proper funeral rites and dissolved her body into the island so it would rest forever with the land she'd presided over. Pomella had thought of singing, but the words and music had died in her heart.

Like Sim and Tibron, Yarina was gone from her life forever. Gone from Kelt Apar. But she still had purpose. Moth needed a High Mystic to guide it and to protect its beauty and its people.

The storm raged harder around her. It was as though the sky knew it had been freed from the tether. Rain and wind surged like a wild stallion. The storm winds battered Pomella as a massive wave crashed against the cliff, showering her with salty mist.

"Seek the beginning to find all ends," she said to herself, recalling a saying she'd once heard.

She made her decision.

Lifting her Mystic staff, Pomella Unveiled the Myst. She pulled deeply from the stone she stood upon, from the Mystwood behind her on the cliff top, from the ocean, from the sky, and from herself. She swirled her staff as though stirring a large pot, churning the Myst around and around.

Crow Tallin had infused her, and nearly all Mystics, with tremendous power. That surge of power had faded when the celestial event ended, leaving them hollow for months afterward. But now, driven by need, Pomella pulled more of the Myst, this time, from the depths of her lifelong understanding and experience. She might be old of body, with not much physical strength left to her anymore, but the Myst was her unwavering companion and it was mighty.

"Calm," she murmured, still stirring her staff.

And at her command, gradually, the storm subsided, leaving dissipated clouds, and revealing the glorious blue sky of the new day.

FOUR

THE SNAKEBITE

The skies above Brigid sang with birdsong. Despite distant storm clouds threatening rain, she didn't think she'd ever seen skies more blue, more perfectly crisp in their reflection of the wide ocean. She stood in a dirt field—*her* dirt field—holding the long handle of a bronze-tipped hoe. She'd have to finish working the modest-sized field soon, before the rain returned, or she'd be hoeing a mud pit.

A flock of white seabirds circled above, crying their song. One of them drifted away from its peers and meandered down to settle on the thatch roof of Brigid's home standing a short distance away. What the house lacked in complexity it made up for with a sturdy frame. She'd built it herself, having refused the halfhearted offers of help from the other colonists. She hadn't been rude in her rebuffs, but she and they both knew everyone was more comfortable at a distance. Their past disagreements were gone, she hoped, along with her old life that had been full of pain. She'd buried those memories in this field along with the darker memories of her husband and the violence they'd endured.

She wiped sweat from her brow using a tattered sackcloth rag she kept on her rope belt. The only sound she could hear, besides the occasional cry from the birds, was the low, steady churn of the ocean.

Freedom and silence. Those were all she had ever wanted.

A pang of concern rose within her. Where was Janid?

She looked back toward the house, seeking her son. It was never good when he was quiet. She generally let him roam free while she worked, and he usually played by himself in a place she could see or hear him.

A familiar cry split the air, igniting her motherly instinct.

She let the hoe fall from her hands, and before it landed on the ground she was sprinting toward her home. She found Janid on the far side of the house, lying on the ground crying beside a large woodpile.

"Myyy-ma!" he cried, his tears coming faster as soon as he saw his mother.

"I'm here, Sunshine," she said, scooping him up to his feet and dusting him off. He threw his arms, long and gangly for his five years of age, around her neck and clung tight.

It must have been a small, harmless tumble off the woodpile, hardly an incident that would keep her awake at night fearing for her son's safety. It was just the two of them living on the homestead, about a mile and a half from the settlement. She scouted the region regularly, and occasionally spoke to some of the other outlying farmers about the dangers presented by the island. From what she'd learned, there was little in the way of real danger in the area besides the usual assortment of hungry animals who might attack if provoked. The exception may've been the strange lizard-people, who lived in the nearby forest but seemed reluctant to interact with the colonists.

Her eyes went briefly to the circular brand burned onto her forearm. Whatever natural dangers her new home threatened her with, they were nothing compared to the horror of her old life.

She eased herself from Janid's tight grip and wiped his face. "What am I going to do with you?" she chided, not without affection. "Myma has to work, and every time I turn my back, you're scrambling up a woodpile. Before I know it, you'll be jumping off the roof!"

Seeing her smile, Janid's eyes lit up. He glanced at the roof of their home and Brigid could already see the boy's mind working on how he could get up there. She made a mental note to ensure there was nothing he could climb to reach the top.

"Are you hungry?" Brigid asked, already knowing the answer, of course. With the rate he was growing, she'd need to plow an entire second field and sow it with wheat and beans just to satiate his voracious hunger.

Janid nodded. The lad hadn't spoken any words besides "Myma" since that terrible day his father had been killed and she'd received her forearm brand. Brigid had many hopes for their new life, one of which was that this island would give Janid the peace he needed to find his words.

With a pat on the behind, Brigid sent him into the house, telling him to portion out two scoops of meal from the wooden bin. "Bring some of that wood in next, while I go to the creek. There's a storm coming tonight, so we'll prepare a fire and read a tale. How does *The Song Thief* sound to you?"

Janid nodded his head vigorously before scampering into the house. She sighed as she saw the state of his pants. A full hand length of pale skin showed around his ankles, reminding her that she had to lengthen his worn trousers. That would require more sackcloth, which meant another trip to the trade post.

She grabbed her bronze bucket that sat beside the house—one of the few remaining items from her husband's trade—and carried it across the field in the direction of the distant western mountains. She'd heard that the colonists had begun naming some of the summits in their new land, and that the sharp mountain to the west had been named after the captain of their ship.

MagBreckan.

It was as though somebody had whispered the name to her. No, that wasn't the captain's name, and it wasn't a name she'd heard the colonists mention, but perhaps her memory was short on account of being tired. Brigid shrugged the thought away. She didn't care what her fellow colonists named things. They could name the mountains after themselves if they liked. All she wanted was her quiet home and life with her son.

The creek was far enough from the house to be out of sight, but still within reasonable walking distance. It ran, smooth and twisting, around the curves of the land, cutting a path between hills. Trees grew along its bank, fir and oak with a scattering of aspen. A dense forest lay to the southwest, but none of the colonists had explored it that she knew of.

The blue skies gave way to swiftly approaching storm clouds. One thing you could always count on here was rain. She came to the edge of the creek where a large, flat rock provided a natural and convenient ledge for her to dip her bucket easily into the water. Brigid hunched down and braced herself as she stretched her arm low over the lip of the rock, holding tight to the bucket as rushing creek water swirled into its belly. The heat from the sun-warmed stone radiated up her arm.

A silver wisp of light from the far side of the creek caught her attention. It was like sunlight reflecting off fog. Two glowing rabbits hopped through bushes, but their passing didn't disturb the foliage. Brigid stared in wonder. Steam-like tendrils wafted off the animals.

A sharp pain stabbed her free hand. It was like a thousand bees stinging her at once. Cursing, she dropped the bucket and yanked her hand back. The strange rabbits leaped away and vanished.

A red-and-white snake, as wide as her thumb, lifted its head from where her hand had been. It waited, poised to strike again if needed.

Instinct took over and Brigid scrambled away, clutching her hand. She looked at her wound and saw puncture marks on the meaty portion of her palm beside her thumb. Already it had begun to swell with an angry, pulsing red. Pain blazed through the wound, hotter and more intense than she would've expected.

The snake lowered its head and slipped from the rock. Tendrils of thin silver steam, like she'd seen on the rabbits, wafted as it moved. Somehow, impossibly, it seemed as if the snake were not fully present in the world. It was opaque, yet not completely solid, either. Its body appeared made of light, but that made no sense. The snake vanished into a hole she had failed to notice.

With her no longer able to feel her fingers, Brigid's heart hammered inside her chest. She'd heard of snakes that could kill a person with a single, venomous bite. She shook her hand, irrationally trying to fling the danger from her hand. She put her mouth over the wound and tried to suck out the venom, but all she tasted was the tinge of her own blood.

She abandoned the bucket. All rational thought flew from her head as the tingling sensation spread up her arm. She stumbled and ran back toward her house, calling for Janid when she got close.

She found him inside just as she finished tying a long strip of cloth tight around her forearm. The boy was hunched on the floor, trying to scoop up a pile of meal that he'd accidentally dumped on it.

"Myma," he said, his voice full of apology as he pointed to the pile of oats.

"It's OK, Sunshine," Brigid said, her voice cracking from worry. "Leave it. We have to go. Come here."

"Myma?" Janid said.

She grabbed his hand into her own uninjured one and hurried him to the door. "We have to go to the settlement." He still had his thin, handwoven shoes on, which was good.

Her mind raced as they hastened to the colony. Storm clouds surged from the west. Janid kept pace without complaint. This wasn't the first time she'd grabbed his arm and told him to hurry.

She risked a glance at her wounded hand but looked away quickly upon seeing that the edges of the puncture marks near her thumb had turned a slight shade of purple. It still burned like fire.

"Hurry, Sunshine," she said to Janid, and pulled him faster.

They arrived at the outskirts of the colony, which bustled with people making last-minute preparations before the coming storm. Naturally, the first person Brigid saw was one she despised most.

Engatha's imperious glare—a holdover from her noble upbringing—was as haughty as ever. Life as a struggling colonist had grayed her, but her hawklike eyes contained the same intensity. Upon seeing Brigid, those eyes narrowed. But before Engatha could scold Brigid for showing her face in the colony, Brigid hurried to her and spoke first. She had no time for past conflicts.

"I need you to watch Janid," Brigid gushed. "Please."

Engatha's expression softened. She was a mother of five, Brigid knew, and despite her jealousy and petty misplaced anger, she was a mother who recognized one of her own.

The other woman carried a wide basket of potatoes, beets, and cabbage in her arms. She shifted it to her hip. "What happened?" Engatha asked.

"Where's the hobbist?" Brigid asked in a rush.

"Are you all right?"

"I just need you to watch him, please." She debated telling the woman about the bite, but Janid was scared enough as it was.

"I can't explain," she said.

Engatha considered her, and for a moment Brigid was certain she would reject her. Engatha's husband, who Brigid heard had been gored in a hunting accident last year, had attempted to force himself onto her shortly after the voyage, in those first terrible early days of the colony. When Brigid had rejected him, he'd turned the colony against her, claiming that she'd offered herself to him in ex-change for protection and assistance. Being a widow with a young child in a new land was hard enough, but from then on Brigid had to contend with the judgmental stares and not-so-quiet mumbling from the other colonists.

Yet all along, Brigid had seen something in Engatha's expression that told her that Engatha knew the truth. No one could hide from their partner's all-seeing heart forever.

"He's in his house," Engatha said, pointing south toward the edge of the colony. "Janid will be safe."

Brigid passed Janid's hand from her own into Engatha's. "Thank you."

Engatha nodded, and Brigid noticed the other woman's gaze flick to her wounded hand.

"Myma?" Janid asked as she pulled away. "Myma!"

"I'm sorry, Sunshine," Brigid said, her voice cracking again. "I'll be back soon."

She knelt to meet her son eye to eye. His eyes were light like hers, and his hair had a reddish tinge to it. He resembled his father in stature and size, but his face was hers.

Brigid willed herself not to show her fear. She wouldn't let her son's final memory of her be filled with sadness or anguish.

"Stay with Engatha; she'll take care of you."

"Myma," the boy whimpered.

She hugged him fiercely. "I love you, Sunshine."

Before Engatha could question her more, and trying to ignore Janid's sudden cries that followed her, Brigid ran toward the hobbist's house.

The main portion of the settlement consisted of approximately twenty structures, mostly homes, along with a smith, and a lumberer. They'd had plenty of farmers, of course, and a silver merchant, who'd proved his usefulness in helping the colony establish a fair system of barter among themselves.

And there had been a hobbist.

Brigid found the man's house on the edge of the colony. Even by the lowly standards of the settlement, his hut was sadly dilapidated, with a poorly thatched roof that was certain to leak once the rain broke over the island. A bundle of dry herbs and purple-budded flowers hung from a nail on the stick-thin door.

"Hello?" Brigid called out. The pungent scent from the herbs washed over her. Sandalwood, she recognized, and the flowers were lavender.

"Hobbist? It's me, Brigid. I need help."

The door opened and a scraggly man with a tangled gray beard opened the door. "Ah, yes?" he said, squinting at her.

A stifling odor of untold herbs wafted over her.

"I've been bitten by a snake," Brigid said, lifting her hand to show the man. Her hand shook as the hobbist peered at it.

"Ah, come in, come in," he said, stepping aside. He licked his lips and brushed his beard with his hand as if suddenly conscious of his appearance.

The hut was filled with herbs hanging from the crooked ceiling, warped clay pots overflowing with strange powders, and an assortment of animal furs that served as both wall decoration and practical floor rugs.

"Bring it to the light," the hobbist said.

Brigid held her hand near the hut's lone lantern. The hobbist, whose actual name she either couldn't recall or had never known, held it and peered so closely that his nose brushed her wrist. Red lines now crept up her forearm, toward her elbow like swiftly growing ivy.

"Mmm," he said, "looks bad. When'd it happen?"

"Less than an hour ago," she said, her heart beating faster.

"The venom works fast."

"Can you do anything?" Brigid asked.

"Possibly. Tell me 'bout the snake."

She couldn't worry about that now. She told the hobbist everything she could remember about the snake, even as she worried he may not believe a word she said about ethereal snakes and rabbits.

The hobbist listened with a concerned expression upon his face. "I've never heard of such things before," he said. "But most of the island's creatures are still strange to me."

A lump formed in Brigid's throat. "I have a son. He needs—" She choked on her words.

The hobbist patted her shoulder. "Sit, sit. We will try to pull the venom out."

He bustled around the hut, mumbling to himself and grinding herbs into a smelly concoction. Brigid sat as patiently as she could until he applied the odd, green paste to her wound. The pain pulsing from the bite wound hadn't subsided, and the herbs didn't help. She winced as the hobbist applied a thick dose of the paste until her entire thumb and wrist were covered.

"Rest, rest," he said, motioning her to lie on a fur rug before he began prepping tea.

Brigid gritted her teeth. Was this all he could do for her? Apply some stinky herbs and make her drink tea? Shouldn't he be cutting the wound open to drain the venom? Her mind raced with other, more extreme solutions, too. How long did she have before she'd have to sever her arm? If it kept the venom from her heart, perhaps that was the only solution.

She was about to ask when movement by the door caught her attention. It was gone in a heartbeat, but for a brief moment Brigid had seen a young woman, with long dark hair and wearing a dress that shone like snow beneath a spring sun, her eyes glimmering in the lantern light.

Brigid shook her head, fearing that the venom was causing her to hallucinate.

The hobbist handed her tea. "Drink," he urged.

"Are you certain this is how to treat a serpent bite?" Brigid asked.

"The tea will help you rest," the hobbist said. "It will slow the poison."

Reluctantly, Brigid drank the tea and sat back. The hobbist

chatted at her, but Brigid quickly lost track of what he was saying. Her mind became foggy and soon she drifted in and out of sleep.

"Will I die?" she mumbled.

"No, no," the hobbist said. "I will stay with you. Tell me about your son."

Brigid spoke, but her mind was lost in a fog. "I . . . don't . . . have a son. Only a brother. And . . . and, no, I have a sister, too. But . . ."

Sleep pulled her into its embrace, and she dreamed of fire, and sickness on the ocean, and pain coursing up her arm. She twisted and moaned through her dreams.

A pressure on her arm woke her. Her eyes fluttered, not wanting to open. The room blurred into focus and she found the hobbist sitting beside her, examining her forearm brand.

Anger flared within her. She knocked his hands away.

"Mark o' the Dragon King," the hobbist said in a low voice. "Didn't know we had any o' you aboard."

"I'm . . . not . . . my past," Brigid said. Her mouth was too stuffed with fog to speak more clearly. "The bite. What . . . I do?"

"You need to rest," the hobbist said. He pressed her back down. "Sleep, sleep. It will help the medicine."

Pain pulsed through Brigid's arm still. She had to do something. She wouldn't sit idle. People who gave up and rested in the Dragon King's warrens never got up. She and Janid and her husband had only escaped that labyrinth because they'd kept moving.

We do what we always do. We move, and we survive.

Brigid sat up, and shoved the hobbist away when he tried to ease her back down again.

"I can't stay here," she said, forcing herself to articulate the words.

"You need—"

"I need a cure for this venom!" she snapped. Her frustration helped clear her head. Helped her focus. "If you don't have something to help me, then I'll find it elsewhere. But I won't die waiting around."

She wobbled to her feet and made her way to the door, clutching her wounded hand to her chest.

"The southern forest," the hobbist said.

Brigid paused at the door.

"I haven't seen animals like you described," he continued, "but I gathered a flower in the forest. The petals were like flowing rain, and light dusted off each one. I powdered it and drank it in my tea and slept better than I ever have. Woke the next morning feeling decades younger. Perhaps this flower is like the snake and rabbits you described. Perhaps it will help where my medicines will not."

"Will you show me?" Brigid asked.

The hobbist dropped his gaze, unable to look at her. The shamed expression on his face told her all she needed to know. He was afraid.

"Thank you," she muttered, and left the hut.

It was late afternoon, and the storm clouds had arrived. An occasional raindrop landed on her, promising more of its kind. Brigid considered going to get Janid, but even with the hobbist's concoction covering her wound, it still burned like fire and didn't look any better than before.

She had to find another way. Perhaps the flower would be the answer. Where else could she go?

Time and again she'd survived on her own. This would be no different. She didn't need these people.

But Janid did. If this venom was going to kill her, he would need them.

"Onward," she muttered to herself, and took a step toward the forest. "Find a cure and come back to your son."

FIVE

THE UNCLAIMED MYSTIC

Mia didn't like this plan at all.

It was one thing to hold secret rituals, and another to try and hide it right under the Hunters' noses.

The storm had raged through the night and into the morning, but she didn't think that it would dissuade the Hunters from making an unannounced visit to their little conspiratorial gathering. She sat on a stool in the corner of the cabin near the door. She kept her elbows propped on her knees while her hair spilled down either side of her face. Dronas and the other Mystics fidgeted.

"For a bunch of Mystics," Rion mumbled, "they sure cower a lot."

Her brother leaned against the wall beside her. His arms were crossed over his chest and one of his knees popped out as he rested his foot against the wall. She glared at him. Rion had very little respect for Mystics. He reminded her of their mother in that regard.

They were in one of the older cabins, which meant it could have been a century and a half old, and it was especially cramped. The shuttered windows made the room stuffy, and limited the daylight streaming in. But they dared not let themselves be seen like this. It would raise too many questions with the Hunters.

Everyone had heard the news by now. Mia suspected none of them had slept. She certainly hadn't.

Finally, Master Kambay broke the silence by standing and clearing his throat. The dim light of the room played upon him.

"Here we go," muttered Rion with a conspiratorial wink at Mia.

"I'm glad we've gathered to talk about this," Kambay said with his thick Keffran dialect. "I've lived on Moth for twenty-five years. Though my time here has mostly been in the mountains, and wandering the forest, I always knew this domain was well cared for under Mistress Yarina's watch. I'm glad I knew her, and could call her friend. Now, I'm honored to be the first to call her Grandmistress."

"I'm sure he'll enjoy being one of the highest-ranking Mystics left," Rion muttered. Mia slapped at his leg but missed. He shrugged at her as if to maintain his innocence but kept more mutterings to himself.

Dronas nodded and raised his Mystic staff. "To Grandmistress Yarina."

There was a shuffling of wooden staves as each Mystic and apprentice raised theirs. Mia joined them, not wanting to stand out.

"Grandmistress Yarina," the others whispered in unison. Kambay sat, settling himself beside his red-haired apprentice, Shillo.

Dronas coughed softly and unnecessarily for attention. "Thank you, Master Kambay. Perhaps some of us could share stories about her while—"

Mia didn't hear what Dronas said next because Rion suddenly stiffened beside her and snapped his attention toward the door. Dronas continued on, but Mia kept her attention on her brother.

Rion wasn't a Mystic, not exactly, anyway, but he sensed things nobody else could. Her heartbeat quickened, raising her anxiety. She didn't like when he had that look on his face because it reminded her of their father, whom Rion had begun to look more and more like every day.

She fixed him with a questioning look, but Rion ignored it.

"So, who's the new High Mystic?" Ovelta asked. She was the

youngest of the apprentices, barely eighteen, a year younger than Mia, who was also her cousin. They'd come to Kelt Apar at the same time, three years ago.

"Vivianna, I would assume?" said Kirane, Vivianna's caretaker.

Laithen, a scarred and wild-bearded Mystic from the baronies of Rardaria who had no Mystic staff, shook his head. "She didn't wake up, right? And she's . . . inside the tower now, right?"

A quiet fell on the room. Kemba and Mia had discovered the locked door before sunrise. Vlenar had explained to them what he and Mia's grandmother had witnessed the night before when the door closed.

"It hasta be Mistress Pomella then, no?" Shillo said. He was supposedly Mia's age, yet he looked several years younger, not fully out of boyhood yet.

At mention of her Amma, most faces turned toward Mia. She shied back into her corner.

Rion still stared at the nearby door leading out of the cabin. To anybody else he might've looked odd fixing his stare at the wood, but Mia knew better. He somehow saw beyond all that. She wanted to ask him what it was, but not here, not with other people around.

"I don't know," Master Kambay said, answering his student. "I believe that decision will be made by others." His voice and expression darkened as he added, "Like most things in our lives now."

Rion shifted to face the door directly. His hand drifted toward the small of his back where Mia knew he wore a knife. She tried to discreetly reach toward her brother to prevent him from doing something stupid, but another Mystic spoke, and she snapped her hand back to her lap.

"What about the Hunters?" Laithen asked. "And the Accord?"

Dronas shuffled his feet before answering. "Mistress Pomella will handle all that soon," he said, sounding as if he were trying to convince himself.

"I don't know Pomella's thinking," Kambay said, "but without a successor, then the baron and baronesses of Moth can declare Kelt Apar vacated and claim the land."

"What?" Shillo said. His face blanched, making his scattering of freckles stand out. "How can they do that?

"Because of the Accord," Kambay said, glancing from Shillo to the rest of them. "You're too young to remember the years after Crow Tallin. Ever since the Change, the tension between Mystics and, well, everybody else has been strained, to say the least. There was a time, when Yarina and Vivianna and Pomella were much younger, where Mystics were respected and admired. Nobles bowed to us, treated even the shabbiest, dirt-crusted Mystics as dignified guests, and listened when we offered advice. But all that went away when the human and fay worlds merged. The fay became rampant. The rangers of old did what they could, but it wasn't enough. People got scared. Fingers were pointed. Nobody really knows how the Change occurred—that knowledge may've died with Yarina—but all Mystics share the blame now. Eventually, after enough years had passed, one thing led to another and we were rounded up. Some rangers changed their ways, becoming the first Hunters. Hunters of fay, they said, but really it was Mystics and the Touched that were their prey."

Heavy silence fell upon the room.

"You know the rest," Kambay said after a moment. "We've each lost teachers or peers to the Hunters and their culling. Because of the Accord, which was presented to us as an act of mercy, we're little more than prisoners, kept in a location where the local lords can keep an eye on us with their watchdog Hunters."

Mia realized with a start that Rion was gone. She snapped her head around, not seeing him. He must've passed through the door while Kambay had been speaking.

She stood up, grabbing her Mystic staff and everyone's attention.

"Mia?" Dronas asked.

She shook her head in quiet reply, then hurried out of the cabin.

The scent of dew-laden grass greeted her, along with the lingering bite of nighttime cold. It had stopped raining, although the air was still thick with moisture. The first pink rays of light pierced the clouds, like the sun cracking open a single eye. Thousands of fay lights sparkled the air.

"Rion!" she called in a cracked whisper.

But her brother didn't respond. She looked in vain in every direction, but all she saw were silent cabins floating in a sea of fay-filled morning fog.

Mia ran onto the wider grass. A well-defined footpath in front of her led to the central tower and also branched off to the northeast and southwest. She peered down each pathway, wondering where her brother might've gone.

Her heart hammered in her chest. She didn't like when Rion vanished, especially when he looked like a hound who'd caught a rabbit's scent. She didn't know what he'd do if left unchecked.

She closed her eyes, and fought her rising anxiety in order to find calm, something she wasn't very good at, despite Amma's training. She forced herself to use the techniques she'd learned. First, she slowed her breathing and took long, calming breaths. She relaxed the tension from her body by consciously loosening the muscles in her face and working down her whole body. She let herself *float* in stillness.

When at last her pulse slowed, she inhaled the Myst.

For some Mystics, sensing and Unveiling the Myst came as naturally as breathing. She'd learned early in her life that her grandmother had been naturally gifted at this, not because of any special breeding or blessing she'd received, but simply because some people had an affinity for it just as others could run faster, or had a more sensitive sense of smell. Mia had very few, if any, natural affinities. What she'd learned as a Mystic, like everything else in her life, had come through tenacity and tears.

Rion, however, was a prodigy in his own way, although nobody but her knew it.

The Myst rose around Mia. She didn't really know what to do with it, though. Amma always said that the Myst was a teacher, and that the more time you consciously spent with it, the more intuitive your understanding of its workings became.

One thing Mia did know was that when she held the Myst she could sense Rion better. Now, with the Myst swirling around her like fog stirred by a wind, she felt a *resonance* in her mind. She turned northwest, toward Oxillian's Wall, where that strange sense told her Rion was.

Lifting her robes with one hand and holding her Mystic staff with her other, Mia ran in that direction. Mud splattered her as high as her knees, but she hardly noticed, as it didn't take long for her to see where Rion had gone.

On the edge of the clearing, where the grass met the Wall, five Hunters led a disheveled man from the north tunnel entrance by an iron chain around his neck. His hands were bound behind his back, presumably also in iron, and he struggled to keep pace.

The exposed parts of the man's skin were dark, marking him most likely as either Keffran, Qina, or possibly virga. Brown and gray mud caked his body. It was hard to judge his exact number of years, but his thin frame and gray hair marked him at around Amma's age.

The group was almost fifty paces away when one of the Hunters noticed Mia. Like all of their kind, they wore long leather dusters. Four of the Hunters were Mothic, judging by their light skin, but the final one was Qina. Mia thought she knew some of their names, but she definitely knew Nabiton, the Qina Hunter.

He was the one who saw Mia. He ran half the distance to her and lowered his glaive in warning. The iron atop the staff gleamed.

"Go away, Mia!" Nabiton hissed.

He spoke in Continental, which was strange for her to hear, considering they'd both been born in Qin.

Now that she was closer, Mia understood what was happening. She'd seen the Hunters do this before. They were bringing in a newly captive Mystic. Nothing else would explain the use of the iron bindings, which had been forbidden from Kelt Apar for centuries. And nothing else explained why five Hunters would be dragging a single old man into Kelt Apar.

Mia's heart raced as she watched the scene, but it was her brother who captured most of her attention. Rion stood not far from the Hunters, pointing his knife at them. An angry wind stormed around him, rippling his clothes, but nobody else's.

"Look, Mia!" Rion shouted in Qina. "They've captured another Mystic! Now's your chance! Strike while they're distracted!"

Mia shook her head vigorously as if to deny the words entering her ears.

Another one of the Hunters turned his attention onto Mia and Nabiton. Mia's heart skipped a beat as she recognized him from his wide-brimmed hat. Carn, the leader of the Hunters. He strode up beside Nabiton and leaned in to listen. Nabiton talked quickly, although Mia couldn't hear what he said.

Behind them, the man in chains tripped, and two of the Mothic Hunters dragged him to his feet. Another punched him in the face.

"See what they're doing, Mia!" yelled Rion. He pointed at the old Mystic. "This is your fault if you don't do something!"

Nabiton stepped forward while Carn loomed behind him. "Go back to your cabin," Nabiton called to Mia. "Stay out of this!"

Carn signaled the others to continue taking the old man away. Nabiton kept his glaive pointed at Mia.

"Now, Mia!" Rion screamed.

The Myst surged around Mia in a sudden flood. It was all too much. She clawed at her hair and fell to her knees. Rion's screams berated her. He always wanted her to hurt the Hunters. He said she could conjure wondrous, powerful Unveilings with the Myst if she would just *listen to him*. He always said he was just trying to help her.

Carn approached, and Nabiton lingered a step behind. The pressure on Mia's chest made her gasp for air.

"What's wrong with this one?" Carn asked.

"She's always been emotional," she heard Nabiton say. "Let me deal with her."

Carn must've nodded in agreement as her former friend knelt beside her. "Ulammia," he said, using Mia's full, formal name. "What's wrong?" He spoke Qina. Their parents had been friends and business partners. At one point, Mia was sure they were going to be paired up and encouraged to marry. Amma's arrival to Qin had changed all that, of course.

Mia could feel Carn's eyes burning into her.

"You can tell me," Nabiton continued. "Don't worry about the old man. We found him in the woods. He'll be safer here."

"Safer?" Rion shouted. He loomed above them. Mia hadn't seen him arrive. "They were beating him!"

Nabiton placed a hand on Mia's back, but she flinched away from it. It was meant to be a comforting gesture, she was sure, but it was as though he'd burned her.

Mia leaped to her feet, anger contorting her face. The sun had broken through the clouds finally, warming the morning and burning away her fear. She could hear Rion laughing nearby.

Something in her expression caused Nabiton's eyes to widen. He stumbled to his feet and held up his glaive.

"Now, Mia!" Rion yelled, rage painting his voice. "Incinerate them!"

Mia raised her Mystic staff and sensed the Myst shift with it. It was as though she'd pushed a knitting needle into the woven fabric of reality and now she pulled the strings. A twist here, and the air could change to fire. A pull here, and Nabiton's thread could unwind.

Rion's scream echoed across Kelt Apar. *"Do it!"*

Mia locked eyes with Nabiton and saw panic rise in his face.

Suddenly the flood of Myst drained away from her, vanishing as quickly as moisture on a scorching day. Mia stumbled, knocked off-balance by the sudden loss of energy.

Nabiton and Carn stared past her, over her shoulder. They pointed their glaives at whatever was behind her.

Disoriented and confused, Mia turned.

Amma approached them, regal despite her obvious exhaustion. She wore her black gown as always, and leaned on her Mystic staff. Ena buzzed nearby.

"That's enough of whatever is happening here," Amma said. She gestured at the Hunters. "Put those sticks away."

"Your apprentice was about to assault us," Carn said, keeping his glaive out.

"Oh, buggerish," Amma said. "You know as well as I do that Mia would do no such thing. Perhaps if you and your hound hadn't scared the skivers out of her, she wouldn't be so upset." She peered at Mia, her brown eyes crisp and shiny. "Gather yourself, Mia."

Mia's heart still hammered, but she began the calming ritual again by slowing her breath. Nearby, Rion threw his hands up in exasperation.

Mia's mind raced. She couldn't remember ever having so much of the Myst under her control before. Moreover, she didn't know how her grandmother had drained it from her.

"The girl's hysterical!" Carn snarled.

"There's no issue here, Carn," Amma said. "Except that you've brought a man to Kelt Apar in iron. Where are you taking him?"

"To the barracks," Carn said. "He's filthy. We'll send him to you after he's been bathed."

"After you interrogate him, you mean!" Amma snapped. "I'll

remind you that harming a Mystic in Kelt Apar violates the Accord."

Carn stepped toward her, and a sense of pride filled Mia that her grandmother didn't wilt beneath his nasty stare.

"So does a Mystic leaving Kelt Apar," Carn said. "Why are your clothes wet? Where have you been?"

"Resting," Amma said.

Carn lifted a finger to Amma's nose. "You're lying to me. . . ."

They held each other's glare before Carn stalked away, tossing his glaive over his shoulder and calling for Nabiton to follow. Their passage across the lawn toward the east-side barracks seemed as unnatural as an iron forge in a garden. The morning fog and the tiny, ever-present fay slunk away from them as they passed.

"Mia?" Amma said, and with a start Mia realized her grandmother had been repeating her name. Mia turned to her and lowered her eyes.

"Are you all right?"

Mia nodded.

"Did they hurt you?"

She shook her head.

"Were you going to hurt them?"

Mia dared a flicking glance to the spot behind her grandmother where Rion stood. He quirked his eyebrow at her as if to say, *Well? Were you?*

Mia remembered the pain, and rage she'd felt when she saw the Hunter punch the old man. She hated them. She hated that they'd recruited Nabiton to their ranks. She hated that Nabiton had so easily succumbed to their hateful rhetoric.

She shook her head and returned her eyes to a downcast position.

No, she wouldn't have hurt anybody. She hoped she would never have to. Fortunately, she'd never had to hurt anybody like that before.

"Except me," Rion said, reading her mind, as always.

Amma looked over her shoulder toward the place Mia had looked. She couldn't see Rion, of course. Nobody except Mia could.

Then her grandmother's attention returned to her and she continued. "Then it is done. Did Kambay and Dronas speak to the others?"

Mia nodded.

"Thank you. We have much to prepare for, including, apparently, the arrival of a new Mystic. Find Ovelta and prepare a bed for this man. One of the smaller cabins. He's new and will value as much privacy as we can give him."

Mia nodded again and moved to the cabins.

"And Mia?" Pomella said.

Mia stopped and waited. A light breeze caught her long hair. She tucked it behind her ear.

"You Unveiled a remarkable amount of the Myst. We will work on your control, but I am glad to see you progressing."

Mia forced a false smile and let it slip away after she turned around and started walking to the cabins to find her cousin Ovelta.

Rion walked beside her, silent.

Later that day, as the sun crested behind clouds that seemed determined to regather their stormy strength, Pomella waited on the outskirts of the large garden where just yesterday she'd strolled with the High Mystic.

So much had happened in the last day, with even more to come. Her conversation with Willwhite consumed most of her thoughts, but now she also felt a rising concern for Mia. Pomella's granddaughter was rarely able to Unveil the Myst at will. She generally shied away from it like one did from an overly large bonfire. The thought of what Carn would've done to the poor girl had she attempted to Unveil the Myst against him sent chilly bumps across her skin.

She shifted her weight and debated whether to Unveil a seat of ground to sit on. She was so tired, but she stubbornly refused to let the Hunters see that exhaustion consume her.

As if summoned by her thoughts, Carn and a handful of his minions exited their barracks along the eastern edge of the grounds, leading their prisoner who now wore black robes. Pomella studied the man as they approached. He was perhaps her own age, with dark skin and a shaved head. His body was frail, and he moved with the slowness she herself had become used to. Faded tattoos in the Keffran tradition peeked out from beneath his shirt, marking him as former nobility. That didn't surprise her. Any Mystic their age meant he had been born to a noble house.

Only he was no longer a noble or a Mystic. His shaved head and filthy manner marked him as an Unclaimed.

Outcast, shunned, and deprived of all possessions and legal rights, the Unclaimed were those who had generally either committed a horrible crime, or caught the ire of the nobility. The Change hadn't done any favors for their status, and, if anything, had worsened their lot. She suspected this man was one of the many outcasts living in the Murk outside the eastern Wall.

The man kept his face downcast, staring at his knobby hands, which were still bound by iron manacles.

"Take those wretched things off him!" Pomella hissed through her teeth. "By the Saints, he's not going to harm you."

Carn's lips curled in a cruel smile, but he complied, taking his time with the task. With the bindings removed, the man lifted his face toward Pomella.

She had to take a slow, calming breath. The man's face was swollen and bruised. His left eye hid behind a mass of inflamed flesh, while blood oozed from his lip.

Pomella's eyes narrowed onto Carn. "How dare you? The Accord—"

Carn spit onto the ground. His leather coat creaked as he shoved the man forward. "Save your righteous jabbering, *hetch*. He'll survive. At least until he dies of old age. Seems to be happening a lot lately."

Pomella ignored them and gently took the man's hand. "All will be well," she whispered. "You are safe now. Let me take you someplace comfortable."

Pomella slowly turned a hard-wilting expression onto Carn. "Where's his staff?"

"Didn't have one," Carn said.

"Then how do you know he's a Mystic?" she asked, incredulous.

Carn sniffed. "I can sense a Mystic as well as you." He gestured toward the other Hunters. "Come on."

"Can you walk?" Pomella asked the man, holding an arm out to him. "It's just a bit further."

He nodded and licked his parched lips. "Thank you." His accent matched his Keffran tattoos.

They walked slowly across the grass, his arm looped through hers. Pomella welcomed the slower pace. The man had a pleasant demeanor about him, battered though he was.

"What's your name?" Pomella asked.

"Kilpa," came the quiet reply.

"Where did they find you?" Pomella asked.

"In the Mystwood, near my home."

"In the Murk?"

The man shook his head. "No."

Pomella eyed him. During the years immediately after the Change, homesteaders had come to the Mystwood, knowing that the Hunters protected it from the worst of the fay. The numbers grew as families brought their Touched children to live there. Most of those came seeking the Kelt Apar Mystics, hoping for a cure. In almost every case, when they learned there was no curse or disease, and therefore no cure, they simply remained in the Mystwood, trying to eke a living off the land. And so the Murk began.

"Have you lived there long?"

Kilpa stopped walking and Pomella turned to face him. He stared at her, cocking his head slightly.

"Do you not see me?" he asked, and a wave of familiarity washed over her, although she could not place it.

Kilpa shifted his grip so that he held her hands. "We held hands here once before, in another time, in another world. Do you remember, Pomella-my?"

His last words triggered the memory. Pomella gasped, unable to help herself. It had been a lifetime ago, but she saw it now, past the bruises, through the years and hollow cheeks.

"By the Saints," she whispered. "Quentin."

SIX

THE HALLS OF INDOLTRUNA

The sun lifted above the horizon, bathing Hizrith, *Zurnta* of Indoltruna, Supreme Steward of Lavantath, and Grand Keeper of All That She Has Touched, in life-giving light. His scales soaked in the warmth, raising his body temperature. Beside him, he felt the abundance of decorative ferns and vines swell with heat as well.

He kept his eyes closed as he sunned himself upon the wide balcony overlooking the Scalla river and the surrounding forest but extended his tongue to taste the morning. The high humidity, laced with spice, surged through his body as his tongue retracted, bringing the forest to him.

Today's sunrise would reveal a good day. Last summer's eggs had begun to hatch and should continue to do so in earnest. At the same time, the youngest generation would molt and Awaken to their sentience soon, bringing a close to the restful season of union, laying, and hatching. A rising joy filled him. Year by year his people hatched new generations of lagharts that were not born into indentured captivity. Never again would *kanta* be seen dragging stone under the threat of a human whip. But never would they forget.

He raised the Myst around him, letting it fill his senses as much as the sun. *Always greet the sun and Myst together*, he remembered

Ehzeeth, his long-dead *Zurnta*, saying, *for they both shine eternal, and fill us with life.*

Hizrith lingered a minute, then opened his eyes and stood with the help of the *Ismara*, his Mystic staff. The heat outlines of the sun and plants and other life filled his vision more quickly than the emergence of the visual light, but his slitted pupils adjusted quickly.

He reached out his hand and opened his talons, palm upward. "Hemo," he muttered, and swirled the Myst.

The air quivered with energy and moments later his familiar soared up the length of the massive Indoltruna superstructure. Hemosavana burst into the air before him, flying upward, face first, with his great wings pulled tight to his body and long multi-hued tail streaming behind. The fay bird lifted into a graceful back loop, spread his wings, and swooped to a landing onto the balcony.

Hizrith held out his hand for the fay to nuzzle. His shimmering plumage was as soft as silk. How strange, Hizrith thought, that once, before the Merging of worlds, it had taken great concentration to feel a fay creature through physical contact for so long. Certain fay previously had the ability to slip between worlds, but now, with Fayün and the so-called human realm merged, Hemo was as present as himself.

"We will ride tonight," he promised the bird, and turned away. Two round-pupiled servants approached him from the distant edge of the balcony. They draped his naked body in purple and white robes—the same colors as their scales—as he entered the fortress.

By the time he'd crossed the massive open archway that led from the balcony to his vaulted personal chambers, he was dressed, and the servants retreated.

Kumava waited for him inside, already dressed and holding her own staff. The pale blue of her robes matched the shade of her scales almost perfectly. Small, darker blue and black scales accented the outer edges of her eyes, and down the spiked crown of her head. The coloring pattern was unusual, especially for a slit-pupil like her.

Her tongue tasted the air as she bowed. "You taste aroused this morning, Master," she said. Hizrith could hear and taste her amusement. "It's a little late in the season for water bonding, however."

He smiled, knowing she was teasing him. She was far younger than him, but they had water bonded in three consecutive seasons. To some of the older lagharts, the ones who, like him, had been born *kanta*, the idea of hatching children together with somebody not of your own generation was taboo. But much had changed with the Merging of worlds, the freeing of the *kanta*, and the downfall of the false People of the Sky. The old ways had burned in Seer Brigid's fire, giving way to new traditions, new ways of living.

Hizrith touched Kumava's forehead. He leaned in to smell her scent and let his tongue flick across the scales on the crown of her head. His apprentice and former water mate tasted of purified water and lavender. "Every day," he said to her, "the lagharts and our new world make me feel young again."

"There were more hatchings last night," Kumava said, standing straight. "The count is not complete, but it is over a thousand. By the next full moon, they will all be hatched."

Hizrith beamed with pride. Some of the new hatchlings in the hatchery were his and Kumava's, though lagharts, unlike humans, did not parent their own offspring. They were tended to by a community of caretakers for the first year before their sentience Awakened, at which time they were given a vocation based on their affinities.

"Walk with me," he said. "What other news do you have to share?"

"The baroness of Moth has agreed to speak with you this morning. Her Mystic lit the candle an hour ago. She waits for you now."

Hizrith tasted the air with his tongue as he considered this. "Then she is considering our offer," he mused.

"I will tell her that you will speak with her after the morning meal," Kumava said.

"No," Hizrith said, waving a talon to dismiss the idea, "I will speak to her now. She is not to be kept waiting any longer."

It took them only a short time to reach the Candle Chamber. Despite Indoltruna's massive sprawl—it was said that it would take somebody a month to explore the entire fortress—Hizrith had insisted that his private chambers be adjacent, or at least as near as possible, to the other rooms he frequented. Thus, the Grand Receiving Hall, Steward's Library, Relic Sanctuary, and Candle Chamber were all within a short walk on the upper ninth level.

Lagharts of every background bowed as Hizrith and Kumava passed through the opulent halls. An honor guard of the Unbroken accompanied them, which Hizrith was thankful for. He did not fear for his safety, but he appreciated how the Unbroken prevented a seemingly endless tide of thankful lagharts' reaching for him to touch or taste. He was older now, and even a brisk walk wore on him.

More of the Unbroken waited outside the wide, gold-trimmed double doors leading to the Candle Chamber. Sanktarin, Hizrith's Watcher and the captain of the Unbroken, stood first to greet him. The Unbroken wore plates of bronze armor over the vulnerable parts of their body, and carried curved swords with serrated teeth. Sanktarin's scales and eyes were all white, even his milky, slitted pupils, a truly rare occurrence.

The Unbroken bowed, Sanktarin held the door, and Hizrith and Kumava entered the Candle Chamber.

There were no windows in the circular, vaulted room, but it was well lit by evenly spaced light spheres. Each sphere was housed inside a golden cage with mirrors placed in such a way so as to expand the light springing from it. The glowing orbs themselves shone steadily from the Myst. It had been High Mystic Yarina who had shared with Hizrith how to conjure and maintain them.

Like almost every room in Indultruna, this one was filled with ornate furniture of the finest artisanship. It had all been here waiting for them when the *kanta* had stormed the palace shortly after the Merging.

The rebels had come, preparing to die if necessary, to fight the mighty People of the Sky, the legendary beings who ruled all of Lavantath. The People of the Sky commanded the Golden, who in turn led the Bronze Ones, who oversaw the indenture of the *kanta*.

But when the rebels finally arrived in Indoltruna, they had not found the People of the Sky. They found no one.

Not a single living person, laghart or human, lived within Indoltruna's walls. Like so many other tools used by the Golden, the People of the Sky had been a lie. The Golden swore, even beneath the touch of fire irons, that they hadn't known that the palace was empty. Only the Crowned Golden had ever been allowed to speak with the People of the Sky. But he'd taken his own life when he saw the hordes of laghart *kanta* sweeping through the jungles, cutting down his army with sheer numbers, and so no one had been able to question him.

But Hizrith didn't need to question the Crowned Golden. He already knew the answer. There were no People of the Sky, and Indoltruna—the grandest palace in the world—had somehow remained empty and pristine for centuries, leaving immaculate rooms fully furnished for Hizrith and his people to claim.

The only significant additions that Hizrith had made to this room were the multitude of candles arranged in concentric rings on the center table. His tongue tasted the air, bringing him a concentrated mix of wax and incense and various floral fragrances. Each candle was a different color, and each was bold and vibrant so that they could be more easily distinguished. Hizrith's eyes had grown weaker with age, a fact he found annoying in part because both the round-pupils and humans could supposedly distinguish color much easier than the slit-pupil lagharts like himself. But so it was. There were, of course, far greater ways to sense the world.

Stepping into the Candle Chamber raised his body temperature slightly, but the only visible heat sources within were small tongues of flame burning atop five candles. Those five waited in the outer rings of the circle. Those represented audience requests from Hizrith's various generals or administrators. He rarely responded to those personally, opting instead to delegate those tasks to Kumava or another assistant.

His attention shifted to the candles located in the center of the rings, the tall, thick ones that represented the High Mystics of the eastern Continent and, of course, the High Mystic of Moth. None of those were lit today.

But there was one candle, located very near the center, just outside the circle of High Mystic candles, that bore a small, steady flame. The candle was dark green, nearly black to his vision, and represented the request from one of the baronesses of Moth.

The heavy doors to the chamber shut, wafting the candle flames lightly with wind.

Hizrith tapped the *Ismara* against the floor, and the Myst rose in response. The flame on the green candle grew until it was nearly as tall as himself, and wide enough to hold the shoulder-to-shoulder visage of a human woman.

Baroness Norana ManHinley's skin, like that of all humans', was smooth and unscaled, her coloring light, which was typical for humans on Moth. She had long black hair that descended well past her shoulders, marking her as part of their noble caste. The hair contained streaks of gray that arose due to her age. She wore paint upon her face, including dark lines edging her eyelids, which Hizrith had always found amusing. In so many ways, humans aspired to be like lagharts, going so far as to paint their faces to resemble laghart features, or appropriating their inventions, such as the Mystic staff, and, of course, learning to Unveil the Myst to begin with. But rather than admitting to mimicking these parts of their culture, humans preferred to take credit for them as their own.

The baroness was the only person visible, yet she undoubtedly had a Mystic near her in order to Unveil and activate the candle.

"Greetingsss to you, Baronesss," Hizrith said in the awkward human Continental language. It was an unfortunate reality that humans lacked the biology to speak most of the laghart languages, which meant the burden had always fallen on the lagharts to learn *their* way of speaking.

"High Mystic Hizrith," the baroness said, "it warms me to see you again."

Kumava's tongue struck the air in repeated fashion, but Hizrith ignored her. He was glad the baroness could not see his apprentice's amusement. The baroness had clearly been taught that specific saying, which was a rough translation of a common laghart greeting. Being a human, however, she did not realize that coming from her, the greeting was an insult. Human bodies regulated their own body heat, and thus this saying lost all its meaning and significance.

Then again, it was always possible the baroness knew this, and was attempting to play him for a fool.

"Thank you for accepting my sssummons," he said. "I believe it isss time we ssspoke of our mutual desiresss. Sssomething hasss occurred that affectsss usss bottth."

Norana's face hardened. "Tell me." She had a reputation as a fierce ruler and Hizrith understood why. She'd inherited a barony, and a world, in the midst of chaotic change. Four faded scars covered one side of her face. Hizrith had heard conflicting stories about the scars' origin, but all agreed that she'd received them at a young age from a fay creature. He was uncertain whether they had been from before the Merging or after, but if they had come from before, she would have been extremely young, perhaps even less than a year old. The baroness was part of the first human generation to grow up without remembering the separated worlds. And she was part of an ever-dwindling number of un-Touched humans.

"I have reccceived newsss," Hizrith said, "that High Mysssstic Yarina isss dead."

The baroness's face remained stony, and although she was not there for Hizrith to taste, his tongue could practically feel her surprise radiating from her. Humans were terrible at hiding their emotions. They scented their true thoughts constantly, having no biological means to realize they were doing it.

"Where did you get this information?" she said, trying to maintain her mask.

"I have my meansss," he replied.

"When?" Norana asked, her voice hard and commanding.

"Yesterday."

The baroness's eyes narrowed before she looked to her side toward what Hizrith assumed was one or more of her advisors. "I have not heard from Kelt Apar yet," she said. "If her death occurred yesterday, I will know of it soon."

"Of courssse," he said. He didn't expect her to know or understand how significant it was that he was even speaking to her during these days of hatching, but he was not about to explain the sacred nature of nesting. And there were, of course, other reasons—preparations that needed to be made swiftly—that he did not wish to share with this human. "I wisssh to begin our new year-generation wittth an allianccce."

"What do you propose?" Norana asked.

"You know of Yarina'sss apprenticcce?"

Norana nodded. "The Hunters report that Vivianna is physically well enough for her age, but her mind has begun to decay. She's been given a caregiver."

Hizrith's tongue tasted the air, trying to give the impression that he was pondering this for the first time. Human minds, compared to those of lagharts, were weak. They so often lost focus and cognition before their bodies withered. Such things occurred far less frequently with lagharts.

"I have learned ssshe may be dead," Hizrith said.

"If that is true," Norana said, "then Kelt Apar—"

"—isss without a massster," Hizrith said, unable to keep the eagerness from his voice. He tasted Kumava's surprise at his eagerness. "If a High Myssstic cannot claim the tower, then by right I may do ssso."

"And why would I allow that?" Norana said.

"Becaussse," Hizrith said, "then I can give you the ressst of Moth."

Norana's lips tightened as she considered the offer. This wasn't the first time they'd discussed these plans. But the time had come to make decisions.

"The other baron and baroness will not allow it," Norana said. "Besides, Pomella will inherit the tower."

"No," Hizrith said. "She isss not in the direct line. Only Yarina'sss direct apprenticcce can claim the lineage. If ssshe cannot, then there isss a vacancccy, and I will take it."

"How?" Norana asked.

Even without scent, he could taste her hubris. "Be prepared," Hizrith replied. He would not share his plans with this human. "I will come to the island."

"When?"

"Our forerunner shipsss are already on their way."

Norana turned to consult with her unseen advisor. Eventually, she nodded and fixed Hizrith with a long look. "And the other barons?" she asked.

"I havvve not ssspoken to them. My allianccce isss with you alone."

He knew what she would choose. She was not foolish enough to decline this offer. Not only would it put her at risk if she did, and make him her enemy, but it would give the other baron and baroness of Moth the opportunity to accept the same offer. For as united as they claimed to be, humans were easy to divide.

"They will not agree to letting you land on Moth," Norana said. "I cannot overcome them alone. They will push you out. And there is the ceon'hur to consider."

"The ceon'hur serves the High Mystic, ssso there isss no concern there. We will combine our mighttt," Hizrith said. "The other baronsss will be no challenge. You will rissse above them. By winter, we will havvve a united island in which you rule the humansss, and I will peacccefully keep the tower."

Kumava's amused scent would've revealed his lie if Norana had been present and able to taste her emotions.

SEVEN

THE EXILED

He no longer called himself Quentin, which Pomella understood.

Throughout her life, she'd learned continually that names mattered, and they changed. Knowing a Mystic name allowed you to resonate and connect with that person or place. Some Mystics had many names throughout their life, especially as they themselves changed. A true master could see into the Myst and pull forth the perfect name for their student, and, on some occasions, themselves.

But Quentin—who now called himself Kilpa—was no Mystic.

Pomella reflected on all this as they sat together at her small table in her cottage. Kilpa slowly spooned soup from the wooden bowl to his lips, his hands involuntarily trembling. He'd been at Kelt Apar for three days now, and they'd settled into a quiet routine. His wounds hadn't fully healed, and he had frequent night terrors, something he said he'd had "since the Change." So Pomella had offered to share her cabin, humble as it was, so she could tend him back to health. Mia and Dronas had offered to bring a second bed into the little cabin, but there was no room. So Pomella and Kilpa just shared hers, which was just wide enough for two.

It had been many years since Pomella had shared a bed space with another person, but this was an entirely different circumstance than when she'd been married. Sleeping beside Kilpa, a broken old man, came with no expectation or even a discussion of intimacy. They were, in all practical matters, just there to sleep.

Now, as Pomella watched him slurp his soup, she stirred the Myst, watching in fascination as silver and gold threads, invisible except to her eyes, wafted toward Kilpa. The tiny tendrils approached his skin, hovered above the faded tattoos that he'd had since his youth, then disintegrated like fog on a hot day.

The Myst reacted this way because Kilpa was Unclaimed. Over the years, she'd helped many Unclaimed, and never had she seen an instance where they didn't push the Myst away. She'd never fully understood it, but when a person became Unclaimed—when they received a punishment and became forbidden to touch another person or own anything beyond what they could carry— their mind so powerfully associated with that low status to the point where their self-identity cracked. It became a self-inflicted mental barrier against the Myst.

"Do I have paint on my face?" Kilpa said slowly, spooning another mouthful. "Because you stare at me like I'm framed artwork."

"Oh, buggerish," Pomella said, blinking back to the present. "Got lost in my thoughts and didn't realize I was staring. What a dunder I am."

He smiled. "We've lived long lives. Our minds are full of thoughts that always need sorting."

"You paint, then?" Pomella said after he'd taken another bite.

He finished his soup in silence, then nodded. "It passes the days."

Most of their conversations went like that, which Pomella enjoyed. She suspected he took pleasure in them as much as she did, but he was difficult to read. He'd sit by the window in her cabin, gazing out for long periods of time. Pomella wondered where he went, what he saw, when he looked that way.

With Kilpa not requiring much from her besides tending his wounds, Pomella could focus and prepare for all the other pressing matters she had on her mind. The full moon wasn't for another four days, so she still had time to prepare for her journey by meditating and fasting.

"You haven't asked me," Kilpa said, "how I came to be here." He stared into his soup, dipping the wooden spoon to stir.

Pomella watched the Myst swirl toward him before suddenly retreating, like reluctant waves too afraid to come all the way to high tide. "The last time I saw you," she said, "was right before Crow Tallin. You were enthralled by Mantepis. I don't know how, but clearly you escaped him. I figured you'd share more when you were ready."

He nodded, still looking at his soup.

"And you're Unclaimed," Pomella said, her tone flat. "The Continent has, if anything, become more unfriendly to the Unclaimed since we were young. You cannot return home to Keffra because your family exiled you. So you've hidden on Moth, but not in the Murk. Perhaps you've joined some of the Unclaimed communes hidden in the Ironlows, but with the Hunters and barons and fay all expanding their territory, you were forced out into the open."

Kilpa shook his head. "Exiled," he mused. "Unclaimed."

Pomella waited while he finished the last of his soup, knowing he had more to say.

"I am both of those things, and beyond that. I am free."

"What do you mean?" Pomella asked.

"You, of all people, should know," he said. "As a Mystic, don't you seek to transcend titles? I suppose most things never change." He shrugged. "You surmised most of the story."

"What I don't understand," Pomella said, "is why the Hunters arrested you. You aren't a Mystic."

He nodded. "Your High Mystic saw to that, long ago."

"And for good reason," Pomella responded, unable to keep the heat from her voice. Despite over sixty years having passed, Pomella would never forget the trauma she'd gone through where he'd betrayed her in a conspiratorial effort to overthrow Yarina.

Recognizing her fiery emotions, Pomella took a breath to snuff them out. "I don't believe you would have willingly come to Kelt Apar to shake up a bundle of trouble."

It was more than a hunch. Unless he was an unparalleled master of the Myst who could conceal or mask his emotions, Pomella knew for certain that his intentions were peaceful and honest. The years she'd been exposed to the Myst, and a lifetime of delving deep into its heart, daily, through ritual and practice, had taught her how to Unveil the most subtle of shifts around people when they brought forth powerful thoughts or emotions.

"No," he said, and finally looked at her. "I would never harm you. Nor could I, I suspect, if I tried."

The air, and the Myst around them, stirred in the slightest of ways, like a hum in the air that only Pomella could hear. "You let yourself be caught," she said. "Why?"

He smiled, the first time she'd seen him do so since arriving, and suddenly she saw him as she had in those early days at the apprentice Trials, handsome and charming. "Let's walk," he said, and held out his hand.

They strolled through Kelt Apar's grounds, trying to enjoy the waning autumn warmth. Pomella walked slowly, carrying her Mystic staff in one hand and lending her other to Kilpa so he could walk more easily. She hoped it wouldn't rain later, but this was Moth, after all, so you could never tell for sure what the weather would decide.

"Brittle knees," Kilpa said by way of explanation for his slower pace. He'd been given black robes to wear as well.

"I remember a time when you showed off those knees by performing *kenj* forms in front of me," Pomella said with a small smile. He'd been devastatingly handsome then, not to mention shirtless.

Kilpa returned the smile. "Did I?" he said, shaking his head. "A lifetime ago, it seems. I spent my entire youth learning that art. Most of it's gone now."

He looked toward the ground. "Pomella," he said, and once more, his voice aged itself to a weary sigh, "I never apologized for what I did during the apprentice Trials."

The smile faded from Pomella's face. She still occasionally had nightmares where Ohzem, the Iron Mystic who attempted to lay siege to the central tower, loomed over her with a snarling face, cursing her with spittle flying. In those dreams she was often locked in chains in a cave near MagDoon's summit. Chains that Kilpa—Quentin—had placed on her. The dreams came less often now, but that did not diminish them from her memory.

Now that Pomella heard Kilpa voice the incident out loud, a part of that pain returned to her, like a scab being unexpectedly torn from her skin. She took a long breath and grounded herself, then patted his arm. "As you said, it was a lifetime ago," she said. "Angry memories are the heaviest to carry. Let's make room for newer, lighter ones."

They walked in silence as the sun illuminated a crystalline world of silver and gold overlaid atop Kelt Apar. Pomella tucked the memories away and tried to enjoy Kilpa's company. Despite the constant stress of the last three days, she found stability in the familiar routine of her everyday life. These daily walks, along with working in her various gardens and meditating in her cabin, all helped to ground her in the here and now. A part of her mind screamed that Yarina was dead and that she needed to *do something*. But the better part of her consciousness—the part that had trained as a Mystic her whole life—knew there was nothing to be done until the full moon arrived. Nothing good or productive would come from reacting to the situation until the time was right. That time loomed in her mind, however, and soon, as certain as her next breath, it would fall upon her.

So she rode the energy of every passing moment, letting herself sense its immediate needs. And what she found, time and again, was there was no need to panic. She would not let her mourning period for Yarina be tainted by worries of an unknown future. There would soon come a time for action and response, but until then, she would continue to live in the moment, trying to make every minute one that was free of fear or anxiety.

They rounded the southern side of the central tower and beheld a wide, looming figure. Kilpa paused and gaped at a massive, silver-shining tortoise sunning himself on the Kelt Apar lawn. The fay creature lay flat on his stomach, legs outstretched, and yet was still five or six times the height of a human, and double that size wide.

Kirane stood beside him, holding peaches for him to eat. A basket of the fruit rested in the grass near her feet.

Kirane bowed to Pomella. "Mistress."

"Hello, Kirane. Hello, Tuppleton," Pomella said.

The great tortoise lowered his head to Pomella. Silver-and-golden smoke rolled off his scaled face.

"You know this fay?" Kilpa asked Pomella.

"I know all of the great fay who still reside on Moth," Pomella said, placing her hand on Tuppleton's head in greeting. "This one is bonded to Vivianna. We had some adventures together during Crow Tallin."

Kirane peeled another peach and offered it to the giant tortoise. "He hasn't left the side of the tower since Mistress Vivianna fell asleep."

Tuppleton shifted his head toward Kilpa and his nostrils flared again as he breathed his scent.

"I have seen many fay on Moth," Kilpa said, "but never one this grand."

Before Pomella could reply, Ena flew from the sky and buzzed in front of her, wafting silver-and-gold smoke that matched the tortoise's. Tuppleton swung his head in the little bird's direction, perhaps sensing the same urgency that Pomella felt from her familiar.

Pomella's heart sank. From the moment Ena had arrived, carrying the news, she knew the time had come. Turning to the east, looking across the lawn, Pomella saw an entourage of soldiers and Hunters leading four ornate carriages flying the dark blue and gray banner of the Fortress of Sea and Sky.

Baroness Norana had arrived. There could be only one reason for her unannounced visit.

"Summon the other Mystics," Pomella said to Ena. "And bring Mia to me immediately."

The hummingbird raced away, leaving a trail of sparkling dust that joined the other motes drifting in the air.

Pomella turned to Kirane. "Ready yourself."

She returned her attention to the approaching entourage. "I'm afraid our stroll is at an end, my old friend," she said to Kilpa. Even from this distance she could sense the iron in the soldiers' weapons and the Hunters' glaives, as well as in the wagons.

Kilpa stepped away from Pomella as if to give her room. She could feel his energy dry up, like a flower wilting, as he returned to being just another broken Unclaimed.

The time of waiting was over. Now it began.

The wagons and horses fanned out across the lawn, trampling grass and wildflowers. Plate-mailed soldiers hid behind helmets that concealed their faces. Each soldier carried a lance tipped toward the clouds, and every tenth one bore the banner of the southern barony. These were the renowned Shieldguards, the most disciplined and accomplished military force on Moth. Sheathed swords hung at their waists. Walking beside the soldiers were the Hunters with their gleaming glaives and grim expressions. Carn strode at their front, leading the largest of the wagons.

Pomella waited patiently, letting everyone fuss and posture. The Myst roiled around her, riled by the presence of so much iron.

Mia, Kambay, and the other Mystics approached her from behind. Mia's worried expression caught Pomella's attention, so she offered her granddaughter a comforting smile. Kambay radiated calm, yet Pomella sensed the Myst rising around him, too. Shillo and the other young Mystics waited farther back, yet Pomella could feel their restless energy.

At last, the wagons were arranged, the soldiers lined up, and the baroness revealed herself.

Norana ManHinley, in a wide gown of deep ocean blue trimmed with gray, descended two steps from her carriage and strode toward the gathered crowd. She resembled her mhathir strongly, with her long dark hair and narrow features. It was through her mhathir's family that Norana had inherited the southern Mothic barony. Pomella had known the baroness for the younger woman's entire life. The first time they'd met had been shortly before Crow Tallin, when Norana had been a wee tyke, only about a year old, and tormented by a fay creature who'd given her the scars she still bore on her face. Pomella had rocked her in her arms and sung to her on that occasion, breaking the tether binding her to a malicious fay creature. Now four pale lines inking their way from Norana's forehead to her neck were the only record of that meeting.

Norana stopped ten paces away from Pomella. Carn stood behind her. Neither of them bowed.

Norana's parents, Kelisia and Pandric, had been good rulers, and lifelong friends to Pomella. But seeing Norana's eyes now,

Pomella was reminded that their fondness for her had not passed to their daughter.

The baroness turned her hawklike gaze from Pomella to the Mystics gathering behind her, to the central tower itself. She lingered her gaze on Tuppleton, who sat as unconcerned as ever.

Pomella opened her mouth to greet her when Norana spoke over her. "This is the first time I've come to Kelt Apar and not been welcomed by the High Mystic," Norana said.

"That's because the High Mystic isn't here," Pomella said. "She died, which is why you've come."

Carn glowered at Pomella, but she ignored him and focused instead on the baroness.

"The world is better for her loss," Norana said.

"You disappoint the memory of your parents, Norana," Pomella said. "They would have understood that Mistress Yarina deserved better than to have her funeral be a storm of blades and iron defiling the land she cherished."

"You speak of her as though Yarina were already one of your precious Saints," Norana said. "But there is blood on her hands. This abomination of a world"—she gestured to ribbons of fay twirling in the air around her—"is due to her. How many lives were ruined? How many families torn asunder for her meddling with powers beyond her comprehension? She was weak, and the world suffered for it. In the end, my parents knew that, too."

"Why do you fear this world, Norana?" Pomella said.

The scars on Norana's face screamed louder than ever. "Enough," Norana said, "this was debated years ago. The Accord stands, and you are in violation of its decrees."

"The Accord will never rule us!" somebody shouted from behind Pomella.

It was the boy, Shillo, Kambay's student. Pomella's heart sank.

Norana's eyes flicked in Carn's direction, and that was enough for the Hunter. He nodded and two other Hunters strode forward, brandishing their glaives.

"Don't harm him!" Kambay yelled, the fear plain in his voice. "He's only a boy!"

One of the Hunters kicked Shillo's knee out, dropping him. The other dragged the youth before the baroness, so he knelt between Pomella and Norana. Shillo's long red hair tumbled over his face. One Hunter held the boy's Mystic staff, while the other kept the iron blade of his glaive at the back of Shillo's head.

"Leave the boy, Lady Baroness," Pomella said to Norana. "His youth speaks louder than his wisdom. Your debate is with me."

Norana looked back over her shoulder and motioned for somebody to come forward. Another woman, bent with age, stepped from one of the carriages and approached. She leaned heavily on a staff with a three-forked top. Pomella's skin pebbled as the Myst rippled in the air between them. The woman was a Mystic, and one she could not recall ever meeting.

The old woman had dark brown skin that had aged to wrinkled leather. Time-weathered Keffran tattoos covered her exposed skin except for her face. Long, tightly woven braids of gray hair were held back by sharp pins that were as long as Pomella's forearms.

Pomella sucked in her breath. The woman had bars of iron piercing her arms and neck. An Iron Mystic.

"Tell me, Ellisen," Norana said to the newcomer. "Are Mystics not taught to contain their passions?"

The Myst shifted in a curious manner around Pomella. There was a tightening around her skin, as though she suddenly wore a shirt that was too small. The shift was directional, however, and Pomella followed it with her gaze until it settled on Kilpa, who huddled near the back of the gathered Mystics. There was something between him and this Iron Mystic, but Pomella had no time to unravel it.

"There are many approaches to Unveiling the Myst, Lady Baroness," the Iron Mystic, Ellisen, said in a deliberate, scratchy voice that revealed its noble roots, "but I have always believed, especially in this Changed world, that one's emotions lead to undesirable outbursts, and uncontrollable personalities."

Norana fixed Pomella with an arrow-like expression. "Whose protection is this boy under?"

"Mine, as are all who dwell at Kelt Apar," Pomella said.

Norana cocked her head. "You claim to be High Mystic then?"

"I've claimed nothing."

"Then who presides over Kelt Apar?" Norana said. "Where is Vivianna?"

The old Mystic Ellisen shuffled forward, her movements stiffened by age. Pomella estimated she and the other Mystic were roughly of the same age, which made it even stranger that she didn't recognize the woman. It also struck Pomella as unusual that Norana would employ a Mystic at all.

The other woman fixed Pomella with a calculating eye. "The baroness asks the wrong question," Ellisen said. "It is not Vivianna Vinnay's absence that intrigues me." She reached into the folds of her robes and pulled forth a knife, no longer than Pomella's finger, and drew it across the thick sole of her palm.

Pomella inhaled sharply as blood flowed from the wound. Her mind raced, realizing what the other Mystic intended.

"How dare you bring an Iron Mystic to Kelt Apar!" Pomella snapped at the baroness.

But her words were lost as Ellisen snapped her wrist toward the ground, flinging blood onto the trampled grass.

A silent tension filled the clearing. Nobody, except the carefree fay, moved.

"Explain yourself, Ellisen," Norana said after an extended silence.

"Where is the Green Man?" Ellisen called loudly for everyone to hear. "Blood is spilled onto Kelt Apar soil and yet he does not come!"

"And this is significant how?" Norana demanded.

"It is significant because the lineage of High Mystics is broken!" Ellisen declared. "The Green Man, the mighty ceon'hur, is tied to this land, but now his allegiance is broken. The island of Moth lacks a High Mystic."

If Norana was surprised, it did not show on her stony face. "Then on behalf of the barons of Moth, I claim this region of Kelt Apar and the surrounding Mystwood as part of the southern barony, effective immediately. Henceforth, all uninvited Mystics are exiled from here and shall be arrested and punished if they trespass upon the grounds. Carn." She motioned to the Hunter, who brandished his glaive, and the other Hunters mimicked him.

Pomella stepped forward. "No," she declared, and the Myst surged in that single word. A wind howled through the clearing, snapping the banners atop the Shieldguards poles.

"Take me," she said. "Leave the others."

Footsteps approached from behind. "Don't do this, Mistress," said Kambay. Pomella appreciated the younger master's words, but she did not turn to look at him. He would understand, eventually. Pomella prayed to the Saints that Kambay and the others would care for Mia.

The baroness pursed her lips. "Carn."

The Hunter looked to his mistress.

"Arrest this one. Kill the others."

A hoarse scream rose in the back of Pomella's throat. The Myst raged around her, but before she could Unveil it the blunt end of Carn's glaive smashed into her jaw. She tasted blood and dirt as she slammed onto the ground. Somebody rolled her over onto her chest, spiking pain throughout her body. The cold snap of iron shackles bit into her wrists, binding her hands behind her back.

Carn's knee pressed down on her neck, pinning her roughly to the grass.

"No!" she managed to gasp through a mouthful of blood. "Mia!"

Chaos consumed her vision. From her crooked angle on the grass, Pomella watched as a Hunter sliced downward with his glaive, decapitating Shillo.

Pomella would have screamed, but with Carn's knee upon her neck she could not breathe. The Myst raged like a stallion around her, too wild, too untamed, to grasp.

"Ena!" she managed, but she could not see or sense her hummingbird.

"Stop struggling, *hetch*!" Carn snarled in her ear. "You're too old for this. Don't make me hurt you more."

Calm. Pomella had to find calm. Even among the chaos, she could tame the stallion and help those she loved. She had to!

The iron manacles holding her hands seared like fire on her skin. And where had her staff gone?

"Round up the others, quickly!" the Iron Mystic, Ellisen, said.

Finally, Carn's knee left Pomella's neck. She sucked in air, trying to find breath. Strong hands hauled her to her feet. Blood still flooded her mouth. Her head spun. Two Shieldguards wrapped a line of heavy chains around her torso and pulled them tight.

Oxillian.

"Ox," she moaned through the pain and blood and shortness of breath. "Help."

"He will not aid you," the Iron Mystic said, stepping close. "He owes you nothing."

Carn snarled a short laugh beside her. With the chains secured around her, he shoved her toward the waiting wagons. "Some friend of yours if he won't help unless compelled," the Hunter said.

Screams filled the air. Pomella tried to look over her shoulder to see what was happening to the other Mystics, but Carn backhanded her.

It was all Pomella could do not to rage or weep. It couldn't end like this. What had she done?

"This is on you, *hetch*," Carn said as he shoved her into one of the carriages. "Your legacy. Your kind. Today, decent folk will see the end of Mystics."

He slammed the door of the carriage, locking her in darkness.

EIGHT

MIA IN THE MYSTWOOD

Mia ran alone through the Mystwood, her Mystic staff heavy in her hand.

Whispering voices spoke to her from every direction, including the ground under her heels. She couldn't understand the words, but sometimes she thought they sounded like her father, or her mother.

She'd never been comfortable in the Mystwood to begin with, despite Amma's insistence that the forest was special and benevolent. That might've been true for the older woman, who'd lived there most of her life and who'd always had a bond with the fay, but Mia was a stranger and a foreigner, having only arrived in the past three years. And now, with Yarina gone, and the lineage of Moth broken, the Mystwood had no reason to continue the pretense that Mia was welcome.

She ran faster, fleeing the voices and the Hunters who surely pursued her. She was somewhere in the southwest forest, where the trees counted their age in centuries, and where their branches formed an unbroken canopy above, blocking all but the most stubborn of sunbeams and rain. The air thickened with humidity. Heavy fog drifted around the moss-covered trunks and jutting roots that twisted around one another.

Her grandmother's old green cloak wafted behind her. She'd

grabbed the cloak earlier when Ena had summoned her, thinking that Amma would need it. But there hadn't been a chance to give it to her before everything had—

She lurched to a stop beside a tree, leaning on it to gulp air. How long had she been running? She didn't trust her sense of time.

Shillo. Dead.

Ovelta. Her cousin. Cut down by a glaive.

Mia pressed her hand harder against the tree to keep it from shaking. Dry blood pinked her fingertips.

She yanked the hand back and shook it, trying in vain to get the blood off.

How had it gotten there? She couldn't remember. There had been so much chaos.

Kambay yelling at her to run.

He'd Unveiled . . . *something* . . . and torn a gaping hole in the side of the Wall, allowing her and some of the other Mystics to escape.

Mia could only manage shallow, ragged breaths. She tried to steady her breathing, but now her whole body shook.

Ovelta.

Sweet, kind Ovelta who had once painted Mia's face to look like a rabbit, had collided into her when they ran for the hole Kambay had Unveiled. That's where the blood had come from. Mia had tried to carry her, but she was too heavy.

"Run, Mia!" Rion had shouted.

"Run, Mia!"

Mia started and looked around.

"Run!" Rion screamed at her from nearby.

She ran, not knowing where she went.

Eventually she had to stop. A cramp in her side made her wince. Her breaths came far too quickly.

"*Ulammia*," whispered a voice behind her.

She spun, lifting her staff in a defensive gesture, but could not find the speaker. Drips of moisture rained from tree branches that swayed gently from storm winds that shook them on the outside of their protective canopy.

"Ulammia."

She spun again. Nothing.

"Ulammia."

"Ulammia."

"What do you want?" she said, dropping her staff and covering her ears.

"Ulammia!"

"Mia."

"Ulammia!"

"Ulammia!"

"Mia!"

"Leave me alone!" Mia screamed, speaking in Qina.

"Mia?"

The last voice silenced the others, and the abrupt change startled Mia more than anything else. She pulled her hands away from her ears and turned around.

Rion stood there, wearing the formal black tunic and pants of their house. He was dressed impeccably, down to the polished pointed shoes, which had come into Qina fashion. With his black hair slicked and combed, it struck Mia again how much he resembled their father. She shuddered.

"Are you all right?" Rion asked, also in Qina. "Why are you running?"

She looked at him in confusion. "You told me to. And . . . the Hunters," she said, still catching her breath.

"You don't have to run from them," Rion said. "They should fear *you*."

Mia shook her head. "No, Rion, no. I won't hurt them."

He stepped toward her and his expression darkened, much like Father's did. She backed behind an oak tree but kept him in view.

"Why are you afraid?" Rion asked. "I'm trying to help you, but you won't listen. You have a power that nobody else has. By not protecting yourself, and by not protecting the others, you're hurting people you care about. Don't you see?"

Mia cowered further, blocking him entirely from view. A fay bug with hundreds of feet crawled over the mossy trunk. Tiny wisps of silver-and-golden smoke wafted off it.

"You can't hide from your power," Rion said, suddenly beside her, speaking directly into her ear.

Mia yelped and stumbled back, tripping on the oak's root, falling onto her backside. Rion loomed over her. She scrambled backward.

"Why are you here?" she cried.

His expression shifted to one of genuine hurt. "Don't you want me here? I'm your brother. I'm doing for you what you won't do for the others."

A spark flickered in Mia's mind. She sneered and stood up, finding her Mystic staff as she did so. But even with the staff in hand, she found herself unable to keep the tremble from her hands. She balled her free hand into a fist to keep it from shaking. "If you want to help me," she said, "help me find the others."

"The Hunters have them," Rion said.

"No!" Mia snapped, surprised by her own fierceness. "I don't believe you. They're still out there. Running, like me."

Rion shrugged as if it were of no consequence whether the others had been captured or not. Father used to do that, and it had always infuriated Mother.

"You accuse me of not helping, yet you don't even care," Mia said.

"It wasn't my idea to leave home and come to this tiny island," Rion said. "These are *your* friends, not mine."

"Then help *me*," Mia said. "Help your sister."

"When are you going to help yourself?"

"I—" Mia swallowed a sudden lump in her throat. "I need your help, Rion. Please. Where are they?"

Rion smoothed his already-well-groomed hair with his hand. A frown played upon his face as he looked at his shoes. There wasn't a single splatter of dirt or mud on them.

Finally, he answered by pointing behind her. "That way," he said. "Near the fork in the creek, beside the shallow falls."

He raised his other arm and pointed in a different, near-opposite direction. "And more that way. Over the rise, within a hollow filled with boulders."

Mia stood frozen by the two hands pointing away from each other. Her heart raced with indecision. Two groups. But which one should she go to? She thought of what Amma would do.

"Where's Master Kambay?" Mia asked.

Slowly, Rion dropped the first arm he'd raised, leaving the other.

Not wasting time to thank him, Mia ran again. She knew her brother helped her not from generosity, but because he would extract a payment later. He always did, and he always reminded her when he helped her.

His laughter hounded her as she ran.

She found the hollow easily enough, and slipped behind one of the nearby moss-covered boulders to hide. Peering around it, she saw, just as Rion had said, a party of three Hunters approaching a handful of Mystics with their glaives up. Mia recognized an apprentice named Najungotep among the Mystics. He was Keffran and had his long arms around Kirane protectively. Two other Mystics had their backs to her, but she couldn't recognize them from her angle.

"Kneel and put your hands up!" one of the Hunters demanded.

A fist clenched at Mia's heart when she saw one of the other Hunters was Nabiton. Why did it have to be him? Why had he joined those vile people?

"Here's your chance," Rion said, suddenly beside her, also in a crouch. He wore colorful attire now, the same that he and Father donned when they hunted. It included a hat with a curled-up brim. The outfit was loud and obnoxious, and one of the only places in Qina culture where such frivolousness was generally tolerated. Mia had never understood her family's obsession with hunting for sport.

Or much about her family at all.

"They'll be killed," Mia said, her heart sinking.

"Yes," Rion said. He faced her directly with a fierce expression. "So what are you going to do about it?"

"Maybe I can lure the Hunters away, double back, and . . ."

She stopped. Rion was shaking his head and muttering.

"What?" she said.

"You're not thinking again, like always!" Rion said, raising his voice.

"I was just—"

"No," he said. "I'm tired of you tiptoeing around your problems! It's pathetic! Your friends are about to be killed and you want to throw rocks to distract their captors? What are you, a child? Maybe you can disguise yourself as a Hunter and fool them into thinking you're one of them? Huh? How's that sound? By the ancestors, you're helpless."

Shame burned on Mia's cheeks. She looked away from her brother, toward the prisoners.

"Stand up for something for once in your life," Rion continued. "You're a Mystic!"

"I'm just an apprentice," she managed.

"And that's all you'll ever be if you cower behind rocks!" Rion yelled.

"Stop shouting at me!" Mia cried, putting her hands over her ears.

"Stand up!" he screamed.

His words bounced around the forest hollow, echoing back toward Mia from multiple directions.

"*Stand up!*"

"*Stand up!*"

"*Stand up!*"

"Stop it, stop, stop!" Mia cried, rocking back and forth.

A heavy boot suddenly shoved her back, pinning her to the rough ground. Mia's mind snapped back into focus. A glaive hovered inches from her face, held by a Hunter. Mia tried to scramble away, but the Hunter pressed harder with his boot.

"Move and I'll cut your throat!" the Hunter snapped in Continental. It wasn't Nabiton, but Mia suddenly wished it was, irrationally wanting somebody familiar. He'd understand and not hurt her.

Mia's eyes jumped to the place where the Mystics were being held. Nabiton and the third Hunter were rushing over, leaving the prisoners alone.

The Myst rose around Mia. It warmed her skin, like a newly lit campfire, shifting to a low burn. Her heart and breathing raced in unison. She tightened her grip on her Mystic staff.

Nabiton and the other Hunter arrived, iron manacles in hand. Nabiton's eyes widened when he saw Mia, but immediately narrowed in anger. Rion stood beside him, his eyes aflame, watching her.

Please, Mia mouthed silently, although she didn't know if she spoke to Rion or Nabiton.

Nabiton's face hardened, and any flickering light of warmth snuffed out. "Lock her up," he said.

Mia screamed, the Myst raged, and her mind went blank.

She didn't know where she was. Pushing herself up from the ground, Mia discovered she lay on the soft forest ground.

The Mystwood. Yes.

It was still light, but the deep shadows cast by the canopy of trees made it difficult to determine the time of day. The fog had thickened, frizzing her hair. Figures moved around her, and she feared they were Hunters.

Memory flooded back, and she recalled all that had happened. Rushing through the forest, and coming across Kirane and the other Mystics. The Hunters. Nabiton. She'd screamed, but after that, she recalled nothing.

Her rapid breathing returned. Where was Rion?

"Rion!" she tried to call, but her voice failed. She wobbled to her feet.

"Easy, lass," said a voice.

Mia whirled around to find Master Kambay holding his hands out gently toward her. The black stripes crossing his brown face revealed an expression of gentle sympathy. He held a metal cup whose contents steamed like the Mystwood fog.

"You're safe," the master Mystic said.

Mia opened her mouth to ask about Rion and the Hunters and everybody else, but she snapped her mouth closed. She reached a trembling hand toward the cup, but it shook so badly she couldn't grasp it.

Kambay eased the cup into her hand and slowly closed her fingers around it. "Careful," he said. "The tea's still hot."

It did indeed burn her hand a bit, but Mia paid it no attention. She took a sip, tasting simple oak bark, but was grateful for the bitter warmth.

"Better?" Kambay asked.

Mia nodded, not truly feeling it, but answering such because she didn't want him further fussing over her. She looked around, trying to find the others.

"The rest of us are nearby," Kambay said, watching her carefully. "We're all fine for now. You caused quite a stir."

The tea in Mia's stomach churned. What, by the ancestors, had she done?

"You don't remember, do you?" Kambay said, seeing the question in her eyes.

She shook her head, and he sighed. "Maybe that's for the best. Come. There's water and clean cloth. You can clean yourself by the stream."

Mia followed Kambay east into the Mystwood. She wanted to ask him where they were going, and where were the others, but the questions died on her lips. She'd find out soon enough.

He brought her to a wide, spring-fed pool resting beneath an open sky. Storm clouds blanketed the forest, drizzling a light rain. A swarm of tiny fay critters hovered over the water, buzzing and spinning in time to music only they could hear.

Kirane, Najungotep, and a handful of other Mystics waited nearby, each sitting or standing quietly with uncertain expressions on their faces. On the opposite shore of the pond, Dronas moved among several covered mounds that, to Mia's horror, looked like human bodies.

"We cannot retrieve the bodies of those who died at Kelt Apar," Kambay said. "The ones you see here succumbed to their wounds here in the forest. This is the first chance we've had to rest. We will stay here tonight, and honor Sh—the dead." His voice cracked at the end.

Mia found Nabiton, sitting with his back to her, near a spruce tree whose roots trailed through the mud into the water. No chains or rope bound him, but a black bandage encircled his head. Kilpa, the old Keffran Mystic her grandmother had befriended, squatted shirtless beside Nabiton. Seeing a pile of rags beside him, Mia realized he'd used strips from his black robes to create the bandage Nabiton wore.

Kambay's hand rested on Mia's shoulder. "Will you be OK?"

Mia's heart thundered, but she managed a nod. She needed to know what had happened.

"I'll leave you with him," Kambay said, and left.

Kilpa eased himself away from Nabiton. He nodded once to Mia. His faded tattoos swirled across his chest and arms, going up his neck.

She knelt beside Nabiton and touched his hand. He flinched. "Don't touch me!" he snapped in Continental.

Mia pulled her hand back as she realized what the bandage over Nabiton's eyes meant.

"He cannot see you," Kilpa said. "He will never see again."

Tears burned on Mia's face. Had she—?

"Do you remember what happened?" Kilpa said.

"Mia?" Nabiton said, realizing who she was. He continued in Qina. "Is that you?"

Mia tried his hand again, easing hers over Nabiton's and squeezing.

Nabiton snarled, and yanked his hand away. "Don't touch me ever again! You've—" His voice suddenly broke with emotion and loss, the anger sliding away like soft mud. "You've ruined me."

Mia went to touch his face, to lift away the bandage to see what happened, but retrieved her hand.

"We found you laying beside two Hunter bodies," Kilpa said to Mia, softly. "They'd been burned alive. This one, too, but only his eyes."

Mia sobbed into her hand, desperately trying not to make a sound. How could she have done this? She had no memory of it. She'd *burned* them? How? She'd never done anything like this before.

Had she?

The line of Nabiton's jaw tightened behind the bandage.

A new voice approached Mia and Kilpa. "The Hunters would've killed all of you," the newcomer said.

Mia turned to see a Touched man in rough homespun breeches and a woolen shirt. In place of a human nose and upper lip there was a hooked beak. White feathers crested back from his cheeks, temples, and forehead. His eyes were human and shone with a vibrant golden light.

"This is Riccan," Kilpa said. "He and a group of scavengers from the Murk freed us from our Hunter captives. Kambay led us to you."

Mia nodded to the newcomer to acknowledge his help, but she didn't feel much beyond that. It had been a long time since she'd seen a Touched, despite that most people born after the Change had merged with a fay while in their mother's womb. She, like Nabiton and Ovelta, was a rare exception. Celebrated as young children for being supposedly pure human. And therefore celebrated by the nobility and groups like the Hunters that valued such things. Only, Mia had proved to be less than ideal in other ways.

Riccan spoke up. "We were gathering food near the Wall when we heard the fighting from your side. We found the hole that had been ripped in its southern side and followed the tracks to Kilpa." He nodded to the older man. "The Hunters were taking you back to their commander. Carn." He spit.

A thousand thoughts warred within Mia's mind. Nabiton remained where he sat, but he pulled his hand away completely from her.

After a long minute, Kilpa and Riccan left her alone with her old friend.

The refugee Mystics remained at the pond for the rest of the day. Mia sat away from everyone on the far side of the water, lost in a flurry of thoughts that vanished as quickly as they came. Kambay came to check on her, but she ignored him and he let her be.

Night fell upon the clearing, but the storm clouds concealed the moon, bringing only rain after sunset.

Mia watched from a distance as Kambay gathered the Mystics at the edge of the pond to speak of the dead, including Ovelta and Shillo. Two small points of light, glowing like soft, warm torches, had been illuminated atop Mystic staves to provide light. Nobody questioned Mia for not standing among them, although she knew she should've. Shillo had been her peer, if not exactly her friend. And Ovelta, her cousin, despite their differences at times, had been a kindness in her life.

"It's not like you killed them," Rion said beside her.

She glared at her brother, throwing daggers with her gaze. "You dare show your face to me after what you did?" she whispered in Qina.

Her brother wore formal black funeral attire with a high collar and a single white rosebud affixed above his heart. "I didn't harm those dead people."

"You killed two Hunters and blinded Nabiton!"

He fixed her with a sad expression. "Do we really need to discuss who did that? You know better, Sister."

Mia turned away from her brother and watched Kambay's gathering. She couldn't hear his words, but she could see him gesturing with gentle movements and natural grace. Amma was the same way. The perfect Mystic. Everything she would likely never be. Her grandmother certainly wasn't a monster who blinded her friends and burned people alive.

Tucking a strand of her curly hair behind her ear and not looking at her brother, Mia stepped back into the Mystwood shadows, her Mystic staff in hand. Rion watched her go, the corner of his lips likely lifted in a small grin.

"Stop looking at me like that," she said in Qina.

"Like what?"

She rounded on her brother. "And stop being a culk! I'm tired of you harassing me."

"*Harassing* you?" Rion said, pointing at his own chest. His face beamed with fake indignation. "I empowered you! You'd be dead if it wasn't for me!"

"You bully me! I can't think straight with you around."

"So you want me to leave, is that it? 'Cause I can, Sister!"

Mia's eyes narrowed. "But can you?" she said. "I think we both know that isn't possible."

"Don't be ridiculous," Rion said. "I can leave whenever I want."

Mia looked at the Mystic staff in her hands. It wasn't much more than a nondescript walking stick. Amma always spoke with reverence about how Mystic staves were these sacred *focus points* and so forth. Right now, hers was a stick, and it was heavy. It didn't have a snake carved into it. It hadn't traveled to Fayün like her grandmother's. Mia never had the heart to tell her that the staff was a burden to her.

"I'm not like other Mystics," Mia said softly.

She could practically feel Rion rolling his eyes. He did that whenever she became self-reflective.

Across the pond, which Mia could barely see from the thicket she stood in, Kambay continued the funeral rites.

"I can't keep doing what others expect of me," she went on. "I just hurt them."

"Mia," he began, and licked his lips. "Whatever you're about to do, I think it's a bad idea."

Most of the decisions in her life had been bad ones. Developing feelings for Nabiton five years ago. Refusing to speak to him when he came to her family's estate and opened up to her. Ignoring her family after that. Throwing plates at Mother. Screaming and yelling, shattering windows. And then stubbornly grasping onto Amma when she came to Qin. Abandoning her family for a completely new and unpredictable life in Kelt Apar. Pretending to care about being a Mystic apprentice.

Before she could stop herself, Mia ignited her Mystic staff, pulling heat and the Myst from everywhere to incinerate it. The wood burned quickly, faster than it would have naturally, turning to ash in her hands.

Rion's eyes widened. "What've you done?"

Mia dusted the last ashes of her former staff from her hands. Anger and sadness and confusion swirled around her like the Myst.

She stopped. Someone approached. Her heart thundered. How much had they heard? Had they heard her *speak*?

It was only Kilpa, and she relaxed a little when it appeared that he had just arrived. His face showed no concern, no curiosity about what she'd just done. Certainly, he'd seen the flaring light from the fire? Perhaps that was what had drawn him. She didn't know this man, or his intentions. Amma knew and trusted him, but that was about it.

Kilpa watched her calmly. If he had heard her, he gave no indication that he cared or would say anything. He nodded to her once, then shifted his attention slightly to focus on the distant funeral.

Mia used that as her opportunity to slip away. She passed through a cloud of glowing fay bugs that scattered at her approach, and walked to the far edge of the camp where she found Nabiton, sitting alone with his back against some rocks. The bandage still covered his eyes, but it seemed as though he slept.

Mia crouched beside him. Yes, he was sleeping, judging by his even breathing and occasional twitch. She placed a hand gently on his leg.

He stirred but did not wake. She shook his leg again, and this time his forehead crinkled as if he were trying to force his eyes open and look around.

She squeezed his hand in her own.

Nabiton's expression shifted to one of surprise. Then sadness, confusion, and pain warred on his face before he turned away from her. "I told you to leave me alone."

Mia tugged his hand, urging him to stand. He did not move. She pulled harder, and he brushed it away.

She stood up. Rion was there beside her.

Mia caught her brother's eye and gestured to Nabiton with her head.

"You want me to— No. No way."

Mia stepped up to Rion, nose to nose, her eyes smoldering heat. "Do it," she whispered in the tiniest voice she could muster, low enough only for him.

Rion glared back at her but complied. He bent down and lifted Nabiton to his feet.

"What are you doing?" he stammered, almost falling again but gaining his balance. "*Hetch!*"

She slapped him, not hard enough to harm, but enough to make her point.

He lunged at her, but it had no focus, and she easily sidestepped. He stumbled to a knee. The fight fled from him as quickly as it had come. Mia bumped him with her leg.

Reluctantly, he stood. "You want me to go somewhere? Huh? Well. I—I can't. . . ."

Mia took his hand, and it was as though she hadn't slapped him only moments ago.

Kilpa approached, having followed her. He waited with a small bundle slung over his shoulder. Mia could see he intended to follow them. Perhaps he would be helpful. As long as he didn't try to stop her or alert the others, she would be fine with that.

She led Nabiton into the dark Mystwood, away from the other Mystics, staying well beyond the diffused edge of their light. Nabiton walked uncertainly, holding back as if he expected to stumble over a stone or walk into a tree. Mia kept him safe, squeezing his hand on occasion to assure him.

"Where are we going?" Nabiton asked.

Mia remained silent, but Kilpa spoke up.

"She's taking you to the Hunters," the old man said.

"What?" Nabiton said. "Why?"

"Because," Kilpa said, "they are your only chance to live."

NINE

THE *ZURNTA*

Brigid trekked through open grass-land toward the looming southern forest. The fresh air helped with her dizziness, but there were lapses where she stumbled or found herself staring at visions of dead people covered with inky red veins and sores.

She wasn't sure if the hallucinations were from the tea that the hobbist had given her, or from the snake venom coursing through her blood.

By the time she reached the edge of the forest a handful of miles outside the colony, it had begun to rain in earnest. She shivered but hardly noticed the cold otherwise.

She cradled her burning hand to her chest and entered the grove of hemlock and oak that marked the edge of the forest. It was early evening, so glowing bugs hovered in the air before her. But unlike the ones she was familiar with in her old home, these glowed with a soft silver light. A chill pebbled her skin, and immediately it was as though a heavy blanket had been thrown over her, muffling the sounds of the rainstorm. She had a sense of unseen eyes watching her, and shivered again, but not from the cold this time.

The Mystwood, whispered a voice in her mind. Another hallucination?

"H-hello?" Brigid called through chattering teeth.

When no one responded, she muttered a curse to herself. What had she expected would happen? That the strange lizard-people supposedly living here would rush to her aid the moment she walked into a hemlock grove on the edge of their domain?

Within the first two days of their arrival to the island, the colony scouts had reported seeing man-sized lizards that walked upright, wore clothing, carried tools, and spoke to one another in hissing voices. The creatures had reportedly been as surprised and scared of the colonists as the scouts were of them. Further attempts to find and speak with the lizard-people proved to be futile.

She stumbled through the forest, calling for help. Silvery bugs danced in front of her, wanting to play or annoy her. Brigid sneered and swatted them away, but to her surprise, her hand passed right through them.

Night engulfed the forest and soon she could hardly see. Her whole body shook with cold. The air moistened with rain, bringing a fresh scent of pine and ash and other trees. The pain in her hand dulled to a low ache, and she feared the venom had progressed farther into her.

Exhausted, she collapsed beneath a large, twisted oak that must've been as old as the island itself.

She was so tired. She didn't want to sleep, for fear of not waking. She had to keep fighting, keep moving. Yet she lacked the strength to stand.

"Please," she whispered to nobody in particular.

A bird cawed in the tree above her. Brigid looked up and had to rub her eyes to ensure she was actually seeing it. A crow made entirely of smoky silver light sat on a branch, eyeing her. It cried out again, and flapped its wings, wafting smoke off them.

Brigid stood and took a hesitant step toward the bird. It sounded a third time, then leaped from the oak branch and flew deeper into the forest, seeming to fade into its depths.

Brigid followed.

The crow leaped between branches, and try as she might, Brigid could never quite reach it. The night deepened and the rain fell harder, but neither deterred her from following the silvery creature.

Without warning, the trees opened to reveal a small clearing, no more than ten steps wide. A small campfire, ringed by stones, smoked in the middle. The crow circled the fire once, then came to rest atop a curved walking stick that had been propped up against a large rock. The stick was as curved as a crescent moon, like a hunting bow. But it was the stick's owner that caught Brigid's attention.

A humanoid lizard sat by the fire. Red and white scales formed a mesmerizing triangular-swirl pattern across the creature's exposed claws while black scales outlined its nails. It wore loose gray robes made of wool and kept a hood over its face so that only its snout could be seen.

As Brigid stumbled into the clearing, the creature turned its head to face her. Yellow slitted eyes reflected firelight from within the voluminous hood.

"Hello?" Brigid said tentatively.

The lizard-creature lifted a clawlike hand to its hood and pulled it back. Brigid tensed as the full features of the creature's face were revealed.

More black scales outlined the creature's eyes while short spikes ran from the crown of its head down its spine, growing larger and wider apart as they descended. A delicate lift to the creature's face gave it a distinctly feminine look.

The lizard's forked tongue licked the air, and Brigid had the sense that she was evaluating her.

"I-I am Brigid," she said by way of awkward introduction. "I'm hurt. I was bitten by a snake."

"Food," the lizard said, gesturing to the fire. A clay bowl rested on a fallen tree log that lay between Brigid and the fire. She sud-

denly realized how hungry she was, and before she could stop herself she snatched the bowl and drank its soupy contents. It tasted
of leafy vegetables and mushroom with a sappy sweetness that
may've been sycamore sugar.

The lizard-woman watched in silence on the far side of the fire
as Brigid set the bowl down.

"Thank you," Brigid said. Her mind seemed a little clearer now,
and with that came a stronger sense of caution than she'd had
moments ago. She found herself peering into the empty bowl suspiciously. She had already been poisoned by the snake's venom, and
this creature before her had no cause to further harm her.

The lizard swished her tail, leaving swirls on the bare ground
behind her.

"I sssmell the venom," the lizard said. Her voice hissed the words.
Her tongue coming out again. She stared at Brigid's wounded arm.
A chill ran down Brigid's spine.

"Do you have a name?" she asked.

"Mylezka."

"Can you help me?"

"Are you prepppared to die?" Mylezka asked.

Fear gripped Brigid's chest like a massive claw, but she forced
herself to show strength. "I can't die. I have a son. He needs me."

"Why?"

A surge of wind and rain fell, smoking the fire and filling the
clearing with steam. Brigid narrowed her eyes. "What do you
mean, 'Why?'"

"Isss your ssson in danger?"

"No, but I—"

"Then he doesss not need you right now," said Mylezka with
an infuriatingly dismissive cock of her head. "You mussst tend
yoursssself before you tend othersss."

Brigid forced herself not to clench her teeth. "Look, if there's nothing you can do about the venom, then I need to move on. Can you help me or not? Do you have medicine? The hobbist told me about a glowing flower?"

"I don't have medicccine, but I can help prepare you to die."

"So there's no cure?"

"For deathhh? No. We all die."

Brigid stood. "Thanks for the food, but I need to find somebody who can *actually* help me."

She moved to leave the clearing, but the lizard-woman spoke. "Ssstay."

"No, you—"

"Sssit. Lisssten."

Clenching her teeth, and against her better judgment, Brigid sat.

"Tell me of your ssson."

"What about him? What does this have to do with anything?"

The lizard-woman's tail swished patiently as she waited, her tongue occasionally licking the air.

Exasperated, Brigid sat back down. She cradled her hand and took a deep breath to calm her nerves. "All right. His . . . His name is Janid. He's six years old. He has red hair and—"

The lizard-woman picked up her staff and rapped its end against the ground, startling Brigid. It hadn't been an aggressive action, but the suddenness and focused force of it snapped her attention. Mylezka leaned forward. "Tell me, as hisss mother, about him."

Perhaps it was the intensity of the lizard-woman's slitted gaze, or the hypnotic light from the fire, but an ominous chill settled over Brigid, pebbling her skin. She swallowed the lump in her throat and tried to ignore her throbbing hand.

"He's a quiet child who sees more than others. When he was born, he did not cry, but rather looked around as if to say, 'Why have I returned here again?' He only speaks one word, 'Myma,' for me, because he is afraid of all else. When he smiles, it blooms a light in my chest so much that I wonder why others are not blinded. When he sleeps, he holds my hand, or touches his toes against my legs, never wanting to part from me. He is my reason for living. He is my everything."

"He isss fortunate to havvve a mother like you," Mylezka said. "He needsss you, as all children do, but your attachment to him holdsss you back. It keepsss you imprisssoned."

The hunger, fear, and turmoil of the night had become giant stones around Brigid's neck. "I don't understand," she said. "How can my son *imprison* me?"

"By holding on to him when you die, you take him wittth you. Better to love and releassse and await him joining you. Release your attachments."

Without warning, the world seemed to *ripple*. The phrase echoed all around her, and for a brief moment the lizard-woman was gone, replaced by a woman, sitting cross-legged upon the stone. The woman's robes and silver-white hair blew to one side, caught in an unseen wind.

Brigid knew the woman but could not place her.

Come back to me, whispered a voice in Brigid's mind.

A heartbeat later, it was gone, and Brigid once more faced Mylezka. The lizard-woman watched her carefully, her tongue licking the air.

"What was that?" Brigid said. "Just now, when you said, 'Release your attachments,' I . . . saw something. A woman."

"Memoriesss, too, can hold you back," Mylezka said. "Only by letting them go, along wittth other burdensss, can you prepare yoursssself for deattth."

"What burdens me?" Brigid asked.

"Your posssesssions," Mylezka said, gesturing to the fire. "Disssown them."

"Who are you?" Brigid asked. "*What* are you?"

"I am a *Zurnta*, a laghart, and a Mystic," said Mylezka. "But mossst of all, I am an expression of the Myssst."

Brigid didn't understand what those names meant, but it was clear that this strange woman was a wise elder of some kind. In the Dragon King's realm she would be one of the Blessed.

Brigid's swollen arm throbbed and pulsed with red veins that snaked well past her elbow. It was too late. She would be dead soon. Perhaps this so-called *Mystic* could help her die in peace. If her life had come to an end, she would die warm beside a fire and at peace.

Brigid stood. The fire crackled between her and Mylezka.

"Everything I own," Brigid said, "my possessions, I crafted or built myself. My clothes, my tools, my home."

"How will they ssserve you in deattth, other than to weigh you down?"

Brigid's head spun and her entire wounded arm buzzed with pain. "Very well," she said. If she were to die, then another colonist would claim her homestead. She hoped Janid would inherit eventually, or be paid its fair worth. But he was still young. More than anything, she hoped he was cared for.

"My home will be claimed by another. I do not need it."

"Good," Mylezka hissed. "Your other possessionsss?"

"I have only my clothes," Brigid said.

"They give you warmttth when the rain fallsss," Mylezka said, "but here, bessside thisss fire, and when you die, you will not need them."

"They give me dignity," Brigid said.

Mylezka shook her head. "Your dignity alssso weighs you down. Your clothes are a ssshield againssst fear. Own your ssstrength."

"Then why do you wear robes?" Brigid asked, her eyes narrowing.

The lizard-woman stood, lithe and surprisingly quick, and pulled her robes over her head in one smooth motion, leaving her entirely naked.

"Thessse clothesss keep me warm, as doesss thisss fire," Mylezka said. "But I am not preparing to die tonight."

Brigid thought of the men in her early life who had sought to take advantage of her. The man on the colony ship. Others. Time and again men had taken from her. But no longer. She would not die with fear of them haunting her.

She removed her clothes. A sense of vulnerability prickled her skin, but she let it dissipate like the drifting smoke rising from the flames. She stood there, in the flickering light across from the undressed lizard-woman, feeling an odd kinship.

"Your mate?" Mylezka asked. "Do you ssstill hold on to him?"

"I buried him long ago," Brigid said. "I mourned him, and moved on."

"Good," Mylezka said, nodding. "Now do the sssame for your ssson. Give yoursssself that gift."

"A gift?" she asked. "I don't understand how—"

But then, in a heartbeat, she did. She was unlikely to survive the night. Her last thoughts could be of sadness and anguish over leaving Janid. Or they could be filled with peace, knowing she'd had the opportunity to be his mother. She could rest, knowing he would survive and be strong.

The pain in her arm and the fatigue throughout her entire body became too much. She lay on the ground, just a short distance from the fire.

"I'm ready," she whispered to Mylezka.

"Go in ressstful peaccce," Mylezka said. "Sssleep, Ssseer Brigid."

Brigid's eyes grew heavy, and before she could think any longer darkness engulfed her.

She awoke from a night of vivid dreams, sore, but alive.

The bonfire had burned itself out, yet reddened coals still smoldered within their caves of blackened char.

As awareness dawned, Brigid gasped and bolted upright.

A wool blanket covered her. A fresh bundle of clothes—white

robes—had been carefully folded and placed beside a full bowl of soup on the nearby fallen log. Morning sunlight slanted through the dense tree canopy, shining in distinct beams over her naked body.

Mylezka was nowhere to be seen.

Brigid stared at her arm. The swelling had subsided considerably, and while it was sore, she could feel a tingling sensation across the entire limb. She tapped her fingers together, one at a time, feeling a dull throb with each touch.

A tentative smile touched her lips. Had the lizard-woman healed her? With her mind less foggy now, Brigid tried to piece together what had happened. Mylezka was clearly one of the Blessed: those people who could create wonders by moving their hands or chanting. A *Mystic*, she had said.

But as Brigid thought about it, she realized Mylezka had not done anything other than speak to her.

And the venom had not been deadly. Nourishment and rest were what she had needed.

Or had it? She thought, too, of the ritual-like way that Mylezka had guided her to accept death. She really had convinced herself that she was ready and that Janid would be well without her. She wanted to see him again, but the need seemed less frantic now.

She stood and dressed and drank down the soup. She thought of taking the bowl with her as a reminder of the encounter—it was smooth and well crafted from oak—but then she hesitated. No, she would leave it here. There was no need to hold on to a memento from this encounter. Somehow, it felt right to leave it behind.

With a final look of thanks, Brigid left for home.

TEN

MYSTWALK

Pomella stewed in silent stillness as the prison carriage rattled its way out of Kelt Apar.

Her face throbbed where Carn had hit her. Iron chains bound her movement. She wanted to yell at the two Shieldguards and the Hunter sharing the carriage with her. But she knew it would be a futile gesture that only tired her out and emboldened her captors. The Hunter, a tall virga woman with fierce blue eyes that starkly contrasted with her striped skin, held her glaive at the ready.

As the caravan emerged from the eastern side of the Wall, it wound its way into the Murk. Word must've spread fast, because a crowd had gathered near the road, muttering to themselves. Surely they had heard the commotion. The screaming. The death.

Another wave of anger and sorrow threatened to overwhelm Pomella, but she stifled it. There was little she could do, she told herself. Not yet. Not until the full moon.

But still, she'd seen what had happened to poor Shillo. The screams from Mystics being cut down still haunted her. Tidal waves of terror had surged in the Myst as though she'd been standing on a shore of destruction. She wished she'd been able to see what had become of Mia.

Faces from people living in the Murk stared at her from beyond her small window. At first, it was a small handful of people, all of them Touched, with their hybrid human and fay features standing out prominently.

"The Hummingbird," one whispered, and the name echoed through the uneasy crowd. The Shieldguards shouted orders and a protective ring of mounted soldiers encircled the wagons.

Quickly the crowd surged in size and anger, becoming a mob. More shouting spilled over and Pomella saw rocks being thrown. The people of the Murk had no love for the baroness, the Hunters, or anybody who rejected them because they were Touched or Unclaimed.

Pomella turned away from the window and closed her eyes, seeking stillness. Outside the carriage, the Shieldguards and Hunters hacked a path through the crowd.

The next day, having left the Murk behind, the caravan plodded south and east.

Pomella peered through the tiny carriage window with her non-swollen eye and gazed at MagDoon, the great mountain at the heart of southern Moth, with its snowy summit wreathed in clouds. The mountain figured prominently in Moth's history and culture, as well as her own life. *Mountains are eternal*, she recalled herself saying to Lal in a conversation long ago. *Like the Myst, they existed before our lives began, and will live long after us.* She wondered if she'd ever see MagDoon again.

Seeing the mountain made her think of Sim. It always did. Would things have turned out differently if he hadn't died during Crow Tallin? He'd become a ranger, one with intense determination. Perhaps if he'd lived during the years leading up to the Accord he could've guided the remaining rangers away from the rhetoric that turned so many of them into Hunters. Perhaps, through his leadership and example, he could've helped her.

But he was gone, lost without a monument to mark his passing. MagDoon would have to do.

The weather had done its best to delay them, but the caravan maintained a steady pace. The mud and lumps on the old road leading from the Murk to Port Morrush made for a bumpy journey.

She'd chosen to sleep for most of the journey, building her strength. She'd woken, on occasion, her heart racing, remembering the chaos at Kelt Apar and the riot in the nearby Murk. But she quickly calmed herself with disciplined breathing.

Two days after her arrest, they arrived at the Fortress of Sea and Sky. Wrapped in fog, the imposing stone stronghold looked especially ominous.

For most of her life, the fortress had been a warm and welcoming place to Pomella. Its previous inhabitants, Baroness Kelisia ManHinley and her husband, Baron Pandric, had kept an open door and a roaring hearth for her. Under the ManHinleys, every commoner, merchant-scholar, and noble could attend a celebration when she, the Commoner Mystic, the Hummingbird, came to visit.

But those warm days of welcome were gone. The ManHinleys had passed in their own time, leaving their barony and fortress to their only child, Norana. In their absence, and later, in the wake of the Mystic Accord, the feast hall had been closed, the hearth extinguished, and the mighty fortress gates shut to both commoners and the Mystics of Kelt Apar.

The fortress stood on the edge of a sheer cliff overlooking the sea, acting as both lighthouse and guardian sentinel. Massive waves crashed against the southern cliffs, echoing for miles.

As they approached the fortress gates, fog enveloped the caravan. The ManHinley banners snapped in the ocean-born wind, welcoming the baroness and her entourage home. The high street snaked through the city of Port Morrush, leading up the hill to the fortress. The way had been cleared to make room for the carriages to pass unhindered up the long, winding road to its destination. Pomella suspected that the riot in the Murk had influenced the decision to empty the streets.

The caravan passed through the fortress's portcullis into the inner courtyard and stopped. A knock came at the carriage door, and the Shieldguard sitting nearest opened it, stepping out.

A Hunter Pomella had never seen before motioned from outside for her to get out of the carriage. Nobody helped or offered a hand. Managing as best she could with her chains, she winced at a pain in her stiff hip. She'd almost made it out when her foot snagged on her filthy gown, tripping her. She fell out of the carriage and landed hard. Pain blazed from her right elbow to shoulder.

Pomella struggled to stand, but her arm wouldn't cooperate and her legs and hips had had enough. She could take the humiliation, but she hated the feeling of being a helpless old woman.

Strong hands hoisted her to her feet.

"Get up," a rough voice muttered in her ear. "Show some dignity."

Pomella peered through her swollen eye at the person who'd assisted her. It was a Shieldguard captain, a woman who looked too old to still be wearing a sword and armor.

"There ya go," the captain said when it became evident Pomella wouldn't retort. She whistled and motioned a pair of other Shieldguards over.

"What became of my granddaughter?" Pomella said. It was the first she'd spoken since leaving Kelt Apar. Her throat was scratchy from disuse.

The captain passed the chain connected to Pomella over to the other Shieldguards.

"It's best that you worry about yourself," the captain said.

Pomella worried about Mia, and she wondered where her staff had been taken. Perhaps Norana already had it destroyed. It was strange not to have its familiar weight in her hand.

A cluster of Shieldguards waited nearby, along with the Hunters who'd come with the caravan, the fortress servants, stable hands, and other onlookers.

Pomella realized that fewer Hunters than she'd expected appeared to have traveled with them. Carn was nowhere to be seen.

Norana and Ellisen, the Iron Mystic, descended from their nearby carriage. Norana's expression remained stony and unmoving as she turned to Pomella. She strode away without a word toward the tall double doors of the central keep.

Ellisen lingered a moment longer to sneer at Pomella. She carried two Mystic staves. One of them was Pomella's. Presumably knowing that Pomella had seen what she'd wanted her to, the Iron Mystic followed the baroness.

The Shieldguard captain motioned toward a different multistoried building. "Get her inside." The chains linked to Pomella's manacles clinked as the soldiers led her away.

Nobody looked directly at Pomella as she passed, but nearby people flicked glances in her direction. Rumors had surely already spread throughout the fortress, and likely down to Port Morrush, that she'd been taken into custody.

"Is your arm all right?" the Shieldguard captain asked.

Pomella appreciated the note of sincerity in the other woman's voice. "I don't think it's broken," she said. But her whole arm, from shoulder to elbow, hurt like a horse had kicked it.

The fortress consisted of an inner keep and two other large structures, all made of mortared stone. The two smaller buildings were used for lesser guests, servants, and prisoners. The soldiers led Pomella to the southern, ocean-facing tower that loomed high above the edge of the compound. A cool wind rustled around her before she and her Shieldguard jailers passed inside through the building's lone entrance, a short oak door. Pomella let herself savor the wind, then ducked inside the door, her back and neck muscles complaining.

Steady torchlight illuminated the interior, casting orange-tinged shadows throughout the room. It wasn't unlike the ground floor of Kelt Apar's central tower, although the light from the torches here was harsher than the soft-glowing lamps Pomella was used to. A curved stairwell led both up and down, and it surprised Pomella when one of the soldiers motioned her upward. She'd expected to be thrown in the darkest, gloomiest subterranean dungeon in the fortress.

Another Shieldguard—a shorter man with a bushy beard beneath his polished helmet—waited for them at the top of the stairwell. He greeted the Shieldguard captain behind Pomella with a salute, then unlocked the door at the top he'd been standing in front of.

The door was made of iron and creaked on hinges bolted deep into the stone. Pomella shuddered as she passed the metal door and stepped into the cell beyond. The rounded room was tiny, with a diameter barely wider than her outstretched arms. There was an open slit in the wall near the ceiling, barely passing for a window. Its location high on the wall prevented her from seeing out. A single blanket and a covered night pot were the only other objects occupying the small space. At least, the blanket looked thick. It would likely get cold in here, especially at night.

The bearded Shieldguard kept his face grim as he disrobed Pomella down to her innermost garments. Pomella kept her gaze on the wall, calmly refusing to let the indignity affect her. The man crammed a gray, rough-spun tunic over her head. She struggled to slip her injured right arm inside and hissed through clenched teeth when she extended it too far.

Unconcerned for her pain, the Shieldguard clapped iron manacles around her wrists.

Pomella stilled the storming sense of fear that arose in her stomach. She'd worn manacles like this before during her apprentice Trials. The cold metal touching aggravated her skin, causing discomfort that she knew would eventually become pain.

Her captors fastened a chain to link her manacles to a loop in the wall, then slammed the door shut with a heavy bang. The lock slid into place and she was alone.

She shivered and found herself wanting a chair. The tunic she now wore extended past her knees, but it did little to stop the chilly breeze that sailed into the cell from the window, bringing the briny scent of the ocean.

With nothing left to do, Pomella wrapped herself in the blanket and settled her aching body onto the floor with her back to the wall and tried to make herself comfortable. This was far from the worst place she'd ever had to sleep in her life, but it had been many years since she'd not had a bed. How used to certain comforts she'd become. Despite everything, she found herself smiling. Lal, at least, would've approved of her current humble conditions.

Gingerly, she lifted her injured arm to touch her bruised face. A derisive snort escaped her lips. Humble, indeed.

She closed her eyes, walled her emotions off into a mental cell of their own, and drifted off to sleep.

The next two days passed slowly. Pomella preserved her strength by sleeping and meditating. She received food twice a day, and water four times.

On the second night, she woke in the deep part of the evening, stirred by the chill air carrying the full moon's whisper. Whatever dreams she'd been having rushed away, leaving her with only a sore back and a sense of sorrow.

The time had come.

Pomella eased herself to a sitting position, then used the wall and her left hand to stand. Her iron manacles dragged heavily against the stone floor. The initial itch that they'd caused had deepened to a mild burning, like when she placed her hands too close to a fire. She kept her stiff right arm, which she could no longer extend, tucked close to her body. Deep purple bruises covered it from her forearm to her shoulder.

She used the night pot, then settled herself into a cross-legged sitting position beneath her window. She wasn't sure how long this process would take. Master Willwhite had only said that they'd meet her on the full moon and guide her further. She felt well rested for now.

Pomella closed her eyes and took a calming breath, the same as she'd done countless times throughout her life, and let herself drift into the Myst. It rose around her, through her, saturating her skin. She straightened her back as the Myst infused her, letting her spine elongate and form a straight line from her tailbone to the crown of her head.

For over sixty years she'd meditated daily, and now it came to her as naturally as breathing. The chill from the night air vanished. The aches in her arm and hips and face faded. The weight of her years lifted.

She breathed again, weaving the Myst as one would twine a willow basket. Soon it moved of its own accord, shaping itself. It cocooned around her, until at last Pomella could no longer feel her body.

She opened her eyes. The room had not changed, but her perception of it had. She looked to her left, and then her right, but her physical head remained motionless.

She stood, leaving her body behind. A push of excitement washed over her. It was disorienting to move without a body, and to watch herself sitting on the cold cell floor.

"Get yourself together, Pom," she said. The sensation of air moved through her throat as she spoke, but nothing stirred in the actual jail cell, save for the steady breathing of the old woman who meditated nearby with her eyes closed.

She concentrated again, and molded the Myst, Unveiling a wavering representation of herself around her physical body. It had arms and legs and robes. A softly roiling smoke, silver and golden, wafted off the newly formed illusionary body like fog blowing across a still pond.

Pomella rolled her wrists and tilted her head back and forth, trying to touch each ear to a shoulder. The motions came smoothly and without pain. She lifted her pain-free right arm and snapped it down.

Her Mystic staff popped into her hand. Like the rest of her current form, it was a mental projection, but it had the familiar weight and texture of her real staff. With it in her hand, her illusionary body solidified even more, becoming nearly indistinguishable from her real one.

"There," she said. She wore ocean-blue robes lined with paler, nearly white cloth that felt as smooth as silk but as light as a cloud.

Pomella knelt beside her body, marveling at the ease with which she did so. She peered at herself, noting how haggard she appeared. She must've worn herself out more than she thought.

Sweat and dirt dusted her light brown skin. Deep lines trenched the corners of her eyes. Her forehead bore wrinkles, too, and the skin of her cheeks sagged. Her hair, once wavy and dark, had been almost entirely consumed by gray. Only an occasional, stubborn strand of black hair remained. A muscle in her physical neck stiffened involuntarily, and Pomella wondered what sort of toll this experience would take on her health.

"You're old, lass," she said to herself, then stood and let the Myst surge around her. "But you're far from done."

Silently, she called out to the night, through the cell window, summoning Ena.

The prison walls illuminated with light as Ena zoomed in through the window. She spun once around the room, trailing dust that shone silver and gold before fading away. The little hummingbird hovered in front of Pomella's physical body, cocking her head in confusion.

"Hello, dear one," Pomella said, and shifted the Myst to Unveil herself to the bird.

Ena turned in midair, her wings blazing with her eternal youthful energy. If the hummingbird seemed surprised to see a disembodied version of Pomella standing outside her body, she didn't show it. It wouldn't have been the strangest occurrence Ena had witnessed in her lifetime as Pomella's companion.

"I need to find Mia," Pomella said. "Watch over me while I'm away."

Pomella didn't expect any trouble. She prayed to the Saints that it would be enough time to fulfill her task. She had considered starting this search for Mia a day or two earlier, but she'd needed to gather her strength to Unveil this mental projection of herself, and she also needed to wait for the full moon to meet Willwhite.

Ena alighted onto Pomella's physical shoulder and cocked her head.

Pomella stroked the little bird's plumage with a finger. In this immaterial form, her fingertip passed through Ena with only the slightest sensation of cool vapor.

Her farewell complete, Pomella dissolved her Myst-body into a stream of light and shone away.

Out the window she traveled, across the imposing fortress, over the sleeping city of Port Morrush, and beyond the wave-pounded cliffs of southern Moth. North she blazed, toward the Ironlows where the roots of the mountains sank deeply into the island.

She materialized on a mountainside, with the moon above her, partially obscured by thick clouds fat with impending rain. A wave of dizziness threatened to topple her, but she leaned on her Mystic staff for balance.

The Mystwood lay to the west, and MagDoon towered behind her, looming over her shoulder like a silent, titanic sentinel. The wind howled around Pomella, rippling her hair as though she really stood there, yet its touch was muted and merely cool. This Mystwalk, as she came to think of it, would eventually take her to Kelt Apar, but Pomella wanted to pause here first, to sense what she could.

"Show me my granddaughter," she said to the Mystwood, harmonizing with the Myst and forest.

She closed her nonexistent eyes and stretched out her senses, trying perhaps to hear the sound that could represent her granddaughter's heart. But she heard nothing, felt nothing. The Mystwood remained silent, stubbornly refusing to respond to Pomella's query.

She sighed. With the lineage of Moth broken, the Mystwood would close itself off more and more as time went on. She'd lived most of her life amid these trees and creeks and glens, but now it seemed so distant, so foreign to her.

Releasing the heaviness of her heart, she dissolved into light again. She passed over the Murk and toward the heart of the forest where Kelt Apar's central tower rose from amid a moat of flowers.

She materialized, this time without dizziness, onto the familiar grounds and immediately caught her breath.

Kelt Apar lay in ashes.

Rain had snuffed the fires out, but where her cabin and garden once stood only charred wood remained. The other cabins had suffered the same fate. The old willow tree, which had always stood alone in the center of the lawn, had become nothing more than a burned-out husk of brittle wood and sticks.

Kelt Apar had survived the fires of Crow Tallin and a rampaging fay dragon but fallen to the torches of human Hunters. Norana must have given an order to burn it down. The baroness's wrath had led to this fulfillment of a promised threat she'd made years ago with the signing of the Accord.

But it was not just the burned grounds that caused Pomella's surprise. A thousand fay creatures, tens of thousands, drifted and flew and scurried throughout Kelt Apar.

Winged mice, elephant-eared horses, and other countless critters, both strange and familiar, moved all around her. A dolphin, no longer than her forearm, twisted through the air right in front of her. It leaped and torqued and joined a school of palm-sized bumblebees.

In the far distance Tuppleton, the great tortoise, strode across the grass, swarmed by hundreds of glittering butterflies and bumble-bears.

A smile amid her despair spread across Pomella's face. She'd rarely, if ever, seen so many of the fay together in peace. Her mind spun, trying to understand why they were here.

Perhaps all this resulted from Yarina's passing. With the High Mystic gone, the lineage broken, and no other humans around, Kelt Apar had returned to being unclaimed land. The fay had come to it like ducks to a clear summer lake.

Despite her sadness at seeing her lifelong home ruined, there was an unexpected beauty in the fay dancing across Kelt Apar's ashes.

None of the fay noticed Pomella's presence, but she suspected that they would've ignored her even if they'd been able to see her. While some of the fay were intelligent, and perhaps even brilliant, most acted on animal-like instinct alone, content to live in secluded habitats where they could exist in peace.

She strode past the remains of the burned-out willow tree and came to the central tower. The front door remained locked, as she'd expected. Heavy scuff marks, along with a wedged axe blade, marred the door, marking failed attempts to break it down. Try as they might, the Hunters hadn't been able to breach that barrier, either.

Pomella frowned at the axe head. She Unveiled the Myst to destroy the ugly piece of metal but stopped as her consciousness began to fade with the effort. Distantly, she sensed her physical body pull at her. For an instant she thought of herself as a tired old woman in a jail cell, but she snapped her attention back to focus.

She stepped away from the tower door. She'd have to remember that. The more she tried to affect the waking world while Myst-walking, the heavier the strain it put on her body.

Peering up, she looked at the darkened window at the top of the tower. Beyond it, Vivianna supposedly still slept within the upper chamber. At least, Pomella hoped she still slept.

Curious, Pomella attempted to pass through the stone walls into the tower. But an unseen force held her back, denying her entry.

Pomella frowned. She wished she knew if Vivianna was well, or even alive. What would happen if Vivianna awoke? Would she be able to exit the tower? She didn't know. All she could do was continue forward with her journey.

She moved next to the monument of past masters, walking on her illusionary feet out of habit rather than instantly alighting there. As she walked, an idea occurred to her. She tapped the air to summon Oxillian with the silver bell chime, but again, he did not come. She'd become a stranger, and perhaps an intruder, in her own home.

With the moon obscured by the clouds, the only light to see by came from the soft shine of the collective fay. The burned remains of one of the apprentice cabins were dark, although she could see hunched fay figures lurking in shadows.

At the edge of the monument's grove, Pomella spied another source of light. It shone on her, and despite the lack of a physical body, it warmed her skin.

It was Vivianna's lantern, that ridiculous thing she'd obsessed over, glowing with steady light. The rickety old contraption called to Pomella as if to say, *I am here!* It hung from the same pine branch where Vivianna had left it.

The lantern was a rectangular box framed with whitewashed wood. It was about as tall as the length of Pomella's forearm, with four thin panes of glass serving as its walls. The glass was warped and yellowed with age, but clear enough to see a midnight-blue candle burning within. Its flame gave off more light than its small size normally would. The top of the lantern was peaked with faded, black-painted wood so that the entire contraption looked like a lopsided house.

A swarm of fay moths buzzed around the lantern. Slowly, with trembling uncertainty, Pomella lifted the lantern, and found, to her amazement, she could hold it. A slight tension rose from her distant physical body, but Pomella ignored it. The lantern's light brightened and the familiar sweet scent of Vivianna rose around her.

She turned and looked at the darkened window at the top of the central tower where Vivianna slept. "You've always been there for me, Viv," she said.

With her Mystic staff in one hand and the lantern in the other, she followed the pebbled path toward the monument of past masters.

ELEVEN

THE OCEAN OF MEMORY

The obelisk rose above Pomella, tall and sturdy, and covered, as always, with the carved names of the former High Mystics who had presided over Kelt Apar. The light from Vivianna's lantern shone on the monument's surface, and where it touched, the names flared to life with light and a musical whisper.

Pomella swept the lantern back and forth, watching the light reveal the names. A chorus of voices rose throughout the clearing, wordlessly humming a peaceful harmony that shifted from high glory to deep strength. Pomella didn't know where the music emanated from exactly, or whether it was something she would've been able to hear had she been there in the flesh.

At the base of the monument stood a single yellow candle, the same one she'd placed there the day before Norana's arrival at Kelt Apar.

She lit the candle with a thought and waited. Distantly, she sensed a wave of discomfort gripping her physical body, but she forgot about it immediately as a figure materialized before her.

Silver-and-golden smoke coalesced into a hunched figure wearing robes. High Mystic Hizrith blinked once and licked the air when he saw Pomella.

Pomella bowed. "Master Hizrith. My eyes are old, but I thought I had prepared a yellow candle, and not white."

"You lit the proper candle," Hizrith wheezed. "But Master Willwhite cannot come. They asssked me to attend inssstead."

Pomella couldn't ignore the strain in Hizrith's voice. The Myst always surged near a High Mystic, and it did so now in an agitated fashion, like boiling water rather than a calm pool. Perhaps it was Pomella's imagination, but she thought she saw a tightening around Hizrith's eyes, a little extra intensity to the way he snapped his tongue out.

"Master, are you well?" Pomella asked.

Hizrith waved a clawed hand dismissively. "Age affectsss usss all, laghart and human," he said.

Pomella fixed him with a dubious expression. Something felt wrong. "How did you know I lit Master Willwhite's candle?" she asked.

"Massster Willwhite ssswitched their candle to me. It isss a sssmall thing."

"Are you here to help me?"

"Of courssse."

Perhaps Hizrith was concealing something from her, but she had no time to dwell on it. Her time within this dream was limited.

A white radiance filled the grove from above. With the light came a wind, followed by a large fay bird soaring overhead. His passing wafted Pomella's hair. The creature, massive with fiery plumage, landed beside Hizrith. Pomella knew the great familiar by his reputation and from their meeting years ago during Crow Tallin. He shone brightly, illuminating the monument and the surrounding grove. Pomella noted the amount of power and concentration it would require for Hizrith to not only be present via the candle but have his familiar appear as well.

"Do you remember Hemosssavana?" Hizrith asked, stroking the bird's long beak.

"How could I forget?" Pomella replied. "I've rarely seen his equal."

The mighty bird let out a cry that somehow managed to be both a song and a scream.

Pomella forced a smile, hiding her lingering doubt. She couldn't imagine Willwhite reneging on their word to meet her, but strange were the ways of Mystics, and strangest of all were the ways of the eldest High Mystic. "How do we begin?"

"Sssince the firsssst living Mysssstic walked upon the divided world," Hizrith said with a formal tone, "and likely befffore that, when the worldsss were ssstill merged as they are onccce more, every true High Mysssstic hasss undergone a journey through their land and their experiencesss to become anointed. Within that journey, they learn from their massster the Mysssstic name of their domain, and they inherit the lineage."

Pomella remembered Hizrith cradling his dying master, Ehzeeth, during Crow Tallin, right outside Kelt Apar's central tower. "How did your master pass the name of your domain to you?"

"The name of Indoltruna wasss ssstolen from the laghartsss long ago. It wasss kept, we thhhought, by the People of the Sssky. For generationsss, we had no direct connection to the land. When I returned afffter the worldsss merged, our people tore down the Golden and the People of the Sssky. I journeyed as you are about to, and found the true name of Indoltruna."

"But without a master to pass it to you, where do you find the name?"

"It liesss deep in the Mysssstic Ssskies, in a placcce only you and the land together can disssscover," Hizrith said.

"How will I know it?" Pomella asked.

"You will know it more sssurely than your own name, for ifff the land wasss meant for you, it will ssspeak a language only you undersssstand."

"We met here many years ago, in this very spot," Pomella said. "I am glad you are with me, Master Hizrith."

She bowed, and he inclined his head in return.

"Our friendsssship enduresss," he said. "Are you ready to begin?"

Pomella's hands were full with her Mystic staff and the lantern, so she looped the hook at the top of the lantern into the mouth of the snake carved into her staff. The serpent had been a gift of sorts, given to her long ago, right before Crow Tallin, by the woman who had once been Saint Brigid. The snake head was only ornamental, but it had served as a reminder to Pomella for all these years to be wary of where you placed your trust.

"Yes," Pomella said.

Hizrith's forked tongue lashed as he saw her carved staff. She'd once told him of the carving's origins. The lagharts laid claim to anything associated with Saint Brigid for religious reasons. The Saint's own staff had been destroyed during Crow Tallin. It had belonged to her son, the man who eventually became the corrupt High Mystic Bhairatonix. No matter how many years passed, that revelation still felt surreal to Pomella, who had grown up listening to and singing stories about Saint Brigid.

Hizrith gestured to the monument of past Masters. "Each High Myssstic domain has a monument like thisss. Nobody knowsss who created them, although that sssecret may livvve within the land'sss memory. Touch it, and go with the Myssst."

With the lantern hanging safely from her staff, Pomella pressed her fingertips against the monument. They chilled as they brushed the surface. A fay bug, wafting tiny wisps of silver-and-golden smoke behind it, crawled across the stone.

Pomella stirred the Myst, sensing it swirl around her body, then spiral down the length of her arm toward her wrist, then to her fingertips.

She waited a heartbeat, but nothing changed. She Unveiled the Myst again, probing for an unseen secret to reveal itself. But the monument remained unchanged.

Frowning, Pomella let her hand drop. "Buggerish," she muttered. She eyed Hizrith watching her and wondered how patient he would be. The old anxiety, that nagging doubt that had stalked her for her entire life, that maybe she would fail, and that she was a fraud, crept back into her mind.

Gathering herself once more, she thought of Mia and the other Mystics who were counting on her. She thought of Yarina and Lal, and their memories comforted her. She thought of Vivianna, and glanced at the rickety lantern hanging from her staff.

The lantern light illuminated not only the obelisk but also a patch of dirt on the far side of the grove. On the outermost southern side sat another white pillar, only waist-high but shaped the same as the larger monument. It did not exist in the waking world.

Pomella turned to Hizrith. "What is that? Do you see—?"

But Hizrith was gone, leaving Pomella to wonder if he'd left her, or whether she'd gone someplace else. She exhaled to calm her excitement and nerves.

The smaller monument appeared weathered by time and dirt but was otherwise uncovered. It was cool to the touch, and there was faint writing carved into one of its sides. Pomella squatted to observe it closer.

Like the larger monument of past masters, the diminutive pillar beside her had four flat-surfaced marble sides. But unlike the one she knew, this one had only a single name upon it, carved with clear letter-runes.

Yarina Sienese.

A voice whispered in her ear.

In the vast, unknowable Deep.

It was Yarina's voice, young and strong and full of power. Pomella paused, trying in vain to sense where the voice had come from. She swept the lantern light across more of the clearing. If there was one additional monument, then perhaps—

There. Another monument stood a short distance away, barely visible within the pine trees standing between her and Kelt Apar's western Wall. She approached and found a second name carved into its side.

Ahlala Faywong.

Where faded memories sleep, said a familiar voice. A lump formed in Pomella's throat and she couldn't help but smile. She'd not heard her old master's voice in decades, and although she'd never forget his inflection and accent, just hearing those few words was enough to solidify the memories she'd treasured for years.

She knew now what the monuments were. Holding the lantern up again, she caught sight of the next one, rising just beside the edge of the Wall itself. She approached and found the name of Lal's master, Joycean, who whispered, *I sailed glorious skies.*

Unseen by your eyes, replied Yarina.

A heavy fog had gathered as Pomella approached Oxillian's Wall. The hedge opened at her presence, the bushes and vines unweaving to form a tunnel for her. Beyond it was a world of endless fog, dotted only by the old trees of the Mystwood.

It reminded her of the old painting resting on a shelf in the central tower's library. The artwork depicted a flute player emerging from a fog-enshrouded Mystwood, leading a line of silvery fay animals behind him. Lal had painted it near the time of his anointment.

She found the next small monument, with Grandmistress Ghaina's name carved up on it.

. . . *When all fell apart*, Ghaina's voice spoke.

It shattered my heart, whispered Lal.

Back and back the succession of Mothic High Mystics led her downward into a valley of fog, speaking in fragmented phrases. She no longer saw the trees or forest or anything recognizable from Moth. Her entire world had become a lonely maze of Myst and fog and monuments. She walked a declining slope, taking her time to read the name upon each stone, and as she went she sensed the Myst stirring around her as if in greeting. Soon she lost any sense of time passing. She still didn't know what was expected of her, but she'd learned many times before to trust the lineage of masters.

The fog thickened further until she could no longer see the ground or her feet or even beyond her staff. The blue light from her lantern tinted the smoke around her with a warm hue.

A wind stirred past her, but rather than dispersing the fog, it made it flow like the Creekwaters from her old home in Oakspring.

Pomella followed the fog down, down into herself, and into a place unknown.

"Hello?" she said into the void.

Lights flashed within the fog. Muffled voices spoke from the depths, but she could not understand their words.

The flowing fog gathered speed, and although she felt no pressure upon her dream-body, her mind spun with vertigo.

Another step, and the cloud she walked upon collapsed. Pomella gasped as she tumbled into a vortex funnel.

She flailed her arms and staff, desperate to hold on to something. Nausea threatened to overwhelm her. Lights danced in her vision, and the peaceful ambient music groaned to a harrowing silence.

Pomella's hair and robes were stormed in every direction by a hundred competing winds. She clung to her staff, with the lantern still firmly attached to the snake's mouth but swinging freely. One moment she was descending into the void, and then, without changing directions, she seemed to be falling *up*.

Panic loomed in the back of her mind, but a lifetime of training focused her, bringing calm. She had walked across worlds, ridden the storms of Crow Tallin, and called forth the long-gone masters from the Deep. She would not be undone now.

Steadying her staff, she thrust its lower half toward her feet, as if anchoring herself, and the world slammed back into place.

Smoky walls unfurled around her, rising upward and curling until they met above her, confining her into an onion-shaped enclosure. A seat rose beneath her, forcing her to sit. With her staff in hand Pomella lost her balance, but a small pile of cushions stabilized her.

She was inside a carriage. Gray-and-blue curtains hung from the window, blocking her view. Across from her sat two Shieldguards, and beside her a Hunter. Full metal helmets obscured the Shieldguards' faces and the Hunter's identity was lost in the deep shadows of their hood.

It took Pomella a moment to realize what she was experiencing. She was inside the carriage cabin that she'd recently ridden from Kelt Apar to the fortress. Only this experience was more dreamlike, where the people and the cabin and the curtains seemed only half-present. Moments before, she'd been tumbling through an open sky, but here she was now, reliving a memory she'd recently had. Or at least something that echoed one.

She brushed a loose strand of gray hair away from her eyes. The Shieldguards stared straight ahead. The Hunters gave no indication that they saw Pomella, despite the fact that she'd practically fallen into their lap moments ago. Silver-and-golden smoke wafted from the edge of the windows and the ceiling.

"Where are we?" Pomella asked the Hunter, but as she suspected, the person wouldn't respond or acknowledge her in any way.

The cabin swayed, but it didn't feel like the normal jarring movements of trudging over the road. Instead, it felt as though she were drifting on a child's swing, lazing back and forth.

Her hands were unbound, which was another difference from the experience she'd previously had. She still wore the deep blue robes she'd conjured for the Mystwalk, not the black ones she'd traveled in the carriage with.

Pomella wasn't about to sit still. She had no idea how or why she was back in this carriage, but she certainly wasn't going to discover Moth's Mystic name sitting on this bench.

The Shieldguards and Hunter hardly moved as Pomella awkwardly stood and moved through the cramped cabin to the door. She paused as she reached for the handle.

The Hunter was less than an arm's reach away from her. Although they seemed like a shadow of a person now, the Myst stirred around them in a way that called to her. She hadn't known the Hunter who had ridden in the cabin with her. Before she could stop herself, she yanked back the Hunter's hood.

It wasn't the same person as the one who'd ridden with her from Kelt Apar to the fortress. It was Nabiton, the boy who'd sailed from Qin with her and Mia three years ago. Where his eyes had been, only empty charred sockets remained.

Pomella inhaled sharply. She'd allowed Nabiton to come with them to Kelt Apar because it had been apparent that he lived in a household that abused him. Too common was that scenario in the Qina nobility from what she'd come to learn. She had hoped that Vlenar could make something of him, but Carn had sunk his claws in first, poisoning Nabiton's young mind, luring him with nonspecific promises of revenge against those who abused their power.

Pomella wondered what the boy's damaged eyes meant. Was this experience literal or metaphorical? She wasn't about to stay here, dawdling over the question, though.

But still, she wondered if she could help him.

Reaching out to Nabiton's face, she Unveiled the Myst and soothed the heat from the flesh, trying to ease whatever pain he might have felt. It was a small gesture, and maybe pointless, but the boy had already been through a lot.

Leaving him and the Shieldguards, Pomella swung the carriage door outward and stepped out onto an ocean.

Surging waves stretched to the horizon in all directions. The carriage floated atop the waves, rising and falling with their movement.

Pomella's heart thundered, and she found herself clutching hard to the doorframe with her free hand. Water flooded into the carriage cabin, surging above her knees and waist.

Acting on instinct, Pomella pushed away from the carriage, and watched the ocean pull it down into its depths.

She swam alone in an endless sea. Fear and panic were distant emotions. Not long ago she'd been falling through the sky. She had to remind herself that her body was safe back in the fortress. She was the one creating this experience. She was no victim.

She raised the Myst and lifted her body above the ocean's surface. With a thought, she pulled the water from her robes and hair, leaving herself dry. A cold wind howled past her in force, unbroken by forest or mountains.

Above her, vivid pink-and-orange clouds drifted across a pale green sky. Despite the jarring colors, there was a surprising beauty to it all. The scent of the ocean soothed her, reminding her of more pleasant times.

A wave crashed upward beside her as though it had smashed into a cliff, covering her in foam.

But rather than falling back, the wave took shape, forming itself into the semblance of a man.

Another wave crashed and another person solidified. Then another. All around her, waves crashed and became people. They retained their watery color and substance, but soon she recognized some of the faces. There stood Kambay, his familiar face formed of seawater and foam. Beside him was Shillo, and Pomella's heart cried over the memory of the poor boy's death. Ovelta and Dronas and Kirane and Mia. They were among the last Mystics of Moth.

More water figures emerged, each holding a watery glaive. The

Hunters. Carn's form loomed larger than all others, a tidal wave rising to the height of ten people.

Mounted Shieldguards appeared. Together they charged with the Hunters toward the Mystics, and Pomella cried out as they cut Shillo down again. The wave that had been the young apprentice exploded into vapor.

Pomella raised her staff to . . . what? Destroy the Hunter-waves? She knew of no way to affect them.

Another massive wave rose, larger than Carn's, and this one took on the appearance of Norana. The towering figure loomed over Pomella. "Drown them," Norana commanded.

The same feeling of helplessness that Pomella had felt during the baroness's purge at Kelt Apar returned to her. What could she do? And even if she could stop the Hunter-waves from decimating the Mystic-waves, what would it matter? This was a dream, wasn't it?

More figures rose. Quentin-Kilpa, and the strange Iron Mystic woman who had come with Norana.

Amid the chaos, Pomella looked for Mia and found her backing away, an expression of terror plain on her watery face.

Pomella knew this was a dream. It couldn't be real in the traditional sense. But the experience was vivid and present now, and her fear for her granddaughter gripped her tight.

The wave that was Kambay raced away, dragging other Mystics with him. An enormous wall of water rose around them, encircling every person present. It hung in the air like a mountain, blocking them in. It was like Oxillian's Wall, though far more exaggerated in height.

The Carn-wave struck with his giant glaive at Pomella. She only had time to throw her hands up before the watery weapon crashed upon her, plunging her into the depth of the ocean.

She felt no pain, but the shock of the blow stunned her. For a moment Pomella forgot where she was. She was a child again, swimming in the Creekwaters. She was a young woman, traveling to the apprentice Trials, leaping into the river to avoid corrupted fay wolves.

Memories and emotions swam around her, threatening to consume her. But no, she had to cling to her purpose. She would not drown in old memories.

With a single hard stroke, Pomella shot to the surface, lifted above the water, and settled back onto her feet.

The distant commotion continued as the Hunter-waves decimated the Mystics. Carn and Norana and the Iron Mystic towered above it all.

The Iron Mystic turned her watery expression toward Pomella. Maybe it was the angle, or the unusual light from the oddly hued sky, but the woman's face resembled Kilpa's.

Another familiar presence filled Pomella's senses. It began as musical notes that she hadn't heard in decades. It sang from behind her, so she turned to see a shimmering twinkle flying above the wave tops toward her.

It was a tiny bird, bold and strong. The bird circled her and then hovered in front of her face. All thoughts of the other Mystics faded away as Pomella stared in awe.

"Hector?"

Ena's larger brother had died during Crow Tallin. Pomella lifted a wrinkled hand to the ageless hummingbird, but he didn't land upon it. His movement was erratic, perhaps desperate. She understood.

Hector wanted her to follow him. Away from the chaos. Away from the danger.

Away.

Carn and Norana turned their giant forms toward Pomella and surged toward her.

She bit her lip. She couldn't abandon Mia and Kambay and the others. They *needed* her.

Hector buzzed again.

Far distant, the wave that was Mia stopped and looked back across the water to her. Mia was so distant, so alone, so far away.

The Mia-wave raised her arm as if in farewell and surged out of sight.

It was as though somebody had yanked on a rope tied to Pomella's heart. She wanted to go to Mia and protect her. But the young woman was gone and would have to fend for herself.

Mia was strong. Pomella knew this. Despite her granddaughter's unusual circumstances, she had a tenacity that would enable her to survive. Pomella had to trust that Mia would be OK. Pomella's granddaughter and the other Mystics needed her to find the Mystic name of the island. That was what mattered now. That was what she could control.

Pomella reached out to Hector, much like she did to Ena, and let herself dissolve into his presence. Merging with him, a sense of sadness washed over her.

But Pomella had no time to dwell on it. There was nothing more to be found or discovered in this strange memory. She let herself dissolve fully into Hector, and he lifted her up, up above the waves before plunging down in the depths.

TWELVE

THE HUNTED

Sometimes Mia wondered why she made such unwise decisions. Under normal circumstances, Rion would've called her stupid and grumbled at her until she covered her ears to block out his complaints.

But today, as she and Nabiton and Kilpa knelt on the soft forest floor with their hands behind their heads, Rion remained silent. He leaned against a nearby tree with his arms crossed. An *I-told-you-so* scowl covered his face. Raindrops dripped from the trees, slowly soaking her one plop at a time.

A glaive hovered beside Mia's cheek, its gleaming blade cutting drips of water that fell too close to its edge.

The Hunter holding the blade never took his eyes off her. Another stood in a wide stance with his glaive pointed at Kilpa.

"Bind them," said the Hunter looming over Mia.

It was late morning. After leaving the camp the night before and managing to find a few hours' rest, Mia had led Nabiton and Kilpa back toward Kelt Apar. Rion was reluctant to reveal the way back to the Hunters, but she managed to wriggle their location out of him. Rion had a knack for finding people.

A third Hunter hurried forward and bound her wrists. The cold iron clawed at her skin. She clenched her jaw, and tried to ignore the discomfort.

A fourth figure stepped into view. His breath rose as cold vapor, curling around his wide-brimmed hat.

"Yeh came back," Carn said. His voice was as hard as his square jaw and as rough as his scraggly beard. "Why?"

Mia fought to keep her jaw from trembling, but it seemed like her entire body was determined to shake in fear. She squeezed her eyes shut and tried to focus on her breathing.

Carn hunkered down to her eye level. "I heard yeh were a mutie. Don't talk, they say." He tilted his head, peering at the side of her head and at her body. "Yeh ain't got wings or horns. Don't look Touched on the outside. That's rare these days. Maybe a fay took your tongue." He spit to the side, a violent action that caused Mia to jump.

"Why'd yeh come back?" Carn prompted again.

"She came to save her friend," Kilpa said from beside Mia. She turned to look at him, trying to see the old man through her long strands of wet hair. Hunched over the ground with his hands bound behind his back, he looked especially frail.

Carn looked from Kilpa to Nabiton, who also knelt on the ground as a prisoner. He, too, kept his bandaged face downcast.

Carn motioned to another Hunter. "Clean him up." Returning his attention to Mia, he whistled air quietly through a gap in his teeth. "Why don't yeh talk? Huh?"

Mia found that most people who asked her that question eventually got tired and changed the subject. It didn't take Carn long to do the same. "I'm wont to kill yeh, ya know. To put yeh out of yer misery. But doing that will just rile yer *hetch* grandmhathir. She's likely to sense yer dyin', and we can't have that now, can we? So you're coming with me. But yer friend here . . ."

Mia looked up at Carn, her eyes wide with worry. She shook her head.

Rion pushed off the tree he'd been leaning against and walked over, keeping his arms crossed the entire time. He wore an impeccable red suit complete with black ruffles. Even in Qin it would've been considered outrageous. His slicked hair remained perfectly combed. "He's just trying to scare you. Don't let him."

Mia knew her brother was right. She steeled herself and locked eyes with Carn. His expression shifted to one of mild surprise as he watched her own emotions change. Without breaking her gaze, Mia stood up, struggling only momentarily with the tangle of Amma's old green cloak and her hands bound behind her back.

Carn rose with her. Defiance rolled off Mia in waves.

"There you go, Sister!" Rion said. "Show this old leather strap that he can't push you around! Smack him with the Myst!"

But Mia didn't need to. Carn whistled again softly through the gap in his teeth, then called out to his Hunters, "Pack 'em up!" He leaned toward Mia. "Yeh try to run away and I'll cut your friends open one at a time before slicing your throat."

His words were like water falling on tree roots. She soaked them up, letting them strengthen her.

Carn led most of the Hunters away, dragging Nabiton with them and leaving only two behind to guide her and Kilpa. Mia wasn't sure exactly where they were in the Mystwood, but she was fairly certain they were still south of Kelt Apar. The small band of Hunters traveled in single file, trudging silently along an ancient, moss-covered path.

The Mystwood itself seemed somehow less alive to Mia than what she'd seen of it before. There was more silence, but less light, and, with a sudden jolt, Mia realized there were no fay. Or if there were any, they hid themselves well from Carn and his Hunters.

The clouds gave way, letting the sun drift unfiltered overhead. Over time it moved from Mia's right to left, shifting the angle of shadows and beams of sunlight. By Mia's estimation, they were close to the Murk. The forest was too thick to even attempt to try to see the Wall above the treetops, but there was a thin haze in the air that watered her eyes and smelled of acrid smoke.

"Where are we going?" Rion asked, walking beside her at ease.

Mia eyed her nearest captors. There was a Hunter ahead and behind her, but none, she thought, close enough to hear her and Rion speak.

"We're walking north," Mia muttered, quiet enough for only Rion's ears.

"Yes, I know," he said bitterly. "I'm not stupid. I meant, more generally, where are they taking us?"

"I don't know!" Mia snapped. She was getting tired of Rion's ceaseless pestering. "Go ask them if it's important to you."

Rion held his hands up in mock defense. "Easy there, O mighty Mystic!"

"It's not like they're announcing to me what their plans are," she said. "If you want to know, make yourself useful and find out."

"You know, Sister," Rion said, "that's not a bad idea." He skipped ahead, dodging around bushes and leaping sideways to avoid bumping into the Hunters. Then he was lost to sight, somewhere up ahead near the front of the small company.

Mia yawned. She hadn't slept much, her feet hurt from all the walking, and she hadn't eaten in a day. So much had happened in a short period of time that she'd barely had time to let it all soak in. First the incident with Nabiton when Kilpa had arrived, and then watching Shillo get slaughtered right in front of her. Being chased from Kelt Apar. Smelling it burn and knowing there was nothing she could do about it. And then, the other incident with the Hunters. Had she really hurt those people so badly? Had she *killed*? That wasn't who she was.

Mia was around five years old when she first realized Rion wasn't like other people. Nobody else could see or hear him. She recalled how she'd cried and screamed wordlessly when her mother scolded her, telling her to shut up and that they were alone in the room together, that her brother wasn't standing beside the fireplace and that he'd died before—

She shuddered. Some memories weren't worth revisiting. If it hadn't been for her, Rion would be a living person and not . . . whatever he was. He'd told her once, when they were very young, that they were twins, but that she'd stolen all of Mother's health while they'd been in her womb, letting him waste away, leaving only his spirit to follow her around. She'd been a killer since before she was born.

No. She couldn't go down that path of thinking. Whatever he was, Rion was *real*. He just wasn't like other people. And he wasn't just her fanciful imagination, either.

Maybe if she were better at Unveiling the Myst she could understand Rion. Mia wished that Unveiling were as easy for her as it had always been for Amma. She knew all the stories. Pomella, the Commoner Mystic! The Hummingbird! Amma was a local hero here on Moth. If it hadn't been for the Accord, she would likely have become the patron Saint of the island, cozying up to the likes of Saint Brigid as one of Moth's most beloved daughters.

But Mia had known, from the day Amma had walked into her parents' feast hall in Qin three years ago, that she would never live up to the grand stature of Pomella AnDone. She would never have the same natural mastery of Myst. The same command of the room. The fearless confidence shown by the other woman.

She would just be Mia, the quiet, broken girl.

And that was OK. Because even though her grandmother had been unable to teach her to consistently Unveil the Myst, she'd done something else even more important. She'd loved Mia. And that, more than anything else, was what Mia had craved. She'd realized it right away and come to cherish the lessons with her grandmother. Not once did Amma question her about not speaking. Not once did she demand answers or a response. She simply chatted about her experiences, about the Myst, about her master, Lal, or Yarina and Vivianna. She introduced Mia to Oxillian, who shared interesting tales of long-dead Mystics who had lived in Kelt Apar.

But now, because of the Hunters, it had all come to an end.

"You were right!" Rion said suddenly beside her. "They told me everything!"

Mia quirked an eyebrow. "I suppose you befriended them and then they shared their plans for us?"

Rion pursed his lips and wiggled his fingers. "Not quite, but I listened and maybe prompted them a bit." He winked at her.

Mia tried not to think about how Rion would *prompt* somebody to speak. "Well?"

"They're leading us to meet up with a larger contingent of Hunters," Rion said. "Do you know where Sentry is?"

Mia frowned. "Yes, but I've . . . we've . . . never been there. But it's the closest town north of Kelt Apar and located centrally on the island. Did they say why we're going?"

"Apparently," Rion said, "we're meeting somebody."

"Who?"

Rion shrugged.

"You didn't find out?" Mia said.

"I . . ." Rion fumbled for words, which Mia found to be uncharacteristic. ". . . was trying to observe quietly without being seen."

Mia glared at him a long, flat look.

"Look," he said, suddenly intense, pointing a finger at her. "I don't see you getting us any useful information. They said we were meeting with more Hunters. And something about lagharts. And maybe something about an army."

Mia's stomach tightened as though somebody had tied it into knots. What was happening on this island? An army? Lagharts? She knew very little about the latter except what she knew from Vlenar.

All she knew for sure was that their situation was not improving.

The next morning, a rough boot woke Mia. "Get up."

She sat up, blinking away the deep slumber she'd been in the middle of. For a moment she couldn't remember where she was, but then campfire smoke and the scent of the Hunter's leather brought it all back.

They had made camp in a clearing shortly before nightfall. The Hunters were efficient in their work, and Mia had been relieved that they didn't require her to contribute. She'd gobbled down the soupy oat and acorn meal they'd given her and then promptly fallen asleep.

"Carn wants to see you," the Hunter who had woken her said. He had dark skin, Keffran, probably, like Kilpa. Mia couldn't remember his name, although she'd seen him patrolling the Wall at Kelt Apar before.

The Hunter waited while she'd squatted and washed behind a wide oak, then smoothed her robes and put her grandmother's green cloak on. The cloak had been a gift from Amma when she first came to Kelt Apar. It was worn and patched, but Mia liked the color. She hadn't been allowed to wear it because of the dress code enforced by the Accord. But she'd put it on the day that Norana had arrived, knowing there'd be a chance she'd have to flee.

Carn waited on the northeastern edge of the camp. Two wide knives rested in sheaths on his belt, each curved and longer than Mia's hand. He wore his dark duster and wide-brimmed hat, and was in the process of stringing a bow. A quiver of arrows with black feather fletchings sat near his feet.

"Good morning," Carn said with a crooked smile. Mia came to him like a rabbit approaching a wolf.

"Unbind her," Carn said to her escort, his voice hardening once more. "See that we're ready to move by the time I return."

The Hunter unlocked Mia's wrist bindings. She rubbed the soreness from where the iron had touched her skin.

"That'll be all," Carn said to the Hunter.

"Begging pardon, sir," said the Hunter. "Indrus told me to report something else to you."

"Out with it then," Carn said.

The Keffran Hunter hesitated, flicking a glance at Mia.

"Don't worry about our guest," Carn said. "She's not going anywhere, and she's certainly not about to tell anybody anything. Are yeh?"

Mia ignored his mocking tone.

"Yes, of course, sir," the Hunter said. "Indrus said there's somebody following us."

"Who?" Carn said.

"He doesn't know," said the Hunter. "It's not a Mystic. But it might be somebody from the Murk."

"Mystic sympathizers and Unclaimed shite," Carn said. "Tell Indrus to find whoever it is and take care of it. I want an update when I get back."

"Of course, sir. I'll let him know."

The Hunter left, leaving Mia alone with Carn. He completed stringing the bow, tested the pull, then bent over and tossed Mia the quiver of arrows that had been sitting at his feet.

She fumbled with the catch but managed not to spill the arrows across the ground. A sense of revulsion washed over her.

"It's Mia, right?" he said. "Ulammia." He enunciated her name, but with his haughty tone it just sounded patronizing.

The quiver, and Carn himself, smelled of oiled leather, a scent she'd come to revile these past three years.

"Your old friend Nabiton had a lot to tell me about yeh." He gestured for her to follow.

Mia's twisted stomach feeling returned. Had he hurt Nabiton? She hadn't returned him to Carn just so they could punish him for something he hadn't done. She'd done it so his wounds could get some proper attention. And, in a way, she'd done it as means of showing Nabiton how sorry she was for hurting him.

Slinging his newly strung bow over his shoulder, Carn led her out of the clearing and onto a thin trail that cut through the

Mystwood. Mia was struck once more by the strangeness of the forest, most notably in the lack of fay anywhere. It made her sad, like a pebble piled upon a growing mountain of despair.

"Don't worry about Nabiton," Carn said after they'd walked the path a bit. "Yeh did right by bringing him back. He'll be blind the rest of his life, but I'm sure yeh already knew that."

Carn whistled through the gap in his teeth and shook his head. He walked ahead of Mia so she could only see his back. A sudden, terrifying urge came to her. It would be so easy. She could be upon him in a heartbeat, and she'd end this nightmare by plunging the iron-tipped arrow into the pulsing line in his throat.

Carn looked back over his shoulder. His dark expression cowered her thoughts. "Yeh sure torched that boy," he said. "I'm surprised your grandmhathir didn't teach yeh better control. Or maybe it just proves our point that your kind is dangerous and needs to be looked after."

Mia's grip tightened on the quiver. Anger and fear roiled together in her chest. She looked away and Carn sneered a smile in return. She hated how he mocked her.

"That's why we did it, yeh know," Carn said, still walking forward. "The Accord and all that. I'm sure your grandmhathir has a different telling, but by my Sainted life it's true that we did it to protect ourselves. I was a tyke when Crow Tallin happened. I still remember when everyone was normal and not Touched by fay filth. Mystics like your grandmhathir brought this on us. We suffer 'cause of them. Somebody had to stand up for the common folk."

They followed the trail into the Mystwood. Motes of dust glowed in morning sunbeams slicing through the trees at a low angle. Trees older than civilization watched them pass. Growing up on Qin, Mia heard legends of the Mystwood and all its wonders from the family House Maintainer. Her mother rarely spoke of the forest or of growing up in Kelt Apar. When Mother had learned the House Maintainer was telling Mia bedtime stories of the Mystwood and Saint Brigid, Mother had banished the woman immediately. It wasn't until Mia was eleven that she learned her mother had been born there.

Mia knew her mother and Amma had a falling-out years ago, but she didn't know all the reasons.

Carn led her deeper into the woods, leaving the well-worn trail behind in favor of narrow, overgrown lanes. Branches, boulders, and bushes scraped against Mia's cloak, and more than once she had to catch herself after stumbling on a gnarled root. The air thickened with moisture, causing Mia to sweat.

Maybe she should run, she thought to herself. But where would she go? Kilpa was still back at the camp and she couldn't leave the old man after he'd followed her.

After half an hour of hiking this way, Carn suddenly stopped, holding his fist up beside his head. He unslung his bow and crouched behind a bush and motioned for Mia to do likewise. "Do you sense it? Surely you're attuned enough?"

Mia wondered what he was talking about. There wasn't anything around except the quiet forest and some birds flitting from tree to tree.

Carn shook his head in disappointment and returned his gaze beyond the bush. "Arrow," he muttered, and held out his hand without taking his eyes off whatever he was looking at.

Mia stared at the black arrow she drew from the quiver. She once more considered plunging the arrow into the man's neck but immediately suppressed the urge. She'd hurt enough people already. It would be something Rion would've wanted her to do.

She placed the arrow in Carn's calloused hand and watched as he nocked it and peered harder into the thicket beyond. Mia couldn't see anything, but as she focused she felt . . . something. A slight stir, like a cool breeze on her heart rather than her skin. A wavering resonance as if it were a song being sung far away.

She recognized it then. It was a fay creature. A larger one, from what she could tell.

The resonance grew stronger and she was able to turn her head and peer right at the fay, through bushes, beyond a small cluster of oak and ash, and there she saw it.

It was an elk, grand and powerful, crowned with antlers that had blossomed full trees, complete with leaves and minuscule fay birds that swarmed among those wondrous branches. The elk peered back at Mia, recognizing their connection. His nose twitched.

Carn's arrow slammed into the elk, punching a hole in his chest.

Mia gasped.

The animal crashed to the ground, the leaves of his tiny antler-forest spraying away. He thrashed, kicking in a desperate hope to somehow escape the agony he must be experiencing.

Carn rose from his hiding place and moved to stand beside the floundering figure.

Mia followed, trying not to panic. The elk was even more beautiful up close. He was solid and present, yet silver-and-gold smoke wafted off him like frost melting under the warmth of a newly risen sun. Her heart twisted looking at the poor animal. Here was a creature who, through no fault of his own, had been born to a world that had no room for him. His beauty could be marveled at, but as soon as his Mystical nature was seen he became a threat to be scorned. Hunted.

"I didn't have the upbringing you did," Carn muttered. He readied another arrow. "Lost my mhathir early. No fathir. It was Erksan, the first Hunter, who found me. He was a ranger once. Protected people from the rampaging fay after the Change. He was the first to see the need to cull the fay if there was to be any room for humans anymore. He was the one who showed us that the fay were not innocent like the Mystics claim. They were invaders to our island and a threat to our way of life."

He pulled the arrow, and unsheathed a long knife. Silver-and-golden smoke no longer wafted from the now-exhausted elk.

Mia looked up to see another figure standing nearby, watching them.

Rion.

He wore the same kind of dark duster and leather clothes worn by Carn and watched them with a stony expression.

With casual efficiency, Carn plunged the knife into the elk, stealing his life and the rest of his color.

"And he," said Carn, standing and wiping his blade clean, "saw in me a boy who had witnessed too many horrors. A boy who didn't speak for years and stuttered for many more after that. He saw humanity in me, just as I see it in you. And so, Ulammia, we are more alike than you think."

THIRTEEN

THE SECOND RELIC

Hizrith returned his consciousness to the dimly lit room he had been meditating in. Incense filled the air, but its aroma could not mask Kumava's presence. The scent of concern wafted from his apprentice when she noticed he was awake.

"You are hurt, Master," she said.

As if her words summoned it, a sudden sharp pain stabbed Hizrith's left side, across his chest primarily, but radiating out to his shoulder and arm. He winced, unable to prevent himself from displaying pain.

Kumava hurried forward to drape the heavy cloak of the Supreme Steward across his shoulders. She adjusted it to allow his ridge of spikes to protrude from decorative holes in the fabric running down his back.

"Allow me," she said, gently pulling his arm away from his body, and then unwrapping the loosely draped silk wrap he wore during meditation.

Leaning her head forward, Kumava began to lick his chest, exploring the wound with a repeated and consistent jabbing of her tongue against his burning scales.

"They were formidable," Hizrith said. "But ultimately unprepared. They fell, just as we expected."

"And their followers?"

"The death of a *Zurnta* is often felt by their followers," Hizrith said. "But I was careful. It will appear as though they died in their sleep."

At that, Kumava paused her cleansing ritual to look at her master with a curious expression, her slitted eyes quirking.

"Yes," he said to her unspoken question, "I call them *Zurnta*. Willwhite may not have been laghart, but they were mighty indeed. It brought me no warmth to cease their heart."

It had to have been done, of course. Willwhite had been helping Pomella find the Mystic name of the island, something that could not be allowed under any circumstances.

He had arrived early at Kelt Apar through what *Zurnta* Ehzeeth had called the mind walk. While his body slept in a meditative state, he could travel to places he'd visited before. He had chosen Kelt Apar and the monument of past masters not only because he had been there before, during the days of Crow Tallin, but also because he knew that would be where Pomella would summon Willwhite.

The thin white lines of Willwhite's brows had arched upward in surprise when they materialized beside the candle Hizrith had lit. Hemosavana shifted atop his perch on the monument of past masters. The surprised expression on Willwhite's face vanished a moment later, replaced by the High Mystic's more typical calm demeanor.

"Master Hizrith," Willwhite had said. "Where is Pomella?"

Hizrith had wasted no time. He would not lower himself further by speaking the human's Continental language. All those awkward jaw and tongue movements made him sound like a fool. It was the language of the laghart's oppressors and he would only speak it again to serve a purpose.

Hizrith had not needed to signal Hemosavana. The fay bird knew exactly what to do.

With a piercing scream the familiar struck from atop the

monument, his beak ripping a portion of Willwhite's chest open. Although none of them were physically present together, here, in the mind walk, assaults upon a person's projected self could be made real. And so Willwhite's heart, far distant in Iotepa Falls in Djain, seized inside their chest.

But before they fell, Willwhite retaliated with surprising speed, lancing a blade of silver light through the air, slicing toward Hizrith, who slid out of the way, avoiding being cut in half. His lithe nature saved him, causing him to wonder whether his aged body could've responded in such a way outside of the mind walk.

But even with the twisting dodge, the edge of Willwhite's attack sliced across Hizrith's chest. He felt no pain in the mind walk. He would deal with the physical wound later.

Hemosavana struck again, tearing through Willwhite's head. The High Mystic vanished, and a great surge of the Myst washed over Hizrith like a warm wind.

It echoed across him now, back in the cabin of the ship where Kumava watched him carefully. "I will have a *laven* prepared for you," she said, but Hizrith shook his head.

"No, I will warm myself with the sun," he said. As much as he enjoyed the idea of bathing himself in hot, scented water, there was a more immediate desire he craved. "Is it time?"

"The Unbroken secured the shore with ease," Kumava said. "The legion is setting camp. They will welcome you by evening."

"I will go ashore now," Hizrith declared. He let his scent express his determination. "Ready the Relics."

His apprentice must've sensed the formality of the moment because she stood and stepped away from him, bowed low, then moved to the dim corner of the cabin and returned with his Mystic staff.

Seer Brigid's staff.

At least, a portion of it.

Immediately after Crow Tallin, when the humans were still distracted by the chaotic aftermath, Hizrith had found the remains of Seer Brigid's staff. It had belonged to her son, High Mystic Bhairatonix. His apprentice, the human girl Shevia, murdered her master and incinerated his staff. But not completely. Hizrith found shards, including an intact segment nearly the length of his arm, and brought them back to Indoltruna where they belonged. He'd spent considerable time ensuring that he found every remaining shard within the ashes.

For a year afterward he carefully cultivated the staff's repair. Using masterful Unveilings, he'd fused the Relic remains with his own Mystic staff. He'd *grown* them together until they became something new and sacred.

The *Ismara*, the laghart word for holy union.

Despite his having possession of it for over fifty years, not a day went by where Hizrith wasn't caught up in the sheer power of the Relic.

He looked at Kumava. "Today we take back what was stolen from us centuries ago."

He emerged from the cabin, passing from the candlelit darkness into a daylight world dimmed only by the cover of thick-gray clouds. Ocean scent flooded his senses, along with the tang of burned wood.

Hizrith paused on the threshold of his cabin door and let his eyes adjust to the light. The island of Moth resolved slowly into focus on account of his aging eyes, but when it did he saw the source of the smoke. Thick tendrils rose skyward from a location several miles south. His advance forces had worked quickly, just as Kumava had said.

Sanktarin, his Watcher, and the rest of the crew bowed as he strode to the ship's port side. Kumava offered him assistance to step onto the smaller boat that would row him ashore. He declined her offer but leaned on the railing until he was seated. He settled the *Ismara* across his lap and waited.

Kumava waited for four other Unbroken honor guards, each slit-pupiled, of course, to board, each carrying a corner of a heavily gilded chest. Sanktarin stood greatest among them, honored as he was to be Watcher. The boat was easily large enough for the six of them and the Relic box. Settling beside him, Kumava scented of eagerness. Hizrith wondered if she could scent his similar emotions. It was hard to contain them this day. The Unbroken, each wearing shining bronze armor, heaved the oars in unison, and the anchored ship dwindled away.

Cold water surged against the side of the boat. A cry sounded above, and Hizrith looked up to see Hemosavana gliding overhead, his wavering, partially translucent shadow momentarily sweeping over them.

"When we come ashore," Hizrith said to Kumava, breaking the silence, "you shall keep the second Relic with you at all times, until I need it. No other may touch it."

The only indication of Kumava's surprise was a quick snap of her tongue, which she hid quickly by bowing her head. "You honor me, *Zurnta*."

"You are trained in the use of such a weapon?"

"Of course," she replied immediately. "Its martial uses anyway. I do not know how to utilize its . . . *other* functions, if they exist."

Hizrith eyed the long, rectangular box. They'd discovered both the box and its holy contents when Indoltruna had fallen to his forces decades ago. The box was made of thick cedar inlaid with marble, platinum, and gold. Lagharts carved from jade danced around gem-encrusted dragons. In the center of the glorious lid was a painted rendering of Seer Brigid, its colors only slightly faded by the centuries. Her features were sharper than how she'd appeared during Crow Tallin, less human and more laghart, but she still retained her iconic red hair.

"The Relic is unlike any other weapon," Hizrith said. "It is, in its humblest form, a well-crafted bow. But it resonates with Seer Brigid's *essence*. It is a physical manifestation of her Mystical nature. By holding it, you hold her."

A mix of emotions erupted from Kumava. Excitement, reverence. Fear.

"I will treasure it and keep it safe," Kumava said. "I will not fail you."

"Do not fail *her*," Hizrith corrected.

After coming ashore, they ascended a nearby hill, the highest vantage point in the immediate surrounding area. They'd landed at the northern shore of Moth. A line of twenty Unbroken waited for them, each as still as boulders. Each carried a serrated sword at their side.

Hizrith paused to glance to the southwest where a tall, pointed mountain summit rose above the rest of the island. MagBreckan the second-tallest mountain on Moth, and an important location in Seer Brigid's lore. It was there that her son was supposedly lost, and where she entered Fayün to eventually find him.

Kneeling in the wet grass before them were four humans. Two men, a woman, and a young boy. One of the men was crying and the boy's filthy face had tear streaks. Their rough, homespun clothes and short hair marked them as commoners. Humans on Moth and most of the nearby Continent had peculiar ways of distinguishing their castes.

Thick leather cords bit into each human's wrist, binding them behind their backs.

The Unbroken honor guard rolled out a thick rug across the damp grass and set the heavy Relic chest atop it.

Hizrith tapped one of his sharp nails against the *Ismara*. Kumava, understanding the signal, bowed before the chest, unlatched it, and eased the lid open.

The only sound, beside the wind and nearby ocean waves, was the sobbing of the man.

The Myst stirred around Hizrith. It had been over fifty years since he'd stood upon Moth's soil in the flesh, and he'd forgotten how powerfully and easily it arose here. Bathed in the might of this wondrous island, and standing so close to not one but two of Seer Brigid's sacred Relics, Hizrith knew with more certainty than ever that his time, and the time of the lagharts, had truly come at last.

Kumava lifted the holy Relic from the chest.

It was a wooden hunting bow, sized for a human, with intricate carvings all along its length. The source of those decorations had been lost to time. They had found the bow without string or arrows, so Hizrith had given the order for those to be prepared. The finest craftsmen among the *kanta* had competed to earn the right to weave the strongest bow cord, and craft the mightiest arrows.

Kumava, wearing thin woolen gloves, held the Relic and waited for Hizrith. He turned to the humans. The adults were each about thirty years old, and each was Melded, or Touched, as the humans liked to say.

"What village do you come fffrom?" he asked, hissing in the murky Continental language.

The Melded woman had the pale skin and yellow hair common in this area, and shimmering scales, like a fish, over part of her face and arms. Three blue lines dragged across her neck like gills, although they appeared more like tattoos rather than functional slits.

She stiffened her back and glared defiantly at Hizrith.

"You kneel in the presssence of Hizrith, *Zurnta* of Indoltruna, Sssupreme Sssteward of Lavantath, and Grand Keeper of All That She Hasss Touched," intoned Kumava. "You will ansssswer him."

Sanktarin strode forward, his all-white scales gleaming, and kicked the woman in the back. With her hands tied behind her, she fell facedown into the grass. Sanktarin yanked her back to a kneeling position.

"Whissting Ford," the woman said, defiance still strong in her voice.

"What do you want from us?" said one of the men while the other man sobbed. Thick horns like a ram's curled from his head. He was light skinned as well, as pale as a maggot, Hizrith thought, and wore a beard. But the facial hair was pointed and shaped unusually, giving the impression of a goat melded onto his face.

"Your High Myssstic isss dead," Hizrith said. "Kelt Apar liesss vacant, and we have come, by right and wittth the blesssing of Ssseer Brigid, to take back what isss oursss. One of you will take a messsage to Baronesss Elona AnBroke. Ssshe isss to remain in her easssstern cccity. If ssshe musssters any forcesss aginsssst usss, we will crusssh her."

Because Moth was a small island divided into three baronies, it had been easy for Hizrith to find the most ambitious ruler and exploit their greed. According to Norana, and verified by Hizrith's advance spies, Baroness Elona controlled the second largest and wealthiest barony on Moth, located in these northern regions of the island.

The woman's eyes flicked to the boy, and it was then that Hizrith saw their shared resemblance. She was his mother, and she'd caught the unspoken meaning of Hizrith's words. Only one of them would live to deliver the message.

The woman spit across the distance between them. It splattered on Hizrith's robes.

"Slither back to the water, *snake*. The baroness will skin the scales from your hide."

Hizrith tapped his nail again.

A creak, a whistle, and a wet *thwack* hammered the air as a bronze arrow pulverized the woman's face. Kumava's aim was indeed fine, although he sensed the Myst had helped guide the arrow.

The goat-horned man roared a scream that was cut short by a second arrow that rammed through his heart, killing him before his head slammed onto the ground.

The boy, eyes wide with panic, tried to speak, tried to scream, but no sound came forth. Small nubs grew from his forehead, likely the markings of horns like his father.

The crying man, who resembled the dead woman—her brother, perhaps—sobbed harder.

"Do you remember my messsage, child?" Hizrith asked.

The boy looked back and forth between his mother and Hizrith several times. He mouthed words but couldn't speak. His face crumpled and he cried, too. The front of his pants became wet.

Hizrith Unveiled the Myst, lifted the boy into the air, and pulled him gently closer. The boy, dripping and shaking, cried harder.

"Where does your baroness live?"

Hizrith knew the answer but needed to know the boy could do this.

The boy screamed and shook his head. Human children were so weak compared to laghart hatchlings. It was a wonder they ever reached maturity.

"Hhhow old are you?"

"Leave him alone," the other man said at last. "You've terrified him enough."

Hizrith tapped his fingernail.

An arrow split the air and split the man. The blow knocked him back and spun him around, revealing a bushy red tail curving from his lower body.

"It isss jusst you now, child," Hizrith said. He wove the Myst around and through the boy, stroking his nerves to calm. "You have been chosssen. Like Ssseer Brigid'sss ssson. He witnesssed tragedy, too. I will let you live, but you musssst obey me. Where doesss the baronesss live?"

After some long gulps of air, soothed by the Unveiling, the boy's sobs subsided. "Enttlelund," he said.

"Good," Hizrith said. He shifted the Myst from the ground, tearing a small hole in the grassy hilltop, and lifted a small stone from the dirt. "Follow thisss ssstone. It will protect you and lead you to the baronesss. Tell her what I have sssaid."

The boy nodded, enchanted by the stone and the Myst.

Hizrith set the boy down and watched him follow the pebble down the hill to the east.

"Spread the word. We march south," Hizrith said to Sanktarin in the proper language of his people. "Burn every settlement from here to the town they call Sentry. Kill every human, Melded or not. These are laghart lands once more."

He swept away off the hill, Kumava following, and left the Unbroken to dispose of the human carcasses and stow the Relic chest.

He gave no further thought for the boy, who he knew would deliver his message, before having his heart stop suddenly the moment he finished speaking to the baroness.

Let Baroness Elona come. He and the lagharts would soon be unstoppable.

FOURTEEN

THE LOST APPRENTICE

Pomella plunged from one world into another. One moment she was submerging into the ocean, bubbles and echoing sound streaming up past her, and the next her slippered feet alighted onto a tiled floor. Her staff was still in hand, with its rickety lantern.

The last of the ocean water that had surrounded her moments ago drained away in every direction, leaving her dry. Her hair and blue robes billowed around her, pulled by a heavy wind.

Hector was nowhere to be found, and Pomella wondered if he'd been real. Had *anything* in these experiences been real?

As if summoned by her, the hummingbird appeared once more. She held her hand out for him, wondering if he was more than an illusionary echo of her memory. He seemed to consider landing on her hand but remained aloft.

"Oh, Hector," she said. "I don't know what to think. And where do you think we are?"

She stood in a vast chamber with scattered marble pillars that presumably held up a ceiling that was lost in darkness. She could see no walls anywhere, only seemingly endless emptiness that stretched through the world of pillars. Twinkling stars floated in the void above. For a moment Pomella wondered if the pillars held the vault of the sky itself.

Pomella steadied her mind and tried to get a better understanding of what she was seeing. She didn't know where she was, but she remembered her task. She had come to find the Mystic name of the island. Was it here, echoing somewhere in this seemingly endless chamber?

Lights flashed in the distant hall and muffled voices sounded all around her. She focused her hearing, trying to decipher the words. Perhaps it had been a word. Or a name.

Faces flashed in the distant lights, but they were gone before she could identify them. Another voice came, and this one she recognized.

"Mhathir?"

Her heart leaped. It was Harmona.

A swirling apparition resembling her daughter coalesced near her, just out of reach.

Harmona had always resembled her father. There was so much of Tibron in her that it pained Pomella to see them both reflecting each other in a single face. By the Saints, she missed them both so much.

Pomella took a step toward Harmona. Her staff tapped upon the floor and the sound echoed away into infinity.

"Mona?"

The apparition looked up at her, surprise painting her face. She appeared about the same age as when Pomella had last seen her, in her very late thirties.

"Can you see me?" Pomella asked.

But Harmona looked away, and then walked through a doorframe that was suddenly there, and merged with the muddled light behind it.

Pomella didn't know where the strange doorway led. All she knew was that her daughter had called for her. She paused only a moment before following Harmona through the door. Hector followed.

———

Pomella found herself in a long gilded hallway that curved out of sight before her. Lines of golden inlay edged the marbled floor leading to locations unknown. The doorframe she'd stepped through was gone, leaving only motes of dust drifting in the air.

High arched windows that stretched from floor to distant ceiling ran at regular intervals along the outer edge of the hallway's curve. Sunlight from beyond the windows shone on Pomella's face. She approached and placed her hand against the exquisite cold glass.

Wherever this location was, it soared in the sky, high above a blanket of thick clouds, like a palace honoring the sun. The bright sun caused her to shade her eyes. A lone mountain peak loomed in the far distance, pointed and snowcapped. A whisper-thin shaft of light rose from its summit, beaming into the infinite blue above.

MagDoon. It had to be that mountain, only she wasn't accustomed to seeing it in all its majesty from this high of an angle.

Pulling herself away from the view, Pomella turned back to the hallway, wondering at the fanciful decor. On the inner wall, opposite from the tall windows, paintings and tapestries waited. They all depicted Mystics, both human and laghart, but nobody she recognized.

"Harmona?" she called. Her chest tightened again at the loss. How special, how nice, to have seen her again, even briefly in this strange Mystwalk.

Muffled voices echoed behind her, down one end of the hallway. Startled, she spun quickly, wincing as she braced for the inevitable pain in her hip and knee to flare. But the pain did not come.

She followed the voices. The tapping of her Mystic staff on the floor echoed down the hall. The passage continued on, without any signs of other people. No other doors appeared. As she rounded the curve to the far side of the tower, the distant mountain and beam of light became lost to view.

This was not the ordinary realm she was in, Pomella reminded herself. She'd visited Fayün once in the flesh, shortly before Crow Tallin, before it had merged with the human world. As strange as the fay realm had been, this place she walked in felt even more surreal. Its eerie silence unnerved her.

Some time passed, but it was difficult to discern how much. She was looking for something, but for what? A person? Their name?

"Hello?" she called down the hallway, unable to stand the silence and sense of loneliness.

The voices returned, this time clearer, allowing her to discern two voices.

"Again," said an older voice, a woman.

Pomella's pulse quickened. She recognized that voice.

"Viv?" Pomella called.

She hurried more quickly down the hall, leaning on her staff out of habit.

"It's here with you, always," Vivianna's disembodied voice continued. "It's around you, within you, and indeed it *is* you."

"Vivianna, where are you?" Pomella called. It had undoubtedly been her voice, full of life and strength. By the Saints, it had been too long since she'd heard her friend speak with that confidence.

"I just can't," said a much younger voice, a girl.

Pomella halted.

"Of course you can," Vivianna said. "Everybody has the potential to sense and Unveil the Myst."

"Then why can't I?" said the younger voice. "And if anybody can do it, why don't they? Why aren't commoners Unveiling the Myst? Or the merchant-scholars? Or the Unclaimed?"

"Harmona," Pomella said. She rushed down the long hallway again, cutting through beams of sunlight that slanted in from the tall windows.

"Harmona?" she called again. "Vivianna?"

The voices were so real, and close enough that they seemed merely around the next bend.

"Try again, Harmona," Vivianna said, her voice coming from farther ahead, and betraying a hint of frustration.

"I'm tired. Do I have to?"

The voice came from behind Pomella now, so she came to a stop, her breathing heavy. She glanced around but could not see them.

"You have so much potential," Vivianna's disembodied voice said.

"I must be broken," Harmona replied, coming from a different direction.

"You wouldn't be blocked like this if you focused more on your meditation."

"Why do I have to do this? I'm not sure I even want to be a Mystic."

"It will come eventually. Have patience."

"When can we travel to Sentry again? Or Port Morrush? It's so boring here."

The voices assaulted her from every direction. Pomella gripped her staff, wondering what she was supposed to do.

"You need to break through this," Vivianna said, her voice seeming to come through the inside wall of the curved tower.

Pomella reached out her hand and touched it. Cool, smooth stone greeted her fingertips. But as she pressed, it yielded, shifting its form and letting her fingers pass through.

She slipped through the wall and found herself at the top of a steep set of stairs leading straight down. Gone were the tall windows and sunlight. Small, glowing points of light dotted the walls every handful of steps.

"I don't know how to reach her, Pom," came Vivianna's voice from down the stairs.

Taking a deep breath, Pomella descended, following her friend's voice.

Vivianna continued, triggering memories Pomella held from long ago. "I don't understand," Viv's voice said. "You're her mother. I can sense the Myst all around her, yet she won't reach for it."

As Pomella reached the bottom of the stairway, a doorway came into sight, outlined by light. A simple door handle let her in, revealing a familiar room. Pomella stood now in Vivianna's chamber in Kelt Apar's central tower.

A younger Vivianna, barely older than fifty years, paced the room. Her hair was still mostly dark. She kept it swept up in a casual-yet-perfect bun that Pomella remembered so well.

"Mistress Yarina says I need patience," Vivianna said, still pacing. "She says every student is different, as if I didn't already know that. But I'm running out of ideas, Pom. How do I reach her?"

She turned and looked directly at Pomella, eyes pleading for an answer.

Pomella wondered if her friend could see her as she stood now. What did she think of her, aged in her late seventies, a quarter century older than how she had looked when they'd first had this conversation?

"Viv?" Pomella tested.

Vivianna turned away and moved to the room's lone window to gaze out.

Pomella stepped forward to follow but stopped. She looked down at herself and saw her body was different. Younger, thinner, less hunched. Her fingers had only the faintest signs of knobby knuckles and were smoother than they were in the waking world. She pulled a long strand of her hair around to look at it and saw an equal amount of black as there was gray.

A small smile crossed her face. She, too, was Vivianna's age.

"I've failed her," Vivianna whispered, gazing out the window. "And I've failed you. I don't have what it takes to be a master."

"You haven't failed me, Viv," Pomella said, marveling at the sound of her younger voice. "Harmona . . ." She swallowed and gathered herself. "Harmona wasn't . . . isn't . . . interested in becoming a Mystic. It took me a long time to see that. It doesn't mean you failed as a master."

If Vivianna heard her, she did not show it. "Maybe you should just teach her," Vivianna said. "She's your daughter."

"No, Viv. That wouldn't be good, either."

Vivianna continued to stare outside.

Pomella shifted her own gaze out the window, expecting to see the familiar Kelt Apar lawn. But instead she once more saw the landscape of clouds and the distant mountain peak.

She needed something. Why was she here? She'd come here to find something important.

Vivianna suddenly turned from the window, full of determination. Without looking at Pomella, she strode to the door and picked up her staff that rested by the doorframe. "I'll just have to try harder. There are records and stories of masters who had to overcome great hurdles with their apprentices. Perhaps . . . perhaps I need to be tougher on her. Some apprentices respond better to that. I know she's your daughter, and I love her as though she were my own. But it's clear that I've let my affection for her get in the way. It's gotten in my way of finding the best method of helping her Unveil."

"Viv, no," Pomella said, still trying to puzzle out what she'd been looking for.

But her friend was gone, out the door to the inner spiral stairs of the central tower.

Pomella hurried after Vivianna but halted as soon as she passed through the door. She wasn't in the central tower, but back to another set of stairs, like the ones she'd walked down moments ago. The door she'd just come from was gone, leaving nothing behind but a stone wall.

"In the vast, unknowable Deep," whispered a disembodied voice. "Where faded memories sleep . . ."

Pomella descended these new stairs but stopped after a short distance. On the wall where the door had been was a faint symbol. It was a scorch mark depicting a Mothic knot, circling and twisting around itself to form the shape of a hummingbird.

She frowned at it, wondering what it could mean. But the voices called her, so she continued on, descending the long stairs, past the glowing points of light that lit her steps. Down and down she descended, following Vivianna and Harmona's muffled argument.

Her heart ached at the memories. Harmona had practically been apprenticed to Vivianna from the day she was born. Who else would she have trusted with her daughter's Mystical training? Even Yarina had encouraged the idea as soon as Harmona came of age.

Pomella drifted down the stairs, letting a sense of hope guide her. Hope that she might see Harmona. Hope that maybe, just maybe, this Mystwalk might return her daughter to her.

Like before, a door materialized from the darkness at the base of the stairs, opened at her touch, and led to a familiar place. The eastern road leading away from Kelt Apar, through the Murk, toward Port Morrush.

A simple two-wheeled farmer's cart, pulled by a shaggy ox, trudged away from her. A young farmer, handsome in a scraggly way with light brown hair and beard, walked beside the ox, guiding him. And there, sitting on the back of the cart, her skinny legs dangling off the edge, casually kicking the air, was Harmona.

Beautiful, sweet, stubborn Harmona. Her baby, her darling girl, the light and joy of her life. Her greatest heartbreak.

Pomella stared at her daughter, a rush of emotions nearly overwhelming her. The girl was sixteen, the same age Pomella had been when she left Oakspring to accept the High Mystic's invitation to the apprentice Trials. Harmona's braided dark hair hung low over her shoulder. Her eyes—bold and dark, like Tibron's—stared off in the distance. A small sack of possessions sat on her lap.

"Harmona!" Pomella called, her voice cracking.

"I'm leaving, Mhathir," Harmona said, still gazing away. "It's too late."

Pomella knew the outcome of this conversation. Even without the Mystwalk, she'd relived this encounter a thousand times in her dreams and memory.

Twenty-five years ago Pomella had argued back. Demanded that Harmona stay. But now, many years later, she didn't have the fight in her.

"Why, Harmona?" Pomella said. She spoke softly enough that her daughter shouldn't have been able to hear her. "Was it so terrible here? Was I?"

At this, Harmona looked directly at her. "You left home, too. You left your brother and fathir. Snuck away in the night, never to see them again. At least I said good-bye."

She hadn't said that in Pomella's real memory. Although Harmona appeared young, her tone sounded older.

"My fathir was a cruel, broken man who smothered everything important to me," Pomella said. "If I stayed, I would've crumbled beneath him."

"And Gabor?" Harmona said. "How did that turn out?"

More pain, born of old memories. Pomella couldn't face those, too.

"Did I not love you with everything I had?" she asked.

"Yes, but like your own fathir did for you, you had an idea for what you wanted me to become," Harmon said. "You were so focused on my future that you never considered what I wanted."

"I would've listened to you," Pomella said. "Why didn't you open up to me?"

"The burdens I carry are different from yours, Mhathir." Harmona lifted her sack to indicate it. "I'm not you." The cart rumbled around a curve, taking her from Pomella's sight.

Pomella hurried down the path, waving to her. "Harmona, wait!" Loneliness wrapped itself around her like a cloak.

Hector flew in from somewhere in the fog, silver-and-gold smoke wafting off him. He looped once in the air, then waited for Pomella. Even his presence could not drive her sadness away.

Taking a deep breath, Pomella tried to shake the lingering emotions Harmona had stirred up. She'd kept that sadness, and the disappointment, for so long. Now she'd lost her daughter again, leaving her with nothing.

Harmona would go to Qin. Find shelter with the remnants of Tibron's family. Eventually she'd marry into another noble house and have children of her own, including Mia.

Mia.

Thinking of her was like seeing bright sunlight after a storm. Pomella remembered her granddaughter's face. She remembered . . . more. The fog surrounding her dissipated, and with it, her mind cleared.

The name of the island.

She was here to find the Mystic name of Moth.

She stood now on the edge of a cliff overlooking an ocean of clouds. There was no telling how tall the cliffside was, or how far the plunge would be if she leaped. The lone mountain with the beam of light atop it loomed above her, closer than it had been before.

Hector zoomed out across the edge of the cliff and hovered over the roiling ocean of clouds, waiting.

The memories of Harmona still sat in her chest, heavy and full of pain. But she saw them for what they were. Burdens. Not the people or the memories themselves, but her attachment to them.

How tempting it was to get lost in those memories, to reach and cling to them, and secretly hope that maybe this time there could be a different outcome. She thought of all the things she would say differently.

The ocean of fog roiled silently beside her. The fog stirred by gentle winds. It called to her in the voices of the past masters, *In the vast, unknowable Deep, where faded memories sleep . . . !*

She had to continue. To go *deeper* into this dream. Closing her eyes, she leaped from the edge and called to the Myst to carry her far across the roiling clouds.

FIFTEEN

DAUGHTER OF NONE
BUT THE WOODS

Shaking off the last of the wet morning chill, Brigid returned to the Enttlelund colony where she'd left her son. She huddled her shawl around her shoulders and glanced at the sky, glad to see the sun finally breaking through the storm clouds.

Enttlelund.

She hadn't heard that name before, yet it came to mind as soon as she thought of the colony. It had a different name, didn't it? But no matter how hard she chased the thought, she couldn't think of its proper name.

Her hand still throbbed where the snake had bitten it the day before, but the angry swelling was gone, along with most of the pain. She still couldn't believe what she'd been through during the night. It was as though the strange lizard-woman, Mylezka, had been a dream.

Despite the gradually clearing sky, thunder rolled across the sky. With it came the wind, which swept like ocean waves across the grasslands.

Brigid pulled her windswept hair back behind her head. Silver apparitions slid through the air like fish, only existing for a brief time. She'd seen them often since waking alone beside Mylezka's campfire. She was eager to get back to Janid, but she couldn't keep her mind from wandering. The world was far stranger, far more mysterious, than she could've ever imagined. From the little she'd heard, the colony seemed afraid of the lizard-people living in the woods. But her experience suggested that at least some of the lizard-people were peaceful.

Right now, though, her focus was on getting Janid back. She strode into the colony.

Listen once, hear me thrice.

Brigid stopped dead. She'd only taken a couple of steps within the colony. The voice, a woman's, had seemed to come to her on the wind. She strained to listen.

. . . I cry; I call; I plea . . . Come back to me.

Echoes of memory rolled through her mind like the thunder she'd just heard. She spun around, trying to see if somebody was calling her. "Hello?" she called, but heard no reply.

Had she imagined it? The voice sounded familiar. And while she'd never heard those specific words before, they resonated within her. Perhaps it was her mother. Her Myma had died when she was very young. Or so she'd been told by those who had kept her as a child.

An image came to mind of a humble woman with blond hair, a round face, and sad blue eyes. But the image faded, taken by forgetfulness.

Had that been real? Was that her mother?

She stood still, keeping her eyes closed, trying to hear the voice again, but only the wind spoke to her.

With only a small pang of disappointment, she moved deeper into the colony settlement. A surprising silence greeted her. It was nearly midday, yet not a single person moved about.

She peered through a shuttered window of the nearest dwelling but only saw an emptiness. Beginning to worry, she ran to another home and banged on the front door. Nobody answered, so she pushed her way in.

"Is anyone here? Where is—"

She covered her mouth with her hand.

Flies buzzed above a body lying on the floor. It was a man, his dead eyes staring at the ceiling.

Brigid stumbled out of the home and sprinted toward the place where Engatha lived. Which house was it again? The homes in the tightly built colony weren't arranged in any particular fashion, and they all looked the same to her.

The sky had darkened again with storm clouds. More thunder sounded, but Brigid hardly noticed.

Come back to me.

A single snowflake drifted from the sky in front of Brigid. She barely paid it any mind. Finding Janid was all that mattered.

By the time she found Engatha's home on the far end of the colony, near its northern edge, the snow was falling at a steady rate.

Brigid burst through the door. "Janid?" she called, then gasped.

Engatha sat in a chair by the hearth, head tilted back, mouth wide open, with eyes staring at the ceiling, dead. A fire crackled in a nearby hearth. Beside the fire, a heap of patched clothing lay bundled in the corner of the room, shivering.

Her heart fluttering with hope, Brigid ran to her son. "Janid!"

His eyes were wild, but as soon as he recognized her he sobbed and clung hard to her. "Myma, Myma, Myma!"

"Shhh, shhh, I'm here, Sunshine," she soothed, stroking his head. Tears welled in her eyes. For a moment she thought she had lost him.

Unbidden, she thought of Mylezka's message from the night before. *Release your attachments.*

She clung closer to Janid. She would never let him go.

They left the settlement, walking across a fresh layer of snow. Circling whirlwinds spun flurries ahead of them. Brigid wrapped a blanket from Engatha's home around Janid's shivering body and tightened the one around her own.

Her boy still wore the homespun clothes Brigid had made him, which were sufficient for warmer weather, but they were useless in snow. He and Brigid had lived on this island for a year but had never seen anything as peculiar as this sudden flurry.

As far as Brigid could tell, everyone in the colony except Janid was dead. Her mind spun trying to comprehend what could've happened. Red blotches covered Engatha's exposed skin. Brigid hadn't lingered in order to study her more closely. Janid said nothing else to Brigid, of course, except to mumble "*Myma*" now and again.

Perhaps it was her imagination, but as they left the colony the whirling snow flurries seemed to take shape, revealing hideous faces that blended between human and lizard. Claws reached for her and Janid, but she pushed on, knocking them away if they came too close.

She needed to get home. The farm lay to the west a little over a mile. She wasn't certain that—

A figure formed of snow flurries materialized in front of them, startling her. She stepped back, sheltering Janid. The wind howled harder and the figure further coalesced into the thin shape of a young woman. A gown of snow and silvery light whipped around her as if caught by the wind. The woman held her rippling gown in place and spoke to Brigid, but her voice was nothing but the wind.

Brigid didn't know the woman. And yet—

A village from long ago. High in the mountains where voices echoed between towering peaks. A lovely girl, with soft eyes. Eyes that Brigid had later closed forever.

A little wooden carving of another, different woman.

Banishing the memories, Brigid tucked Janid's head to her chest and hurried around the apparition. The woman remained where she was, but she called out again, pleading with her silent voice.

More apparitions rose around them as Brigid and Janid ran from the colony. Hands reached for them, howling their wind-voices.

Brigid left them all behind, and fled the colony town.

Later at home, Janid finally slept. Brigid sat on the floor of their tiny farmhouse and rocked him as best she could with his long, lanky frame.

She had started a fire, and she found herself appreciating the heat as much as she had the previous night when she'd stumbled upon Mylezka's camp. Whether it was the flames, or the warmth, or something else, no more apparitions haunted them. Still, just to be sure, she kept her longest knife within arm's reach.

She didn't understand what was happening. Those ghastly beings, whether they were human or something else, had groped for her in a desperate, menacing way.

Janid twitched in her arms, startling her, but slumbered on. Brigid stroked his hair. He was growing so quickly. With the colony gone, they were all alone now in this strange land. No longer could she rely on somebody from the colony to help her repair a broken tool. Or trade her surplus crops for other food. She only had herself now. And Janid. In time, he would grow strong and she could rely upon him. Right now, he needed her. Perhaps she needed him, too.

She dozed on the floor, startling awake at a sound from outside. It was in the deep hours of night and the fire had spent itself.

Janid slept beside her, still wrapped in the blanket from Engatha's home. Easing herself away from him, she picked up her knife and peered out the cottage door.

A man stood there, a stone's throw away from the house. At first Brigid thought his body was formed of snow like the apparitions in the colony, but now she saw this man was made of slow-swirling silver and golden light.

The man's features were familiar to her, but she could not place him exactly. He was young, perhaps not much older than twenty. He wore rough clothes suitable to an outdoor life.

She stilled her fear. Opening the door, she advanced to face this person or creature or whatever it was. She spared only a quick glance back at Janid to ensure he still slept.

"Who are you?" she demanded.

The silver-and-golden man watched her, his only movement a slight tilt of the head.

Brigid tightened the grip on her knife. The cold bite of the night's chill grabbed at her, but she ignored it.

"Who are you!" she repeated, shouting this time.

"Brother." The apparition spoke and then gusted away like sand scattered by the wind.

Brigid spun in place, looking for the man, but found only the landscape of her homestead and the far-off hills and even more distant mountains.

Sleep eluded her for the rest of the night, but dawn and its early warmth helped to dispel her fears and the immediate memory of the apparitions. They lingered in her mind, but Janid woke unexpectedly happy and full of energy.

She finally let him go out to play while she set about the morning chores. The sun was already well up, which meant she was behind with her routine. In a time when the world was dissolving around her, there was nothing like hard work to ground one's self in reality and to banish dark memories.

She fetched water from the river, taking care to watch for snakes hiding in the rocks. She placed her handwoven fish traps by the water, showing Janid how to set them. In the afternoon she cleared the rest of the oak tree that had fallen during a recent storm.

All in all, the day went by as normal. Perhaps it had been a dream? She considered returning to the colony but decided against it. If her experiences had all been real, then there was nothing she could do for the dead. The colony's spare supplies tempted her, but the memory of those ghastly dead faces haunted her too much. She had nowhere to flee, no means of leaving this island, nor any desire to do so. Winter would soon be upon her and that was a reality she could not face without preparation, especially if she was alone. This was her home and she wouldn't let anything chase her out.

The day passed without incident, and then, at last, the week. The season gave way to winter, with the fallen aspen leaves dissolving into the ground beneath the nearly endless rain. Brigid had prepared well, though, and the island's climate was such that, despite her recent experience in the colony, the only snow she saw lived atop the mountains that shone through the crisp, cold air.

Spring raced back to the island. Janid continued to grow quickly, forcing her to improvise clothing for him. She used her abundance of wood from the fallen oak to carve herself a hunting bow. The wood formed easily in her hands, revealing itself as though it were eager to become a new shape. Cord and feather-fletched arrows followed until she had a passable tool, one that worked well enough for her to fell deer. That meant meat and clothes for Janid.

By the following summer Janid became more and more restless, eager to explore beyond the boundaries of their homestead. It made Brigid uncomfortable to let him go far on his own, so she'd often range with him, teaching him what she could and learning much on her own through careful experimentation and exploration.

Janid's sixth year arrived and already he was as tall as her shoulders. He still didn't speak, yet Brigid could see his mind working, deftly solving problems. She read to him daily, sometimes multiple times when she could, and she saw his eyes lining the words, soaking them up. Soon he was looking at her small collection of books on his own, and while she couldn't be certain for sure, it seemed to her that Janid could *read*.

No other mysterious incidents occurred, no apparitions, and no word ever came from potential survivors from the colony. For Brigid, those brief days of terror drifted away into a distant memory like those of her childhood and the nightmares she endured during the days of Revolution.

By the time a year had passed, Janid had long since mastered the fish traps, so Brigid let him do that task without supervision. She let him roam a reasonable distance from the homestead so that she could work uninterrupted. She crafted a slingshot for him and was surprised to see him bring home a rabbit and a squirrel within the first week of having it.

"Myma!" he called out, running to her with a dead hare clutched in his fist. "Look!"

The word startled her. It was the first word beside her name that she'd ever heard him speak. She hugged him, tears of happiness in her eyes. He probably assumed they were for the hare.

More words followed, slowly at first, until he had a small vocabulary of regular phrases. Brigid was almost able to have a true conversation with him. They ranged farther together on dry days, joy filling her heart.

At night, she found herself smiling as she sewed clothing for him. Her mind drifted as she worked, looping the needle in and out of the wool, endlessly repeating the pattern until the task was done. Sometimes the smile would fade and it seemed to her that her life was like that needle. Running in and out, working toward something.

Then Janid would shift in his sleep, he would mutter, and Brigid would be glad he was with her. The smile returned to her face and soon she would go to curl up next to him and sleep.

Those were the happiest days of Brigid's life. The snakebite, the dead village, the apparitions, and Mylezka's campfire were all but forgotten until the day came when Janid did not return home.

It was late fall. Brigid yielded to Janid's plea and let him explore the nearby waterfall they'd recently come across. She watched him scamper off, heading west, youthful joy giving wings to his feet. He took his slingshot and deer hide pouch of stones with him.

Beyond him, looming in the far distance, was the mountain that had no name. As Janid vanished out of sight she thought that perhaps during the following spring she would take him there and they'd explore it together. It would be a round-trip journey of several days, but with enough preparation it could be done.

The sun reached its zenith, but Janid hadn't returned. She went looking for him, already berating herself for letting him go alone to the waterfall, which was maybe too far for him after all.

But he was nowhere to be found. No footsteps. No sign of his presence.

"Janid!" she called, but only the heavy rumble of the falls replied.

Worry gave way to genuine fear. She hurried back to the homestead, hoping he'd gone back and their paths hadn't crossed. But the house was still and quiet, with no signs of his return.

By now the afternoon was well upon her, and she feared that with the later season nightfall would come swiftly. Grabbing her bow and cloak, along with a canteen of water and some provisions, she marched out from her house, determined to find him. The wind gusted her hair, so she tied it back with a length of spare bow cord.

She would find him, no matter how long it took.

Six years passed.

Six long, agonizing years that would come to define her life.

To Brigid, the goal never wavered. At all cost, beyond all reason, she would find Janid, her beloved son, her Sunshine. The boy who called her Myma. The boy with a sharp, brilliant mind.

In some moments, it seemed to Brigid as though she'd lived a thousand lifetimes, walked the same steps over and over, searched every lead, fought every foe in an endless loop that she couldn't break free of. Perhaps the course was a bit different, but every passage led her to places and events that echoed in a familiar way to her.

And yet, on days like today, that felt impossible, and the weight of those six years pressed upon her like a singular, unrelenting burden that she'd carried far too long. One lifetime of this had been enough. A thousand was incomprehensible.

She walked through the Great Forest on the southern end of the island. Her cloak hung from her shoulders, but with its strange material she hardly sensed its weight. She preferred the forest and solitude to anything else. In her life of violence and ferocious searching, only the forest with its quiet glades and whispered secrets had brought her any semblance of peace.

Outside the forest, there were people. And where there were people, there was conflict. In the six years of her search, since the catastrophe of that first colony, more people had come to the island. A small port colony had been established at the southern tip of the island, and it seemed to grow every time she visited. She tried to avoid going there as often as she could, yet trouble always seemed to find her.

After years of conflict and betrayal from the new colonists, only the lagharts welcomed her now. From the very beginning, they had been the only ones to embrace her as something close to a friend and not as a rival, or enemy, or symbol to be taken advantage of.

Most of them anyway. A certain contingent, a vocal minority, resented how Mylezka had welcomed a human to their velten.

But now she had returned to that velten, to the *kelta*, their holy ground. She adjusted the soggy pack slung over her shoulder and wiped her nose. No matter how hard she tried, the stench of death filled her nostrils. It had long since seeped into her clothes, perhaps into her skin.

She walked through streams of sunlight lancing through the tree canopy. Where the beams fell, they dissolved the ever-present fog that seemed to hover perpetually in the forest. Small fay critters, squirrels and rabbits, darted through nearby bushes, but she paid them no heed. She knew the way to the *kelta* like she was going home.

Two shadows slid onto the path, blocking her progress. They wore leather of greens and brown and carried stone-tipped spears.

Brigid lifted her hands, palms outward to show she was unarmed.

"Zyhen," she said, "Echlith."

The lagharts licked the air, tasting her scent to confirm her identity.

They'll only smell death, she thought to herself. Always death, but undoubtedly . . . her.

Zyhen's clawed hands moved, signing a welcome they'd come to share. He followed with another sign where he dragged his claw in a long horizontal line and sketched a triangle at the end. A long journey and an arrowhead. The laghart way of saying her name.

"Thank you, Zyhen," she said, lowering her hands.

Zyhen and Echlith, the *kelta*'s two strongest warriors, were hatchling mates, or brothers from the same egg clutch. They eased their weapons. Echlith, whose green scales were so dark they were nearly black, scratched at a place beneath his armor. As always, Zyhen eyed the bow slung across her back. His tongue flicked out as if trying to touch it. The soiled bag that Brigid carried bounced awkwardly against the bow when she walked, but it was still better than carrying the weapon for days and endless miles.

Zyhen's gaze shifted suspiciously to the stained deerskin bag she carried. His tongue snapped out, smelling its contents. "You brought ittt," Zyhen said.

Brigid's expression darkened. "I will speak to the *Zurnta*."

Zyhen motioned to Echlith, who led them the rest of the short distance through ancient trees and large ferns to the *kelta*.

They emerged onto it, a wide, circular grassland that was sloped slightly like a shallow bowl. Robed lagharts carrying staves milled around, mostly in pairs, although occasionally in clusters of three or four. A ring of stone monoliths rose from the center of the clearing. The *kelta* itself.

Brigid eyed the robed figures with suspicion. Mystics. It was the word they'd chosen to describe themselves in her language. Mylezka and the other *Zurntas* taught strange methods of manipulating the world, which they called Unveiling. Mylezka had offered to teach Brigid, which supposedly was a great honor, but Brigid had refused. She remembered all too well what the pre-Revolution Blessed had used their powers for. No matter how much she tried, and despite her fond affection for Mylezka, Brigid could never completely trust anybody who used the so-called Myst. Sometimes it surprised her how strongly she felt this. But it was as though a small voice in her conscious warned her against fully embracing Mystics.

For their part, hardly any of the laghart Mystics trusted Brigid. Only Mylezka seemed undisturbed by her quest, and by the upheaval she brought to the island. There had been some manner of great debate when she'd first arrived, seeking assistance in finding Janid. The Mystics had debated within the center of the *kelta* for most of the day, but in the end they agreed to assist her. Brigid was more than reasonably sure it was only because Mylezka had insisted.

"Welllcome back, Daughter of None," Mylezka said when

Brigid and her escorts had arrived at the *kelta*. Two additional *Zurntas* sat beside Mylezka, each sitting upon a flat stone rising out of the grass.

Brigid's skin pebbled. She always felt a strange rush of peculiar energy when she was around the masters. She placed her right palm over her heart and bowed. "Thank you, *Zurnta*," she said.

"Your quessst wasss successsful?" Mylezka prompted. She wore robes of white wool that matched most of her scales. Her eyes, which, like the spikes running down her back, were outlined in red and black, flicked to the bag on Brigid's shoulder.

Brigid unslung her bow and held it with her off hand. That, too, caught the attention of every laghart present. They craved Dauntless. And perhaps they had the right to the Relic, as it was part of their mythology and culture. But she, and not they, had won it.

"Yes," she replied. She unslung the wet bag from her shoulder, unraveled the knot, and held the dripping contents aloft.

"I found your Lor Gez, the All-Seeing."

Hissing sounded all around her as the lagharts looked upon the severed head of their enemy.

"Why do you bring hisss blood to our *kelta*?" one of the *Zurntas* hissed. Brigid did not know the master's name.

"Is that not what you wanted?" Brigid shot back. "This creature hunted you for sport. He stole not only this bow, but your teachings, twisting the Myst around him for hideous purpose." She flung the head onto the ground between herself and the *Zurntas*. It was covered with human eyes, each a unique color. Most of the eyes were open, but some were closed. She'd been too sickened to count them, but there were at least fourteen or sixteen covering nearly every inch of his skull, peering in all directions. Among the horrors she'd seen in her lifetime, Lor Gez stood among the most hideous.

"And now he defiles our sssacred ground," the *Zurnta* countered.

Other la08harts outside the circle of stones had gathered, hissing to themselves. The air crackled with energy, and Brigid could practically feel her hair curling as it surged around her.

The intensity of the hissing increased when the confrontational *Zurnta* stood from where he'd been sitting on his rock and stepped forward. His staff was tall and bent at hard angles in multiple places.

"I told you," he said to the gathering crowd, "that ssshe isss a harbinger of deattth. Ssshe—"

Enough.

In a single, fluid motion, Brigid drew Dauntless. Her fingers found the impossibly smooth string and drew it to her cheek. There was no arrow, but also no need for one. She aimed skyward and released.

Thunder boomed from a cloudless sky throughout the *kelta*. The lagharts silenced immediately, staring in outright shock or terror or amazement.

Brigid strode forward, meeting the gaze of every *Zurnta*. She rested a boot on Lor Gez's head.

"I may have struck the head from Lor Gez, but he is dead because of you. You call me death, yet I was the executioner of your justice. How dare you judge me for the actions you desired?"

She swept her gaze across every laghart present, driving her point home.

"A new age is upon us," she continued. "The Tyrant King of Dragons has fallen. His Vastness shattered, leaving the Continental lands in disarray. More humans will come to this island. Some seeking refuge, and others seeking opportunity. They will come like the torrential rains, washing away your way of life because that is their way. Unless . . ."

Again, she held their attention.

"Unless you join with me. For I have crushed every so-called king who stepped onto these shores. I broke them so that you, the *kanta*, the People, could live in peace. I have turned against my own kind for you."

A gust of wind howled past Brigid. For a moment the circle of monoliths vanished, replaced by a great stone tower with a conical green roof looming above her. Storm clouds raced in to cover the unseasonably clear sky. The remains of burned lagharts lay at her feet, disintegrated to ash in many places.

Kelt Apar.

The name rushed to her in a flood, and other faces—human faces—flickered around the clearing. The charred lagharts became human. One of the figures still lived and clawed toward her seeking, what? Salvation? A cure?

Her hand found her forehead, which throbbed with an aching pulse. This wasn't right. She'd seen this before. Again. The dead lagharts. The bodies.

A roar rose within her chest and she let it loose, screaming her confusion and frustration toward the clouds.

When she was calm, the dead bodies and the tower were gone, replaced with the monolith circle and Mylezka. The other lagharts were nowhere to be seen.

"Where—where did everyone go?" Brigid asked.

Mylezka, the wisest of *Zurntas* and the closest thing Brigid had to a friend, eyed her carefully. "You've never been part of thisss world. You are nottt laghart and you don'ttt belong wittth the humansss. Not anymore. The Myssst hasss alwaysss moved around you in profound waysss."

"I don't need the Myst," Brigid sneered. "I just need—"

"To find your ssson, yesss," Mylezka interrupted. It surprised Brigid to hear her jump in like that. Normally Mylezka had the patience of a blooming flower.

"How long have you sssearched, Brigid?"

"Six years."

To Brigid's surprise, Mylezka shook her head. "It hasss been far longer than that."

Brigid's eyes narrowed. "What do you mean?"

"We've had thisss discusssion countless timesss," the laghart said. "Alwaysss I find you wounded in the forest wittth a sssnake-bite. Alwaysss I offer to teach you to Unveil the Mysssst. Alwaysss you refussse and travel the island, killing and sssearching for ss-something you know isssn't there."

Anger rose in Brigid. "You claimed you could help me find him! Every task I've done has been for the benefit of the *kanta*!"

"But hasss it?" Mylezka said. "Or hass it been for you to prove sssomething?"

"And what would that be, O great master of the Myst?" Brigid snapped.

"That you are who you thhhink you are."

"What does that mean?"

"It meansss you are trapped. You are losssst. And you will never have peaccce until you dissscover the truth."

"And how do I do that?"

"Go to the place that callsss you. Go to the one you hear."

Brigid waved her away. "I'm done here. You speak in riddles. I'll find my own way." She turned and left, heading for the forest.

"The Namelesss Saint," Mylezka said. "Ssshe waitsss for you atop the mountain. Jussst as ssshe alwaysss hasss."

Brigid stopped and looked back over her shoulder.

"I don't know what you're talking about," she said, and left.

The *Zurnta*'s voice followed after her. "Then I will sssee you again, after the bite."

SIXTEEN

SENTRY

"Well, this is a quaint little place, isn't it?" Rion muttered.

Mia glared at her brother as a contingent of Hunters, led by Carn, marched her and Kilpa through a tall, arched gate that was, in turn, guarded by more Hunters.

The town of Sentry had stood for centuries within the north-eastern outskirts of the Mystwood. Mia knew it by reputation as a cozy hamlet that marked the very edge of the northern barony. Norana's territories lay to the south. At least, they had. The baroness's banner hung from the top of the wooden wall, spilling over its outer edge, displaying silver and blue.

The pungent smell of burning wood lay thick in the air. Sentry, Mia saw, was a conquered town.

As they passed through the gate under the watchful eyes of the Hunters, Mia couldn't help but marvel at how naturally the town harmonized with the surrounding forest. The Mystwood had decided that the presence of a large town wasn't enough to stop its business of growing. Oak and aspen, cedar and fir, all encircled its wooden walls. The outer wall wasn't as tall as Oxillian's Wall surrounding Kelt Apar, but all of that carefully placed lumber was still impressively assembled. The buildings crammed inside the town were typical of those on Moth, with wooden structures, peaked thatched roofs to let the endless rain slip off, and shut-tered windows to let the inhabitants peer outside longingly while it poured.

Kilpa had been especially silent of late, seemingly withdrawn into himself. He shuffled forward, eyes down, like a condemned man going to his execution.

Mia worried about him. The Hunters had pushed them hard through the often-uneven terrain of the Mystwood. Even with her youth, it had been hard on her physically, so she couldn't imagine the challenge that the older man had to endure.

But at every brief rest, Mia placed a hand on his knee to silently inquire about his condition, and he would just smile in his charm-ing way and pat her hand reassuringly.

So it continued each day.

The morning they arrived at Sentry, Rion informed Mia that Carn had received an update on the mysterious pursuer from the day she and Carn had gone hunting. According to the Hunter's report, they'd lost track of the mysterious lurker and believed he'd left them. From what Rion described of Carn's stony expression, she doubted the Hunter leader believed them.

Within the town walls, Sentry appeared relatively well orga-nized. The sawdust scent of freshly cut lumber mingled with the lingering stench of the recent burnings. Straight, perpendicular avenues created right-angle intersections with homes and shops and stables and other buildings filling in the blocks. It wasn't a large town, certainly not the size of Port Morrush or any of the great cities of Qin, but Mia could appreciate Sentry's attempt at being an important location on the island.

A tall, four-sided wooden tower rose from the center of the town, looming over the other buildings. It had a peaked cap, sim-ilar to Kelt Apar's central tower, with the baroness's flag fluttering on a pole atop it.

"You have to admit," Rion said, "she has impressive ambition."

Mia glared at her brother but decided not to start an argument with him.

Facing out from the top of each of the tower's four sides, a round-faced disk with regular hatch markings had been hung. Straight arrow-arms pointed to different marks.

A clock. Mia's family had one in the parlor back home that was as tall as a person. But the massive clockfaces alone on Sentry's central tower were taller than her family's entire piece. Small windows peered out beneath each of the impressive clockfaces.

Despite its being midmorning, only a bare handful of people bustled around, presumably going about their chores. Most people kept their heads down and moved quickly so as not to catch the unwanted attention of the Hunters. The latter patrolled in groups of three or four.

It took her a moment to realize what was unusual about what she saw. All the villagers were Touched. Now that she was aware of it, she made a point to look for any Untouched people as the Hunters led her into the heart of the town. But she saw only people with antlers, hooves, feathers, beaks, talons, or other obvious Touched features.

The Hunters, who were all Untouched of course, stood at every intersection, holding their iron-tipped glaives at the ready. Their numbers were bolstered by soldiers wearing the blue-and-silver markings of the southern barony. Norana's Shieldguards, then.

"So morbid," Rion muttered. "Those soldiers look as though they might skewer somebody for sneezing."

There was always violence when people took land that they wanted, but strangely, Mia saw no indications of widespread fighting. No bloodstained streets or piles of bodies to be burned. There was only the scent of burned buildings, although she didn't see any charred ruins.

Her stomach rumbled. She hadn't eaten since yesterday because she'd given her portion, and some of her water, to Kilpa. Her feet were sore from days of marching.

Their entourage arrived at the wooden clock tower. Past a double-door entrance a foyer yawned wide on the ground floor. The Hunters led her and Kilpa to a smaller, minimally furnished side room and they were given water and damp cloths to refresh themselves. Later, a Hunter tossed a fist of bread to Mia and grunted about that being the only food they would receive for a while. She and Kilpa chewed their meal in silence.

The room lacked elaborate furnishings, having only a long table, some chairs, and a handful of paintings on the wall. No fewer than six Hunters watched over them.

Rion roamed around the room, arms folded behind his back, peering patiently at both the artwork on the wall and, on occasion, one of the unsuspecting Hunters.

Normally Mia disliked when he did that, putting his nose just a fingertip's distance from a stranger's face, but as she had no love for these Hunters, she decided to let Rion have his fun.

Most of the paintings depicted abstract scenes from the Mystwood, or slashing approximations of the Ironlow Mountains. But one painting in particular caught her attention more than the others.

It depicted Kelt Apar and the central tower, as seen from a distance near the Wall across the lawn. The artwork depicted the tower in an idyllic fashion with windswept grass creating a sea and the central tower a lone island among the emerald swells. A sky of wispy, cloud-swept blue dominated the canvas, and at the top of the tower, radiating from a tiny window at its summit below the conical roof, a circular aura of light rang out. The artist had made the ring of light subtle, so it completed the artwork rather than controlled it.

It was a beautiful painting, Mia thought, but it didn't feel like the Kelt Apar she'd known. What she had known were a little over three rainy years of oppression at the hands of the Hunters. Sometimes she regretted coming to Moth with Amma. The Hunters were terrible and no sane person would willingly subjugate themselves to them.

But what other people didn't understand was that despite living in a wealthy household, she was, in many ways, even more repressed in her old home. As in so many other noble Qina homes, her parents were as cold and unloving as winter mountains. Her silence made her as invisible as Rion at times to the rest of her family. Nobody calmed their shouting when she was near. Nobody held back with their criticism and name-calling. Nobody showed her affection. Until Amma arrived, anyway.

Maybe the Kelt Apar shown in that painting had existed once, in the near-mythical high days of spring when her commoner grandmother strolled onto the lawn barefoot and won the heart of an old master and, later, the heart of the people of Moth. Those days were gone, burned away by Crow Tallin and its aftermath long years before Mia had ever drawn breath.

The Kelt Apar in that painting was a dream from last night, and now, in this moment, it had become the sad time of afternoon when dreams were distant and forgotten.

Mia pulled her eyes from the painting and found Kilpa watching her carefully.

Before she could wonder more about it, the door across the length of the table opened. Two more Hunters entered, taking up positions on either side of the doorway, followed by Carn, and three lagharts.

What were lagharts doing here?

The first of the lagharts was clearly a soldier or bodyguard, armed with vicious swords and armor that fit snugly to his form. Every exposed scale on his body was silver-white, and his slitted pupils were clouded over, opaquing his eyes, though they scanned the room with obvious clarity. The other two lagharts were Mystics.

Mia had never seen laghart Mystics before, but it was clear enough which was the master, and the other, the apprentice.

The apprentice had pale blue scales accented by darker blue. She wore robes of purple and gold, the same as her master's, if less elaborate in design and decorative lining. She stood a step behind the elder Mystic but watched Mia carefully, her slitted eyes taking in every detail that she could. Her tongue flicked out, its tip snapping the air.

The master leaned heavily on his tall staff, clunking it down hard with every step before using it to leverage his body forward. He wheezed slightly as he neared Mia. Carn entered with them and made his way directly to Mia.

"Stand up!" he snapped, knocking the end of his glaive against Mia's chair. "Show respect."

Mia hastened to her feet, silently remarking that it was the first time Carn had insisted on any respect for any kind of Mystic.

Mia lowered her eyes, as was proper in Qin, but she did not bow. Kilpa eased his way up but neither bowed nor lowered his eyes. Rion was nowhere to be found, and Mia could understand his reluctance to be present now.

"Thisss isss the giffft your baronesss spoke of?" the apprentice scoffed. "You wassste Massster Hizrith's time wittth—" Mia could not understand the final word she spoke, but it was clearly an insult from its harsh tone.

"Baroness ManHinley offers this one to you as an affirmation of your agreement," Carn said, nodding toward Mia. He paused for what Mia could only assume was an attempt to build a light suspense. "This girl is, as you might see, the granddaughter of Pomella AnDone."

The apprentice Mystic's eyes narrowed and her tongue flailed the air.

If the master, Hizrith, showed any surprise, Mia could not see it. He peered *through* her the way Amma could do at times, like Yarina had once done. By this, Mia knew she stood in the presence of a truly powerful Mystic, one who understood the Myst more deeply than perhaps she ever would.

"And the ottther?" Hizrith said, not even bothering to glance to Kilpa.

"Just an old man," Carn said. "We kept him alive only so the girl wouldn't blubber and slow us down."

Mia knew that wasn't true. The real reason they'd kept him unharmed, she suspected, was because they'd seen what had happened to Nabiton and weren't about to risk her wrath. Hunters could control Mystics to an extent with their iron, but perhaps there were limits to what they could prevent.

"Leavvve usss," Hizrith commanded the guards, raising one gnarled claw finger. Most of the Hunters filed out of the room, leaving Mia and Kilpa with the Mystics, Carn, and the lone laghart bodyguard. Apparently the white laghart was above the normal rank and file. An elite bodyguard then.

"What is ssshe called?" Hizrith said, though he addressed Mia.

Mia kept her eyes downcast. Master or not, she would not give this Mystic what he wanted.

The Mystic apprentice stepped forward. "You will ansssswer His Highnesss!" she snapped, but her master lifted his claw again, and she halted.

"You will get no answer from Ulammia," Kilpa wheezed, speaking for the first time in days. "Her voice has given way to other gifts."

Hizrith turned to Kilpa for the first time. He stepped toward the older man, and his tongue flicked out, tasting the air between them. "You ssscent of the Myssst," the master said. "But it hasss abandoned you. Why?"

"The High Mystic saw to that long ago," Kilpa replied.

Hizrith considered this a moment, then returned his attention to Mia. "Ssstand there," he said, and gestured toward a more open part of the room away from the table. With only a quick glance at Kilpa, Mia made her way to the indicated place.

The master Mystic circled around her, eyeing her like a nobleman might examine a potential sculpture for his courtyard. Or a wolf stalking a lamb, right before the assault.

"What ussse would His Highnesss have fffor thisss girl?" the apprentice asked Carn.

But it was Hizrith who answered. "Tell your missstress that I acccept her generousss gift."

His claw reached out, and perhaps it was Mia's imagination, but his claw seemed to tremble before touching her cloak, the old patched green one. But before Mia could determine why, he pulled back.

"Sssee that ssshe bathesss," Hizrith said, turning away to leave the room. He gestured to his white bodyguard and spoke quickly in their native language.

The menacing bodyguard revealed some iron manacles and moved toward Mia.

"No need for those," Hizrith said. "The Myst gathers around her, but she is raw still. An apprentice. She is no threat to our forces. Treat her with respect."

The elite bodyguard gestured for Mia to exit through a different door. Mia noted he did not touch her.

"And the other?" Carn said.

Hizrith did not look back. "He is yours. Do as you will."

Mia gasped and moved to stand guard over Kilpa, but the laghart bodyguard snarled and pointed a jagged sword toward her.

Hizrith left the room, followed by his apprentice and, finally, a grinning Carn and Kilpa, whose face had once more become downcast and resigned.

The white-scaled bodyguard locked Mia in another room in the clock tower. Like the one she'd just been in with Kilpa and Hizrith, the room hardly had any furnishings. In this case, a lone chair sat by a small, high window. The lock thunked into place, but Mia could see other forms through the gap beneath the door. Lagharts.

"Great," Rion said in Qina. "We've gone from being prisoners of the Hunters to being laghart captives. Nicely done, Sister."

"Well, you weren't any help back there," she retorted, also speaking in Qina.

"Me?" he said, incredulous. "I'm not the one who volunteered to become a prisoner to begin with. Don't lecture me."

His tone was so much like their father's that Mia had to walk away. Not that there was anywhere to go. She stood in the farthest corner that she could from her brother.

"So what's your plan now?" Rion said. He lounged in the chair, one arm thrown over the back.

"I don't know," she confessed.

"They'll kill him, you know."

Rion was right. Carn and the Hunters would likely torture and hang Kilpa. It was mid-autumn, which meant evening had already arrived. She prayed to her ancestors that Carn would stay Kilpa's execution until morning. But she doubted he would. There was no reason for it.

"You do this to yourself," Rion said. "Every time. You think you're doing the right thing, like trying to save that boy, but all you did was further endanger him. Now you're getting the old man killed."

"His name's Nabiton, not 'that boy,'" Mia said.

"No," Rion pressed, "he's 'that boy.' Different from the other boy before him years ago that caught your fancy. You have a soft spot for the handsome ones, don't you? Like the injured mice you used to find in the cellars. But they withered in your care and Father had to wring their necks to put them out of their misery. I'll tell you this, Sister, that boy's and the old man's biggest problem isn't Hunters or lagharts. It's *you*."

Mia's eyes squeezed shut tight. "Leave me alone," she said.

"There you go again. Getting yourself *emotional* and hoping that your mean brother will leave you alone. Well, hope's a poison, Sister. You can just sit there passive, *hoping* all night for somebody to save the old man, or you can *do something*."

"Like what?" she said, and hated that her voice betrayed a note of desperation.

"Like figuring a way out past those lagharts to start with," Rion said. "Oh, and the locked door."

A spark of an idea floated into the room, drifting downward like a glowing ember toward dry grass. Mia watched it fall, her mind racing.

"I am locked in here . . . but you're not," she said, and looked at him.

He blinked in surprise, then shook his head as he realized what she was talking about. "No way. No."

"Now who's the one doing nothing?" Mia said.

Rion crossed his arms. "I refuse."

The spark that had landed on dry grass caught fire. Mia's eyes blazed with its flame as she stepped toward the chair Rion lounged in.

"You say I'm afraid; I think it's you who are filled with fear," she burned. "I wasn't the only child in our family that cowered from Father. For all your verbal abuse, you're just as affected as I. But where I sought refuge in solitude, your armor is of polished silver, mirroring the abusive behavior that you see. You *will* do as I say, Brother. By sweet or strap, you will obey me."

She loomed over him, a storm fire of righteous power. Rion's eyes were as wide as her fists. He leaned farther away from her and fell off the chair.

Mia kicked it out of the way, sending it skittering across the small room.

"Get up," she said.

With what was likely a supreme act of courage on his part, Rion replaced the expression of naked fear on his face with steady calm. He rose to his feet, dusted himself off, and said, "Very well. No need for all the drama. What, then, shall I do for thee, O Mistress of Sparks?"

Mia looked toward the door. "First," she said, "my chair."

She didn't see him, but she could imagine Rion rolling his eyes at her behind her back. But, just as she'd commanded, he obeyed, and placed the chair she'd kicked beside her. She sat, took a deep breath, and closed her eyes.

"Are you sure about this?" Rion said.

"Yes," Mia said, although in truth, she wasn't certain that this plan could be done. He grumbled about it, but Rion frequently spied on other people or fetched her objects and information. Sometimes, when he let her, she could hear through his ears and sometimes see through his eyes. So what if Mia . . . *went* . . . with him more fully?

She evened her breathing, just as Amma had taught her. The righteous inferno within her subsided, but glowing embers remained, hot in their core, pulsing with the evenness of her breathing.

"OK," Rion said. "Where do you want me to go?"

Mia let the Myst wash over her. Let her consciousness shift from her physical body to Rion. There was a rush, and a moment of vertigo, but then she saw that she stood by the door, looking back at herself.

Her body sat on the chair, and despite the calm, meditative expression on her face, the fatigue lines lay heavy below her eyes.

"We find Kilpa," she commanded. Together, they passed through the door.

There was a mental trick to moving with Rion. It involved two parts.

For the first part, they did not walk. Perhaps her brother would appear to do so when he was around Mia, but when she moved as part of him that wasn't possible. It was as though their twin presence weighed them down, preventing them from moving in a way she was familiar with.

They could not step or move in a small, gradual manner. They had to *surge*. Mia would turn their attention to the place she wanted to go to, and initiate a rush of movement. The world around them blurred, colors streaking like smeared paint for a single heartbeat, and then they would be there together.

The second part of knowing how to move with Rion was to not think of herself as separate from him. Every time she began to think of herself as *Mia*, and him as *Rion*, they pulled apart and the awareness of herself sitting on a chair in an empty room became stronger.

So it was a constant test of her willpower and ability to exist in a state of calm focus to remain merged with her brother.

At first, as they stood outside the door of the room she was locked in, it took exceptional will on Mia's part to keep them together. Either Rion chose not to speak, or he was unable to, and Mia found herself strangely wishing for his voice. Even so, without words, she sensed his presence, silent and encouraging, if perhaps a little harsh, urging her forward.

Two laghart warriors guarded her door, though neither of them was the white bodyguard who had escorted her earlier. The two warriors also had an elite look about them, with their heavily decorated armor and fierce weapons supporting that idea.

They stood with their clawed hands near their weapons, and their slitted eyes constantly roved the foyer.

Mia focused her joined energy with Rion and *shifted* their location to the middle of that foyer. Carved wooden pillars decorated the space, with slatted lanterns hanging from iron hooks. This tower with its working clock must have been a location of significance to the people of Sentry, perhaps an official building conducting the business of the town.

A heavy weight pulled upon her consciousness, blurring her sight, and for a terrifying moment she thought she would lose the connection to Rion. But she let go of the idea that there was a *Mia* who lacked knowledge of Sentry, and a *Rion* who carried her awareness. There was only a single whole, held fast by her concentration.

The foyer returned to focus, their combined pulse slowed, and once more, they found themselves in control.

More guards stood watch over a handful of other doors, each seemingly trying to outdo the others in their ability to be constantly vigilant.

They needed to find Kilpa. But how?

The feeling that was Rion in their awareness pulsed, like a warm light seen at the edge of their vision.

They turned in that direction, toward the warmth, and surged out of the building, into the darkened avenue. No more townsfolk walked the streets, but whether that was due to an enforced curfew or a desire to remain inside and avoid trouble they did not know.

The only visible figures were laghart warriors, standing at street corners, watching the night warily. The lagharts patrolled this northern part of Sentry while the Hunters occupied the southern. That left the town and its poor inhabitants as the meeting ground between two militant forces.

Shifting their location again, they moved south, toward the human-occupied district, leaving the clock tower behind them.

They arrived at an intersection with more laghart warriors, so they shifted farther, wondering exactly how many lagharts occupied Sentry.

Mia-Rion came to a street where a large gathering of lagharts waited. These warriors had the additional markings of the elite guard.

On the immediate other side of the street, eyeing the lagharts with open mistrust, was a gathering of Hunters. Some of them rested their hands on their glaives and knives and bows, while several had already drawn their weapons, just in case.

For a moment Mia-Rion stood in the middle of the intersection, equally distant between the two factions. Waves of aggressive energy crashed from either side. It was all they could do to remain stable in their merged form.

Harnessing their attention, they shifted again, crossing to the southern human side.

While they didn't know precisely where Kilpa was being held, they assumed he would be with Carn. And with Carn not on the front line, he'd likely be wherever the Hunters kept their command. And that meant finding the largest cluster of them.

It proved to not be difficult. A gathering of Hunters had congregated outside a large building, many of them holding torches aloft. There had to have been hundreds present, more than Mia had ever known to exist.

The Mia-Rion union wavered again, but this time it was the Rion portion who pulled his sister back into alignment. The action lacked anger or frustration but still remained firm in its resolve.

The questions of where the Hunters had come from, and how they'd managed to recruit so many to their ranks, dissolved. Regardless of the methods, there would always be a means to gather those who harbored disdain or fear of others.

Glaives and torches jabbed the night sky. The merged siblings shifted through the crowd, streaking past blurred faces and shouts.

Carn stood at the front, his heavy duster and hat laid upon him like a heavier darkness than the night.

"What we have here," Carn called to the crowd, "is a fallen Mystic!" He gestured with his glaive to a line of people behind him. Kilpa's hands were tied above his head to a pole that had been driven into the middle of the crossroads. Beside him was another person, also tied to a pole.

Nabiton.

The part of the union who was Mia became alarmed, but they remained whole.

"And beside him," Carn continued, "is what yeh might call a fallen Hunter."

The crowd erupted with shouts, hyping themselves into rage by Carn's lead. Carn himself, for all his hatred, remained utterly calm and in control.

An energy shift came from a nearby rooftop. Mia-Rion wondered what it could be. It wasn't movement that they could see, but someone lurked atop a nearby building.

"I don't know—" Carn began, but the jeers from the other Hunters drowned him out until he was able to settle them somewhat with hand gestures. "I don't know about yeh, but I'm not sure what I despise more, a filthy Mystic, or one of our own who defends them."

Torches and glaives and bellowed curses punched the sky in response. Carn's grin spread wider.

The Hunter leader began to pace back and forth in front of his crowd. "When the Mystics brought Crow Tallin upon us, and slammed our worlds together"—he demonstrated with his glaive and free hand—"mixing two things not meant for each other, they gave us tainted blood. They *infected* our tykes! Drove us out of our homes in order to make room for what? *FOR WHAT?*"

The replies came in thunderous waves, yet not a single answer could be clearly heard.

"For the *jagged fay*!" Carn screamed, putting every bit of spite he could into his words. He spoke faster now, frothing the frantic energy into a frenzy.

"Our founder, my mentor, the great Erksan, didn't purge this island of fay vermin just to have their half-human *spawn* steal our homes! He didn't take on the *righteous* task of wiping out infestations, ridding the land of terrors like the snake Mantepis, in order to see their places taken by axthos and talking rodents! We didn't drown our babies in the river, sparing them cursed lives, just to see ourselves betrayed by our own kind! Thanks to Erksan, there are laws in this land now! Laws commanded by our great Baroness ManHinley, who was a survivor of a vicious fay attack when she was a tyke.

"And these laws are very clear! All Mystics *must* remain in Kelt Apar. Those who leave that shelter *spit* in our faces. When one of these blood traitors commits a crime so terrible that even the Mystics kick them to a ditch and brand them Unclaimed"—he gestured to Kilpa—"well, you know that's just about as low as you can go."

Jeers rained down. Kilpa flinched as a stone thrown from the crowd struck his torso. But Carn had saved the worst for last. He shushed the crowd. The energy swirled through the crowd like a caged beast testing the bars of its prison.

The figure on the rooftop that Mia-Rion sensed earlier moved again, vanishing as quickly as they'd arrived.

"Well, maybe there's something lower than a rejected Mystic," Carn said, "and that's a Hunter who loves one."

Shouts landed like physical blows upon Nabiton, who bore the full brunt of their anger.

"So what do we do with 'em?" Carn screamed back to the crowd. "Huh? What justice is there from the true sons and daughters of Moth? From the great order of Hunters? *Tell me!*"

The crowd burst forth, swarming past Carn, who had his arms stretched wide, glaive in one fist and a beseeching open hand for the other.

The merged consciousness of Mia-Rion rushed ahead with them, passing the crowd by to arrive between the poles holding Kilpa and Nabiton. There was no time to think. Only time to move and react. How could they unbind the prisoners?

They pulled the Myst to them, from the air, from the stones underfoot, from the garments worn by the attackers, from their very thoughts, and from all the universe beyond the stars. As the first attackers reached the captives with their knives and fists and torches, Mia-Rion directed the Myst at them.

The first knife strike, aimed at Kilpa's chest, met a forceful gust of the Myst, pushing it toward a nearby Hunter.

A torch meant for Nabiton's face met a Hunter's instead. Fists flew to the wrong targets, triggering enraged retaliations against the offenders. Wave after wave of assaults aimed at the captives went astray, sowing new chaos.

Carn turned to see what the unexpected trouble was all about. His face hardened when he saw his Hunters fighting one another, then suspicion when he saw Kilpa and Nabiton still unharmed.

Mia-Rion Unveiled the Myst again, leading daggers not to other Hunters, but to the rope bonds that held the captives in place.

An enraged glaive gleamed through the air, reflecting torch-light, but the Myst led its wooden handle down, slicing the last of Kilpa's bindings free.

There were too many Hunters, though.

As the Hunters swarmed the prisoners, a new figure—a laghart—emerged from the shadows. He wore leather armor and a wide-brimmed gardener's hat.

Vlenar, Mia-Rion recognized. It had been him on the nearby rooftop.

The retired ranger had a small walking stick in one hand and a sword in the other. The rabid Hunters saw him and attacked, screaming obscenities.

Vlenar moved with surprising speed. He deflected the first attack with his staff and sliced with his blade, dropping the first Hunter. He dodged an incoming glaive strike, shifting his head precisely the right amount to make the attack miss.

As graceful and fast as he was, even in his old age and with a twisted knee, Mia-Rion knew he would not survive without help. They raised the Myst, and pressed it forward, knocking Hunter strikes away, or distracting an attacker, giving Vlenar time to slice them down.

Finally, the first wave subsided and Vlenar stood there, covered in human blood, his mouth open and tongue flicking. He could not see Mia-Rion, but it was plain from his searching expression that he'd sensed the assistance they'd given him.

"Gettt the boy and run!" Vlenar hissed at Kilpa.

The old man unlashed the last of Nabiton's bindings, then led him toward the dark shadows that the Hunter's torches wouldn't reach.

Carn strode through the rioting crowd. Many of his Hunters still fought each other, having been fueled by the anger he'd fed them. His deathly eyes focused on Vlenar.

The old ranger turned his staff and blade toward the approaching Hunter. "Fffor Kelt Apar," he said.

The distance closed between them, and Carn struck with his glaive. Vlenar deflected the attack with the ease of a master bladesman and crouched low to counterattack. But as he bent, his twisted leg gave out, and he wavered. Carn took advantage, knocking Vlenar's sword away. Three other Hunters pounced on the ranger, pinning him to the ground.

Carn calmly peered into the shadows, searching for signs of the true disturbance. He sniffed the air, and whatever he found pulled his attention toward the place that Mia-Rion existed.

Fear rippled through Mia, shaking her connection to Rion. Carn was different somehow. Set apart by *something* that elevated him above other Hunters. Whether it was pure cruelty or a more devious method, he sensed them. Recognition and rage covered his face.

He knew. Somehow, he did.

Carn motioned for the Hunters holding Vlenar to move. With a snarl, he lifted his glaive into the air and plunged it downward.

Before Mia-Rion could scream, their merged consciousness ripped apart.

It was like having an arm torn from her body. The shock and pain raged through Mia. Her eyes burst open.

Her body was whole, but she'd been struck and knocked backward over the chair she'd been sitting in.

Desperately, she tried to gather herself. Her gaze focused on the beamed ceiling as two scaled faces slid into view. The laghart master and his apprentice.

"Ssso there isss power in you," Hizrith said. "It isss a ssshame then."

He spoke again to his apprentice, who jerked her clawed hand downward, sending Mia into darkness.

SEVENTEEN

THE BOTTOM OF THE WORLD

The ocean of clouds beneath Pomella's feet solidified into stone. All that was soft and welcoming became cold and oppressive. Light gray puffs shifted into angular planes of deep brown. She found herself crouched upon a single knee in a vast cavern, dark and ominous. Her staff was still gripped firmly in her hand.

Shadows loomed around long stalactites that reached from the ceiling toward the distant ground. Torches with blue-white flame burned in standing sconces that had been bolted into the floor.

The cavern was packed with people, all facing away from Pomella, who was at the back of the crowd. She stood and checked her hands and hair. She'd returned to her actual age, or at least significantly closer to it. White-gray hair, knobby fingers. Seeing that, she leaned into her staff instinctively, though she didn't feel the usual assortment of soreness in her knees and hips.

A murmured tension filled the stone cavern. She'd never been to a place like this, and indeed it didn't truly seem real, or at least familiar. The flames were an unnatural blue, casting strange shadows, and the cavern was angled and slanted in a way that seemed impossible. None of the people in the crowd seemed to notice or care. Their attention was fixed on the people standing on a distant raised dais.

Leaning upon her lantern staff, Pomella moved through the crowd. Her presence went unacknowledged, but the crowd seemed to unconsciously make way. It was a thick crowd, hundreds of people at least, so it took some time for Pomella to reach the front.

Three banners hung above the dais, green and gold bearing the laurel-crowned harp of House AnBroke. A white sword on a split field of orange and brown from the ManYelt barony. And in the middle, a dark blue and gray banner designating House ManHinley.

The two baronesses and the single baron of Moth sat on stone chairs beneath their banners. Norana sat in the center chair, younger than Pomella had last seen her. The baroness's face was as impassive and hard as the chamber itself.

Each seat was formed from a single piece of stone, as if they'd been carved directly from the cave. A slab podium rose in front of each ruler holding stacks of parchment. House guards and clerks lined the edges of the dais, all dressed in their respective colors.

In front of the dais, between the nobles and Pomella, yawned a wide pit, as dark as midnight's shadow, descending to depths unknown.

The sight of Norana raised Pomella's anger. There sat the woman she'd known since infancy, a woman she'd held in her arms and sung to. A woman who'd ordered Shillo's death and condemned every Mystic on Moth.

Equally as upsetting were the swarms of Hunters arranged throughout the cavern, along the walls and behind the dais. Their iron glaives menaced in the flickering blue light. One of them moved with authority among the others, patrolling their ranks, and Pomella knew it was Carn, the prime Hunter, the faithful apprentice who'd spawned from his master Erksan's tutelage and brought the order to prominence.

"We will have order!" boomed Kylen ManYelt. The baron sat beneath the orange-and-brown banner featuring a sword. The other noblewoman sitting on the dais, Baroness Elona, sat quietly and withdrawn.

Nobody had been speaking and order had already been established in this eerie place, but with the baron's command Pomella suddenly knew what she was about to witness. The baron had used the same command to begin the trial that resulted in one of the worst days of her life.

"It's gone too far, m'ladies and lord!" shouted a bodiless voice from the crowd. "The world ain't natural no more!"

Baron ManYelt raised his meaty hand. "We've heard what you've said. At great length." He glanced at Norana, then back to the crowd. "And we've made our decision."

Pomella tightened her grip on her staff as a clerk hurried forward and handed a stack of parchment to Norana.

As the baroness reviewed its contents silently, Pomella turned her attention to the crowd once more, catching only fleeting glimpses of shifting faces and identities. Among them she saw Yarina, weathered and exhausted, with Vivianna behind her, aged hands on her mistress's wheeled chair. As quickly as Pomella glimpsed them, though, they wafted away, replaced by indiscernible people.

Norana stood. The surrounding shadows shifted with her movement, reaching toward her. She seemed to grow in stature, but Pomella couldn't tell if the baroness enlarged or if she and the room shrank.

"The world has changed," Norana intoned. "In this, we all can agree. Cast from their ruined realm, the fay have invaded our world. Some call it refuge, but the world is wide, and yet they flock to our small island and curse our children."

Few among even the Mystics truly understood what had happened with the merger of Fayün and the human world at the end of Crow Tallin. And fewer still, beyond her closest confidants, knew that Pomella had been at the heart of it. Even if she had taken personal blame it wouldn't have mattered. The people of Moth wanted somebody to blame, and the Mystics were an easy target after centuries of being perceived as being elite and more revered than even nobles and merchant-scholars. Who else was there to blame? Who else could cause such a problem?

"It may already be too late," Norana continued. "Only the rarest of newborns are untainted, untouched by the corruption of a parasitic fay seeking a living host to feed upon. And thus, by the authority of a majority of barons, we declare that a new Accord will be enacted, effective immediately. All Mystics on Moth shall come forth and register themselves and their lineage. They shall no longer own land or possessions beyond what they carry, and they shall take up permanent residence at Kelt Apar. There they shall remain in order to quietly and peacefully conduct their activities, so long as it does not affect the outside world."

The crowd cheered around Pomella. She remembered this day three years ago, when the Mystic Accord had been enacted. The proclamation had not occurred in a strange cavern, but in the grand hall of the Fortress of Sea and Sky. But the cheering had happened, just as it did now.

She had just returned from Qin with Mia. Norana, Elona, and Kylen ManYelt had waited for Pomella's absence to meet and vote on the Accord. Then Norana insisted on waiting until Pomella had returned to Moth to make it public. By then the fight had gone out of Yarina. And with Pomella away at Qin, there'd been only minimal dissent. Decades of slow suppression had finally caught up to the rights the Mystics of Moth had entertained for centuries.

On that day three years ago, Yarina, Vivianna, and herself had all been "peacefully escorted" back to Kelt Apar by the Hunters and given black robes to wear.

As the cheering continued, Norana used a feather and ink to

make her mark upon the parchment Accord itself, then passed it to Baron ManYelt, who marked it and passed it to Baroness AnBroke.

Baroness Elona, the oldest of the Mothic rulers, hesitated over the document. Her eyes lifted and found Pomella's. That, too, had actually occurred three years ago.

Elona was similar in age to Pomella, and had nearly become a Mystic herself. She'd been expected, all those years ago, to receive High Mystic Yarina's invitation to the apprentice Trials. Every year in her youth Elona had marveled the villagers from Oak-spring and other northern barony villages with her Unveilings of lights and sound. She would've made a fine Mystic, probably, but it had been Pomella who went to the Trials instead, and Vivianna who became Yarina's apprentice.

After Pomella went in Elona's place, it was said she never used the Myst again and instead turned to the task of governing her people.

They met again, years later, when Pomella was apprenticed to Lal. Pomella remembered the nervous energy coursing through her before their reunion, but it had been Elona who greeted her with a genuine smile and put her at ease.

"Pomella," Elona had said with a bow that had left her practically gawking, "it genuinely gladdens me to see you. I must say, I've thought of writing you, but I felt this needed to be said in person. I'm sorry for how I treated you during that Springrise. We were practically children, and I'm sorry my pettiness got the better of me that day. Can you forgive me?"

Now, as Elona shifted her gaze away from Pomella back to the parchment Accord, she firmed her expression and made her mark.

Perhaps, in the end, Elona had not lost her bitterness toward the Mystics. Or maybe she had, but the pressures put upon her by those she governed, and by the other barons, were too much. Regardless of the reason, her mark sealed the Mystic Accord, transforming it from a piece of parchment into an act of law that would affect all Mystics on Moth, and become the model document other countries on the Continent would use to draft similar Accords.

While it was Elona's and Norana's and Kylen's signatures upon the parchment, it really represented the people of Moth. It had been signed as a reaction to the fear and uncertainty brought by the new world that Pomella had personally brought about.

After Crow Tallin, nobody told the tale of Pomella's Trials. Nobody invited her to sing and dance at lively inns, or called her the Hummingbird and begged to be apprenticed to her.

For nearly fifty years the world had gradually shifted to become more entwined with the old Fayün. More and more Touched children were born until they became the vast majority, nearly an entire generation of humans sharing a symbiotic relationship with the fay.

"It is done," Norana intoned. "And so let it be known all across our great island of Moth."

"No," Pomella said. The Myst rose around her, filling her with energy. Righteous anger flared within her. She could easily suppress it. She could remain passive. But not this time. She refused to let this travesty occur again.

Lifting her staff, she Unveiled the Myst, shining it forth from her lantern until it filled the room with a vibrant light. The shadow crowd cringed away from her. The barons flinched and the cave shuddered.

"I will not allow this!" Pomella cried out.

The cave shook harder.

Her arm hurt. The muscles in her chest clenched. She struggled to take a breath.

Hector appeared at her side, radiating urgent concern. Pomella ignored him.

This was her memory. Her world. Perhaps she could change the outcome. Perhaps within these depths of the Myst, by changing something here, she could affect the outside world. The name of the island was important, but what could be more important than eliminating the hateful Accord?

Laughter came from the dais where the barons sat. Norana stepped forward, shielding her eyes against the light from Pomella's lantern.

"Sit down!" Pomella called to her.

The cavern went dark, and for a moment she was back in her physical body, eyes closed. Fear raced through her, and she refocused and returned to the cavern.

Her heart thundered in her chest.

Norana continued her laughter. "Let it be known that this is your fault, Pomella. The Mystics of Moth will wither and die because of your hubris. One day, Kelt Apar shall burn and you will only have ash to weep upon."

Pomella gritted her teeth. She could change this. She had to. Maybe it would tear her from the Mystwalk to do so, but perhaps it was necessary.

Hector spun in the air beside her, frantic.

The Mystwalk shuddered around her. In a moment, it would vanish.

It would be worth it. The Myst roared like an inferno within Pomella. Perhaps it would tear the fabric of reality apart to alter this moment, or rend her mind, but she could undo the signing of the Accord. She could sacrifice herself for this one thing. The Change had been her fault. She had to make this right. She would give herself so that the Mystics of Moth could be free.

She moved her staff and began to twist the Myst throughout the cavern, smearing the vision like dragging a finger across wet paint on a canvas.

An arm touched her shoulder. She turned and saw Mia. She stared at her, willing her silently to remember herself.

Hot tears formed at the corners of Pomella's eyes but burned away as they slid down her cheeks. "I have to fix this, Mia," she said. "For you. For all of them."

Mia squeezed her shoulder harder. As Pomella looked at her granddaughter, she remembered one of her oldest lessons.

There was nothing to fix.

Like Mia, the world was not broken. It was different, unfamiliar, but not inherently wrong. It was the world Mia and her generation had been born to. And now Pomella was trying to force it to become something it no longer was.

There'd been that moment, during the peak of Crow Tallin, when she'd existed in harmony with the Deep, and made the instant decision to fuse the human world and Fayün together permanently. She'd never truly understood why she made that choice, but she'd known it was correct. Within that perfect moment all doubt and fear had melted away, revealing a harmonious sense of purpose.

As terrible as the signing of the Accord had been for the Mystics of Moth, it was another note in the symphony of the Myst. To act now against that was to bring discord.

The guilt she'd been holding clung to her like a storm cloud. Yet it stayed only because she held tight to it. In order to move on, to move deeper into the Mystwalk, she needed to let go.

Reluctantly, Pomella lowered her staff. The lantern light faded, returning the cavern to darkness. The pain in her arm and chest subsided, and the Mystwalk dream solidified around her.

Mia smiled at Pomella. By the Saints, reliving these experiences brought forth all the same emotions that she'd carried for years. Now she had to accept them. She could remember the feelings but could not carry their weight any longer.

The vision of the cavern had resumed its previous shape. The crowd around Pomella shifted, as if shuffling themselves. Two of the barony banners and their respective rulers smoked away, leaving only Norana to preside over the gathering. Mia removed her arm from Pomella's shoulder and vanished.

Most of the Hunters disappeared, but more guards materialized, including three of them upon the edge of the dais, leading a fourth man, gagged and bound in chains.

Somehow, Pomella now stood at the forward edge of the crowd itself, right on the rim of the pure black pit. She stood more upright and her hand holding her staff was smooth and young. Despite the grim cavern's oppression, she marveled at her unblemished hand. At her youth.

She looked up and saw that it was no longer Norana upon the dais. It was Norana's mhathir, Kelisia, young and vibrant in her own strength. She stood alone beneath her family's banner. By the baroness's age, Pomella quickly estimated that Norana was a wee tyke and she herself was only a handful of years older than what she'd been at Crow Tallin, twenty-six perhaps.

A tightness rose in her chest as she realized what that meant.

Then she saw something else she'd mistaken. Where before there'd been a banner depicting the gray fortress emblem upon a field of blue representing House ManHinley, there now hung a different banner. Twisting lines and curves of sloppily painted whitewash formed the shape of a Mothic knot depicting a hummingbird over a field of deep blue.

The man who'd been brought forth in chains collapsed to his knees under the force of his guards.

Kelisia stepped forward, dominating the cavern. "This man is accused of kidnapping, enslavement, trafficking, torture, and murder. I have seen and heard the evidence against him and deemed it to be overwhelming."

She turned her gaze downward to the man kneeling in front of her. Bent over his knees as he was, he faced away from the baroness and had to glance over his shoulder to see her.

"You have said nothing in your own defense," Kelisia said.

"Not a single word. Before you hear my verdict, will you speak, Shadefox?"

One of the guards yanked the gag from the man's mouth. He worked his jaw and scratched his scraggly beard against his shoulder before steeling his expression and gazing out among the crowd. His eyes found Pomella, and her heart lurched.

It was her brother, Gabor, only three winters past twenty, and already the most notorious slaver and criminal on Moth. Pomella had seen him and identified his role during Crow Tallin. She'd seen him wearing that hideous mask and leading the same bandits she'd spent years tracking down. After Crow Tallin it took years for her and Tibron and Kelisia's Shieldguards to track his whereabouts and apprehend him.

The hummingbird banner loomed over Pomella's brother's head.

"If you seek a reason for my deeds," Gabor said, his voice harsh from disuse, "ask my sister."

He had not spoken during his trial, even at the end, so now, for her to hear this, Pomella felt as though she'd been punched in the stomach.

"Then by my authority as baroness of Moth, I find you guilty of all counts," Kelisia intoned. "Your final justice shall be dispensed in the morning."

She motioned to the guards, who shoved Gabor into the dark pit. He tumbled forward without sound, rolling at the last moment to lock eyes with Pomella before being consumed by the darkness.

Kelisia turned her formidable stare to Pomella. With the shadows dancing across the hard planes of her face she looked amazingly like her daughter.

"His actions were his own, but he did not become the Shadefox by himself."

"Let go," Pomella whispered to herself. She would not change history. But she could accept it. The name of the island waited somewhere, deeper with her. She would find it.

Into the memory, into the pain. She stepped forward and fell into the pit.

Once more, the darkness beneath Pomella's feet became stone. She found herself in a circular pool of light about twice the width of her outstretched arms. A narrow corridor stretched in one direction into darkness.

The heavy oppression of memories weighed on her. Mournful moans and cries of despair drifted through the hallway.

Down the corridor she found a door with a small barred window cut into it, just large enough for her to see the room's occupant. It was a man with dark hair and beard who seemed familiar to her, but he cowered in the far corner and clawed at the walls.

"I—I dd-did it for Char-Charliss," he rambled, and clawed at the walls some more.

Pomella shuddered and was about to move away from the door when the man turned more fully toward her and she at last recognized him.

It was Zicon, the leader of the Black Claw mercenaries who had conspired to kill Yarina during Pomella's apprentice Trials. The horrible man had been thwarted and eventually brought to justice, but here he apparently remained in her Mystwalk, over sixty years later. His blue eyes, wild and desperate, tried to pull her in like a drowning man clawing for life.

Pomella walked away from the cell and its occupant and moved farther down the corridor. More cell doors lined the walls, each containing a person she knew, or might've known. They were all criminals she'd brought to justice over the years. Slavers, and, from later in her life, rogue Mystics who agreed with the Hunter's notion that the fay were an infestation to be exterminated, even if it meant destroying the humans they'd bonded with.

As she passed each door, the moans of despair thinned until

no sound remained. She passed a cell where a bald, scarred man sat. He watched her with pure spite. Plates of metal jutted from various parts of his body, including the dome of his head. It was the Iron Mystic who worked with Zicon and the Black Claws. She refused to say or even think of his name because of all the pain his memories brought back. Old fear welled within her, but she turned away from the cell and breathed it out.

All these people were gone. They couldn't hurt her any longer. She found her hand trembling, and so she evened her breathing until it calmed.

If anything, she should have compassion. They might've done terrible things, and harbored great hatred for her or others she loved. But in the ultimate sense they were as much a part of the Myst as she was. They were a part of her, and she was a part of them.

At last, the corridor came to an end, and one final cell door remained. Only the sound of her breathing and footsteps and Mystic staff tapping the floor could be heard.

Upon the door, carved into the wood above the barred window, was the Mothic hummingbird emblem. Pomella paused, knowing who was inside. She took a final breath, and Unveiled the Myst to open the door.

She found him sitting against the far wall, elbows resting on his knees.

"Hello, Sister," Gabor rasped.

She loomed in the doorway, blocking the only light in the cell. This was a true memory, as close to the actual experience she'd previously lived so far.

She'd come to him again on the morning of his execution.

They waited in silence, neither wanting to speak. The fight had gone out of Gabor. When she had visited him in her waking life, she remembered being struck by how scared he'd been.

Pomella shook her head as she pondered all this.

"I've lived this memory already, Gabor," she said to him.

He peered up at her and a small beam of light from the corridor shone upon his face. Fear danced in his expression, but there was defiance, too.

"This was my existence," he said. "From the day I woke and found you'd left home, I knew I'd end up like this."

"Oh, buggerish!" she snapped. "Quit the shite, Gabor. Fathir might've been a culk, but nobody ever forced you to enslave the Unclaimed or to murder people who crossed you. And nobody forced you t'seek that life t'begin with!"

She found it so easy to slip into her old slang in her brother's presence.

"Sure, Sis. Go on. Lord over me as I go to the headsman. It musta been nice to receive a fook'n' invitation from the High Mystic, inviting you to a new, wondrous life. I sure as shite woulda loved that opportunity. Maybe in my next life, I'll learn t'talk to owls and trees so I can be just as *special* as you."

Pomella bit her lip and had to turn her face away from his. "I can't do this, Gabor," she said. "I can't face you again and argue."

"Then you're weak," he said.

She turned to him. "You know nothing of me and what I've done. I would not be here, walking this dream-within-a-dream, if I were weak."

"Perhaps. But it's just words now. You have to show that strength again. You have resolve now. Good. But it can't always be joy and peace and all that other shite the Mystics taught you. Norana and the others took your home. Your way of life. They've killed. Doesn't that make you *angry*?"

"I feel—"

"No! Stop it!" he snapped. "Stop *feeling*. Start *acting*." He scrambled to his feet and lurched toward her, as far as the chains would take him, falling short of reaching her.

"You want to know why I chose this life? It's because it was the only way I could be more than nothing. The only way I could be remembered. Nobody will remember Fathir. Nobody would've remembered me. Without an invitation from the High Mystic, I would've wilted."

The familiar phrase she'd often used punched at Pomella.

"Judge me as you will," Gabor continued, "but I was admired for what I did. Men cheered my name. Others trembled at it. Women climbed into my bed. My life was short, but at least I found meaning!"

Pomella took a final, lingering look at her brother. She stepped forward and took his head into her cupped hands. He flinched at first, but she drew his forehead to her lips, and kissed him.

"Good-bye, twerper," she said, using an old affectionate name for him. "I'm sorry for any wrong I did to you."

She turned and left the cell.

"Stop!" Gabor screamed. "Come back! Sister! *SISTER!*"

The door behind her closed, and the enraged screams followed her, just as they had so many years ago.

"Filthy *hetch*! You made me! *YOU MADE ME!*"

She shut the cries out from her heart and walked away. Time slowed as a heavily hooded executioner, eyes downcast and carrying a long axe and wearing the standard of the Mothic hummingbird, passed her in the corridor. The executioner nodded to her as he drifted past. She eyed him in return but otherwise passed in silence.

Gabor's screaming laughter continued. "You'll die here! He follows you now! He will devour you!"

She stopped and turned around.

Who would devour her?

But the executioner had reached the door and dissolved with it until she was left again in the shallow pool of light.

EIGHTEEN

THE GARDEN OF LOVE AND FIRE

Encroaching shadows inched toward Pomella, consuming the stone walls and cells of the corridor.

She did not fear the dark. The light from Vivianna's rickety lantern, dim as it was, was enough to keep it from overtaking her.

The fatigue wore on her. By the Saints, she was tired. She sat on the stone floor and laid her staff across her lap. Light from the whitewashed lantern played over the youthful skin on her hands.

Despite her not truly having a body in this place and feeling no physical discomfort, the weight of her recent journeys had taken a toll. Reliving her memories, distorted as they were, was like reopening old wounds and feeling them bleed fresh.

Having to watch Mia flee without being able to help her. Losing Harmona. The signing of the Accord. Watching Gabor dragged to his execution, knowing she had been the one to arrest him.

It was all too much.

She was tired of being strong. For so many years, ever since Sim vanished, and later after Tibron's passing, and especially now with Yarina's death, she'd felt so alone. With the lineage of masters at stake, and the fate of all Mystics of Moth in question, she had to continue.

A familiar humming sounded behind her, and a moment later

Hector alighted onto her staff. He stared up at her and cocked his head, seeming uncertain.

"I suppose I could use your help," Pomella said, and held her finger out to him. With only a slight hesitation, he hopped onto her finger.

"You're a bit bigger than I remember," Pomella said, smiling at the hummingbird. She stroked the plumage on the back of his head, and a ripple of rainbow-colored lights shone beneath her finger.

Pomella's smile faded as dark thoughts intruded upon her mind. Perhaps she should step out of this Mystwalk entirely. Maybe she should return to her physical body and try to learn more about what had transpired in the world.

She didn't know how much time had passed since she'd begun. What if she'd been here too long and Norana's guards discovered her? What would they do with her if they found her in her meditative state?

Her attention drifted away from Hector over to her younger-than-normal hand. So often, especially as a girl and now still occasionally as an old woman, she was impulsive, leaping to action before fully thinking out the consequences.

"It's how we got into this mess to begin with," she muttered to Hector.

Pomella peered into the darkness. She couldn't see how merging the worlds had created a better reality for anybody. For over fifty years she'd rationalized her actions. She had to continue believing that her decision would ultimately bear fruit.

For that reason, she had to continue with this Mystwalk. There was nobody else left to do it.

"OK, I suppose that's enough rest," she said to Hector, and nudged him back into the air where he buzzed away.

Leaning on her staff, she stood. The weight of her fears and the pressure of her quest threatened to keep her grounded, but she'd had enough. Lal's voice, from so long ago, returned to her. *We create our realities, Pomella.*

And her brother's words, said with spite, but containing a surprising bit of practical wisdom: *Stop* feeling. *Start* acting.

They were both right. She could wallow, or she could act.

She took a deep breath, lifted her staff, and raised the Myst around her. It came to her with ease, and she was reminded that it was another old friend, but one that was ever present and never hesitated to be there for her. She circled it, feeding her fears and anxiety into the growing maelstrom.

Joyful memories of the loved ones she'd had to let go rose around her. She fed them into the maelstrom. Regardless of how things ended with each person, it did not negate the happier memories. Harmona's youthful joy as she ran barefoot across Kelt Apar. Sneaking away with Gabor as children to catch tadpoles near the Creekwaters. Laughing with Sim during their early adulthood. Sharing her garden with Vivianna and Mia.

As she recalled her garden, the lantern hanging from her staff flared to life, eradicating the darkness of her environment.

When her eyes adjusted, she found a garden of flowers and light. A sweet and familiar scent washed over her. Birds sang.

Pomella smiled.

At last.

She walked through the garden of her own making, letting the full bouquet of scents fill her nose. All of Pomella's favorites grew there, tulips and lavender, marigolds and lilacs, roses and daffodils. Meandering paths wound between mesmerizing clusters of flowers.

The sound of a waterfall trickled from nearby, although Pomella could not see it yet. She moved in that direction, allowing herself moments to stop and check a flower, or tend a tangle-branch. Hector swooped overhead, exploring the landscape.

It was all she could've ever hoped for in the grandest garden.

And yet it wasn't.

Beautiful as it was, this wasn't the humble patch of soil she'd tended for years outside her cabin in Kelt Apar, nor was it the larger one she'd created in the space that once housed Lal's cabin. This one spread wider, as far as she could see. A golden-blue sky with clouds softening a warm sun presided over her. Rosebushes and an assortment of tall trees blocked most of her view of whatever horizon lay beyond the garden's borders. A short distance away, a willow tree rose above the rest of the garden, its drooping limbs swaying like a lullaby in the wind.

Beside her on the path stood a rosebush. She touched one of its outstretched blooms, and breathed in its fragrance.

This was beautiful, but it was a distraction. She needed to find the Mystic name of the island. She couldn't let herself become caught up.

"Pomella!" came a voice.

She lurched at the sound of her name, scraping herself on a thorn. "Shite," she muttered, and looked to see who had called her.

Tibron, young and handsome with his long dark hair, stood at the top of a nearby hill, just up the garden path. He wore sandals and cream-colored robes highlighted by slashes of the same light blue she wore.

Forgetting her fresh cut, Pomella hurried to him, but he ran away from her down the far side of the hill, out of sight.

"Find me, Pom!" he teased.

A smile bloomed on her face. She hurried after him, and followed him into a small grove of apple trees. She peered around one of the trees just in time to see him slip farther away, but not before offering her a playful grin of his own.

"Don't tease me, Tibron," she called, feeling tears of sadness and joy well up. "If you're really here, don't stay apart from me a moment longer!"

And then he was with her, solid and strong, gentle and tender. His scent, mixed with the garden's, flooded Pomella's senses. His arms wrapped around her and she found herself folding into that familiar place in his chest that was just hers. His lips touched the top of her head and he squeezed her in a loving embrace.

"My love," he said.

Pomella looked up at him and marveled at his youth. He appeared to be around the age he'd been when they first met, in the days right before Crow Tallin. She pulled away from him and looked down at herself, taking note for the first time of her own appearance.

She was nearly as young as he was, probably twenty-three. A wave of excitement bubbled through her and she leaped at him, throwing her free arm around his neck and kissing him full on the mouth.

It had been the life of the stars since she'd done anything this passionate and she found herself laughing as she kissed.

"What?" Tibron said, smiling but clearly perplexed.

A lump formed in Pomella's throat. "I've missed you, Tibron. So much. Tell me this is real. Tell me we can stay this way."

She knew, though, of course, what needed to happen. But she refused to acknowledge that truth. For just a little while she needed to bask in a memory that didn't hurt. They always did in the end. But for now, she wanted to remain here until the world's last rains ceased.

They lay on a patch of grass beneath the willow tree, snuggled into each other's arms. Her staff lay across her lap, its lantern resting in the grass. Tibron had been silent, matching her need to simply exist in the same space. Pomella's eyes grew heavy, though she did not truly sleep. Idly, she wondered if she could sleep in this strange multilayered set of dreams.

"Did I suffer?" Tibron asked her, twirling a strand of her hair in his fingers. She had always loved how he'd done that.

The lump formed in her throat again, but it was surprisingly easy to speak of his loss. "Not for long. The disease grew unseen within you. You were in pain in the end, but Yarina was able to ease that."

He died in the early summer, when the goslings learned to swim in Kelt Apar's pond, almost exactly twenty years ago.

"You passed quietly in the night as I lay beside you," she finished.

"Well, that doesn't sound so bad," Tibron mused. "All things considered, it could have been much worse."

A smile found its way to Pomella's lips. "Yah," she said. "You had some close calls over the years. Scared the skivers out of me."

"There was nothing I wasn't prepared to handle," he said. "Because I had you."

She squeezed him tighter. He was right. The dundering fool had gotten himself into plenty of tussles that she'd had to save him from.

"The only time I truly thought we'd all die," he said, still twirling her hair, ". . . when I thought the whole world would die, was Crow Tallin."

Pomella nodded against his chest. "Shevia," she said.

"Yes," he said. "I never forgot the heat of those flames. The anger. The rage. The fear. I wish I could have done more for my sister."

Pomella pushed herself up to an elbow. "Did you have any regrets? Harmona?"

"Harmona broke both of our hearts. Her Qina blood called to her, though. I believe I understood that better than you at the time. I died knowing she lived her life, and not that of her mother."

Even in death, Tibron told it to her straight. Pomella had loved him for that, even when it made her grind her teeth.

"If I had one regret, however," Tibron continued, "it was that I never reconciled properly with Shevia and our brothers."

Pomella nodded, remembering how that had haunted Tibron, especially in the years immediately after Crow Tallin. He outlived his triplet brothers, Tevon and Typhos, who had each come to tragic ends. Shevia destroyed Tevon during Crow Tallin and she maimed Typhos. The latter wandered Moth, living alone in the Ironlow Mountains by whatever means he could find. Pomella never understood why he didn't return home. There couldn't have been anything but pain and hardship for Typhos on Moth. Surely he would've found support had he returned to his family in Qin?

Tibron had eventually tracked him down, but Typhos rejected his aid. Years later, they received word that Typhos has been found dead in the wilderness, having fallen down a steep ravine in the central Ironlows.

"And me?" Pomella asked. "Any regrets?"

His answer was slow in coming. "Only that you stopped singing."

It was this that brought tears to Pomella's eyes. "I sang to you as you slept," she said. "The night you passed. Your disease was beyond Yarina's healing ability, and far beyond mine. All I could do was sing."

That night returned to her again, the agony, the overwhelming sadness. But she pushed it away. Why did every memory end in sadness? Why did joy ultimately lead to pain?

Another memory, this one of Lal, came to her. *When sad, we live in the past. When anxious, we live in the future. Only in the present do we have peace.*

"It was the last time I ever sang," Pomella said. "For after I lost you, I had no music left in me."

Tibron shifted around to look at her directly. He stroked her face. "You *are* the music," he said. "Sometimes, you just need to remember it."

He spoke something in Qina and kissed her forehead. Pomella had learned a sprinkling of the language from him, but it had been too long, so she couldn't discern what he'd said.

They lay there for a while, but Pomella couldn't judge if it was an hour, a day, or the length of a single breath. "How long will this last?" Pomella asked as she thought about it. It was as though thinking of time solidified it, snapped it back into focus.

"It's your Mystwalk," Tibron said. "But you know better than I ever did that memories like this are fleeting. All experiences must end."

Despite his words, the urge to remain here forever became stronger. In her past memory, Pomella had wanted to change it. Now, she wanted to linger.

The air warmed, and a sickening scent breezed past Pomella. She looked up and saw the colorful skies had darkened. The soft clouds that had previously lazed over the garden now roiled with thick smoke as dark as night.

A roar sounded, and flames tore across the heavens, heating the air and Pomella's skin to near burning.

Pomella covered her face. "Tibron!"

Glowing embers danced around her. The willow they'd dozed beneath had become an inferno. Pomella scrambled out from beneath its cover, just as a flaming branch collapsed onto the place she'd been lying.

The sky rained fire now, burning her robes, hair, and exposed skin.

"Tibron!" Pomella yelled. She couldn't see him any longer. She watched in horror as her garden caught fire, smoking and burning as she watched. By the Saints, what was happening?

A thunderous crack sounded behind her. Pomella spun in time

to see the willow tree explode in a fireball of sparks and flaming branches. By instinct she raisde her staff and the Myst, and an invisible wall deflected the fire.

Where the willow had stood a massive shadow churned. It rose through the fire, and Pomella's heart clenched. She'd seen this creature once in her waking life, during Crow Tallin, and countless times in her dreams. It haunted her memories no matter how much she'd tried to bury it.

The shadow coalesced into a scaled form four times the height of a man, and ten times as wide from wingtip to wingtip.

The dragon. Lagnaraste.

She wanted to panic and run, but decades of training and experience straightened her spine and lifted her chin. Tibron was nowhere to be found. A part of her felt sadness for that, but the dreamy enchantment of their lovely garden stroll had evaporated in the heat of the dragon's fire.

Vivianna's lantern swayed from the wooden loop that dangled in the jaws of the snake carved in her staff.

"Lagnaraste!" she called, raising the Myst around her.

The garden was gone. She stood alone now in a gently sloping valley of fire. The dragon stomped forward, pulling its wings close to its body. Its scales shimmered a dark iridescent black, with hints of orange and red slipping through. It walked on four legs and had a neck as long and thick as a tree. Slitted golden eyes blinked at her, and its tongue flicked out, not unlike a laghart.

"You are not welcome in my dream," Pomella said to it.

The dragon charged at her, its maw wide to consume her. Pomella punched her staff out and caught the creature with the Myst. She spun, and slammed it to the ground, which shook with its impact.

The creature thrashed. Pomella strode forward and placed her foot onto its scaled face.

"I bind you," she said. "You have no power here."

The dragon ceased its movement. Its face shifted to what Pomella thought might've passed for an amused smile. "Once more, I am yours to command, Pomella AnDone, the Hummingbird, She Who Merged the Worlds."

It was the first time Lagnaraste had spoken to her in this form. Crow Tallin had happened so quickly, with so many staggering events happening in a short time that Pomella had never learned more of Lagnaraste's true nature. There had only been fire and chaos and the Deep Myst.

Lagnaraste lowered its head and slid it closer to her, molten saliva running along its bare teeth. Lal had told her that nearly a thousand years ago the dragons had dominated the world, but they waged war on one another, driving themselves to near extinction and sundering the world into Fayün and the human realm.

"What purpose do you have here?" Pomella asked. "You will not bar my way, for I claimed your power and dispersed it."

"Dissspersed does not mean gone," Lagnaraste said. "Like your memoriesss, like thossse that you love, I am here, eternal and waiting, and all you musssst do is call."

"Do you know the Mystic name of the island of Moth?" Pomella asked.

Fire belched from the dragon toward Pomella, but she shattered it away with a wave of her hand. The flames only served to ignite her anger until she realized Lagnaraste was laughing.

"I knew it once," Lagnaraste said, "but it was ssstolen from me. And it hasss changed."

"Changed?" she asked. "How?"

The dragon slid around her, gliding on its belly like a snake. "When you merged the realmsss, you altered the fundamental nature of the world and itsss contents. Over time, the name of Mothhh became sssomething new."

Fear gripped Pomella as she realized the truth. "Is that why the anointment ceremony failed? The name that Yarina tried to pass to Vivianna was wrong?"

"Perhapssss," Lagnaraste hissed.

"How do I find the new name?"

"Find the one you lossst."

"What do you mean?" Pomella said. "Speak plainly."

Lagnaraste arched its neck back, exhaled, and exploded into black smoke. The dark fog roared around Pomella. Then, as quickly as it began, the smoke rushed back in, coalescing into a human form, a girl, no older than eighteen or nineteen. She had long dark hair that curtained down her face and down her back. Her olive-colored skin gleamed with the same iridescent shimmer as that of the dragon. She wore a dark red dress and had a twisting Mothic-knot-style dragon tattooed on her shoulder and upper arm.

Shevia. Tibron's sister, and the Mystic prodigy who had been the focus of so much trouble during Crow Tallin.

"Go back, further into your memories," Shevia-Lagnaraste said in a human voice. Her beautifully strange lavender eyes gleamed. Thunder rumbled in the churning clouds above. "There is no separation between our deepest selves and the Myst. Find yourself and you will find what you seek. Go there, you will find everything."

The young woman dissolved back into a cloud of smoke, which lingered for a heartbeat before rushing downward, shrinking and condensing until it was a single flower growing among the still-smoldering valley floor. Where the endless garden had been now lay a wasteland of ash and embers.

Another memory came to Pomella, again from Crow Tallin. When she'd awoken after the passing of the Mystic Star, moments after the worlds had been merged, she'd found a single flower among the ruin.

Here that flower, a lily, now grew. A gentle light, as pure and clear as any she'd ever seen or imagined, shone from inside the heart of its core.

Pomella knelt beside it, letting the warm fire-wind catch her dark, youthful hair.

She reached to the lily and cupped its bulb in her hands.

"Deeper," she whispered to herself.

The light grew, the Myst swirled, and Pomella merged with the flower.

NINETEEN

THE CIRCLE

Mia awoke with a throbbing head-ache. She lay on her back on a hard surface and tried to discern where she was. It was dark, although she couldn't tell if that was from being indoors or whether it was night.

A nearby fire warmed her, and as her vision and thoughts came into focus she determined that, yes, she was inside after all. She moved to sit up but found her wrists and ankles bound to a table by unyielding iron shackles.

Fear and panic loomed in the shadows of her mind, prowling at the edge of her consciousness. Her pulse raced. She had to get out of here.

She wracked her memory trying to remember what had happened. She'd merged with Rion, and moved through the streets of Sentry. Carn. The rally. Kilpa and Nabiton. And then . . .

Vlenar!

No. Her mind rebelled against the pain of losing her friend. He'd been kind to her since the day she arrived in Kelt Apar. She'd rarely seen a laghart before meeting him, and never one so quiet as he. They'd been content to work in mutual silence beside each other in the garden. She recalled a time they'd played a game of Stone and Pebble on the ground. Amma had always spoken about how brave and magnificent he'd been as a ranger.

Then Mia had watched him die.

Mia wanted to scream, to call out for help, but she knew there was nobody coming.

"Ssso at lassst you awake," said a voice behind her, out of sight.

Mia craned her neck around. A figure came into view. It wasn't Hizrith. It was his apprentice. The laghart carried an elaborate longbow at her side. It was strange to see her holding such a weapon, rather than a Mystic staff.

"*Zurnta* Hizrithhh will be pleasssed to sssee you awake," she hissed.

Mia tried to slow her breathing, but it was difficult. She hated being bound, and the iron bit into her wrists like a vice growing tighter by the moment.

The apprentice's tongue licked the air, a mere finger length from Mia's face.

"Hisss Highnesss sssaid your consciousssness exisssted beyond your body when we found you. Did your grandmottther teach you that?"

Mia hated that her lip trembled. But she would not be abused by this laghart. She, too, was a Mystic apprentice. She locked gazes with the laghart and sneered in defiance.

The laghart leaned even closer. "I am called Kumava," the laghart whispered. "My massster, His Highnesss, is great and powerful. But he doesss not teach me as he ssshould. He withholdsss secretsss such as how to Mysssstwalk."

Mia studied Kumava, trying to understand her point. She gave the laghart a confused look and shook her head slowly.

Kumava closed her eyes. The blue scales surrounding her slitted pupils pressed together and remained closed. The Myst stirred, lighter than a feather's whisper, and when she opened her eyes the slitted pupils were gone, replaced by rounded ones.

At first, Mia did not understand.

"Like nearly all laghartsss, I wasss one of three eggsss that hatched from a clutch of ten. My mother asssigned me one of the three hatchling namesss. My sssiblings reccceived Ssstrength and Wisssdom, and I wasss givvven Myst-senssse. Thusss has it alwaysss been for the *kanta*, the laghart people, and why we havvve the Pattern-of-Three upon our bodies." She traced a claw along her long snout, indicating the swirling triangular pattern of scales present on all lagharts.

"Yet I wasss diffferent," Kumava continued. "Only a fffifth of the *kanta* have round eyesss. When I awoke to my conscioussssness at a year old, I knew I wasss different by the way I wasss treated. Unveiling the Myst came easssily to me and I quickly learned how to hide my round eyesss, eassily and effectively."

Mia didn't understand why Kumava shared all this with her. Could it be some sort of trick? A trap designed to . . . what?

Kumava long-blinked again, and the slitted eyes returned. She leaned in, the side of her snout brushing against Mia's ear.

"The world isss abouttt ttto change again," Kumava continued. She held up the bow gripped in her claw. "My time hasss arrived. Agree to teach me Myssstwalking, and I will fffree you."

Mia's mind raced. She couldn't explain how she'd done this so-called Mystwalk any more than she could explain how she dreamed. Rion was essential to the process. It wouldn't work without him, at least, using her method, so she didn't know how she'd teach that to anybody.

The sound of a door opening pulled Kumava away from Mia. She heard the other apprentice's robes rustle as she bowed in welcome to her master.

Hizrith and his elite bodyguard strode into view. The master gestured and the iron shackles gripping Mia opened and fell to the wooden floor. "I trusssst you know better than to attempt esssscape," he said. A statement, not a question.

"Sssit up," he commanded, and moved deeper into the room.

Mia did as she was told. She rubbed her wrists and noted the raw bruises left by the iron.

Kumava and the bodyguard placed themselves off to the side, a tail's length apart. They were in a high-ceilinged room lit by at least fifty candles. Carved beams of aged dark wood provided support, as was the style in Sentry. On the far side of the room, away from the table Mia sat on, Hizrith walked into a ritual circle, complete with cushions and an altar. The chalked circle was elaborate, swirling diagrams dominating the space.

Hizrith eased himself down onto one of the cushions and set his Mystic staff across his lap. "You are about to witnesss a great moment in hissstory," he said. "But fffirst, tell me of thisss cloak."

He gestured with a claw, and a folded garment floated off the altar and hovered above the center of the chalked circle. Hizrith shifted his wrist and it tilted, unfolding itself. It was the old green cloak Amma had given to Mia.

Mia fixed Hizrith with what she hoped was a defiant stare, but suspected it appeared more confused than anything else.

Hizrith licked the air and Mia jolted off the table and flew toward him before lurching to a stop. The wind rushed from her lungs. She hung, feet dangling, beside the cloak as an unseen force gripped her neck and shoulders. She gasped but managed to draw a breath.

"I know you can ssspeak," Hizrith hissed. "You will fffind I have lesss patienccce for your impertinenccce than your coddling human masssters. Tell me of thisss cloak."

Mia clawed at the unseen force at her neck. She knew the effort was useless, but what else could she do? She shook her head defiantly. He would get nothing from her. Besides, it was just an old cloak that Amma had worn when she had left home to try to become a Mystic apprentice.

"Very well," Hizrith said. "My way will be lesss comfortable."

The room darkened, though Mia didn't know if it was because the candles dimmed or something else. All she knew was a sudden pressure upon her mind, like being plunged underwater, deeper and deeper, the pressure growing until her ears would burst. Discomfort gave way to pain, and a moaning squeak escaped her lips.

Hizrith remained silent for long, agonizing moments while Mia hung in the air, grasping for breath and focus. He rummaged roughly through her mind, seeking to steal answers. Desperately, she shook her head as if to fling him away. When that failed, she attempted to sharpen her mind, to protect herself, but every time she marshaled mental tenacity the force set upon her by the master swatted those defenses as if flicking a bothersome fly.

Mia managed to turn toward Kumava but found only indifference. Like the bodyguard beside her, Mia saw that she'd get no help from the apprentice.

She lurched her gaze to the other side of the room, irrationally hoping she'd find Rion there, lurking in the shadows, arms crossed and shaking his head as if to say, *Don't look at me; you got yourself into this mess.*

But her brother was nowhere to be found. She was on her own.

The pressure in her mind grew until she couldn't contain a cry of pain. She thrashed her head back and forth, trying to purge the presence from her skull.

As quickly as it had begun, the presence vanished. Mia dropped to the floor.

Kumava walked past Mia, who knelt, trying to catch her breath. The apprentice looked down at her but spoke to her master.

Their hissing words, spoken in the laghart language, passed through Mia without leaving any meaning. Hizrith sounded frustrated while Kumava seemed cold and calm.

Kumava slipped to the floor, placing her bow reverently across her lap. She addressed Mia in Continental. "We do not ssseek to harm you. It hasss been a long journey ffrom Lavantath. His Highnesss isss tired.

"We know thisss cloak belonged to your grandmother. Ssshe wore ittt to her apprentice Trialsss?"

Mia continued to collect herself but allowed herself to nod.

Kumava nodded in reply, both confirming what she already knew and acknowledging to Mia that she appreciated the gesture of cooperation.

"Wasss this cloak givven to you as a giffft?"

Mia shrugged.

"Wasss it gifffted to your grandmothhher?"

Again, Mia shrugged.

"Wasss it givvven to the perssson before your grandmothhher?"

Mia shook her head no. Amma had told her that her friend Bethy had made it for her. The lingering ache of Hizrith's assault fogged Mia's mind, but it was quickly fading, returning her to her normal senses.

Hizrith spoke to his apprentice in their language. Kumava's tongue tasted the air between herself and Mia. "Wasss the cloak crafffted by the perssson who gave it to Pomella?"

Mia nodded.

Again, Hizrith spoke in the laghart language.

"We believe," Kumava said to Mia, using a friendly tone, "that thisss cloak hasss a connection to Ssseer Brigid. Like her bow." She indicated the weapon sitting across her lap. Hizrith hissed a short word, perhaps warning or forbidding Kumava from continuing, but the apprentice went on. "And like His Highnesss's staff. Whether or nottt thisss cloak wasss worn by Ssseer Brigid herself, it carriesss a . . ."—she paused to consider the right word—"a scent, that matchesss the other two Relicsss."

Mia wondered what they wanted from her. Since arriving at Sentry she'd been "given" to these lagharts, thrown in what was essentially a cell, knocked unconscious, tied to a table, and then assaulted by a High Mystic. Now they wanted to reason with her without saying what they truly wanted?

She gathered her strength and stood in the middle of the chalked circle. Hizrith and Kumava did the same. Mia noted the master's burned and knobby staff. It looked strange in the laghart's grip, but if it had once belonged to, or *scented* like, Brigid, then she understood why he carried it.

A familiar shift in the shadows caught her attention. Relief flooded her, but she carefully concealed it. Rion hid behind the altar, his back pressed against it. He twisted around, pressed his finger to his lips, then slipped back out of sight.

Reaching out to the still-floating cloak, Mia gently took it down and draped it around her shoulders while the lagharts watched.

Hizrith's tongue flashed out, eagerly tasting the moment. Mia nodded to him and held out her hand expectantly.

He hesitated, but finally Hizrith handed her his charred staff and motioned for Kumava to pass the bow.

She expected a jolt of power at holding what were supposedly two priceless Relics that belonged to a Saint, but they just felt like unusually heavy sticks.

Both master and apprentice flicked their tongues out, and their slitted eyes widened. They retreated slowly outside the chalk circle. Hizrith hissed commands to Kumava in their language before lifting a clawed hand. The candle flames roared higher.

"We begin," the master hissed.

It took a lifetime of training for Hizrith to contain his excitement. Here, at long last, his life's work would come to fruition. Since the day he'd prostrated himself before Seer Brigid during Crow Tallin, when she'd called upon him to "*call our people home*," he'd undertaken every action he could to make this moment a reality.

He was glad the girl had chosen to work with him. Somehow, she knew instinctively what he needed her to do, though perhaps if she knew the full extent she would be more hesitant. He did not fear her, though, even though she held the Relics.

He wished Hemosavana could have seen this event occur, but the great fay bird had other duties.

Hizrith hissed a command for Kumava to seat herself onto a cushion. The Myst flared around the room. How easily it arose here on the island, further evidence that the land belonged to the *kanta*, and that his mission was the will of the Myst. It sang here now, coursing through him toward the girl who would trade herself for Seer Brigid.

"Clossse your eyesss," he hissed in the human speech. "The ritual will not hurt or take long."

Three Relics. And the girl.

Such was the cost of the ritual, which he'd uncovered from the deepest libraries of Indoltruna. Three Relics of might and significance belonging to a timeless Saint. With Seer Brigid walking beside the *kanta*, no one, not even the barons of Moth or the combined realms of the Continent, could hope to prevent them from taking back their home. Perhaps, with time, they could bring their peaceful way of life to the Continent itself.

With Seer Brigid, anything and everything became possible.

Soon he would have the name of the island as well, a gift he'd present to the Saint.

Ehzeeth, his *Zurnta*, had died in ecstasy upon seeing Seer Brigid in the flesh during Crow Tallin. He'd been older and in poor health during an extraordinary time. Hizrith would not suffer his end upon seeing the Saint again.

He had prepared the ritual circle as soon as his forces arrived in Sentry. The advance team had scouted and prepared this central room of this central building for him, finding candles and crafting an altar to his specifications. All was correct. He'd had a lifetime to review and memorize every part of the ritual, making sure not to leave out a single detail. He'd brought two of the Relics. And his divinations back in Indoltruna had assured him that the final one would present itself to him upon reaching Moth.

Now, at long last, it would begin.

He pulled on the Myst, wavering only slightly due to his lack of a focusing staff. But he was not an apprentice reliant upon such things. With hardened focus he shaped the Myst to the exact parameters, coursing it through candles for energy, infusing it with life through his own breath. He wove it into the girl and into the three Relics: bow, staff, and cloak, the items that had defined Seer Brigid's rise to Sainthood.

The girl's eyes closed as the Unveiling took hold. Her toes lifted off the ground, and she slowly rotated in place, arms outstretched with each holding a Relic. Her upturned face expressed a peaceful look, and Hizrith was glad for that. He had no specific love for humans, but she was just a girl, mostly innocent in all of this. Great potential resided within her, but whatever it was that blocked her speech would surely prevent her from reaching full bloom.

Her death would become the vessel for which Brigid could return.

The shape of the girl's face shifted, becoming somebody else's. The transformation lasted less than a heartbeat, vanishing before Hizrith could see the Saint's detailed features. His tongue zipped out, dancing with excitement.

A harrowing wind blew throughout the room, flickering the candles. The scent of sandalwood and holly filled his nostrils. New excitement washed over his body. He felt decades younger. Full of power. For the first time in long memory, a stirring rose within him, and he wondered if perhaps, when this was over, he would water-bond with Kumava, as they had done long ago. Such was generally not the way after lagharts passed twenty years of age, but this was a momentous occasion.

"My lady," Hizrith said in his native language, "Seer Brigid, Beloved Saint, I return you to us. I have done as you commanded of me on Crow Tallin, dedicating my life to bringing our people, the *kanta*, home. Come forth and lead us to our promised glory!"

The staff and bow blazed with silver and gold light, mixing the color energies of old Fayün and its reflected solid world.

The girl's face flickered back and forth from her own to another, never stopping long enough on either for Hizrith to see it.

"Seer Brigid!" he called. The culmination of the summoning ritual had peaked. This was the moment.

The girl's face flashed once more and held on a familiar Mothic complexion, then snapped back to the girl.

She opened her eyes, herself and not Brigid, and for the first time since beginning Hizrith experienced doubt and a twinge of fear. She was just an—

The girl leaped in place, and spun, swinging the two heavy Relics in a wide sweep. The Myst exploded from her in a tidal wave of force, knocking Hizrith back end over end. The candles snuffed out, and the carefully controlled ritual energy vanished. He tried to scramble upward, but his old body wouldn't cooperate. For a moment he'd become a husk of an old laghart, devoid of power. Sadness, then rage, filled him.

The girl ran, still carrying the Relics. Sanktarin met her at the door, his sword drawn. But the girl had found her power somehow, and swept him aside.

Kumava ran after her, shouting ahead to the other guards to assist. Hizrith wondered why his apprentice did not attack with the Myst in order to stop the girl, but he did not dwell on the thought. He stood at last, breathed once, and purged himself of his insecurities, his fear, his weakness.

He was the High Mystic, *Zurnta* of Indoltruna, Supreme Steward of Lavantath, and Grand Keeper of All That She Has Touched. His life's work would not be undone by a child.

He summoned the Myst once more, and lashed out, gripping the girl in its fist. She lurched at the change in momentum, remaining fixed in place.

"Sanktarin," he commanded.

His Unbroken Watcher regained his feet and strode toward the girl, sword ready.

"Do not damage the cloak."

The Watcher struck just as the near door burst open and a body flew into Sanktarin, knocking him to the floor.

It was a human, an old man, along with a Hunter who had bandages on his eyes. Hizrith stared perplexed at the strange rescuers. The girl spun once more with the Relics, clearing a space around her and the humans who had come to her aid.

"You cannot have the Relicsss!" Hizrith shouted in Continental.

He thrust his hands out, willing the Myst to bring the staff and bow to him. They lurched toward him, but the girl held them tight.

The girl's grasp slipped, but she was strong, and used the Myst against him as well.

Hizrith hissed his frustration and commanded Kumava to help him.

"Stop her!" he screamed, but at that moment both he and the girl lost their strength. The staff flew from her hand to his, but she retained the bow.

The old man was slow getting up, and he was clutching his chest through his torn black robes. He, along with the blind Hunter and the girl, fled the room, leaning on one another. Hizrith opened his mouth to command his guards, but suddenly his consciousness tore out of his body.

TWENTY

THE SON OF MOUNTAINS

Pomella emerged from her journey through the flower to find herself in the most familiar of places, her home for the past sixty-one years. Kelt Apar's lawn, green and splendid and just as she remembered, sprawled before her like an ocean of grass.

But not everything was like she remembered.

Oxillian's Wall was nowhere to be seen, and there were fewer cabins than there should have been. High above, a golden-yellow sky glowed beneath a blue-white sun. Purple clouds drifted east on their journey from the sea to MagDoon. But even more strange than the sky was an emptiness that took her a moment to identify. There were no fay.

"Well, I'll be buggered," she muttered to herself.

Looking down at herself, she saw she wore an old work dress, only somewhat disheveled from use. Her eyes widened and a smile spread on her face. It was the Springrise dress she'd sewn herself before leaving for Kelt Apar. She couldn't remember the last time she'd worn—or fit in—this old thing.

Her bare feet nuzzled the grass, practically jumping with excited energy. She laughed. By the Saints, she felt so . . . young. Examining the rest of her visible body, she estimated she couldn't have been any older than seventeen or eighteen years old.

A sudden bark nearly made her jump out of her skin. She turned to see a slobbery brown dog crouched playfully behind her. He barked again, clearly wanting something from her.

Pomella's eyes widened. "Broon?"

At the sound of his name, the big dog sprinted away, then stopped, looking back at her expectantly.

Then she remembered. Early in her apprenticeship years, Lal made her run around the perimeter of Kelt Apar for long stretches of time until her legs were sore and she could barely move. Broon had been her eager companion on those runs, somehow always demonstrating a longer-lasting constitution than her own.

The dog barked yet again, his wagging tail betraying his impatience.

"We're really doing this?" she said to the dog. "You better hope I've forgotten how to run!"

With only the slightest awkward stumble to begin, and still holding her lantern staff, Pomella ran after the dog, who sprinted away the moment he saw she was indeed going to join his game.

At first, she winced at every pebble or twig that her bare feet encountered. She kept expecting her hip to pop or her knees to collapse.

But they didn't.

The wind from the strange sky blew behind her, urging her forward. Broon stopped, waiting with his wagging tail.

"OK, Pom," she said to herself, "go for it."

She opened herself up, stretched her legs, and sprinted. Life and energy and joy surged through her. She dug in, pushing herself faster. Broon ran beside her, his legs pumping as fast as hers. The lantern on her staff felt as light as air as it swung wildly with the movement. Hector flew from somewhere in the sky and spun around her as she went.

She laughed and ran faster.

They circled the wide borders of Kelt Apar, tracing the path where Oxillian's Wall stood in her waking life. She couldn't see anybody except Broon and Hector, and that was fine by her.

Oh, stars and Saints, what a wonder to be young like this again! How simple a pleasure to run as a girl once more with an old, beloved companion and experience the sheer bliss of exhausting yourself.

Sweat drenched the back of her neck. Her calves burned, and by the time she stopped, her ribs ached with a stitch. Her lungs heaved and it felt amazing. Pomella closed her eyes and savored the moment. Even Broon collapsed onto the grass beside her, his tongue hanging out as he panted.

Gradually her breath returned to her, and Pomella saw she'd come, out of apparent old habit, to Lal's home. The building was as old as it had ever been. In her later life, this dilapidated cabin had become a toolshed for her garden. But here, in this memory and beneath these strange skies, it was still her old master's hut.

A trickle of fear rose in her gut. She'd already had to face her husband, her brother, her daughter, and lose them all over again. Lal almost certainly waited for her inside.

But why did she feel this fear? She'd faced so much already. Lal died during Crow Tallin, fifty-four years ago, and while it had been a bittersweet passing, she'd long ago come to peace with it. She honored his training by gracefully releasing him and not dwelling on the loss.

Yet here she was, standing outside his little house, dread clawing its way through her ribs like ivy.

She bent over to pet Broon, making sure to scratch his belly. He rolled to his back, leg twitching, content with life.

Pomella took a deep breath, and pushed open the door.

As always, the single-room building was dim, just how Lal had preferred it. She remembered how he kept it that way because he liked to meditate by the light of a single candle. She differed from him in that she'd always preferred an open window, even when it rained, because the light and fresh air revitalized her. That, and because dim light always made her sleepy.

A harsh, sour scent washed over her, bringing memory and sadness. Lal sat in a loose, meditative posture on his mat in the far corner of the room. His head lulled, swaying slowly back and forth.

The sight of him paused her. She'd never truly forgotten his face, but seeing him again after so long caused an ache in her heart. She'd forgotten small minutia about his features, like the tiny curl of his ears, and his scraggly eyebrows that she had always wanted to pluck and straighten.

While she knew this was her Mystwalk, here he was, her master, the great grandmaster who had taken her as an apprentice a lifetime ago.

"L-Lal?" Pomella ventured, feeling like that nervous apprentice again.

A light snore was his only response.

Pomella navigated her way across the room, toeing her way around clothes and dirty dishes. She thought of all the times she'd cleaned his house. For all his wisdom and kindness, Lal had never been a particularly tidy person.

An empty bottle lay uncorked on the floor at his side. She picked it up and sniffed, recognizing the horrid scent of chi-uy, Lal's strange homemade liquor.

She placed the bottle in the small wooden crate that she'd used to clean up after him. Following that old habit, she moved around the cabin, picking up clothes and dishes and tidying his few possessions, her thoughts racing.

"Pomella," Lal breathed, and her heart lifted. How long had it been since she'd heard him speak her name? For how many years had she longed for his guiding voice?

She set the bin aside and turned to him from across the room. His eyes were still closed.

"Finished running?" he asked.

"Yes."

"Good. Meditate now. Find Crossroads."

Pomella bit her lip. Before the Merging of worlds, the Cross-roads was that place, or perhaps a state of mind, where a person could hover between the human realm and Fayün. For years Lal had pushed her to meditate until her mind went there, to reside in that peaceful fulcrum in order to drift within the Myst and saturate in its presence.

As an eager young woman, appreciative of the opportunity he'd given her to learn, Pomella had been an ideal student, at least when it came to effort. Vivianna hadn't taken as well to the meditative portion of their studies, but Pomella had rarely skimped on it. Now, with long decades of experience behind her, she appreciated what Lal had been trying to teach her. The cosmology of the Crossroads changed long ago, but after a lifetime of daily practice, reaching the meditative state, even while going about her daily activities, came to her as easily as breathing. Even now, maintaining this Mystwalk required that constant so-called second attention.

But as she looked at him now, Pomella saw Lal in a new light. Interestingly, he seemed younger than she remembered him, but that may've been due more to the years separating them. She estimated he was around seventy years old in this memory, which was seven younger than her physical body was now, as well as seven younger than when he'd passed away.

As always, his head and face were shaved, with only some gray stubble designating a few days of growth. His brown skin was darker than her own, and darker than Tibron's had been.

An empty wooden cup lay in his lap.

How many years had she looked the other way with his drinking? How many times had she silently cleaned him up and tucked him in? She told herself it was because she loved him and that she didn't wish to pass judgment. He was a grandmaster, and while his methods were unconventional, who was she to say that he didn't have supreme awareness and control over his actions?

"No, Master," she finally replied. "Meditation will have to wait. I am here for another reason."

Lal opened his eyes, and for a brief heartbeat Pomella saw past the inebriated haze, and saw a spark of something deep and powerful. But the glazed and droopy expression returned.

"Run again," he said. "Until you cannot. Run until Broon falls asleep."

Pomella moved to the space opposite him and slipped to a cross-legged sit. "I've run so far, Lal," she said. "I'm tired. This body I'm in now hums with youthful energy and vigor, but inside is an old woman who only wishes to tend her garden. But I can't. As you said, I need to keep running. To keep searching. I have to find the Mystic name of the island."

Lal's back straightened. She could see him trying to blink away the haze and see her.

"Yah," Pomella said. "I know you see me, Master. More than ever, I need your guidance."

Lal stared at her, barely containing his surprise; then his face broke into a restrained sob. His body rattled like a willow sapling in a storm. Tears slipped down his face. "Ah, Pomella. You come to me, across time. I see you. From the day you walked into Kelt Apar, I knew. The Myst shines in you so brightly. Knew you would come, one day, into the Deep, for anointment."

He shifted around and prostrated himself before her, forehead touching the ground.

"You honor me with your presence," he went on. His words tumbled around themselves with his heavy Qina dialect.

Pomella stared with wide-eyed shock. This wasn't what she'd expected. Her master, a grandmaster, was *bowing to her*. She'd wrongfully assumed that his tears were those of embarrassment and self-revulsion. How wrong she'd been. How easily she'd let her quick judgments taint her view. Even across all this time, he taught her in every moment.

She inhaled a breath, and with it the Myst, raising it within her mind and tongue.

"Master," she said, speaking in his native Qina language. "I don't deserve this honor. You are my teacher. It is I who should honor you."

She did not have the ability to speak fluent Qina in her waking life. But here, in the Mystwalk, with the Myst so heavily around her, she could communicate meaning and intention and let the Myst form the words for her. For once, she could speak his native language, and give him the opportunity to express himself fully.

He straightened and looked at her with a curious expression. He touched his palms together at his chest. "The student defines the master," he said in Qina. "Did I ever tell you how I came to be the apprentice to my master, Mistress Joycean?"

Pomella shook her head. "You rarely spoke of her at all."

"She was a great woman, defined best by her kindness. She walked among the poor and sick, healing and tending to their needs. Every day during her tenure as High Mystic, people lined up to visit her in Kelt Apar, if she was not already out among the villages and towns of Moth."

Pomella longed for such a time. For most of her years living there, Kelt Apar had been open to any who sought the High Mystic's advice or blessing. But few people had ever come, and none since Crow Tallin.

"I was headstrong and proud when I came to my apprentice Trials," he continued. "Arrogant. Like so many noble-born candidates, I had been given everything in my life except the inheritance of the family title and estates. Those went to my older sister, and I was very angry about it. So, I came burdened by that to my Trials."

"And yet you were chosen to become Mistress Joycean's apprentice anyway?" Pomella said.

Lal nodded. "I am forever grateful to her. She guides both of us now. Never forget, Pomella." He tapped the center of his forehead and then tapped hers, just as he'd done in years past, and for a moment Pomella forgot she was anything but a sixteen-year-old apprentice again.

"Why did she choose you to be her apprentice?" Pomella asked.

"Can we ever truly know the minds of our masters?" Lal said with a whimsical smile. "Perhaps you have a student now, too, Pomella? Selecting an apprentice requires seeing beyond the surface. It is not about the weight they carry up their mountains but about their capacity to shed it, and about your capacity as a teacher to show them how to willingly take it off.

"I was born Ahlala Faywong, which means Son of Mountains, during a spring night of the Huzzo when chants echo between the summit peaks. A bold, powerful name. One that had been shared by kings of the past. Warriors."

Hearing Lal speak the name Huzzo sent a ripple of energy through Pomella. "My Mystic name," she whispered. He'd gifted it to her at the side of a creek.

"Yes," Lal said. "We give a part of ourselves to our students when we name them."

Pomella nodded, remembering the name she'd given Mia, and also the name she'd given another person, an even longer time ago.

She'd given the name Lina to Mia, which meant hidden. And to Shevia, she'd given the name Lorraina, after her grandmhathir, who had chosen a life of personal peace.

"I arrived at Kelt Apar with a soldier's haircut and attitude on my shoulders," Lal continued. "I did not want to be chosen as the apprentice, but my sense of duty prevented me from not trying.

"When I Unveiled the Myst for the first time, the universe opened before me. All the bitterness I'd held drained away as though a dam had been broken."

"What was your first Unveiling?" Pomella asked. It surprised her that she'd never heard this story, or asked him about it.

Lal met her eye and once more a smile spread across his weathered face. "My first Unveiling was like yours," he said. "I sang. It was the night of the Huzzo back home, although I was far from there, in Kelt Apar. I found a secluded place here on the grounds and sang the Huzzo. Mistress Joycean was watching secretly from the shadows, listening. Like she had known I'd be there somehow. I was embarrassed and angry, but she asked me, gently, in just the right way I needed to hear at that moment, to continue. So I did, and I Unveiled fay butterflies and other creatures of Fayün, who were drawn to my voice. The High Mystic smiled at me and left, knowing I was forever enchanted by what I had done. From that day forth I forgot about my worldly inheritance and understood that the only true birthright any of us have is the Myst, which is freely given."

Pomella smiled, caught up in the story's charm. But it faltered quickly. She sighed and reached out slowly to take Lal's hand. It was old and leathered, knobby with age, much like hers was in the waking world. She savored the feel.

Lal looked at her, wide-eyed, and she saw a mixture of surprise and sadness well in his face.

Pomella gave his hand one last fond squeeze and stood. "Thank you for the story. But it isn't true, is it?"

Lal sighed and spoke in Continental, his familiar dialect returning. "I lived to see Yarina become High Mystic and now I witness this. Tell me, are you embarked upon your anointment?"

"Yes," she replied. "At least, I believe so."

"You Unveil me then," Lal said. "What you experience is your version of me. And perhaps what you want me to be."

"I only want you to be who you truly are," she said.

"I am," Lal said carefully, subtly punctuating each word, "and always have been, the Myst. Same lesson as your first day. No separation. All of us, everybody, create our own experience. Our own world. Only in here, during anointment, you witness past and re-experience it through new eyes."

"I don't know if this anointment journey is like yours or Yarina's," Pomella said. "The lineage is broken. I have to find the name of the island before another does."

Lal sighed and nodded. He wobbled to his feet, steadying himself against the wall. Pomella popped up to assist him, but he held up a hand to forestall her.

"Seek the beginning, Pomella," he said, "and you will find the end." The statement resonated with her.

"Come," Lal said.

He led her out of his cabin, and across the lawn. The strangely colored sunny skies were replaced by an ominous, twisting canvas of darkness and color. Broon slept in the building's shifting shade, twitching as though he, too, walked an unfamiliar landscape.

The wind howled, pulling the grass and Pomella's hair in a uniform direction. Motes of dust flew by her face, along with leaves and faint glowing points of light that reminded her of lantern bugs.

Lal staggered across the windswept lawn, holding his hands up to shield his face. Pomella followed, using her staff to steady herself when a particularly heavy gust threatened to knock her over.

Nobody crossed their path or greeted them when they arrived at the central tower. The stone building was a beacon of familiarity to Pomella. In a strange world and time, where she walked beside the memory of her dead master, the tower remained unchanged.

Almost, anyway.

The green conical top of the tower was wreathed in a swirling fog, concealing its topmost floor.

She was surprised to see Lal open the door without effort and gesture her inside. Warm air gusted around Pomella as if the tower had sighed.

Before Pomella could enter the tower, Hector's presence rose in her mind. She turned back to the windy grounds and saw him flying toward her, buffeted by the glass howling eastward across the lawn.

The bold little hummingbird buzzed to Pomella. She held out her palm for him to rest on, but Hector hesitated as if not sure. "It's all right," Pomella assured him. "I'll keep you safe."

Hector acquiesced by alighting onto her palm.

Lal gestured for Pomella to enter the tower. "Once, my student. Now, my successor, my teacher, and my predecessor. Enter in peace and with wisdom."

As she stepped to the door, Lal stopped her by touching her shoulder. He leaned in and whispered, "Beware, Pomella; you are watched."

Holding on to Hector, Pomella kept her suddenly shaken nerves in order. She smiled at him and crossed the threshold. Her skin pebbled. An overwhelming sense of familiarity arose within her, giving her that distinct feeling that she'd been here before, crossed this same threshold, worn this same dress, and appeared just as nervous.

She stepped in all the way, and the door shut behind her. An indomitable silence consumed the foyer. Lal was nowhere to be found.

The glowing lights that normally drifted above the room were absent, leaving only the unevenly spaced windows leading up the stairwell to illuminate the chamber. She lifted the shutters on the lantern hanging from her staff and it cast a wider, warmer glow.

Pomella wasn't sure why Lal had led her here. She tried opening the tower door to leave, but it wouldn't budge. A sudden flash of worry rippled over her. Was she trapped? Had she been lured into some sort of prison?

Looking around the foyer, she saw that the stairs were blocked off. While they normally spiraled upward to the first landing, these terminated in a pile of rubble, denying her a path to ascend.

"What do you see, Hector?" she asked the little bird. He looked at her but gave no sign that he understood what she meant.

"Well, buggerish," Pomella muttered to herself. Hector leaped from her palm to explore the room. Pomella sat on the stone floor, adjusting her work dress and laying her staff across her legs. The lantern rested on the ground beside her.

She closed her eyes, cleared her mind, and tried not to dwell on whether she'd been intentionally trapped or if this was just another curious obstacle laid out before her on this strange journey.

Hours passed. Perhaps days. In a strange way it was as though she slept, although Pomella was aware of every heartbeat. She let herself float in that space of timeless nothing, trusting that the path forward would reveal itself when the time was right.

Lal had brought her to the central tower. The path upward was blocked and there was nothing else of note in the foyer. She had asked him to help her find the new name of the island. Could it have been as simple as the answer being in the tower? Had she journeyed all this way only to learn that the answer could be found in the heart of Kelt Apar? By the Saints, there was a whole *library* upstairs that could somehow hold the name.

But if the library contained what she sought, then why were the stairs leading to it blocked? No. If the tower did indeed hold the Mystic name of the island, it kept that secret buried.

Buried.

Pomella opened her eyes, and knew the answer. At least, partially. She stood and stretched her back. She tapped the stone floor with her staff wondering if there was something below the tower. She had no knowledge of a basement of any sort in the waking world, but here who knew? Lal said this was her reality, created by her Unveiling of the Myst, so why not?

She lifted her staff again and, with a shrug toward Hector, knocked it harder against the floor. As she did, she channeled the Myst downward with the strike. The floor rumbled beneath her feet, bouncing loose pebbles and dirt.

She struck a third time and a fourth, and on the fifth strike light blasted from a crack.

"Aha," she muttered. "I will undo my reality." She struck again, hard.

Her final strike rippled the whole tower like a rock splashing a calm pool of water. The entire floor disintegrated into dust and Pomella found herself falling. Hector zoomed after her. Pomella slowed her descent and alighted gently onto a patch of cool dirt. The roof above her rebuilt itself, leaving her in a stifling muddy tunnel. The lantern light illuminated the walls ahead. Behind her was only more solid rock.

Pomella followed the sloping passage into deeper darkness.

"Crawling through a dirt tunnel," she muttered to the humming-bird. "How typical of my life."

It was hard to tell how far she'd gone because of the nature of the Mystwalk. Every step was like walking through fog, displac-ing time as she moved. At last the tunnel widened into a stone chamber.

The air here was dry and the space cramped, requiring Pomella to hunch low in order to avoid scraping her head along the rocky ceiling. She was once again grateful for her young body that had no difficulty crouching and weaving between low-hanging out-croppings.

As her lantern light illuminated the cavern, she saw silver and golden letter-runes scrawled, or maybe painted, across the exposed stone. Pomella could read both the commoner runes and noble, but none of the writing here matched what she knew, although much of it seemed familiar, like the memory of a dream from several nights ago.

Dominating the chamber was a smooth, bone-white obelisk stretching down from the cavern roof to the floor. More runes covered its surface, and they pulsed faintly in time to her breathing.

Pomella recognized the pillar. The monument of past masters, although curiously, it was wider here than she remembered it from Kelt Apar. As she looked at the ceiling, it dawned on her that this was the subterranean base of the pillar, or at least an extension of it.

"It's about time," said a voice.

Pomella jumped and hit her head on the dirt ceiling. "Ow, shite," she yelped, unable to help herself. The pain radiated from the crown of her head, but she quickly gathered herself and remembered this was a dream. With hardly a thought, she dismissed the pain, and turned her attention to the person who had spoken.

It was Vivianna, in her current old age, sitting cross-legged in a meditative posture on the far side of the monument. She wore a beautiful flowing gown of dark blues, lavender, and white. Her long white hair flowed behind her like a silk curtain. Her eyes were bright, focused, and powerful.

"Viv?" Pomella said.

"Hello, Pom," Vivianna replied. She nodded to an open space on the floor next to her. "Have a seat."

A swell of happiness washed over Pomella as she sat beside her friend. Vivianna beamed at her through a smile.

"Well, look at you," Vivianna said. "Young as a lamb and cute as a kitten."

Pomella grinned. "I'm hardly young, Viv, but it's been nice having working knees again. You wouldn't believe it, but I was running with Broon, you remember Lal's old dog? We were galloping around like gazelles earlier."

"Oh, I believe it," Vivianna said. "I watched you do it plenty of times. You always loved those lessons of his, even though you grumbled."

"I never *grumbled*," Pomella grumbled.

Vivianna arched an eyebrow and they both laughed. When it subsided, Pomella looked carefully at her friend. This is how Vivianna could've been if she'd retained her razor-sharp mind and more easily been able to inherit Moth's lineage. This was the High Mystic she could have become.

"Is this really you, Viv?" Pomella asked. "I keep asking myself that and the others I meet on this journey and I don't know if I'll ever really know the answer."

"What do you think?" Vivianna asked.

Maybe it was the teenage body she inhabited, but Pomella had to restrain herself from rolling her eyes at the unhelpful answer. And perhaps she did so anyway, just a little, because Vivianna shook her head.

"You're hopeless, sometimes," Vivianna said, not without affection.

Pomella ignored the comment. "Why are you here?"

"I've been here waiting for you," Vivianna said. "Ever since my anointment went so horribly wrong."

"Are you well?" Pomella asked. "In your physical body, I mean?"

"For now," Vivianna said. "I would've died if I had returned to my body."

"What happened?"

"I think you already know," Vivianna replied.

"Lagnaraste told me that the Mystic name of the island changed," Pomella said. "But I don't fully understand."

"The Mystic name of Moth is not a word anybody can speak," Vivianna said. "Think of it more like a melody. Or perhaps a grand symphony, because it is more than a single sound but a harmony of countless lives united. The High Mystic of Moth can hear that symphony and host it within their heart. And in normal times it is passed to their successor here, within what you call the Mystwalk."

"But the name changed somehow," Pomella said.

Vivianna nodded. "When you merged Fayün and the human realm, the name *began* to change. The song shifted its melody. Slowly, note by note, over time, it shifted. The change was subtle, and I believe Mistress Yarina did not notice. The same is likely true for all the other High Mystic domains on the Continent. After more than fifty years, the name had changed so much that it no longer resembled the name that Lal had long ago passed to Yarina."

Pomella let all this settle over her. "What happened when Yarina tried to give you the old name?"

Vivianna's face sagged in sadness. "The resonance of the outdated name killed her," she said. "And nearly killed me. Yarina held too tightly to the name she knew. She'd spent her lifetime protecting and preserving something that no longer existed. The power of that attachment, and the energy of the new one, proved to be too much for her."

"I'm so sorry you had to experience that, Viv," Pomella said. "You deserved better."

"*Deserved?*" Vivianna scoffed. "You know better than to use that word. We are Mystics. We accept what comes to pass with no judgment upon it. By letting go of what we think we *deserve*, we free ourselves from the pain that it brings."

"You would have made a fine High Mystic," Pomella said. "The past masters would be proud."

"They are," Vivianna said. "Of both of us." She indicated the obelisk behind her.

"I didn't know it extended into the ground," Pomella said. "Does it exist in the waking world?"

"The 'waking world'?" Vivianna said. "You merged all worlds, Pomella. And with the Myst, there is no separation. This monument, this cavern, your plucky teenage body, it's all as real as what you would call a kick in the shins. I'm sure you've had a long and challenging journey to come here, but don't let the experience dull your memory of those early lessons: everything is the Myst, and a true Mystic is one who always understands and remembers that. In every moment you are sixteen-year-old apprentice Pomella, and twenty-three-year-old Crow Tallin Pomella, and thirty-five-year-old mother Pomella. Apprentice, Mystic, master. In every moment you are reborn in all times and places."

They sat in silence and Pomella let it all soak into her.

"Viv," Pomella said, breaking the silence, "did you ever learn the new Mystic name of the island?"

Vivianna shook her head. "I chose not to look for it."

Pomella gaped at her friend. "You didn't? Why not?"

"Because it's not mine to find, Pom. I knew I had to be *here*."

"How? And why?"

Vivianna raised an eyebrow and fixed her with a firm *just-think-about-it* expression. "To be here for you, of course."

"I don't understand," Pomella said, her mind spinning.

Vivianna straightened her back and turned her expression toward the submerged obelisk. "The answers you seek are already within you," she said. "Go deeper. Into your past. Into your future. Find the Nameless Saint."

Pomella frowned, trying to remember where she'd heard that name before. "From the Brigid tales?"

"Yes. The one who is beyond time. She knows the name of *all* things."

"Where is she?"

"Do I really need to say it?"

Pomella opened her mouth to snap a reply, *yes*, that would be really damned helpful, but she caught herself. Vivianna was right. She already knew the answer. Like everything else she had discovered on this journey, the answers were within her.

She shifted to a meditative posture matching Vivianna's, a task as familiar to her as breathing. Closing her eyes, she said, "Thank you, Viv."

"You're welcome, dear friend. And you may call me by my Mystic name, Baylew."

The name rang through Pomella like a drum. She knew that name, from years long past, during the days of Crow Tallin, when Lal had passed away. Pomella had descended into her master's mind to try to save him and it had been Vivianna's chant, *bay-lew*, that had anchored her and helped her return back.

Pomella reached across and squeezed Vivianna's hand. Hector buzzed nearby. "My beloved Baylew," she said.

Leaving Vivianna and the cavern behind, she focused on the monument and dissolved herself into it. The cavern melted away, along with Vivianna and the rest of the dream, forming a space of timeless presence that was utterly devoid of darkness.

Her final steps in this journey had begun.

TWENTY-ONE

THE MYSTWOOD HETCH

Faded visions of a woman with blue eyes and fierce red hair lingered in Mia's memory as she and her would-be rescuers burst from a door out onto the center of Sentry. Looking up, Mia caught sight of the clock tower looming above them. They'd been inside it the whole time. Morning sunlight gleamed off the clockface, blinding her.

Two surprised laghart guards drew weapons. She pointed at them with the stolen bow, motioning for Rion to knock them aside. He smiled as he leaped toward them. Mia didn't bother to look at the outcomes. She trusted him not to kill them. What was important was that he cleared a path for their escape.

She quickly checked Kilpa's wound, which bled through his black robes. A wide gash oozed blood. She swallowed some bile upon seeing it. He leaned heavily on Nabiton, who seemed unsure of where to go because of his blindness. They were quite the pathetic bunch, she thought to herself.

Kilpa must have sustained the wound when he attacked the white bodyguard. She marveled that the old man was still alive. He labored to breathe but waved Mia away when she looked at him with concern.

He had to be around eighty years old, Mia estimated. Adding to everything, he hadn't truly had a good rest since Kelt Apar, and he'd been abused. Yet somehow he'd taken down an elite laghart warrior. She knew of Kilpa's old warrior tattoos, and what they meant, but it was still impressive.

"Looks bad," Rion said, looking from Kilpa's wound to his own swollen knuckles. The way he said it so casually, Mia suspected that he was referring to his knuckles.

He wore a dramatic outfit now, complete with a billowing black cape and an eye mask, reminiscent of the old hero sagas her House Maintainer had read to her as a child.

"Any idea how to get out of here?" Rion asked. "They'll be here at any moment."

Mia looked around, her heart hammering in her chest. They'd earned a hard-fought moment's advantage. But it would evaporate like a puddle in summer when the next wave of guards or Hizrith, Kumava, or their elite bodyguard found them.

They needed a place to hide quickly. And then they needed to find help for Kilpa or he wouldn't survive.

The old man tugged Mia's sleeve and pointed up a street leading east. "That way. There's a—" He winced and caught his breath.

Mia didn't wait for him to finish the statement. She tapped Nabiton's shoulder and tugged him in the direction Kilpa had indicated. The two men moved as quickly as they could, but it was still a shambling pace. Mia's fingers squeezed the bow with a death grip. She wanted to scream in frustration.

"I know this is hard," Rion said to her as they hurried, "but you can't risk being caught again. You might have to leave the old man behi—"

Mia rounded on her brother, cutting him off by stabbing her finger to his lips. She glared directly into his eyes, burning him with a look that made it clear he was not to ever suggest that idea again.

"Fine," Rion said. "But you can't just move in the open. What are you going to do?"

Laghart patrols sounded from around the corner. In pure desperation, Mia yanked Rion's ridiculous black cape from his back, snapping the thin clasp holding it in place.

"Hey, be careful with that!" he cried.

Mia called to the Myst, and pulled her companions into a crouch beneath the cape. Nabiton grunted and Kilpa collapsed with a muffled moan of pain. Sweat poured from his forehead, soaking his neck and untamed beard.

Mia peered from a gap in the cape toward the laghart warriors who had just rounded the corner. They stopped and looked multiple ways, trying to determine which way Mia and her companions had gone. Tongues licked the air, and soon the warriors were rushing down the street directly toward them.

"What have you done, Mia?" Rion said. He was still standing outside of the cape, while Mia and the others were beneath it. "They can smell you!"

Mia made an urgent shooing motion toward her brother.

He stared at her, eyes wide with surprise. "You want me to *what*?"

She jabbed a finger telling him to get moving.

Cursing a horribly offensive word, Rion fled in the direction Mia indicated, taking their scent with him.

It was now or never. Mia huddled as small as she could under the cape and prayed to her ancestors.

The laghart patrol rushed by, passing them, pursuing Rion. Mia waited a full minute before she was certain she couldn't see or hear any other nearby patrols. She got her companions to their feet but kept the cape draped over them as well as she could.

A lone figure came running around the bend from the opposite direction to where the lagharts had gone. It was Rion. He stopped in a huff, hands on his knees. "I hope you're satisfied," he said. "I nearly got skewered on at least three of those swords. It's a good thing my constitution is well-conditioned."

She glared at him and gestured to her two companions.

"Right," he said, wiping sweat from his forehead. "Let's go. Can I have my cape back?"

She didn't give him the satisfaction of answering. The cloak obscured them from sight, so long as they remained beneath it.

Mia navigated her desperate party eastward through streets by peering through the thin gap in the cape. Rion scouted ahead, occasionally throwing a patrol off with their scent.

As they neared Sentry's eastern wall, Kilpa touched Mia's shoulder and whispered, "Wait."

She leaned him against the side of a wooden building. A cat stopped licking water from a nearby puddle and looked directly at them before scampering away. For a panicked moment Mia wondered if the cat seeing them meant the lagharts could, too. She dismissed the thought and hoped it had just heard them.

"Rose and oak," Kilpa muttered. His eyes rolled back in his head and he fell unconscious into Nabiton's arms.

Mia glanced at Nabiton, hoping to learn more. She touched his arm questioningly.

"We—" Nabiton swallowed to wet his throat. "We found a house. Kilpa did, I mean. After we escaped the Hunter's rally. He said he had to find a specific sign on a door. He found it eventually and they took us in. They were Touched. They knew a way out of the city, said they could help. But Kilpa insisted we go back to find you. He wanted me to stay, but I insisted on coming." He found Mia's hand after a moment. "For you."

Mia's heart swelled. She kissed his fingertips and touched his cheek.

Rion, who apparently had been standing there, rolled his eyes. "Rose and oak. Right. I'll see what I can find," he muttered, and left.

Mia bent to examine Kilpa's wound again. His entire chest was covered in blood. A lump formed in her throat. He wouldn't last long. His chest rose and fell slowly in unconsciousness.

Nabiton knelt beside her and felt Kilpa's chest rising and fall-ing. "I'll carry him," he said. "Lead the way."

Mia helped Nabiton lift Kilpa. The younger man wasn't very tall, but his body was solid and he lifted the frail older man with relative ease. Mia peered out to the streets again and saw Rion waving to her from a block away.

Mia moved as fast as she dared. Individual lagharts stood on the street corners, hands on their sheathed swords, tongues snap-ping the air as they peered into the morning light, searching for Mia and her companions. A large patrol roamed a block away, me-thodically combing every portion of Sentry. Rion was practically prancing with impatience when they finally arrived at his location down one of the side streets. They'd come to the side of a small nondescript wooden building. Upon the door hung a wreath of oak branches decorated with red rosebuds.

Mia hurriedly knocked on the door, and again, more urgently when nobody answered.

She was about to bang on the door a third time when a Mothic-accented voice inside said, "Who?"

Mia opened her mouth to reply but bit her lip.

Nabiton spoke up. "It's us, Higren," he said. "Please. Kilpa's wounded and won't last."

The door cracked open and Mia lowered the cape, which she handed back to Rion. He huffed to himself about disrespecting fine clothing.

The door opened wider and Mia ushered Nabiton through with Kilpa in his arms before slipping in and shutting the door.

The home belonged to a young couple, both Touched, who had a young child. Goodness Higren, who had the ears and nose of a doe, took Kilpa from Nabiton's arms and rushed him to a back room that doubled as a small sun-room for growing flowers. She was a stout woman, and Mia could see she was determined in her nature by the way she moved without hesitation.

The husband, who quickly introduced himself as Gonlen, was tall and had a mane of flaming red hair running between two thick ram's horns curling from his forehead. He held their child, a sleeping boy less than a year old, who appeared like a typical Untouched pale-skinned Mothic tyke except for two faint nubs on his forehead where horns like his fathir's might grow someday.

Mia nodded in greeting but swept past him to follow Higren into the sun-room. She estimated by the organization and quantity of flowers growing there that the family operated as flower merchants. They were commoners by the looks of them, so they likely kept the operation intentionally small in order to not raise the attention and ire of the local merchant-scholars.

"Clear t' table," Higren commanded in the thickest Mothic accent Mia had ever heard. She complied, glad to be able to do something useful. The woman laid Kilpa down on the table, then practically yanked the old green cloak off Mia's back before easing it behind the old man's head. Behind them in the doorway, Nabiton explained the situation to Gonlen in hushed tones.

"Hand me that jar, love," Higren said. "And pass me t' shears."

Mia did all she was told. Higren sliced Kilpa's robes open, exposing the wound. His frail chest rose and fell with great effort.

Higren set to work with a practiced eye. "Dark blood," she observed. "There may be a chance. Keep apply'n' pressure to t' wound. Don't let him bleed any more than he already has."

Mia pressed a clean cloth against the wound and wondered where Higren had learned such skills.

Nabiton found Mia and muttered in her ear, "We won't be safe here, long. The Mystic laghart will have means of finding us. We have to get out of Sentry."

"You can go east, into t' last edges of t' Mystwood," said Gonlen. He shifted his grip on the sleeping baby. "From there, you can cross t' Ironlows. Enttlelund hasn't fallen yet, as t' lagharts have primarily pushed south. Baroness AnBroke will let you in"—Higren scoffed at this comment but continued setting a concoction of herbs and leaves against Kilpa's wound—"and, if yer desperate enough," Gonlen continued, "you can take a ship to t' Continent."

Mia shook her head. She wasn't about to flee Moth. Not without her grandmother and Vivianna and the other Mystics.

"They won't move quickly enough and they'll just get caught," Higren said. "Enttlelund won't do. They need to go to t' Hetch."

Mia quirked an eyebrow at the doe-faced woman.

"Yes, I know it's a vulgar term, but it's what she calls herself. She can help you. Gonlen can get you safely to t' Mystwood and set on t' right path."

"What about Kilpa?" Nabiton asked, echoing Mia's thoughts.

"I can stabilize t' wound. The Hetch can see to t' rest. If anyone can save him, it'll be her."

Higren led them to a small storage room at the back of the house. There she moved a basket of gardening tools aside and pulled away a circular rug revealing wooden floorboards. She fumbled around and opened a cleverly concealed door that hinged open.

Below lay a wide tunnel descending into darkness.

Higren looked from Nabiton to Mia. "It's a long tunnel," she explained, possibly more for Nabiton's benefit because he'd be carrying Kilpa. "Just stay straight and it'll route you outside t' city. Gonlen'll meet you with Rosie on t' other side. From there, he'll send you onto t' Hetch."

Mia guided Nabiton down the ladder, then helped Higren pass Kilpa's frail and unconscious body down to him. She gave Higren a hug good-bye and led Nabiton down the dim tunnel. The floor was dirt, having been packed tight from generations of traffic. Mia chose not to imagine what this passage had been created and used for in the past.

Thick wooden beams braced the walls and ceiling, along with the occasional stack of stones. A lantern with fresh oil hung on a peg on the tunnel wall near the ladder, but Mia left it where it was. Rion waited farther down the passage, holding a different lantern. That would be sufficient for her.

After walking awhile, Nabiton called to Mia, "Wait, please. I need to rest!"

He set Kilpa down gently and sat, leaning his back against the stone tunnel wall.

Mia sat beside him, grateful for the rest as well, but eager to get to safety, too.

"Do you trust them?" Nabiton asked.

Mia nodded and squeezed his hand in reply.

"I don't trust anybody anymore," Nabiton said. "Blind trust only gets you hurt."

He caught himself. "*Blind.* Trust." He snorted a derisive laugh. "I'll probably think twice before using that word again."

Mia turned to him. Rion was scouting ahead, so there was no light to see by. Yet this close she could discern the outline of Nabiton's face, and the filthy bandages he wore over his damaged eyes. He looked so worn, so different from the handsome and brash youth who'd charmed her when they were young. His normally clean-shaven face had over a week's worth of growth. It made him appear older, which, Mia admitted to herself, wasn't all that bad of a look.

"Ulammia," Nabiton said after a moment. He squeezed her fingers and switched to speaking in Qina. "I'm sorry for hurting you. And I'm sorry for my cruel words. I've paid a price"—he touched the bandages covering his eyes—"but it can never be enough for the way I treated you. For abandoning you to become a Hunter."

A lump formed in Mia's throat. He was wrong. He'd suffered

too much, and the damage she'd done to his body was cruel. Violence had begotten more of the same.

Her fingertips traced up his arm, to his cheek, and to his eyes. Slowly, she brought her lips to his damaged eyes, and pressed them there, as gentle as a whisper. He tilted his face up toward her. Her lips found his scruffy cheeks, and then his lips. They lingered there, letting the kiss settle.

"Mia," Nabiton began, his body trembling, "may I—?"

In reply, Mia pulled him closer, increasing the intensity of her kiss. Heat burned beneath her hands, and she let herself fall into Nabiton's strong grip.

"We should go," Nabiton said a short time later. "We've lingered too long. Gonlen will wonder what became of us."

Mia wished this nightmare would end. She longed for a peaceful place to rest, where she was safe and could sleep and dream uninterrupted.

She nodded into Nabiton's chest and stood up, gathering the laghart bow. She helped him stand, and together they got Kilpa settled into Nabiton's arms and set out along the tunnel.

They didn't have very far to go before they reached the end of the tunnel where Rion waited with the lantern at the base of a ladder leading up. A knowing smile played upon his lips, but he wisely said nothing.

The ladder led to a rickety wooden shed resting in a narrow thicket of oak trees. It was nearly midday now. Although she couldn't see Sentry's walls to the west, Mia could hear the distant muffled commotion of the large town.

Gonlen hurried over to them as they exited the shed, clearly relieved that they'd finally arrived. For her part, Mia was glad Gonlen didn't ask what had delayed them.

The flower peddler had brought a mule and cart whose bed was strewn with flower petals and leaves. He helped them load Kilpa onto the wagon and made him as comfortable as possible with blankets that he'd brought.

"I had no problems coming through t' walls," he explained. "T' lagharts searched us thoroughly, o' course, and they expect me back with a haul of wildflowers, like I normally do."

"Thank you," Nabiton said to the man as he settled himself beside Kilpa in the wagon.

Mia sat next to Gonlen in the driver's seat. They moved eastward a short distance, then turned south. The trees grew thicker and the familiar damp chill of the Mystwood settled over them. This was the eastern edge of the forest, Mia knew, resting in the morning shadow of the Ironlow Mountains.

"My wife found this place half a decade ago," Gonlen told Mia as they rode. "Full of wildflowers it was. Imagine her surprise when an old woman stepped out of t' trees and shooed her away! But my wife, you met her, so you know what she's like, wouldn't have it. 'I need these flowers,' said she to t' old woman, who responded, 'They're mine from my garden and not for pluck'n'!

"But Hilgren, my charming wife, she sweet-tongued that ol' crone till she laughed, and t' crone agreed to let her take some flowers to sell, so long as she agreed to grow them herself so as to spread their beauty. Hilgren did as she said but kept coming back to learn from the old Hetch—that's what she calls herself, the Mystwood Hetch. Funny name, but she prefers it, so who am I to judge what a person's to be called? Business's been blooming, if you don't mind t' expression, ever since. T' Hetch's taught Hilgren more than just flowers, mind. She's told Hilgren all about care of animals, how to count sums, and how to read noble runes." He flicked a glance at Mia, suddenly tight-lipped. There were still laws on Moth forbidding commoners from reading noble runes. But he obviously decided she was safe enough to trust them, because really, what would they do otherwise?

"She even taught her how to stitch a man up," Gonlen said,

nodding to Kilpa, "which certainly benefits this poor fella. When he and your friend first came to our door, t' old man said he knew t' Hetch and recognized t' oak rose wreath. I admit, if you'll excuse me, that I wanted to turn them away, but Hilgren insisted we take them in. I'm glad we did. Just hope there's time for your friend, and hope nothing gets back to t' lagharts about my family."

"We appreciate your bravery," Nabiton said from the back of the cart. Mia nodded her agreement and patted Gonlen's leg in thanks.

As the sun crested to its zenith, they came to a clearing of wildflowers, just as Gonlen had described. The red-maned man halted the mule with an "Easy there, Rosie," though the animal clearly knew the destination and had come to a stop before he'd spoken.

"Are we there?" Nabiton asked, staring upward.

"Yah," Gonlen said. "Come. T' Hetch'll come soon. Always does."

He went to help Nabiton and Kilpa while Mia glided into the middle of the wildflowers. She carried the laghart bow with her. A strange presence lingered in the field. Butterflies and fay bugs flitted around her. A pair of robins skittered between trees.

Energy stirred around Mia. She looked for Rion, but strangely, he was nowhere to be found. She had a bad feeling about this place, and for the first time began to regret hastily trusting the idea of this "Hetch" helping them.

She clutched the bow in both hands, holding it like a Mystic staff. Then, as if the wildflowers had bloomed to life all at once, a strong fragrance filled her nose. Her mind clouded, and sudden fear gripped her chest.

Mia turned back to look at the cart and saw Nabiton and Gonlen collapse to the ground just as darkness overwhelmed her.

More dreams of the red-haired woman. She wanted something, that woman. With bow and staff and cloak she sought it, across time and lives. Her determination was real, visceral, and present in Mia's mind. She reached to Mia, extending her longbow to her. Imploring her for help.

Mia awoke.

It was the second time in recent memory that she'd risen from a drugged stupor. But this time, instead of being strapped to a table, she found herself in a comfortable bed. Her head cleared quickly, the fog blown away swiftly as if caught in a sea breeze.

The bed she lay on rested inside a lavishly decorated room full of flowers. Paintings hung on the log walls depicting everything from butterflies to mountains to the dense swath of stars that stretched across the night sky.

Mia swung her feet out of bed and found her now-worn-out shoes waiting for her on a soft, plush rug next to a pair of thick slippers. As tempting as the slippers were, she opted for her shoes and made her way to the wooden door that led from the room. The laghart bow rested against the doorframe, waiting for her. She grabbed it and proceeded out.

She emerged to the main portion of a cozy house that was even more elaborately decorated than the room she'd awoken in. More paintings decorated the walls along with woven baskets and wreaths decorated with all manner of flowers. A large stone fireplace dominated the far side of the room and upon its mantle were wooden carvings of squirrels and other small animals, a pile of old books, and some wooded instruments. And of all things, a long animal spine stood upright against the stone of the chimney.

Nabiton sat on a chaise near the fireplace, sipping a steaming beverage from a small cup. His long hair had been washed and combed and the bandages over his eyes replaced with clean ones. He had been speaking in a low voice but stopped and tilted his head in Mia's direction as she approached.

Another figure rose from a chair with its back facing Mia. She was tall and thin, with gray hair pulled up into a bun. She wore a gown of finely woven and embroidered maroon cloth and held a steaming cup similar to Nabiton's. Swirling tattoos peeked out of her long sleeves, down her wrists and on both sides of her hands. Her neck, too, was covered in intricate tattoos.

She turned and Mia couldn't help but gasp. The woman was Qina, like her and Nabiton, with strange lavender eyes. Mia sensed power radiating from her like heat from a fire.

"Ulammia," said the old woman. Mia estimated she was near Amma's age, though she stood with a straighter back and moved with a more graceful motion.

Mia curtsied out of habit of showing proper respect for older Qina women.

The Mystwood Hetch sneered a laugh. "No need for that frivolousness, girl. You are welcome here in our home. I am grateful for you returning my husband Kilpa to me. I generally prefer that the locals refer to me as the Mystwood Hetch, but all things considered, since we are related, you may call me Shevia."

TWENTY-TWO

THE THOUSAND LIVES OF BRIGID

Despite her desire to avoid the location, Brigid found herself at the base of the great mountain. After six years of searching, it was her last hope. All other options were exhausted, all other trails long since cold.

The lagharts had a name for the mountain, but it was impossible for her to speak with her human tongue. The mountain loomed higher than any other peak on the island, casting its long shadow at dawn across the Great Forest and across the eastern foothills at dusk.

She sipped from her water flask, and checked the straps holding Dauntless in place on her back. It would be a long climb to the summit, where Mylezka, after trying for a long time to convince her, had assured her she would find what she sought.

"At the sssummit," the *Zurnta* had told her, "you will ffffind the namelesss one. Sssshe who isss beyond time, transsscendant."

"A Saint?" Brigid said.

"Yesss," Mylezka said. "Ifff that isss your word for sssuch personsss."

Now, as Brigid looked up at the distant summit, the sky shone bright and clear. The summer sun was already warm despite the early hour. It would be a long, hot trek to the top.

She had come alone, although she had considered asking Zyhen and a handful of other laghart warriors to join her. They would've followed her, she knew. Not just because she carried Dauntless, but also because they'd come to adore her. The lagharts had a dizzying array of legends and omens they saw everywhere, and for some reason Brigid seemed to somehow always say or do the right thing that made them stare at her in awe. It seemed to her at times that much of their mythology had been written for her, so that when she defeated a creature like Lor Gez, or befriended the lucklesslings, or tamed the mountain valley tythons, she was fulfilling some sort of preordained prophecy.

She didn't care about any of it, though. She wasn't here for glory. All that mattered was finding Janid.

The climb began as expected, and Brigid fell into the familiar pace of travel. One step at a time, breathing through the slow burn in her muscles. A portion of her mind remained ever vigilant for danger, but she expected little trouble on the mountain. It was a sacred place to the lagharts, and only the elders occasionally came from the nearby velten to pay homage at the summit.

She hiked the path on the western side, following switchbacks scratched through bushes and around debris of fallen stone. At one point she looked back and saw much of the Great Forest laid out before her like a blanket. It was beautiful, but her eyes couldn't hold on to that. She only remembered the pain and the battles she'd fought beneath that canopy of trees.

There would be more of it, too, once the humans made their way here. They would come and cut the trees and build a city. Sentry, they would call it, right on the northern edge of the woods, not far from her long-abandoned homestead. And they would burn the velten there, killing the unsuspecting lagharts. . . .

She shook her head, coming back to the moment.

Sentry? A town? What was she thinking? There wasn't a human colony in that area. Why had that come to her so clearly?

She hiked on, not dwelling on the thought.

After a thousand thousand agonizing steps up the mountain, Brigid came at last to the cave at the summit where the reclusive Saint dwelt.

Brigid's well-worn boots crunched atop sandy stone just outside the entrance. A heavy wind raced across the summit, catching her cloak and fiery hair. From this height, she could look down onto the fog-drenched Great Forest, to the twinkling ocean beyond. She allowed herself a moment to savor the fresh air. So peaceful, yet she had no time to linger.

As she watched, her shoulder itched, like she expected somebody to touch it.

She spun, her small belt knife in her hand, ready.

But there was nobody there. Only the rocky summit and the yawning cave entrance.

Memories flashed in her mind. Zyhen, the laghart warrior, was supposed to be there, wasn't he? Hadn't he and the others traveled with her to the summit?

No, of course not. She hadn't asked them. She'd come alone.

Brigid peered into the cave. What secrets and wonders were within? She sheathed the knife and fingered an arrow resting in the hide quiver opposite her knife before deciding against it. One did not walk into the dwelling of a Saint with an arrow nocked. She kept Dauntless in her hand, though, just in case.

She squeezed through the cracked entrance, trying not to cut herself on the sharp rocks. She slid along the long, cramped tunnel that was no wider than her arms outstretched. It eventually widened into a large chamber filled with darkness. Brigid suppressed her fear. She couldn't stop now, even if this place made her feel like she'd just been swallowed into a stomach of shadows.

A warm gust of wind rushed past her, coming from within the cave. It carried the stinging scent of ash.

Memories of other places, other times, stirred. For a moment she thought she saw a figure looming in the shadows. A pair of beckoning lavender eyes gleamed before fading away.

"To the Saint within!" Brigid called into the darkness. "I am Brigid the Red, Daughter of None but the Woods."

She wished she'd thought to bring a source of light, and briefly considered leaving the cave to craft a makeshift torch. But her eyes adjusted to the light, and the walls glowed dimly. A silver algae grew upon them, partially covering runes and primitive drawings. Small silver fay scuttled across the stone, trailing misty smoke behind them. In the farthest corner of the cave, she made out a small alcove.

Brigid approached, her boots echoing across the cave floor.

The corpse of an old woman waited in the alcove. She sat cross-legged on the stone, her chin drooped toward her chest. Cobwebs covered her mostly naked body, the skin faded to a dull gray-white. Her few shreds of clothing were aged beyond recognition. An old, nearly disintegrated tome collected dust beside her.

Brigid's heart raced. This couldn't be right. Mylezka had assured her that the Saint still lived.

Brigid knelt anyway and pressed her forehead to the ground. A Saint still deserved respect, dead or alive.

Brigid lifted her head and looked more closely at the woman she'd traveled so far to see. The Saint's closed eyes rested in sunken sockets. Gray hair spilled down her face and back. Her mouth hung slightly open, revealing decayed teeth.

"You cannot be dead," Brigid whispered. "The Corenach claimed you lived!"

She stopped. The Corenach? The name was vaguely familiar to

her, but she had never encountered such a person. Or creature. Why had she said that? Everything about this cave kept her off-balance.

A silvery centipede crawled over the Saint's hair. Sitting on the ground in front of the Saint was a cornucopia filled with fresh rice, nuts, and grapes. Likely offerings from the laghart elders. Reluctantly, Brigid eased to her feet. There was nothing here for her.

"Prisoner."

Brigid froze. The word had floated to her as a thin strand of sound whispering across the air. She held her breath, not daring to move.

The Saint's lips moved slowly, puffing dust from her lungs. "Again, you come."

Hope, like the glorious dawn, filled Brigid's heart. The woman was alive!

The Saint's head shifted to face Brigid. A tendril of smoke lifted from the center of the Saint's forehead. Like a trickle of dust, it vanished, revealing a thin line that slowly opened to form the shape of an eye. The eye was outlined in silver with a golden pupil and sketched like a tattoo upon the Saint's dull skin. It blinked once, slowly, and focused on Brigid, studying her.

Brigid fell to one knee. "Beloved Saint, I pray for your help."

"So you say, time and again," the Saint whispered.

Brigid licked her lips. What did she mean? "I've come for my son," she said, "Janid. He was taken from me."

"He is not yours."

A low rumble filled the cave. Streams of dirt and stone trickled from the shadows above. Brigid ignored them.

"I am his mother. Of course he is mine."

"You do not yet see," said the Saint. Brigid had to strain to hear the quiet voice. "How many more loops of the needle until you do?"

"The *Zurnta* told me you held the answers to how I could find my son," Brigid said. Her patience waned like the receding tide. "Please, how do I find him?"

"Release yourself. Release your attachment."

"I don't understand," Brigid said.

"Then you are not ready."

"Help me then," she pleaded.

"What do you offer?"

"For the path to my son? Anything." She set her flawless bow on the ground between them. "I would offer Dauntless, won in a contest against Lor Gez, the All-Seeing. I'd offer my cloak, woven from the spring grass by the lucklesslings and given to me in thanks. And I'd give the Fire Branch, bestowed upon me by—"

She stopped. *Fire Branch? What was that?*

"Trinkets will not free you."

The cave shook again, and this time Brigid had to steady herself. She looked around, wondering if she was truly in danger. She gritted her teeth. The blood-charred tomb could collapse for all she cared, so long as she got what she came for.

"What must I do?" said Brigid.

"Return to me."

The shaking became more insistent. A large stone crashed between them, crushing the cornucopia of offerings. The Saint tilted her head back. Her eyes opened, revealing cankered orbs that seemed to stare through the ceiling. The surreal movement chilled Brigid's skin.

"It awakens," hissed the Saint. "Leave, Daughter of None! Awaken, Prisoner of Time!"

"Tell me, I beg you," Brigid said, raising her voice against the growing noise. "Tell me how I can learn of the Myst and find the path to my son!"

"Leave your bow, cloak, and branch," commanded the Saint. "Revoke your name and quest. Lay claim to nothing and let nothing claim you."

Brigid looked at the treasures in her hands. Each had been hard-won. Friends had died to help her gather them. For six years, she had searched. For six years, she'd hunted, going where nobody else dared travel. She'd seen terrors that would bend kings and battled enemies no person could conquer. No person, except a mother who desperately wanted her child back. How could she let him go?

"I cannot," she whispered.

"Release your attachment. Embrace only the Myst, and all will be found. Now go!"

A heavy tremor shuddered through the cave. Brigid rose to her feet, bow held firmly in her hand. "Will you tell me your name?"

The Saint whispered, but the shaking cavern stole the words from Brigid's ears. The central eye on the Saint's forehead stared straight at her.

Brigid stepped away from that gaze and ran, fleeing the tremors and the Saint's impossible demand. Unbidden tears fell from her cheeks. Up ahead, the cracked entrance seemed farther away than she remembered.

The cave collapsed behind her, rolling dust and thunder across her path. The entrance ahead loomed like the mouth of a stone tython clenching its jaw.

As she ran, Brigid thought of Janid. She saw his gentle eyes smiling up at her as she climbed over fallen stone. A stone jostled Dauntless in her grip and the bow caught her legs, tripping her. The entrance collapsed, the world rushed, and everything turned to darkness.

The needle lifted, looped, and wove again.

After a thousand thousand agonizing steps up the mountain, Brigid came at last to the cave at the summit where the reclusive Saint dwelt.

Brigid's well-worn boots crunched atop sandy stone just outside the entrance. A heavy wind raced across the summit, catching her cloak and fiery hair. From this height, she could look down onto the fog-drenched Great Forest, to the twinkling ocean beyond. She allowed herself a moment to savor the fresh air. So peaceful, yet she had no time to linger.

She couldn't remember the last time she'd stopped to *savor* anything, and after a full year of searching for Janid she wouldn't stop now.

She squeezed through the cave's cracked entrance, trying not to cut herself on the sharp rocks. She slid along the long, cramped tunnel that was no wider than her arms outstretched. It eventually widened into a large chamber filled with darkness. Brigid suppressed her fear. She couldn't stop now, even if this place made her feel like she'd just been swallowed into a stomach of shadows.

She lit a makeshift torch she'd made from wood found outside the cave and found the Saint in a small alcove. At first, she thought the woman was dead, but her ancient head creaked upward, turning toward Brigid's light.

The Saint's lips moved slowly, puffing dust from her lungs. "Again, you come."

Brigid's skin pebbled. Somehow, she'd known the Saint would say that.

"I've come for my son," she said, "Janid. I—I think he may've been taken from me."

"You have no son, Prisoner."

A low rumble filled the cave. Streams of dirt and stone trickled from the shadows above. Brigid ignored them.

"Of course I have a son."

"Return to me when you can see," said the Saint.

The shaking became more insistent. A large stone crashed between them, crushing a cornucopia of offerings that had been left. The Saint tilted her head back. Her eyes opened, revealing cankered orbs that seemed to stare through the ceiling. The surreal movement chilled Brigid's skin.

"It awakens," hissed the Saint. "Leave!"

"Tell me, I beg you," Brigid said, raising her voice against the growing noise. "Tell me how I can learn of the Myst and find the path to my son!"

"Leave your bow, cloak, and branch," commanded the Saint. "Revoke your name and quest. Lay claim to nothing, and let nothing claim you."

"My bow?" Brigid asked, thinking of her small, handcrafted weapon she'd left outside the cave. She had no idea what cloak or branch the Saint referred to.

"Release your attachment. Embrace only the Myst, and all will be found. Now go!"

Brigid stepped away from that gaze and ran, fleeing the tremors. Unbidden tears fell from her cheeks. Up ahead, the cracked entrance seemed farther away than she remembered.

The cave collapsed behind her, rolling dust and thunder across her path. The entrance ahead loomed like the mouth of a stone tython clenching its jaw.

As she ran, Brigid thought of Janid. She saw his gentle eyes smiling up at her as she climbed over fallen stone. But her distracted mind caused her foot to slip, and she fell. The entrance collapsed, the world rushed, and everything turned to darkness.

The needle lifted, looped, and wove again.

After a thousand thousand agonizing steps up the mountain, Brigid came at last to the cave at the summit where the reclusive Saint dwelt.

Brigid's well-worn boots crunched atop sandy stone just outside the entrance. A heavy wind raced across the summit, catching her cloak and fiery hair.

Not sparing even a moment to look at the twinkling ocean to the west, she squeezed through the cracked entrance, trying not to cut herself on the sharp rocks. She slid along the long, cramped tunnel that was no wider than her arms outstretched. It eventually widened into a large chamber filled with darkness. Brigid suppressed her fear. She couldn't stop now, even if this place made her feel like she'd just been swallowed into a stomach of shadows.

"Again, you come," said the decaying Saint. Her lips moved slowly, puffing dust from her lungs.

Brigid's skin pebbled. "I've come for my son," she said, "Janid. He—"

She stopped. He what? For a moment Brigid had almost said, *He was taken by the fay.* Only, she had no idea what the fay were.

"Do you see yet?" the Saint said. "You do not yet know what you truly seek."

A low rumble filled the cave. Streams of dirt and stone trickled from the shadows above. Brigid ignored them.

"Of course I do," Brigid said. "And I need your help."

"Then leave your bow, cloak, and branch," commanded the Saint. "Revoke your name and quest. Lay claim to nothing, and let nothing claim you."

"I-I don't know what those things are."

The shaking became more insistent. A large stone crashed between them, crushing a cornucopia of offerings that had been left.

"It awakens," hissed the Saint. "Leave!"

Brigid's head spun. This encounter was all happening so fast. "What awakens?"

"Your Prison."

"My what?"

"Release your attachment. Embrace only the Myst, and all will be found. Now go!"

Brigid stepped away from that gaze and ran, fleeing the tremors. Up ahead, the cracked entrance seemed farther away than she remembered.

The cave collapsed behind her, rolling dust and thunder across her path.

As she ran, Brigid wondered what the Saint said about a Prison. Was this cave to be her prison?

The entrance collapsed, the world rushed, and everything turned to darkness.

The needle lifted, looped, and wove again.

After a thousand thousand agonizing steps up the mountain, Brigid came at last to the cave at the summit where the reclusive Saint dwelt.

"Again, you come," said the decaying Saint, lips puffing dust from her lungs.

Brigid's skin pebbled. "I've come for—"

She stopped, lost for words.

"Do you see yet?" the Saint said.

A low rumble filled the cave. Streams of dirt and stone trickled from the shadows above. Brigid ignored them.

"I don't—" Brigid said. "What's wrong with me? I came here to ask about my son, but now . . ."

"You have left your bow, cloak, and branch," said the Saint. "Do you revoke your name and quest?"

The shaking became more insistent. A large stone crashed between them, crushing a cornucopia of offerings that had been left.

"My what? I don't understand."

"Then leave, Prisoner. It awakens."

"What do you mean? Tell me."

"Continue to leave your attachments behind. Soon you will be ready."

Brigid stepped away from that gaze and ran. The cave collapsed behind her, rolling dust and thunder across her path. Everything turned to darkness.

The needle lifted . . .

looped . . .

and paused as if to consider . . .

and then wove again.

One last time.

After a thousand thousand lifetimes, the humble woman came to the cave at the summit where the reclusive Saint dwelt.

"Welcome, Prisoner," said the decaying Saint, lips puffing dust from her lungs.

The Prisoner's skin pebbled. She knelt in front the ancient woman and bowed her forehead to the ground. "Beloved Saint," she said.

"Do you see yet?" the Saint said.

"No, but Mylezka the *Zurnta* said to come and to expect nothing."

A low rumble filled the cave. Streams of dirt and stone trickled from the shadows above. The Prisoner ignored them.

"You have left your bow, cloak, and branch," said the Saint. "Do you revoke your name and quest?"

The Prisoner swallowed. She missed Janid so much. It had been years since she'd seen him, but her heart told her that he was still alive.

"Yes. If that's what it takes. I'm just a farmer. And a mother."

The shaking became more insistent. A large stone crashed between them, crushing a cornucopia of offerings that had been left.

"It awakens," the Saint said.

"The mountain?" the Prisoner asked.

"Your Prison. The needle readies itself to weave again."

The Prisoner did not understand, but she pressed on.

"What must I do?"

"Remain here. For that has always been your path. The silver road always brings you here. To me."

"Who are you?" the Prisoner asked. "Will you tell me your name?"

"I am she who has sung to you for countless lifetimes. She who waited for you atop the mountain you've endlessly climbed. I am she who sits and waits and loves you."

"Sitting Mother," the Prisoner whispered.

The cave collapsed around them, rolling dust and thunder through the chamber. Everything turned to darkness.

When the rumbling stopped, a heavy silence blanketed the Prisoner. She coughed and rubbed dust out of her eyes. The cave-in had trapped them but preserved a space wide enough for them to sit facing each other.

An eerie silver-and-golden light bloomed to life around her, emanating from the woman sitting in the alcove across from her. The ancient Saint, little more than a skeletal figure dressed in ragged bits of cloth, had not moved. Her cankerous eyes studied the Prisoner. A third eye, edged like a silver tattoo, glowed upon the Saint's forehead.

"So this is the Prison?" the Prisoner said, looking at the collapsed stone. There was no way she could dig herself out, even in— She swallowed. Even in a hundred lifetimes.

"The Prison is your life," the Saint said.

The Prisoner coughed a laugh. "It's often felt like that," she said. It was strange to laugh, even in self-derision. There had not been much humor or joy in her life.

"You sense it now," the Saint said.

"I—" The Prisoner stopped. She had so many questions. So many thoughts.

"Ask," the Saint prompted with all the patience of a woman who'd lived in a cave for untold years.

The questions fought for priority in the Prisoner's mind. *Where is my son? How do I find him? Can I trust the lagharts? What is the Myst? How will it lead me to Janid? Who are you?*

"Who am I?" she asked at last, in a rush. She could not have said why she chose that, of all questions, as the one to ask first.

The Saint smiled, the slightest curve of her lips, and the room brightened further with her light. "You are the Prisoner of Time. The lost one, trapped, as Janid once was, as Brigid once was."

"But my name is—" The Prisoner stopped. "Then, who—?"

"Listen."

The Saint closed her two milky, human eyes while the third on her forehead remained open.

The Prisoner closed her own and shifted her awareness to her hearing. The collapsed mountain pressed complete silence down around her. The Saint's light warmed her, comforted her, and the Prisoner found herself more content in that silent basking than in speaking.

She didn't know how much time passed. Time no longer seemed like a tangible concept to her. It was as though she existed only in this stone enclosure. Soon she forgot about the walls, about the mountain, and why she'd come there to begin with.

At last, after another hour, month, year, or cycle of lifetimes, the Prisoner once known to themselves as Brigid opened their eyes. The mountain was long gone and all that existed was the Nameless Saint, sitting and radiating an aura of glorious light in an empty void of stars.

The Prisoner breathed in slow unison with the Saint. They knew, somehow, that should their breathing change, they would lose their harmony with the powerful being before them.

"Who am I?" the Prisoner asked again. They were not Brigid, although they had lived her life. Lived all of her experiences count-less times.

"Where am I?" the Prisoner wondered. They were not in the

mountain, although they had climbed it many times. Climbed many mountains across many lives.

I was Brigid, and I was somebody else, thought the Prisoner. *I was a mother. I was a brother. I was champion of the lagharts. I was a blacksmith. A woodsmith. A ranger.*

I was trapped.

In a tower.

The Tower of Eternal Starlight.

The Prisoner opened their eyes. Their real eyes.

They were inside an empty, circular stone chamber with a single window. Two long bladed sticks, each covered in blood, rested on the hard floor beside them.

The Prisoner sat up, and realized they'd been lying down. The Saint's warmth still glowed upon their skin. They could still feel her, but she was nowhere to be seen.

The Prisoner stood, and their legs wobbled.

Memories of countless lives, of light and darkness, of hope and despair, of quests and conquests, of love and sacrifice, flooded into them.

And foremost of all of them came one other, more immediate life. That of a blacksmith who'd left home and become a ranger. A ranger who'd lived in the mountains and then walked into the Tower of Eternal Starlight during Crow Tallin and—

The Prisoner turned and saw the decapitated body of a woman. A woman who once had flaming red hair.

The Prisoner looked at their own hands. A man's hands.

From beyond the lone window, a voice sang out. It was a soft chant, calling to him. Calling a name.

His name.

The Prisoner stepped to the window. A bright beam of light shone from the outside.

The voice called him again. It was not the voice of the ancient Saint, but that of a young woman.

He turned one last time to the room, feeling the Saint's presence still there.

"Thank you," he said to the Nameless Saint.

Closing his eyes, he took a deep breath, grabbed the sticks from the floor beside him, and let himself dissolve into the voice that was calling his name.

The tower vanished, and the Prisoner became free.

TWENTY-THREE

THE LAST AND FIRST MEMORY

Pomella awoke from one dream into another deeper dream. She drifted in darkness. Small glimpses of light blurred through cracks as if she were opening her eyes.

Only, her eyes weren't closed. They were . . .

She removed her hands from her eyes and the world focused around her. She was in a large garden, with tidy rosebushes taller than her. Full blooms of red and white and pink loomed over her like noble sentinels. By the Saints, the flowers were as large as her combined fists!

A woman's voice from somewhere else in the garden sang to her. *"One, two, three, you can't hide from me!"*

A giggle escaped Pomella's lips before she could help it. A giggle! Another one threatened to sneak out, but she clamped her hand firmly over her mouth to stifle it. An overwhelming sense of mischief washed over her. She had to hide!

She looked around the garden but didn't see anywhere to go. The paths were pretty narrow and the voice was getting closer.

"Pommmelllla," the woman sang.

There. She spied a little hollow under one of the rosebushes just a short distance away. She scampered that way but realized she was holding something big and heavy.

A stick.

A big stick with an ugly old lantern on top.

"Found you!"

Pomella screeched with delight and ran, finding the strength to drag the giant stick along with her out of pure adrenaline. She leaped for the hollow under the rosebush, but the big stick snagged on one of the oversized rose branches and its weight and the jarring motion dragged her down. As she fell, pain from a thorn lanced across her cheek.

She crashed into the ground and the big stick clunked her on the head. Unable to help herself, she let out a wail, and immediate tears spilled out.

"Ohhh, no, dearie," said the woman who had been chasing her. Her shadow loomed over Pomella. Still crying, Pomella looked up.

The concerned face that looked down at her immediately caused Pomella to cease her crying. A ripple of energy rolled across her body. Before her was a face she had nearly forgotten, remembered only in the most silent and peaceful of times in her life.

It was her grandmhathir, Lorraina, the woman who, along with her fathir, had raised her after Mhathir died.

Grandmhathir's features were dark, her skin deep brown, with short, tight, curly hair haloing her head. She was plump and stooped and smelled of dirt and sweat and marigolds and love. She wore a homespun work dress, similar to the one Pomella had worn in her previous memory.

"Are you OK? Let me look at that," Grandmhathir said.

The last of Pomella's mind fog cleared and she realized where and who she was. She peered at her tiny four-year-old hands, then to the normal-sized roses she'd mistaken for giants.

She marveled at Grandmhathir, whose face and eyes looked so much like her own, she realized, then charged forward into the older woman's arms, allowing herself this treasured reunion. In the waking world, she was probably at least two decades older than this woman, but it was her grandmhathir.

Grandmhathir thumbed the scratch on Pomella's cheek and kissed it. Her lips were wrinkled and sweet. "All better?" She spoke with a heavy Keffran accent. Pomella noticed traces of black ink near the base of Grandmhathir's neck, hinting at tattoos that she'd never seen, or at least never remembered, before. It made sense, however. Grandmhathir had been born a Keffran noble, so of course she would have the tattoos marking her house and individual accomplishments. Knowing what she did of the Keffran nobility and their famed dedication to family, Pomella found it even more remarkable that this woman had defied tradition and married a commoner.

Perhaps defying law and tradition ran in the family, Pomella mused.

Pomella nodded in response to the question, and indeed her cheek no longer stung.

"What do you have here?" Grandmhathir asked, looking at Pomella's staff and running a hand along its smooth length.

"It's my stick," Pomella said. Then, laughing at her own ridiculousness, amended, "My Mystic staff, I mean."

Grandmhathir replied with an exaggerated nod. "Very impressive. I always knew you'd become a Mystic. There's just so much life in you. Why don't we go into the house and you can tell me all about it."

"OK."

Grandmhathir stood and gently held the rose branches aside for Pomella, not minding the thorns.

Pomella had to use both hands to carry her staff, as it was over twice her height. Hector buzzed around the garden, but Pomella put him out of mind.

They emerged from the garden, which Pomella realized wasn't nearly as enormous as she'd thought it had been. Really, it was nothing more than a small patch of dirt quartered off from the side of the house. Scraps of wood and metal lay nearby, waiting for her fathir, the village cooper, to finish making them into barrels.

"Storm's comin'," Grandmhathir said, looking skyward.

Pomella nodded, likely appearing far more serene than her four-year-old physicality suggested. Midnight-black clouds outlined in silver quilted the sky, moving like fog rolling in from the ocean. The sun, which was black and glowing along its edges like an eclipse, descended toward the western sky. The wind carried a light gust of moisture hinting at another heavy Mothic rainfall.

If Grandmhathir noticed the black sky and clouds, she gave no indication.

The house was just as Pomella remembered, although smaller and more worn. A heavy pall rested over the place and Pomella could sense the Myst swirling there, waiting.

Grandmhathir held the door for her and helped her navigate her heavy staff into the common room, which made up most of the building.

"Where's Fathir?" Pomella asked.

"He took your wee tyke brother to see Goodness AnClure. That leaves us with some special time together."

They settled before the fire, which had a small iron pot hanging over it. "Supper's almost ready," Grandmhathir added, bustling around the room, leaving Pomella.

For a moment a hopeful thought stirred in Pomella's mind. Would her mhathir be here? She turned to ask Grandmhathir if she would, but she stopped short.

She could conjure no memory of her mhathir, not even her face. Like so many countless others, Ellis AnDone had died of the Coughing Plague that had swept across Moth when Pomella was very young. Pomella only knew her by reputation and would never know or remember her touch, her voice, or her mannerisms. She'd long ago made peace with this, but still, a sense of sad longing hummed around her now.

"Now," Grandmhathir said, returning to sit by the fire. She eased herself down, favoring her knee and hip, wincing an expression

Pomella recognized all too well. "Tell me about your Mystic staff and that little fella." She gestured to the nearby window where Hector had alighted onto the sill. "Seems like you have quite the story."

Pomella settled herself cross-legged opposite Grandmhathir while the older woman waited patiently. She laid her staff across her lap and accepted the plain wooden cup of tea offered to her. Together, the two women blew on their cups at the exact time in the exact same way.

"His name is Hector," Pomella said. "He's my fay bird. He has a sister, Ena, who isn't here right now. They've been my companions since I was a girl. Hector is strong and fearless. I've needed his strength on this journey. I'm so grateful for him and I think I would be lost if he wasn't here to illuminate my path."

"Is that so?" Grandmhathir said. "And the staff? Did you carve this?" She touched the serpent entwined around the top.

"No, Saint Brigid did," Pomella said. "She gifted me that while she was trapped in the Tower of Eternal Starlight. She did it as a means to gain my trust because she needed my help to escape."

"How exciting!" Grandmhathir said. "Did you help her?"

Pomella shrugged and took a sip of her tea. Grandmhathir had added honey. "Yes, but not in the way either of us expected. It was complicated."

"Well, you've certainly had some adventures!" Grandmhathir said. She leaned in with a sly expression. "Did you meet any luck'ns? Everyone here on Moth chatters about them."

Pomella glanced at Hector, then whispered loudly, "Yes, but don't mention them around Hector. He doesn't like them."

"Oh, I'd never dream of it," Grandmhathir said.

"Grandmhathir," Pomella said. "I have questions."

Grandmhathir sipped her tea and let out a small, resigned sigh. "I know, dearie. And I'm here for you. I know this must be hard."

Curiosity got the better of Pomella. "You do?"

"Of course I know. A grandmhathir always knows, and someday, if you have a special young granddaughter, one who lights up your world, then you'll do everything you can to be there for her."

Pomella's heart overflowed with affection. In that moment she rested at the fulcrum of time, both granddaughter and grandmhathir, alive and loving these two other women, four generations apart, but fully present at the same moment through her.

"Her name is Ulammia," Pomella said suddenly, not intending to bring this up. But perhaps it could be a small gift she could offer the other woman. "We call her Mia, and she's very special. She has the kindest heart, and the gentlest manner. And yes, she lights up my life. We live in hard times, but that's never held her back. I tell her all the time that her moment will come and she should be patient, because she could do anything. I worry about her, of course, and her stubbornness frustrates me at times, but mostly it's because I want to help her so badly. But I can't walk her life for her. All I can do is guide her."

It was then that Pomella saw the tears slipping down Grandmhathir's face.

"Oh, Pomella-my," she said, her accent thick as she used the Keffran form of endearment. "I will remember this always, even beyond our brief reunion now. Your mhathir would have . . . well, she would be proud beyond words. Like her, you are truly a *valiant* woman."

"Is Mhathir . . . is she . . . ?"

"She's always been with you, Pomella," Grandmhathir said. "I know you can't see her. But she lives on in the Myst, just like we've talked about. She guides you, even now, constantly calling to you, waiting with eternal patience for you to just realize you are utterly inseparable, coexisting together in one timeless, perfect moment."

Everything Grandmhathir said rang with truth, echoing lessons Pomella had heard her entire life from her great teachers,

Yarina, Lal, and the masters of the Deep who spoke to her silently in ways too hard to comprehend while awake.

"Thank you, Grandmhathir," Pomella said, pressing her palms together near her heart.

A moment stretched between them. Grandmhathir dabbed her eyes and her cheery tone returned. "So," she said. "I have an idea. How about, before our special time comes to an end, we sing a song."

Pomella bit her lip. It had been so long since she'd sung. The weight of her old insecurities suddenly held her down. But she was with her grandmhathir, sitting by the fire, like they'd always done.

Not waiting for a reply, Grandmhathir creaked to her feet and left the room, returning a moment later with a bundle in her arms. She plunked back down with a slight grunt and held a bulky object wrapped in a blanket out to Pomella.

"Here," she said. "You gave this away long ago, and it's been through many hands since, but it's always really been yours."

Pomella took the heavy bundle and unwrapped the blanket from it. Her eyes widened.

"*The Book of Songs*," she marveled. She opened the old tome, letting the dazzling pages of drawings and poems and handwritten notes brighten her face. It was a simple lesson book, intended for noble students learning of the Myst through rhyme and song. It had likely been made or bought for Grandmhathir when she'd been very young, around the time her family would've hired a willing Mystic to secretly tutor her in the ways of the Myst in order to give her an advantage in the apprentice Trials.

"How did you get this back?" Pomella said. "I last gave it to . . ." She bit her lip. ". . . To Sim."

"Oh yes, Sim," Grandmhathir said. "Did you know that he read the whole book? Even the noble runes. He sang some of these songs on lonely nights in the mountains of Qin. He thought of you. And eventually, the book led him to Sitting Mother."

"Sitting Mother?" Pomella said. "I heard that name recently."

"Yes," Grandmhathir said.

"Who is she?" Pomella asked.

"She is every mother. She is love and patience and guidance. She is inspiration."

"I have to meet her."

"Haven't you already?"

"Well, yes, but in a more practical sense, I need to speak to her like we are speaking now. I need her to tell me the name of the island."

"Oh, Pomella-my," Grandmhathir said. "She can tell you many things. But I'm not certain she can answer that for you."

"Why not?"

"She can guide you, but she can't speak it for you. It doesn't work that way."

The slightest flutter of annoyance worked its way through Pomella. "I'm quite exhausted by things that don't work as expected."

"Perhaps you should take some time by yourself, read your book, and let the answers come to you."

"What about singing?" Pomella said.

"That can wait. I can tell you need a break after all."

"Are you leaving again?" Pomella said.

Grandmhathir leaned in. "My love, I never left."

She kissed Pomella's forehead and the world flashed away.

She found herself now in a pool of light that existed in an otherwise-dark world. Unlike her previous memories, this one extended only thirty or forty steps in any direction. Fog drifted above her, moving with a steady rhythm from one edge of the diminutive world to another. She sat upon a fallen oak covered in moss, which in turn lay beside a wide flowing creek. Soft motes of light, silver and gold, drifted aimlessly in the air, so faint that as soon as Pomella tried to look at one directly it puffed out of existence and was replaced by another just out of sight.

Despite the lack of landmarks, Pomella recognized this location or, at least, the place it approximated. It was where she'd often gone in her youth, before leaving Oakspring to become a Mystic. This was the bank of the Creekwaters, the river that flowed through northern Moth and gave her old village its life.

Tears covered her face, and she noted a pang of sadness clutching her chest, but she didn't know why. Her staff leaned against her, and Hector buzzed above her, exploring the tiny world. On her lap, atop the plain, rough woolen dress, was *The Book of Songs*.

The book was so large, but like her experience in her grandmhathir's rose garden, she realized it was because she herself was so small. She was younger than even before, probably only four years old.

A sense of serenity permeated the memory-world, and despite the strange and fading sadness, Pomella felt very comfortable here. She allowed herself time to bask in the quiet, kicking her feet absent-mindedly as they dangled on the side of the fallen tree.

This, she decided, was her earliest memory. She could only vaguely recall this time, so many long years ago, when she'd run away from home, hiding from Fathir and Grandmhathir because she was sad that Mhathir had died.

It was the first of many visits to the edge of the Mystwood where locals claimed strange and wondrous and dangerous things could be seen. Her fathir would have been very angry if he'd known this was where she ran off to, even though it was just a short walk from their home.

A silver light swirled and coalesced on the water across from her, well out of reach, taking the shape of a curious-looking four-eared rabbit. He perked up, sniffing the air, and looked at Pomella.

As recognition dawned, Pomella smiled. "Hello, Goodman Buttersnatcher," she said to the fay rabbit. Her voice was that of a sweet, high-pitched young child, and it amused her to hear herself like that. "I suppose it's been well over seventy years since we last saw each other, but I hope you've been well."

Goodman Buttersnatcher decided he had other business, so he scampered away, leaping across the flowing river, following it into the soft edge of darkness where this world ended, leaving Pomella alone again.

Pomella sighed in contentment. This tiny world, just her and the Creekwaters, suited her just fine. She had the sense of being at the absolute bottom of a long, deep abyss, at the very needle-point tip. Above her were all the memory-worlds she'd previously visited, and countless others.

But this, her oldest memory, was the foundation upon which everything else she'd become was built. Because this was her memory of the first time she saw the fay, and sensed the Myst. This was when she discovered, at a very early age, that there was a special world beyond her home that called to her, like a song in her chest demanding to be sung.

This was when she realized who she was.

Hector flew to her and landed on the top of the rickety lantern.

"I don't think there will be any more worlds deeper than this," Pomella said to the hummingbird.

The little bird buzzed his wings and tilted his head at Pomella as if asking for clarification.

"If I can't find the name of the island here," Pomella said, "then I don't know where else to go."

She turned her attention to *The Book of Songs* sitting on her lap. The cover was as old as ever. Grandmhathir had suggested she take some time, read the book, and let the answers come.

How could it be that this simple tome, intended for novices, would hold the deepest secrets of the island of Moth?

She opened the cover and its pages illuminated her face. Hector buzzed to her side, hovering above her shoulder.

The book's pages appeared no differently than they ever had. The fanciful drawings depicted fay critters, diagrams of flowers, outlines for simple meditative practices, star charts, basic primers for identifying common medicinal herbs, and an assortment of other practical lessons suitable for a Mystic apprentice. Pomella recognized her grandmhathir's handwritten lyrics scrawled in the margins of many pages. She smiled, recognizing the words to songs like "A Sail to Pull the Moon" and "Into Mystic Skies." The latter made her smile as she recalled that it was Master Willwhite's name for these memory-worlds.

And yet, beyond all of that, there were no great revelations that showed her the name of the island. *The Book of Songs* was, in the end, just a book from her past.

Pomella eyed Hector. "So what do you think?"

The hummingbird kept hovering but gave no other reply. After a moment, Pomella sighed and returned to the book. She spent some time going through each page, humming the melodies to the songs written inside.

Finally, she closed the book and set it aside. She hopped off the fallen tree and walked to the edge of the Creekwaters. Her feet were bare, just as she'd always liked them as a child. She dipped her toes into the water and let its coolness course across her feet.

Hector flew around her, exploring the edges of the tiny bubble of her memory-world.

"I have nowhere else to look," Pomella said to the Creekwaters. "This is where I began. This is where I discovered you. Where I discovered the Myst, and myself. How do I learn the secret of your name?"

She closed her eyes and listened, willing herself to hear a reply, if there was one.

Then an idea occurred to her. In all her travels through these memories, she'd been distracted. There was always somebody special to her, somebody important, who had commanded her attention. She'd had to focus on them, even if it was ultimately to let them go. But not until now had she set those distractions aside and given her attention to the world itself. To the environment.

To the island.

Keeping her eyes closed, she lowered her little four-year-old body into a cross-legged sitting position.

"The High Mystic has moved on," she said. "You have changed. The world has changed. How can I become your steward? I'm listening."

She sat, and waited. The trickling sound of the Creekwaters washed over her. No other thoughts intruded. No worries of the past or anxieties of the future. Pomella channeled her lifetime of practice and focus to not just live in the present moment, but to *become* it.

And there, finally, like the whisper of a bubble rising to the water's surface, she heard a soft musical note. It repeated itself; then others emerged, creating a quiet harmony. The music expanded and became louder, then shifted to a chant.

Pomella opened her eyes as the unspeakable name of Moth sang around her. Her spine and the center of her forehead tingled with energy. Hector hovered in front of her, humming with excitement.

"We did it," she said.

The island's chant resonated in the air, filling the entirety of the world with the musical song of its Mystic name.

She stroked the hummingbird's head. But as she did so, his coloring shifted from silver and gold and green to reveal a rainbow of hues. Oranges and reds and a violet she hadn't seen from him before.

Pomella frowned. "Hector?"

The hummingbird zipped away a short distance. As he flew, he shifted form, expanding and morphing into a gargantuan, multi-hued winged creature that rapidly grew, expanding in size until he dwarfed her and nearly everything else in the small memory-world.

Motes of dusty light wafted off the creature. His colorfully vibrant plumage illuminated Pomella and the creek side.

Pomella's heart sank. "Hemosavana," she said. Hizrith's familiar. "How? Why?"

The massive fay creature cried out, and the sound drowned the music of the island. Hemosavana flapped his great wings, thundering the nearby oak and pine trees like a hurricane wind.

One by one, Pomella made the connections. There could only be one reason that Hizrith would've sent his familiar in disguise with her on her journey. He sought the Mystic name of Moth for himself.

Hemosavana screeched again. He raced skyward with a powerful stroke, then reversed and pulled the wings tight to his body and plunged toward the river.

Pomella reacted as quickly as her little body allowed her. Using every inch of her frame, she swung her Mystic staff toward the bird, and Unveiled the Myst. The Myst looped around the bird's torso just as he reached the Creekwaters. Pomella held tightly to her staff as she was dragged toward the shore.

She couldn't let him escape. If he did, he could switch places with his master, bringing him into her memory.

Where Hemosavana touched the water, a rippled reflection of a wooden building could be seen. Pain shot through Pomella's arm, reaching from her elbow to shoulder in the same location as her wound in the waking world. She cried out, unable to hold on to the staff.

Hemosavana soared fully into the Creekwaters, and the staff was yanked from Pomella's hand. The water settled and the fay bird was gone.

Rising from the same location was a hunched and scaled figure. He coalesced before her, taking shape.

"Master Hizrith," Pomella said in her young voice.

The old laghart hobbled forward, favoring the wound he had

tried to hide from Pomella at the beginning of her journey. It had become worse, or he hid it less now.

"How dare you?" she said, her young voice only partially undermining the seriousness of her accusation.

Hizrith stepped from the water's surface onto the damp forest bank. He peered around the small world, his tongue licking the air to taste it. The island's chant still sang in the air, quietly arising from everywhere at once.

"Ssso you found it," Hizrith said. "Impresssive." He approached her on the fallen log and studied her. "You are a child?"

It took all of Pomella's willpower to tamp down the overwhelming sense of betrayal. "I came to you for help," she said. "We were friends."

"I have profound ressspect for what you've become," Hizrith said. "But thisss isss about far more than you."

Pomella stood to her full height on top of the oak tree, bringing her eye to eye with the laghart master.

"I will not play games with you," she said. "You know very well who I am and what I've become. You will not have the Mystic name of Moth."

The chant filling the memory-world continued speaking the name of the island.

"I come not to ssstart a new lineage," Hizrith said, "but to renew an older one that wasss ssstolen from us."

"The lineage was not stolen!" Pomella snapped. "It was passed freely from a laghart *Zurnta* to the human called Brigid nearly a thousand—"

Pomella blinked and found she was on the ground, her face in the soil. Her vision swam. Hizrith had slapped her, knocking her off the fallen oak and sprawling her across the ground.

"Your blasphemousss tongue isss not worthy to ssspeak her name," Hizrith said. "You dared to asssault her during Crow Tallin."

Pomella stood, and by the time she faced him she had stilled her emotions. "We will not get anywhere with violence. This matter is already settled."

"It hasss not been sssettled for a thousssand yearsss!" Hizrith snarled. His posture changed to an aggressive, coiled stance with claws out. "While you have dallied in memoriesss, my armada hasss conquered northern Moth. The baronsss grovel at my feet, begging mercccy for themselvesss and their twisssted subjectsss.

"And your granddaughter, ssshe speaksss now through screamsss. You ssshould hear her. Ssshe had quite the voice after all."

Pomella knew he was baiting her. Fear rippled the outside of her awareness, threatening to destroy her Mystwalk. The island's chant wavered, but she held its focus by remaining as utterly calm as she could.

With barely a thought, she Unveiled the Myst, merging with the ground, growing with it as an extension of herself. Two saplings burst from the ground at her command, lifting and twisting and wrapping around Hizrith.

The laghart High Mystic tried to jump away as the saplings became full oak trees, but he was too slow. The trunks twisted around him, and their rapidly growing branches entwined his arms and legs and tail.

Pomella waved a hand and she rose into the air with the Myst, until she was once more eye to eye with Hizrith.

"The truth. My granddaughter," she demanded.

"Ssso powerful and clairvoyant," Hizrith said. "Yet you cannot sssee what isss right in front of you. I ssspeak the truth. Moth has fallen. The baronesss gifted your granddaughter and your Unclaimed friend to me." Hizrith's wide mouth spread into a smile. His slitted eyes gleamed. "Mia wearsss your old green cloak."

Pomella sensed only truth from him. A sense of dread crawled over her.

"We have returned home," Hizrith said. "If you dessstroy me

here, which I havvve no doubt you could, my armiesss will purge every human from the land. My apprenticccce will kill Mia and her friend."

"What do you want?" Pomella asked, knowing the answer.

Hizrth's wide mouth spread into a smile. His slitted eyes gleamed. "Nothing I don't already have."

He closed his eyes and the island's chanting grew louder. The oaks binding him in place wilted, allowing him to step gently onto the ground.

The Myst circled away from Pomella. She collapsed to the ground.

Hizrith's expression remained rapturous for a moment longer before he opened his eyes and peered curiously from Pomella to *The Book of Songs*. The book still rested on the log where Pomella had left it.

Hizrith gestured with his hand and the tome drifted to him. Light from its pages illuminated his face when he opened the cover.

Pomella pushed herself up from the ground. "Don't touch that."

He gestured again, and the same oak trees that had previously bound him snaked around Pomella, binding her wrists and arms, lifting her up so she dangled by her hands.

Hizrith leafed through the pages until he came to the center of the book. Then he lifted the tome above his head and closed his eyes. The island sang its name louder, and with it the light from *The Book of Songs* brightened. Hizrith held the book aloft until the name repeated itself. Then he lowered it, and turned the page.

"Thisss will sssuffice for keeping the name," Hizrith said. He peered at Pomella. "Your day hasss ended, your songsss ceased, and today, a new dawn rissses on a refffreshed world."

He turned to new pages in the book and tore them out. They drifted back and forth as they fell to the ground. Then he snatched Pomella's staff from her hand.

"Your deedsss, your choicesss, led here," Hizrith said.

A flurry of fear raced through Pomella as she realized what he was about to do.

Hizrith incinerated her Mystic staff and the rickety lantern atop it. The fire spread from his clawed hands, running the length of the staff until it had become ash by the time the flames reached the ends. He dusted his claws once on his robes.

"Your granddaughter will be ssspared," he said. "But you and the other Myssstics will be executed immediately."

He vanished, leaving Pomella alone and bound in her own memory, with no way to escape.

TWENTY-FOUR

THE HOUSE OF FALLEN EMBERS

Rion stood by the fireplace mantel and poked at the elongated animal spine leaning against it. "I think this is human," he said, but Mia ignored him.

Her attention remained fixed on the severe older woman sitting across from her, back straight, sipping tea. Mia shifted the porcelain cup resting in her hands. How long had it been since she'd held *porcelain* and sipped tea? Such had been her daily life back in Qin before Amma had come and taken her to Kelt Apar.

"So I believe that makes you my grandniece," Shevia concluded, speaking in Qina. "You definitely have something of my brother in your features, but very little of Pomella that I can see. Tell me, has she been a good teacher?"

Mia nodded and sipped her tea. She sat beside Nabiton, who had barely tasted his own. One of his hands rested comfortingly on her knee.

She didn't fear the other woman, but there was something certainly intimidating about her. Mia only knew a little of Shevia from what Amma had told her. That Shevia was her grandfather's younger sister, a prodigious Mystic, and had played a central role in the events of Crow Tallin. And that she'd vanished afterward, never to be seen again.

"And yet here she is," Rion said, now peering at a carved flute that rested on the mantel, "living in a fanciful cabin in the Myst-wood. I've seen nobles live in less luxury." He also spoke Qina.

"I see," Shevia said, and for a moment Mia thought she was responding curtly to Rion's comment before realizing it was in response to Mia's affirmative nod regarding Amma's ability to teach her well.

"Kilpa has some history with her," Shevia said. "He was a candidate with her during the apprentice Trials."

Mia looked at her in surprise.

"And he betrayed her," Shevia continued. "Your grandmother nearly died along with Yarina. Kelt Apar almost became the domain of Iron Mystics. All because my husband was fiercely loyal to the whims of his ambitious family."

She looked over to the room on the southern wall. Inside the room a sickbed had been arranged for Kilpa to rest on.

"Will he survive?" Nabiton asked after a shared silence.

Shevia returned her attention to Mia and Nabiton. Tattoos covered most of Shevia's exposed skin from her hands to her neck, leaving only her face unmarked. The artwork depicted a dizzying assortment of creatures dancing and fighting and celebrating beneath swirling storm clouds. A sinuous black serpent wound its way through the creatures, twisting and spreading up—

"Stop gawking, girl!" Shevia snapped. "Yes, they are tattoos, and yes, they cover the whole of my body."

Mia jumped in surprise, her eyes as wide as the saucer cup she held.

"But I suppose I do understand curiosity," Shevia muttered. "By our ancestors, I do." She sipped her tea, lavender eyes far away, before continuing. "Let's just say that I once had similar markings placed upon me. After Crow Tallin they were . . . removed, so I decided to replace them, but on my terms." Her tone darkened for the last phrase. "Kilpa placed quite a few of these new tattoos on me. He's a remarkable artist. Most of the paintings here in the House of Fallen Embers are his. He occasionally sells them to the wealthier patrons of Sentry and gives the money to people in the Murk."

The painting of Kelt Apar that Mia had seen while captive in Sentry came to mind. Judging by the other framed works of art decorating the walls, works depicting everyday homes and mills, mountains and the Mystwood, Mia had no doubt that it had been Kilpa's work. The blues and oranges of the sky were consistent, as were the soft brushes of gray and green that he used for the grass.

"That's what he does, my Kilpa," Shevia said in a soft voice. "He gives of himself. Always. When I first found him, over four and a half decades ago, he was enthralled to a powerful fay creature, a snake called Mantepis, and had been for some time. I confronted the beast for its cruelty and tamed it with ease. I left it, alive but broken of power, and brought Kilpa into my home.

"He had been known by a different name, but the High Mystic had stripped him of it, leaving him Unclaimed as a punishment for his treachery and crimes against the tower. His mind had been broken by the fay serpent, so he lay in that same room that he's in now. I nourished his body and tended his wounds. I read to him, poetry and song, and summoned the Myst to guide his true consciousness back to his body.

"He muttered in his sleep, 'Kilpa . . . Kilpa,' and only later did I realize he was trying to say 'Kill Pomella,' which was the command the snake had given him, should your grandmother ever return to its lair."

Rion sounded a long whistle. "Wow, that's some heavy stuff."

Mia found the story to be fascinating. It was nearly impossible for her to imagine the kindly old man she knew as either a traitor or somebody who would want to kill her grandmother. But Mia had learned, time after time, that many people held life-altering, and life-defining, secrets in their past.

"His recovery took a year," Shevia continued. "I remained

steadfast throughout that time, and eventually he awoke with a fresh identity. Many of his early memories were lost, but he understood that he had been granted a new chance at life. He'd forgotten about his former enslaver's kill command, but his new name stuck. He liked it, telling me that it had a softer energy than his old one. So I kept its origin to myself, and I believe he's unaware of it to this day."

Mia considered why Shevia was telling her all this. Weren't they strangers to her? What advantage did she earn by telling them these tales?

"I did not plan, nor expect, him to stay long after he recovered," Shevia said. "At first, he remained to regain his physical strength, and then he stayed, so he said, to help me manage the House and my gardens. He began painting, and even dabbled in wood carving. He charmed me, I admit, with his handsome face and broad shoulders. His gentle touch.

"We became lovers, and we gave vows to each other in this very clearing on the autumn equinox.

"I offered to train him in the ways of the Myst, to resume where he had left off, but he adamantly declined, never wanting to do anything with the Myst again. I understood, better than anyone, and never pushed the matter."

They sat in silence for a while until Nabiton spoke up. "What of you, Mistress? Have you lived here since—?"

"Yes," she said, and again her voice darkened. "During Crow Tallin I went places where no human should ever go. I held countless lives in my hand and could have snuffed them out with a thought. I could have done *anything*."

Again, that heavy silence, filled with thoughts unsaid. But then Shevia's expression lightened again.

"It was your grandmother, unsurprisingly, who showed me a different path. I've remained out of her life, and out of sight, for that has always suited me better. Strange to think that I'm so loquacious now. Perhaps your presence here brings out the part of me that is her. Like you, Ulammia, I generally prefer silence, and to listen."

Mia bit her lip. All of this was interesting, but it wasn't helping her to find Amma. She found Nabiton's hand and squeezed it.

"Mistress Shevia," Nabiton said. "We appreciate your kindness to us. But I know Mia wants to find her grandmother. If it's all right with you, we'll stay the night and be on our way in the morning."

"You most certainly will not," Shevia said. "Kilpa nearly died trying to get you here in one piece. I'll not waste his efforts by letting you career back into the Mystwood where a laghart patrol will pick you up. Do you have any idea how well they can track by scent?"

"I'd like to see them track me," Rion boasted. He was cleaning his fingernails with a small knife he'd produced from somewhere.

"Mistress Pomella is likely in great danger," Nabiton said.

"Yes, and what will you do about it?" Shevia said. "Saunter into her prison—wherever that might be—and break her out? Then what? Hide her? Where?"

"She has a point," Rion muttered.

Mia squeezed Nabiton's hand tighter.

"With all respect, Mistress, you can't keep us here. We'll—"

"Of course I can keep you here," Shevia said. A note of laughter filled her voice.

Slowly, Mia stood up. Nabiton reluctantly released her hand. Rion quirked an eyebrow at her. She fixed Shevia with a calm expression.

Shevia pursed her lips and also stood. They faced each other across the table. As much as Mia wanted to rush out and find Amma, she knew Shevia was right. They needed a plan. They needed to confirm Amma's location, and they needed help. More than that, they needed to rest. Fatigue soaked every muscle and bone in her body. She'd been traveling for long days and was physically abused along the way.

Meeting Shevia's eyes, she nodded.

Shevia smiled. "Good. That's settled. There's heated water for you to draw yourselves a bath. I'll have dinner ready after. When Kilpa awakes and is well enough, we'll discuss a plan."

Three days passed in the House of Fallen Embers, a name that Mia found intriguing.

She and Nabiton lay in the bed of their shared room together upstairs. For as reclusive as Shevia seemed to be, there were a surprising number of guest quarters in her home. Their space only stretched wide enough to fit the narrow bed and a dresser, both of which had been carved from pine and still smelled fresh. Moonlight filtered in from a shuttered window and played across Nabiton's bare chest. His body warmed her.

She traced her finger up to his neck and then to his cheek. His bandages sat on a nearby table, exposing the scarring around his once-functioning eyes. On the first night at the House, she had overheard Nabiton ask Shevia whether the older woman could repair his ruined eyesight.

"Perhaps I could have, long ago," the Mystwood Hetch had replied, "but no longer."

The morning after that, Nabiton had gone into the forest and returned with a stout oak limb, which he trimmed and sanded with woodworking tools. It resembled a Mystic staff, though he used it as an aid for navigating while walking.

Mia watched him now, lying next to her. So much had happened over the past several weeks. She loved what had blossomed between them, but there was so much uncertainty about what had to happen next.

"Will you return to Qin with me?" said Nabiton, speaking in Qina.

Mia's finger tracing along his skin paused.

"I love you," he continued. "I would be good to you."

He put so much into those final words. Sweet Nabiton. But he just didn't understand yet.

"I know you want to save your grandmother," he said, "but can you understand how that is an impossible task?"

She heard the sincerity in his voice and Mia found she couldn't look at him.

Nabiton grunted and thumped his head back on the pillow. Mia propped her head with her elbow and touched her other fingertips to his chest. The thick blankets had at first been a welcome relief from the cold night, but after a considerable time with Nabiton beneath them the blankets had become stifling.

They shared each night together, making them a pleasant distraction to the worry and stress. But as nice as the respite had been, she wasn't ready to leave Moth. Perhaps, when they had somehow rescued Amma, or learned of her fate, she could consider going home again.

Mia stretched her face close to Nabiton's and kissed him. Then she nodded *yes*, letting him feel the subtle movement against his lips. The choice wasn't what she had expected, but the world was changing, just like Hizrith's apprentice had said. Kelt Apar was lost, and perhaps all of Moth. They'd never be safe here again, not with her identity and connection to her grandmother known. In Qin, her family—and Nabiton's— would have the resources to keep them safe.

Returning to Qin carried its own complications, starting with her mother, who would be disappointed in her, as always, at anything she did, whether it was decided she would to stay on Moth or return home.

She pitied Harmona. Caught between two generations of Mystics, driving both away.

No, if she returned home to Qin, Mia would have to do it on her own terms. She could face her mother, but she would not be ruled by her decree or manipulations. Perhaps she could build a life with Nabiton, as he suggested. But regardless of how it played out, Mia knew only one other certainty: that her true fate had yet to be revealed. She remained a seed, and she knew not what kind of tree she would grow into, or what soil would nourish her best.

A knock sounded at their door and it pushed open revealing Shevia. Mia pulled the thick blanket higher up herself and Nabiton, but Shevia showed no concern for their nakedness.

"Get dressed. Something has changed."

They joined her in Kilpa's room, which had similar decor to Mia's. Mia and Nabiton sat on chairs while Shevia stood near Kilpa's bedside. Rion leaned against the threshold of the doorway, listening with his arms crossed.

Kilpa had woken a day after arriving and Shevia had hardly left his side since. He now sat upright but looked more tired and frail than ever. Bandages peeked out from under the shirt he wore.

"The island is changing," Shevia said. "This House is endangered." She spoke in Continental now, probably for Kilpa's benefit. A Qina accent tinged her words, but otherwise her fluency was superb.

Nabiton stiffened beside Mia. "Threatened by what?"

"By the new High Mystic of Moth," Shevia said.

Mia's heart hammered, quickening her pulse. The room suddenly seemed more confined. It was difficult to draw breath. She mouthed the word *Amma*, but no sound came out. Rion's face blanched.

"I don't understand," Nabiton said. "Who is the new High Mystic? Shouldn't it be Vivianna? Or Pomella?"

"It is neither of those women. The land is hostile to us now. The wind carries warning to me. The flowers of my garden whisper of danger. A sinister power has arisen. Kilpa told me of the laghart Mystic Hizrith. It could be him."

"Hizrith," Rion said. "By our ancestors, I really don't like that guy."

Mia's heart raced. How could the laghart master have achieved what her grandmother sought? What did it mean for Amma? For herself and for the others in the House?

Shevia placed a hand on Mia's back. "I don't believe your grandmother is gone. She's a very powerful Mystic and I have reason to believe that I would know the moment she died. And so would you. So take that as comfort."

Mia's lungs found air once more, and her hand found Nabiton's.

"Soon, the Guardian may begin his search for us," Shevia said.

"The Guardian?" Nabiton asked. "Do you mean the Green Man?"

"Yes, Oxillian," Kilpa replied.

Shevia spoke with a faraway expression on her face. "If commanded, he will send his consciousness through the soil, seeking our location. Every stone upon Moth, every branch, every flower petal, are his eyes and ears. I concealed this dwelling and the wildflower garden long ago. It is how we've remained hidden all these years. But against the Guardian's assault, the protection will not hold indefinitely."

"And if he finds us?" Nabiton asked.

"The Green Man has always served the High Mystic faithfully," Shevia said. "We cannot expect his mercy."

Nabiton squeezed Mia's hand. "Then what can we do?"

"You must leave the island," Shevia said. "I can provide you with some measure of protection while you travel to a port city, but you must hurry, and I do not know if there are ships sailing for the Continent. If not, you will be stranded. And when my protections inevitably dissolve, it will only be a matter of time before the ceon'hur, the Mothic Guardian, finds you."

"It sounds as though that's our only choice," said Nabiton.

"Is there nothing we can do for Pomella?" Kilpa said, addressing his wife.

"She is almost certainly a prisoner of Norana's, although I have been unable to divine her exact location," Shevia said. "Once I see these two off safely, I will do all that I can to protect her. But the House will fall quickly. And Pomella, too, is undefended against the Guardian's gaze. If he has not already taken her, the High Mystic will have her imminently."

Anger and fear warred within Mia. She checked her breathing, doing everything she could to remain focused, just as Amma had taught. These challenging emotional times were what she had trained for.

"How long do we have?" Nabiton asked.

Candlelight flickered across Shevia's shadowed face. "Rest tonight if you can," she said. "You leave at dawn."

Mia lay awake beside Nabiton, who had somehow managed to find sleep. It was the deep part of the night, when even shadows slept.

She tried to imagine a world where Ox, the gentle giant and her friend, would turn against her. Turn against her grandmother, who had been a young woman when she walked into Kelt Apar, probably as wide-eyed and amazed as she herself had been.

That Hizrith could corrupt Oxillian for his hideous purpose to find and destroy Pomella was practically unthinkable. How, Mia wondered, did that make sense for a Mystic, especially a High Mystic? Was it not their mastery of the Myst, which was a supremely aware and ultimately loving force of the universe, that elevated them? How could the Myst allow this to happen? Surely the Myst would not want to see people murdered and enslaved by its greatest conduits? Why would it allow pain and suffering? She was not a High Mystic, only an apprentice, but for the first time she considered that perhaps the Myst was not as perfect as she had been taught.

She knew she had to sleep. Before they'd gone to bed, Shevia and Nabiton had agreed that Higren and Gonlen's suggestion to go to Enttlelund had been wise. Not only was it the closest port town, but also it had the least chance of being controlled by either the lagharts or Norana. Baroness AnBroke was the most sympathetic of the ruling nobles toward Mystics, so perhaps that could work in their favor in some small way.

Mia conducted simple mind exercises to slow her galloping mind, trying to sleep. She lapped at the shores of unconsciousness like a low tide, drifting gradually toward sleep.

The woman with red hair she'd seen during Hizrith's ritual, Seer Brigid, the Saint, was there again before her. Her face shifted and streaked like a smeared painting before snapping back into focus. This time she appeared as a chiseled man with blue eyes.

The two figures, woman and man as one, reached toward Mia, offering her their bow. They spoke words to her in languages she could neither hear nor understand.

The meaning was clear, though. It was a plea for help.

A bitter chill pebbled the back of Mia's neck as she walked barefoot into the field of wildflowers. A thin fog lingered around the entire House.

It was still late at night, hours before sunrise. Nabiton had suggested they disguise themselves when they left in the morning, so Mia had cut her hair short, leaving her curls to only reach her ears.

Smoke from the House's chimney filled her nostrils, the last remnants of their evening fire. She wore an elegant, Qina-style silken robe of soft yellow and green pastels that Shevia had given her. After three years only wearing woolen black robes, the silk against her skin was a welcome change. She would travel with plain homespun wool in the morning, but for tonight she would enjoy the more elegant attire.

In sharp contrast, Amma's old green cloak lay heavy on her shoulders but offered her additional warmth.

She carried the laghart bow gripped tightly in her hand. Seer Brigid's bow.

Sleep was beyond her for tonight. Not while Amma and the other Mystics were in danger. How could she sleep when a tyrant High Mystic reigned on Moth?

Mia looked northwest in the direction of Sentry. Perhaps it was her imagination, but she imagined shadows moving—searching—within the trees beyond the wildflowers.

"You could end this another way, you know," Rion said. His breath puffed in front of him as he spoke. He wore warm furs in the traditional Qina style. He kept his hands hidden deep in warm pockets.

"What do you mean?" she said.

"You could take the bow and cloak to Hizrith. Plead for Amma's life."

Mia shook her head. "Hizrith has every advantage. If I surrender these so-called Relics, he'll just kill me anyway. If I don't, Oxillian will eventually catch me."

Rion nodded to the object she carried. "That bow," he said. "Legends say it's a power weapon. Perhaps you could return to Sentry and confront Hizrith."

"And do you know how to unlock its powers?" Mia snapped. "Do I look like a warrior?"

Rion lifted his hands, palms out. "It was just a suggestion," he said. He eyed her suspiciously. "Why do I get the sense you plan to do something unexpected and rash?"

Mia shrugged. "Well," she said, "I *am* Pomella's granddaughter."

A chuckle sounded behind her. "Yes, yes, you are."

Mia whirled around and found Kilpa limping toward her. He was dressed in a red night robe, embroidered with black. He leaned heavily on a cane, and clutched his chest where he'd been wounded.

Mia's mouth worked soundlessly. Heat rose to her face. She'd never had anybody witness her talking to Rion. At least, not that she knew of.

"I'm sorry if I surprised you, and more so if I heard something you prefer to keep to yourself. But I suspected you wouldn't be able to sleep. It's been a lifetime since I dabbled in the Myst, but I know what it's like to be a young person with much on their mind."

Mia looked at the bow in her hand, unable to meet Kilpa's face.

"I loved your grandmother in a special way," he said. "It was complicated by a false sense of duty and other terrible things, but there was no doubt she was special. And with all respect, I see some of that same spark in you. Her light shines through you now."

Mia flicked her gaze up to the old man, but she immediately looked back down.

"As you were," he said, motioning with his hand. "I will not interfere."

Mia took a breath, then called to the Myst. It arose from all around her, from Kilpa, and from herself. It Unveiled itself more easily now than it ever had for her before. The bow steadied the Unveiling, acting as a makeshift Mystic staff, and briefly Mia wondered whether Brigid had ever considered using it for that purpose.

Rion watched her from nearby, and Mia realized that he was another steadying presence, like a staff for her, but even more effective. When he was present, the Myst came to her. It was as though—

She blinked and looked again, hard, at her brother, seeing him in a new light.

It was as though the Myst flowed through him. She summoned it, raised it, Unveiled it, but always it channeled through him first. Had there ever been a time she'd Unveiled the Myst with him *not* present?

"Why are you looking at me that way?" he said.

Mia smiled some more, then opened her arms wide, tilted her head back, and moved through the wildflowers, tracing a wide circle, the same that Hizrith had drawn in his attempt to summon Brigid. She began with the outer edge, and as she went, the shape and detail emerged in her mind.

"By our ancestors, you're hopeless," Rion muttered, then began to follow her, turning as she did, matching her step for step.

Glowing points of light floated in the air like lantern bugs. Fay bugs and other translucent floating creatures joined in, brightening the field.

Kilpa watched quietly, leaning on his cane, unfazed by the ritualistic wave of energies being generated. They coursed through Mia now just as they had when Hizrith had forced her into the circle.

The memory of the woman she'd seen, Seer Brigid, flashed in her mind. Also that of the man who flickered across her face.

A new face appeared, too, but this one was here, present physically.

Shevia.

Mia stopped. The old woman stood beside Kilpa, who was muttering an explanation to her. Shevia wore the same red-and-black night robes as her husband. Tattoos peeked out from gaps in both of their robes.

Dejected, Mia lowered her arms. But Shevia flicked her hand, indicating that she should continue. "I think I see what you are creating. There are three focus points. You have Relics to represent two of them. You will need a third."

Shevia approached Mia, who now noticed that the older woman held a Mystic staff made of bone. It was the long spine that Rion suspected had been human.

"Brigid spent her years searching for her son," Shevia said. "He . . . well, he found me much later in his life, but it didn't work out too well for him." She offered the bone staff to Mia.

Revulsion and amazement spun through Mia. She had so many questions.

"See! I told you it was a human spine!" Rion shouted. "Also, that's completely repulsive."

Mia took the bone staff in hand, and immediately the conjured points of light around her flared for an instant to noonday intensity. The Myst surged in tidal forces around her.

She nodded to Shevia in thanks, and resumed her circular path.

Energy from the bow, staff, and cloak charged through Mia. Rion mirrored her movement. Phantom shadow versions of the Relics flowed around him as though he held the sticks and wore the cloak.

Music rose from the wildflowers as though they chanted in harmony with what Mia had Unveiled.

An indistinct vertical line formed in the air directly above the center of the circle. As Mia moved toward it, she reached with the Myst and pulled at the line, trying to open it. The line *peeled* away, revealing a window, no taller than her torso and no wider than her forearm.

Through the window she saw a room made of stone. Upon the floor lay a body and what appeared to be some discarded weapons. Another figure stood in the middle of the room, peering curiously back at her.

The man with blue eyes.

Mia returned her attention to the body behind him. She stifled a gasp and the window flickered, its energies disturbed by her shock. The figure, a woman, had been decapitated. A woman with red hair. Her fiery locks had been cut from the force of the severing strike. Strands of sliced hair lay beside her remains.

Mia had done this to bring Brigid back into the world. To make a bond with her and to convince her to intercede with the lagharts.

But she saw the truth. The Saint was dead. And her murderer was in her place. The scent of sandalwood and holly wafted from the room, filling Mia's nostrils and the fibers of her robes.

The ritual energies wavered, flickered, and vanished.

Shevia watched the girl undergo the summoning ritual and admitted she'd underestimated her potential. Pomella had certainly always had a talent for Unveiling the Myst, and that seemed to have passed to Mia.

A part of Shevia itched to merge into it herself, to get lost in the dance like she once had. The power was still there. It always had been, despite what she'd told Nabiton. The truth, one that she hardly dared admit to herself, was that she hadn't lost a drop of it since Crow Tallin. Over fifty years had passed since then, and not a single day went by where she wasn't tempted to unleash all the might she'd gathered in her youth. But she knew that once she did, once she let go, she wouldn't be able to stop. During Crow Tallin, she'd let herself become possessed, become a *wivan* to Brigid, who was also Lagnaraste, and had nearly destroyed all of Kelt Apar.

That sort of power was better left buried and forgotten. Spending a life helping others, healing illness, purging aggressive fay, it would have led to a place she wouldn't have had the strength to come back from.

Instead, this simple life she'd *chosen* with Kilpa had been happier than she had ever dreamed of as a child.

She'd become free, and it had been Pomella who showed her that path to freedom. Pomella who had given her a new name, Lorraina, that Shevia kept secret in her heart.

And now here danced Pomella's granddaughter—also the granddaughter of Shevia's beloved brother Tibron—dealing with forces beyond what she was capable of, not realizing the price that needed to be paid.

The vertical window in the air above the ritual circle unfolded, revealing a room and a man she hadn't seen in over fifty years. His face and his memory returned to her across time and distance.

Sim.

All of their time spent together rushed back to Shevia. There he was, staring through the window at Mia.

"By the ancestors," she whispered.

"You see it, too?" Kilpa wheezed. "It's not Brigid."

"No, it's not," Shevia said. Her skin crawled as a thought occurred to her. If it wasn't Brigid, then the Relic-totems would be wrong. Mia was trying to summon a dead woman.

Beyond the window, Sim called out, but no sound breached the barrier between them. The window wavered, flickered, and vanished.

The lights that Mia had Unveiled faded away.

"No," Kilpa said.

A heavy silence filled the field. Mia looked around, shocked and confused, then fell to her knees in defeat.

The grand energies Unveiled by Mia were still present, but they were draining away like water from a barrel.

Shevia approached the girl, followed closely behind by Kilpa. She'd never had children of her own, and comforting people had never been her strongest ability. "Stand up, girl," she said, silently admitting to herself that those skills were completely nonexistent.

The girl used both the bow and Bhairatonix's old spine to stand. Now she needed to figure out what to do next and then—

The scent of sandalwood and holly rose from Mia's robes and wafted over Shevia. In a span of a single heartbeat, memory and power blazed through Shevia.

That scent, so deeply ingrained in her, thundered across her mind and heart. She was twelve years old again, in the snowy Thornwood Shrine, speaking visions for nobles. Predicting the rises and falls of dynasties. Her *friend* Lagnaraste, whom she'd thought of as Sitting Mother, whispered words of power and prophecy, imbuing Shevia with a terrible fate.

Then she was nineteen again, healing a sick man with a deadly plague in a cobbled town square in Yin-Aab.

Then she was with him again later, cutting his hair.

Traveling with him across the Ironlow Mountains.

Watching him climb into the central tower alone during Crow Tallin.

Sim. The Woodsmith. The man for whom her visions had once seen no future. The man beyond the window.

"Unveil the circle again!" she snarled to Mia, and thrust a hand toward her home.

"Do it!" she screamed in Qina when the younger woman hesitated.

The girl took a hesitant step but soon became lost in the flows again, repeating the dance.

The tidal forces surged, and the lights blazed to life once more.

Shevia clenched her teeth and willed the Myst to summon the object she sought. An invisible weight filled her hand.

The object she sought flew to her, rushing above the grass and flowers. It was a wooden flute, carved from an elderberry bush. As it arrived, her old hands remembered the feel again and she recalled how she'd bitterly accepted the gift Sim had given her while they traveled to Kelt Apar together during the days of Crow Tallin. She hadn't even bothered to say thank you at the time.

"Take this," Shevia said, still speaking Qina.

She snatched the bone staff from Mia and thrust the flute into the girl's hand. It wasn't a centuries-old treasure like the bow, but it had been carved by Sim's hand.

A bow that had belonged to Brigid. A flute carved by Sim. A green cloak shared in a unique way between them.

Mia spun in her ritual circle, and the energies she Unveiled surged again. Soon the window reappeared, opening to the windowed room.

This time the Relics sang in harmony with the Unveiling. Shevia watched every detail of Mia's movement, and found herself impressed by how natural the young woman was. The Myst followed her movements, but it also followed another point in the circle, as though a second person danced with her.

An arm reached through the window.

"Shevia-my," Kilpa said beside her.

He spoke the familiar term of endearment with a gentle softness and Shevia knew exactly what it meant. For more than forty years they'd lived and loved together. In the whole of her strange life, he'd been the kindest part of it. Now her heart sank as she understood by his tone alone what he intended.

"No," she whispered back.

"What did you think would happen if we let her finish the ritual?" he asked. "We can't let her be lost."

"I can't lose you," Shevia said.

"You've had me for a lifetime. You've taught me our essential nature, and how it relies upon *freedom*. Freedom to choose. Mia doesn't know the cost of her choice. But I do. And I choose to make it in her place. It's one way I can finally repay Pomella for what I did all those years ago."

"No, Kilpa, I—"

"I'm dying, Shevia. You know this. Let me go on my terms."

His hand found her cheek and he kissed her. In that moment they were young again, alone and in love, free to do as they pleased.

In that moment she relived their lives, the countless winters beside the fire, watching the endless Mothic rain. In that moment the sweet summer days of their youth blended as she'd learned to finally love.

And in that moment, Shevia knew she'd forever look back at it, and wish it could be longer.

His lips parted from hers and he whispered, "Until the next life," and he was gone, hobbling as best he could across the circle toward the window.

Shevia watched him go, holding the bone staff in one hand and her husband's walking stick in the other.

Mia reached across time and grasped the hand reaching for her. The blue-eyed man's palm found her forearm and she noted its coarseness. Its strength.

But as they pulled each other, Mia's consciousness slipped away from her body. Darkness encroached all around. What was happening?

"Mia?" Rion called from nearby within the circle. "Mia, let go. *Mia!*"

She cried out, but the darkness grew. Fatigue washed over her, making her eyes heavy. The man's presence surrounded her, but something was wrong. He was—

She lurched back suddenly and landed hard on her back among the wildflowers. When she cleared her head, her awareness slammed back into place. She sat up in time to see Kilpa standing in front of the window, gripping forearms with the man. The stranger's torso emerged through the window and with a final surge he leaped forward, falling on top of Kilpa.

The energy of the ritual exploded out in a shock wave of wind and warmth, and when it settled all that remained were the faint lingering scents of sandalwood and holly.

Mia scrambled to her feet, steadying herself with the bow still gripped in her fist. Shevia ran to the collapsed figures.

In the distance, Nabiton stood on the threshold of the House and called, "Mia?"

She ignored him and watched Shevia help a man sit up. Kilpa was gone, and in his place was a tall, young man, perhaps a handful of years older than Mia. He had scraggly blond hair and a couple days' worth of beard growth. He wore a rough, homespun outfit suited for travel. Even more strange, two onkai blades lay on the ground beside him. The walking-stick weapons were common in the highlands of Qin, but Mia had never seen them outside her homeland.

The man stood, wobbling on his feet, and looked from Shevia to Mia.

"By the Saints," he breathed, looking at his hands, turning them over back and forth.

"No," Shevia said. There was little to hide the amazement in her voice. "By this girl. A Mystic apprentice. Though I doubt any would argue she hasn't transcended that title."

"Who are you?" the man asked, looking at both women.

Slowly, Shevia touched his cheek and turned his attention to face her. She held his gaze until recognition dawned.

"Lavender eyes," the man said. "Shevia—"

His searching expression jumped to Mia. "No, you can't be—where . . . ?"

He swallowed once.

"Where's Pomella?"

TWENTY-FIVE

THE LAST RANGER

The next morning, lost in a maze of memories, Sim roamed the Mystwood, trying to find familiarity in this time and place, as well as in his body. The early sunlight slanted through branches of aspen and pine, illuminating moss-covered trees and hidden springs that bubbled with their steady trickle. Fay butterflies fluttered through the air, silver-and-golden smoke dusting off their wings, and he wondered about this world he'd returned to.

He hadn't been able to sleep, so he left Shevia's House before dawn and before anybody noticed his leaving. He needed to be alone. An odd idea, he supposed, considering that he'd apparently been trapped alone in the Tower of Eternal Starlight for decades.

He let his feet carry him where they willed, having no specific destination in mind. Except for the omnipresent fay, the Great Forest—no, *the Mystwood*—was the same as it had been across all of his lifetimes.

Sim frowned. *Brigid's* lifetimes. He looked at his hands, studying their detail, in order to remind himself that he wasn't that other person. Not any longer, anyway. His forearm lacked the scarred brand Brigid had carried. He rubbed his cheek, feeling the scruff that grew there. He was Sim. Simkon AnClure from Oakspring. Second son of Arabel and Lathwin, brother of Dane and Bethilla.

Arabel.

Had that been his mother's name? No, that had been Brigid's mother. Cana. Cana AnClure had been his mother. Was she alive now? From what Shevia had told him, fifty-four years had passed since his entrapment. Fifty-four years in the blink of an eye. And in that blink, he'd lived lifetime after lifetime, always seeking, always striving, only to find disappointment time and again.

In every life he'd experienced, his own, and the multitude of Brigid's, he always lost those he loved. They died or left, sometimes by his actions. But with every loss he remained. Across the years and the long journeys, from the highlands of Qin to the forests of Moth, he went on, as steady as the tides, while everybody he loved washed away. He had only ever wanted to help, and to protect, and found punishment for it.

With a roar that rose from deep within him, he hurled one of his onkai at a tree. It spun end over end before crashing against an aspen. Orange and yellow leaves flamed downward.

Sim heaved deep breaths. He squeezed his eyes shut. His clenched fist trembled. Why had his life come to this? Why was everything always taken from him?

A familiar buzzing sounded nearby and he looked toward it. It was a hummingbird. Not a fay, and certainly not one of the fay he knew. It was just a normal hummingbird with shimmering green plumage on his chest. He hovered a moment and flew away, returning to whatever task he had.

Pomella.

He hadn't lost Pomella. Shevia and Nabiton had explained about her, about her marriage to Tibron. About her life and the Accord and the fall of Kelt Apar.

Pomella needed him. He knew that with a certainty that went beyond anything he'd known in all his lives. So much had changed, and she was clearly more capable than ever, but still, somehow, he knew his journey would return him to her. It had always been about coming back.

Well, Brother, he imagined his long-dead brother, Dane, would've said, *you've lived one mind-boggingly wild adventure of a life. Well-done.*

Sim relaxed his fist. A small smile crept to his face. So many memories lived in him now, more than a single person deserved.

Remembering an exercise he'd learned from Rochella, his ranger teacher, he began at the crown of his head and relaxed the tension he found there. He moved downward through his body, relaxing every muscle he could. He repeated the exercise, not moving in any way.

Finally, content that he was in control of his emotions once more, he strode over to the onkai he'd thrown. Picking it up, he sighed. He'd named this one Memory. Its twin, Remorse. Two constant companions he carried always since the years when he'd lived in the highlands.

Gripping the onkai firmly in each hand, he twisted them in unison, triggering the tiny mechanism to bare the steel blades hidden within the walking stick. The metal gleamed in the early-morning sunlight.

Leaning into a wide stance, he stepped through some simple forms that Rochella had taught him. He'd only received a little martial training from her, only bits and pieces. The rare times he'd had to fight, he'd relied on luck and stubborn tenacity to survive.

But as he worked his way through the forms, other memories came to him. His feet seemed to move on their own, a muscle memory emerging that he'd forgotten. Flashes of screaming men filled his mind. A self-proclaimed king of Moth who'd tried to defeat him. A rogue laghart warrior who could not understand why a human woman deserved the *kanta*'s respect and devotion. Lor Gez, and his Hundred Eyes.

Sim's pace quickened, his strikes more confident, more powerful. He shifted through the actions he'd taken in each of those battles, remembering the intensity of each one. His blades danced like his memories around him, cutting down the phantoms of his past. Once more he became Brigid as she tore through Moth like a storm, seeking her son, destroying anybody who acted as an obstacle. Mixed with those memories were those of his own, of his charge through the velten with Pomella in the days before Crow Tallin. Fused together, Brigid's life and his own became a dance of death. Together, everyone who crossed their path—enemies and loved ones alike—fell beneath their twin blades.

He returned to the House of Fallen Embers before midday. Shevia sat on a bench near the garden, her back straight. A pile of loosely bound papers sat on a wooden tray on her lap. She scribbled a feathered pen across the pages. Even from this distance, Sim could see the deft motions her wrist made.

He still couldn't quite believe that it was her, aged all these years. To him, it was only yesterday that Shevia was no older than nineteen, beautiful and fierce. She'd had a twisting dragon tattoo on her arm and shoulder then, but now it had been replaced by other, even more intricate artwork. Swirling clouds punctured by a hedge of thorns ran along her arm, the looming eyes of what might've been a black cat peeking over the crest of her shoulder. Her once-black hair had grayed and she kept it in a bun that was pierced by crisscrossed sticks.

Upon seeing him return, Shevia set her quill and tray aside and stood. Only her lavender eyes, so unusual and commanding, had not changed over the years.

"Did you find what you needed?" Shevia asked.

"Perhaps."

"You intend to leave now," the old Mystic said. A statement, not a question.

Sim nodded.

"To Port Morrush?"

Again, he nodded.

"The girl will want to go with you. And the boy, too. He won't be parted from her."

"I know. She's her granddaughter."

Shevia's expression softened. She sighed. It struck Sim as an unusually vulnerable act for Shevia. He reminded himself that she'd lost her husband. He'd met Quentin only briefly, when Pomella had first arrived at her apprentice Trials. They hadn't been friendly then, but after emerging from the tower Sim somehow knew the man, now called Kilpa, better.

He had no memories from the man, not like he did with Brigid, but he could sense a part of him stirring within his heart. He recognized what Kilpa had sacrificed to make his return possible.

"It may not be my place," Shevia began, "but I wonder if you would tell me what happened in the tower. Was it truly only a moment for you? All that time?"

Sim held her gaze a moment, then moved to stand beside her. She'd always been unyielding in her personality, as strong and rigid as steel, yet now he saw that strength warring with grief. More than that, she was no longer the lost girl he'd known. Here was a woman who did not fear releasing emotion, even if it was done in the quiet of night, revealed only to her beloved husband.

"I lack the words to describe the experience," Sim said. "But I carry the countless lives of another with me. One who walked this land seeking her son, only to lose him, time and again."

Shevia's eyes widened. "Brigid," she breathed.

"Tell me," Sim said, "what became of my . . . What became of Janid?"

Shevia met his gaze, and it surprised him to see fear hidden behind her expression.

"Please," he urged.

Shevia's tone hardened. "He emerged from the tower at Crow Tallin during the youth of Pomella's master Ahlala. I don't know how he escaped or why he emerged in the year he did. Perhaps your memories know. Or perhaps Pomella knows. But the High Mystic of Moth at the time sent him into the care of a Qina noble family. I do not know what that life was like for him, but I've long suspected it was harsh. Abusive, likely. Regardless, he became cruel. Terrifying. Mighty. He became the High Mystic of Qin. He became Bhairatonix."

Tears welled in Sim's eyes. His Janid. The sweet boy who'd called him Myma. Sweet Janid, who loved to climb and explore and . . .

He looked away from Shevia.

"That was *her* son," Shevia said. "Not yours."

"My memories say otherwise," Sim said. "You think of me as freed from a prison. But a part of me feels as though this life, right now, is the trap. The jail cell keeping me from finding him."

"That quest is ended," Shevia said, a note of gentleness in her voice. "Rest. Your son has moved on from this world and from this life."

Sim pictured Janid once more. The tall boy with a warm smile for him. Then he remembered from his own experience Bhairatonix, a cruel man and terrifying High Mystic who had discarded him in Yin-Aab and left him to die.

"I do not believe," Shevia continued, "that you would be here if you had not already let him go."

"You sound like the Nameless Saint," Sim said.

"I stopped listening to Saints long ago," Shevia said, "but in this perhaps she is right."

Sim took Shevia's hand in his own. At first, she resisted, her eyes narrowing, but the sincerity of his touch must've convinced her to allow it. He pressed her hand to his chest, directly over his heart.

"I carry another with me now, too, but in a different way."

Letting her hand remain, he pulled her close into a hug. "Your husband still reaches for you," he whispered. "And as long as I breathe, that awareness will live on."

As if sensing her presence, the warmth that was Kilpa inside Sim beat harder, sharing itself with the woman he held.

Shevia leaned into his embrace, and Sim knew it wasn't for him.

They lingered there a moment, then Shevia pulled away. A shallow breath was all she needed to compose herself, but she squeezed Sim's hand before letting go.

"We should see to Mia and Nabiton then," she said, then carried her tray and papers and quill into the House.

Sim insisted that they set out that afternoon, leaving the comfy and secluded homestead behind. Shevia watched them go, standing alone on the southern side of the House, a black-and-crimson shawl wrapped over her shoulders. He knew better than to ask her if she would go with them. If she intended to do so, she would've declared it. Instead, she'd patched their clothes and provided them with water and light provisions.

Pomella's granddaughter, Mia, emerged from the House, wearing Pomella's old green cloak. For a moment he stared at her, seeing some of Pomella's features stand out strongly against the green-hooded frame.

He remembered, too, that Springrise Day, all those years ago, when his sister, Bethy, had sewn and worn that cloak in order to perform the *Toweren*, the play that had become famous across Moth. With her red hair, Bethy had been elated to play Brigid. He himself had dressed in a homemade laghart costume. How strange the way everything had played out since then.

His attention shifted to the bow Mia carried. His eyes narrowed and his fingers twitched. Dauntless. He'd know that anywhere. Even with all of Brigid's memories the bow's origins remained obscured. The lagharts claimed it was crafted by a long-dead *Zurnta*, but Mylezka had told him—*told Brigid*—that it was humans who taught them the making of such weapons. She believed its origins dated back to a time long before the lagharts, in the days of the Dragon Kings.

Seeing the bow again now, he had to steady his urge to yank it from Mia. He could still unlock its power. In his hands, Dauntless was an extension of his might, of his power. No foe, Mystic or otherwise, could stand against him.

He forced himself to look away. He scrubbed his hair once and spoke in the direction of Mia's companion. Nabiton wore a mix of black leathers and one of Kilpa's old nondescript shirts.

"We go over hard terrain," Sim said to them.

"We will keep up," Nabiton replied.

Sim nodded, content. They carried their own packs, having no horse. The animals would only slow them down on the paths and terrain he intended to travel.

With a final look toward Shevia, he turned and walked south. Focusing his mind, he let the silver path emerge.

It shimmered into existence on the ground near his feet, for his eyes only to see. The phenomenon had never been fully explained to him, but it was certainly of the Myst. It had first come to him in the highlands of Qin, when he'd restored the shrine to Sitting Mother, the enigmatic Saint who had both befuddled and guided him for years. Perhaps it was she who created the silver path that rose before him. Regardless of who, or what, created it, the path always led him to the place where he was needed most. So had it always done for all true rangers, according to Rochella.

But the path was not only silver now. Blended into the weave of light was a golden color, shining just as bright. Sim didn't know what it meant, but he supposed it had to do with the merger of the worlds. Shevia had told him of that, too.

Once again, so much had changed, and yet Sim remained the same, as though forgotten and left behind.

The first day was miserable for Sim's traveling companions. He pushed a hard pace, avoiding roads or obvious trails.

To their credit, neither Mia nor Nabiton complained. Not that Sim had expected them to. Mia didn't converse with him, but he heard her speaking in a quiet voice when she thought he and Nabiton were out of hearing range.

Sim had spent years in the silent mountains, honing his attention in order to hear what most people could not. Brigid, too, had learned to sharpen all her senses. But Mia wasn't muttering to herself or speaking because of a broken mind. He'd been surprised to hear she was speaking *to* somebody.

"A horse? Really, Brother?" she said. She walked far behind Sim, with Nabiton carefully following in between. Sim wondered if Nabiton could hear her speaking.

"Where did you get it?" Mia continued. Then, after a pause, added, "Oh yeah? What's her name?"

Whatever the reply, Mia snorted a quiet laugh.

The sound of Nabiton's footsteps told Sim of his presence before he spoke. "How do you know this shorter way to Port Morrush?" Nabiton asked.

"My life led me to the silver path of the ranger," Sim said. "It reveals ways that others cannot see."

Nabiton frowned. He walked with his newly found oak staff to help guide his steps, though his movements were strained because he was unaccustomed to its use.

"I trained as a Hunter for three years," Nabiton said. "The order emerged from the rangers you speak of. Though I'm not sure there's much overlap anymore. With Vlenar gone, you might be the last of their kind. Not even Carn can see Mystical pathways like you speak of."

"Can you?" Sim asked.

Nabition scoffed, "Don't insult me."

Sim stopped and gently touched Nabiton's shoulder. "Wait."

Behind them, Mia also stopped walking. She'd fallen farther behind them, but she paused to give them privacy.

"One of the first lessons my teacher Rochella taught me was that our eyes have little to do with true seeing," Sim said. "The path I follow is one that can reveal itself to you in time. To find it, you must find that which is within you and holds you back. Whatever fear you have, whatever attachment limits you, find that, and let it go. Release your attachments."

"You sound like a Mystic," Nabiton said.

The corner of Sim's mouth curved upward in a smile. "Yah, I suppose I do. I've lived enough lifetimes with them. They've never given me much reason to trust them. But in some ways, they're right."

He placed a friendly hand on Nabiton's shoulder. "A person doesn't need eyes to see that you care for her. You've adjusted to your new arrangement of senses. Keep following that. Seek the path and it will reveal itself to you, even through the darkness."

Gently he took Nabiton's oak staff from his hand and tossed it aside. "That's too heavy. Take this. It is an onkai from a mountain village of Qin, made by a *Huzzoh*. It is yours."

Nabiton accepted the onkai and ran his hands over it, feeling its shape. "Does it have a name?" he asked. The mountain villages of Qin were known in part for their walking-stick blades, and each one always had a name.

"Not any longer," Sim said. "It awaits a new one from you when you discover it. Like the silver path, it will reveal itself when you are ready."

Nabiton bowed his head. "Thank you, Master," he said, his voice full of reverence.

"It's just Sim," Sim said, and returned to the road. "If we're careful and push hard along the path, we can arrive in Port Morrush tomorrow."

They trudged south, steady and hard along the eastern outskirts of the Mystwood. Ancient trees with gnarled roots twisted around one another, making the pathways challenging at times. But somehow the shimmering path at Sim's feet always revealed a passage forward.

Deeper into the forest they hiked, merging into the outskirts of the Murk. Sim kept them well away from any settlements, but several times they had to pause and remain as still as possible. A patrol passed nearby, most of them consisting of Touched individuals. Their human features blended seamlessly with those of the fay animals they'd merged with in the womb. Shevia had explained the growing phenomenon to Sim.

The patrol moved with tension in their stride, and Sim suspected that word of the laghart army must've made its way south. They passed without any indication that they'd noticed Sim or his companions. Yet even if they discovered Sim and his companions, Sim doubted the Murk dwellers would detain them, but any encounter would surely delay them.

Well after dark on the day they left Shevia's homestead, the three travelers passed through a clearing. Although it was a cloudy night, the clouds broke briefly revealing a swath of vibrant stars. To the east, MagDoon's massive shadow blocked an entire portion of the night sky.

They walked all night, eating as they traveled. They stopped only briefly to rest their feet. Sim kept a close eye on Mia and Nabiton, watching for signs of exhaustion or foot blisters that might hamper them. They all wore low traveling boots that Shevia had given them and that helped. Nabiton showed no discomfort, though Mia winced now and again.

In the predawn hours, with exhaustion covering Mia as much as her cloak, Sim turned them southeast, leading them up into the foothills of the southern Ironlows. From there he took them to a hidden path that followed a thin creek. Towering mountainsides covered in moss rose on either side of them.

Sim spoke hardly at all except to provide simple directions. Nabiton had gone into a withdrawn silence.

Late on the morning of the second day since setting out, the sound of the ocean reached Sim's ears. They emerged from the foothills of the southern tip of the Ironlows. In the distance, looming atop its oceanside cliff, stood the Fortress of Sea and Sky. The fortress rested above the trading town of Port Morrush, watching over it like a quiet guardian. A white-masted sailing ship drifted lazily away from the harbor, bound, Sim imagined, for the Continent.

Nabiton tilted his face upward. "The air is fresh," he said. "I can smell the sea."

Sim placed an arm gently across Nabiton's chest to stop him. "The fortress is only a handful of miles south of here," he said. "You need sleep before we continue."

They made a rough camp in a small cluster of pines. As cold as it was, Sim forbade them from making a fire.

Mia had just about fallen asleep when Nabiton spoke again. "The fortress is guarded. Does your silver path show us how to enter?"

"Not this time," Sim said. "Rest for now. I'll keep watch."

As tired as he should be, Sim wasn't ready to sleep. And now that he thought of it, he hadn't slept since leaving the tower. And before that, he hadn't slept since before the culmination of Crow Tallin. His body had lost consciousness in the tower, but that had only been for a handful of moments. Had he truly not slept for over fifty years?

He rubbed his temples. He wouldn't spin his mind any further about it.

Mia and Nabiton drifted off to sleep immediately, leaving Sim alone to watch. He liked the silence. The pines and their scent reminded him of the highlands. He found a nearby sapling and broke off a piece as long as his forearm. Settling beside the others, he used his small knife to begin carving. His hands needed something to occupy themselves.

Pomella was almost certainly inside the Fortress of Sea and Sky. They needed a plan to get in. The silver path stopped here. He'd been surprised because he'd expected it to lead toward the fortress, and possibly right up to the cell where they kept Pomella. He needed to think about what this meant, and what they should do next.

Mia twitched and let out a quiet moan as dreams flicked across her mind. At one point she sat up, although her eyes were still closed. She muttered something, then lay back down to sleep. Nabiton did not stir.

Sim let himself relax into his carving, his mind thinking of all that burdened him. What would he do with his life now? This was Moth, but he had no home to go to. Perhaps he had family, but even if Bethy was still alive her children and grandchildren would not know him. There was only Pomella now, but what would that be like?

Everything but him moved on. Always.

We are rangers. We do what we always do. We move, and we survive. Rochella's voice, from across time.

The day passed, and slowly the pine in his hands took shape.

Later, a soft whispering reached Sim's ears. He peered at Mia, but like Nabiton, she still slept soundly. The whispering came from the south, in the direction of Port Morrush. It shifted and became a chant. Sim could make no sense of what the voice said.

A clear, moonless night fell, revealing crisp stars over the heavy blackness of the ocean. The voice spoke again, speaking words Sim didn't recognize. The voice was sad, perhaps frightened. Then it spoke a single word.

"Myma?" the voice said.

Sim's heart leaped. No, it was his fatigue. Janid was dead. His time, and Brigid's, had long since passed. Whatever lingering memories he had were not his own. He was himself. Not her. Not anymore.

But still.

"Myma."

It came from the fortress. Waves of energy radiated from the building that instantly resonated with Sim in a familiar way.

"Sim," the voice said. "Come back to me."

Sim stood as a wind howled from the ocean, throwing its weight against him. It gained intensity, as did the voice chanting once more from the fortress.

He braced against the wind. It thundered like the storm winds of a mighty gale. The pine trees surrounding their camp uprooted and flew toward the northern mountain they'd emerged from. The ocean surged against the land, drowning Port Morrush and blasting the fortress's walls.

Sim sneered against the wind that threatened to sweep his world away. The sneer became a scream.

He sat up, his own scream having woken him.

It was daylight, perhaps highsun. Only a gentle breeze stirred from the ocean. Mia and Nabiton were awake but lying together. Each had a look of worry on their face.

Chest heaving from the strange dream, Sim stood. Nabiton roused as well. "What is it?"

Sim walked to the same place he'd been standing moments ago in his dream. No storm raged in the air, but the same energy surged from the fortress.

He looked down into his hands at the incomplete carving he'd been whittling. The shape approximated a woman, with long hair, sitting cross-legged.

Sitting Mother.

"Something's happening to Pomella," Sim said.

They needed to get into the fortress. But how? An entire legion of Shieldguards protected it. Sim knew they needed to sneak in unseen and then figure out a way to find Pomella, free her, and get out. It was the kind of challenge that Brigid would've thrown herself at recklessly. The urge tugged at him to follow her ways. But he was a ranger. His ways were more thoughtful, more planned.

"Mia," Sim said. The young woman peered up from her work packing the group's meager possessions. He gestured for her to join him near the edge of the hill overlooking the distant city.

She carried Dauntless like a Mystic staff. Sim eyed the bow, thinking of how he could blast their way past the Shieldguards. Seeing his look, Mia subtly pulled the bow closer to her chest.

Sim suppressed his need for the bow. "Could you help us get into the fortress?" he asked Mia.

When she didn't reply, he added, "I don't know how long you've been a Mystic, but if Pomella taught you, then surely she believes in you, and that's good enough for me."

He knew Mia didn't converse with other people, and he didn't expect her to change that now. She met his gaze, and while there was fear in her eyes, there was also a fierce determination. She nodded to him and stepped away.

Sim watched her walk to the edge of the nearby path that they'd come from. She kept her back to them and appeared to be thinking. Then he saw her head moving slightly. He closed his eyes, focused his attention, ignored the wind, and tried to *listen*.

Mia was speaking. He only caught a handful of words.

". . . Go."

". . . follow you."

"No choice."

And finally, one other word, spoken with a firm tone. "Rion."

Mia turned back to the camp. Nabiton stood ready to go. He, too, had been listening.

When she saw them both watching her, Mia's face flushed, but she kept her chin high. She moved to stand beside Nabiton, then sat down. She tugged Nabiton to join her and gave Sim a pointed look.

We wait, that look seemed to say.

Shrugging in acceptance, Sim sat beside the others.

The afternoon wore on. Rain clouds encroached upon the land from the ocean. Questions arose in Sim's mind along with doubts, but he did not voice them. He'd learned to be patient long ago. Nabiton also remained silent. It was clear the boy would do anything and be content so long as Mia was by his side.

Finally, the wind stirred once more, and Mia's face perked up. She stood, and dragged Nabiton with her. Her gaze focused on something far away. Then she grabbed Sim and Nabiton, pulling them close to her as though hugging them at once.

Sim went with it, understanding only that she was a Mystic working in her strange ways. It was different than he was used to seeing but—

The world swirled around him. Colors rushed. The sky blended with the sea. The ground mixed with his companions. He was falling and leaping at once. He wanted to scream, but as quickly as it had begun, it was over.

A stone wall loomed high beside them. The roar of the ocean was louder, more immediate. It took Sim a moment to recognize where they were.

They were inside the fortress.

TWENTY-SIX

THE STONE DRAGON

Hizrith floated in a void that was neither empty nor dark. He did not see with his eyes or taste with his tongue. His body did not exist in this place. Yet he knew his consciousness was *somewhere*.

The Mystic name of Moth sang from Pomella's book, offering itself to him. Welcoming him home. It was not a word he or any other living creature could possibly have spoken with their anatomy. It sounded to him like warm stones heated by the sun beneath a clear sky. Like water evaporating as he lay stretched out on a sandy shore. It scented of power, and peace, and love.

He focused his breathing and, in doing so, materialized his body along with his staff, robes, and the book. He Unveiled the Myst, willing it to form around him.

Rock and soil rolled open beneath him, then grass and trees and sky above. A tower with a green conical top appeared before him.

Kelt Apar. At last.

"I and the *kanta* have returned to you," Hizrith said.

The land's essence pulsed in harmony with him. He moved toward the tower, and with every step the island honored his arrival. Every windswept branch on the island moved in the direction of his gaze. Every gust that sighed through the forest was his breath. The grass near him turned their blades to face him. Nearby trees bowed.

This was not the physical world, but rather an expression of it. His anointment was upon him.

The door to the tower waited for him. Warmth radiated from its wooden surface, tingling his scales, giving him life.

"Master," the door whispered. "Welcome home."

Within the tower, nothing stirred except the Myst. Hizrith circled this Mystwalk version of the small foyer, tracing the walls with a claw. Energy streamed within the stones, waiting for him to manipulate it.

The spiral staircase rose to the upper rooms. A diminutive library, the High Mystic's personal chambers, and the uppermost ritual chamber awaited him.

He ascended the stairs and entered the upper chamber. A dense fog filled the space. The lone window on the far side lay dark and shuttered. An intricately carved high-backed throne stood in the center of the room and upon it sat Vivianna Vinnay.

He hadn't seen Yarina's apprentice since Crow Tallin, yet it was unmistakably her. She wore an elaborate sleeveless gown, colored lavender and blue, and belted with golden rope. Her long black-and-silver hair had been uplifted in a style similar to how Hizrith remembered Yarina keeping hers for formal occasions. Upon Vivianna's forehead rested a golden crown of leaves. She sat, legs crossed, like an imperious queen with her arms laid upon the sides of the chair.

Hizrith licked the air, tasting her fearlessness.

"Mistress Vivianna," he said, speaking in his own language. In his Mystwalk, she would understand.

"You are a usurper, Hizrith," Vivianna said. "I demand that you give me the book. By rights, the name it contains belongs to me."

The energy filling the Mystwalk laughed around them, mirroring his amusement.

"Your time ended before it ever began," Hizrith said. "Your past masters are dead, your champion defeated. You are but a shadow of yourself, a shade that haunts a lost dream outside of your broken body."

"This is your only chance to surrender the book and to leave this island," Vivianna said. "There can still be harmony."

"There will never be harmony while humans infest Moth!" Hizrith said. "We lived for untold centuries until you tore the *kanta* apart!"

"All conflict is cyclical," Vivianna said. "It is the nature of the Myst. As dawn turns to dusk, as the moon and tides ebb and flow, so does time breathe in and out. See the grander scale, master *Zurnta*, and do not allow lives to be lost in the fights of narrow-time."

"Do not lecture me on the Myst," Hizrith said. "You dare to sit upon a throne and wear a crown and speak as if you are above it all. Arrogant, like all your predecessors. But you are right. The Myst is cyclical, and so this moment marks not only your end, but a new beginning."

He Unveiled the Myst, yanking the energy from the tower, ripping its life-force away. Vivianna screamed, and this time he tasted her terror.

He punched his Mystic staff toward her, blasting away her flesh and muscle and bone until only dust remained. He took a single step backward, and the world rushed away from him. He stood now on the grasslands outside the tower.

Pulling at the core energies of the island, Hizrith commanded the ground to consume the abomination that stood on his land. The ground shook, and the entire tower structure before him shuddered. A single stone fell away, followed by another.

Stone and wood and glass crumbled until the entire tower avalanched to the ground in a massive roar of dust and energy. The ruins of Kelt Apar's infamous tower lay in a heap around him.

With a wave of his claw he brushed the debris away, sweeping a heavy wind of time and Myst across the grassy landscape. The tower's remains vanished with a rumble, as did the primitive human huts and gardens and sheds and walkways. In their place rose jutting stone structures that angled upward out of the ground. Some were simply massive, moss-covered boulders rising out of the grass like oversized turtle shells poking out of a grassy ocean. Most rose to the height of a laghart, while some towered two or three times higher.

Hizrith tasted the air with his tongue in satisfaction. *Yes. This is how Kelt Apar once appeared and how it would again. A true velten.*

When he emerged from the Mystwalk, he would tear down the human abomination that had stood here for a thousand years. The tower had been built for humans by humans. When he came here at last in his body, he would rebuild the structure, making it suitable for the lagharts and their ways. A grand velten, home to the *kanta* and a new lineage of Mystics.

"Ehzeeth," he said to the grassy clearing, "we have done it." He touched his claw tips to the center of his forehead to honor his long-dead master.

The wind shifted again, sweeping away the velten and its stones. Days and years and centuries passed before Hizrith's eyes, taking him back to a time before humans ever came to Moth.

He watched in awe as lagharts moved around the velten, going about tasks or sunning themselves upon the rocks. Clusters of Mystics strolled with their staves, following a *Zurnta* who lectured as they walked.

"Beautiful," said a voice beside Hizrith.

He turned, snapping his tongue out to catch the surprise visitor's scent. There was none, but he didn't need it. He knew the face now beside him, having loved the person most of his life.

It was Ehzeeth, his *Zurnta* who had perished in a moment of ecstasy upon witnessing the glorious return of Seer Brigid during Crow Tallin. Gone was the elder's aged stoop. He stood tall and straight, his scales vibrant with hues shimmering in the sunlight. His Mystic staff was shorter than most, and curved so heavily it resembled a scythe.

"Master," Hizrith said, bowing.

Ehzeeth returned the gesture. "It is you who are the master now."

"Thanks to your teachings," Hizrith said. "Because of your wisdom, we will fulfill Seer Brigid's vision of bringing the lagharts back to our homeland."

"You will drive out the humans?"

"They are invaders," Hizrith said.

"Are they?"

Hizrith tasted the air, savoring the scent of the name of the island.

"Watch," Ehzeeth said, and gestured toward the velten.

Once more the wind rose, coming from the unseen horizons of the Myst, sensed by its passing more than its chill, dusting away the lagharts. The wide grass clearing vanished, replaced by gnarled trees and a small glade with a single wooden building, tall and rectangular. A trio of figures worked outside the building, going about pastoral duties while a pair of graying goats cropped the nearby brush.

"Humans?" Hizrith said. "What are you showing me?"

They had been looking at Kelt Apar in the time before humans. But now all he saw was the tiny clearing with a single human dwelling.

Realization of what he was witnessing dawned on him. Unable to contain his shock, his tongue snapped out in repeated fashion.

"Is this Kelt Apar? From before—"

Ehzeeth's silence answered him. One of the humans chopped wood, while the other two sat in meditative positions. Mystic staves rested across their laps.

The wind swept the glade and its inhabitants away until the forest covered it completely. Where the humans and hut had stood, only trees and a single boulder remained. The boulder rested where the wooden dwelling had been before.

Two lagharts, their bodies exposed without clothing, lay upon the boulder, eyes closed, resting in the shade of the forest canopy.

The wind rose and took them.

"Generation after generation claimed this land," Ehzeeth said. "Drawn to its power, to its mysteries. Before you, the humans presided. Before them, during the reign of the Dragon Kings, when our kind had their favor, we lagharts claimed this as our own. Centuries before that, it was the humans. Before them, the lagharts.

"So it has always been, age after age, for as long as the Myst has been known to our world."

High above the treetops, barely visible through the heavy canopy, the warm sun cycled, faster and faster.

Surprise, anger, and a touch of fear swirled within Hizrith. *No*, he thought. The lagharts were the native inhabitants of this land. It was their *right* to take it back. Wasn't it?

"This changes nothing," Hizrith said to his master. "Kelt Apar was once ours and it will be again. I have the name of the island now. The new lineage begins with me."

"Yes," Ehzeeth said after a short hesitation. Hizirth imagined that if he could scent his master, he would taste, what? Pity?

"What is it?" he asked, unable to keep the annoyance from his voice.

"Your new lineage has begun, but it may not matter," Ehzeeth said.

"Why?"

Ehzeeth fixed Hizrith with a long glance, his slitted pupils seeing through him.

"Because," Ehzeeth said, "when next the wind blows, it may take what you don't expect."

The wind swept across the forest once more.

The sensation of wind passed away, and with it the Mystwalk. Hizrith opened his eyes, not caring where he was. His body shivered with pain.

His eyes focused gradually, but not entirely to perfect clarity. Long had it been since his aged eyes could discern detail as they once had.

He was alone, lying among a nest of comforts. Despite the oil lanterns, a deep chill permeated the room.

He tried to sit upright, but he found little strength and collapsed back. He lay there awhile, trying to find warmth while the memories of his dream lingered.

Soon enough, Kumava entered the room. Upon seeing him awake, she hurried to his side. "Master," she said, scenting concern.

A smile emerged on Hizrith's face. "It is done!"

Fear scented from Kumava, but she immediately hid it. But it had been there, unmistakable. Why fear?

"Master?" she said.

He pushed himself up, straining against a sharp pain in his hip.

They were in the nest room where he slept, near the ritual room where his attempt to summon Seer Brigid had gone wrong. Hemosavana had unexpectedly pulled him into Pomella's Mystwalk right as her granddaughter had escaped.

"How long have I been unconscious? Have you sent soldiers to find the girl?"

Kumava scented of worry.

"It has been six days, Master," she said.

"Six—!" Hizrith snapped. He tried to stand, but Kumava held him down.

"We tried to wake you," Kumava explained. "But you were in a trance. I dared not force it."

"What of the girl?"

"We did not find her, but we are pursuing her."

"The bow?"

Hizrith noted how Kumava's expression remained neutral. "She has it then. We will recover it."

"Help me stand," Hizrith said. "I must drink."

His apprentice gently lifted him and the sharp pain flared. He winced, unable to keep a grimace from his face.

He let Kumava lead him out of the ritual room, down a hallway, to a nearby chamber that his soldiers had converted to a comfort room. Large, communal drinking bowls stood on tables beside blanket-nests and other tokens of rest. He eased his lower mandible into the nearest bowl and drank.

The water, which was room temperature in order to not upset one's constitution, helped blunt the pain he felt from crown to tail.

"Something great has happened, Kumava," he said.

It was still there. The name of the island echoed in his heart. The way that the land turned its attention to him. Even now, inside this hideously unimaginative tower created by humans, he could sense the Mystwood calling out to him. Welcoming its new master. Rejoicing in the return of a laghart *Zurnta* after so many centuries.

Kumava wrapped her claw around his. "Tell me."

After he had eaten and rested some more, Hizrith sat cross-legged in the uppermost chamber of Sentry's clock tower, facing south out the window. Clear skies filled with warm afternoon light shone in the distance.

Though the sun shone brightly now, his storm—the storm of the *kanta*—blew from the north, and soon would cover the southern half of the island.

He closed his eyes to feel the land harmonizing with him. A light wind breezed across his scales. Nearby treetops swayed as they called out to him in greeting.

So far, he had only resided within this newfound connection to the island. Now it was time to reach out and Unveil his vision. He let his consciousness expand, spreading outward until he became the wooden town and the forest and the stones and beyond. He became the sky, and the island turned itself to him, ready and willing to be of service.

With a thought, he condensed the air, and pulled the moisture from the sea-driven winds. From the north he pulled it, bringing the storm southward.

A heavy gust rattled the window resting before him. It began to rain.

This was the beginning. He would wash away the human Mystics and their merged monstrosities. His storm would sweep aside Norana and her militaristic grip on the island. His rains would carve a path for his homecoming to Kelt Apar and the central tower.

"It really happened then," Kumava said behind him. She scented of admiration and awe. "Does the island obey you?"

"Yes," he said. At this he opened his eyes and glanced over his shoulder at his apprentice. "Sit with me."

She settled beside him, her tongue tasting the wind.

"What troubles you, Kumava?"

The faintest scent of surprise filled the air between them. She wasn't accustomed to him addressing her so casually.

"Speak freely," he prompted.

"There is still violence."

Hizrith sat with his emotions, letting them dissolve.

"Yes," he said. "We have visited death upon the humans here. But do you see how it was necessary to reclaim what they took from us? When this is over, we will walk the ancestral memories of Kelt Apar, and witness the atrocities they visited upon us. You will understand then how they drove us nearly to extinction. Chased us to the sea. Watched us drown in the western ocean while only a small number of ships escaped to the horizon. The cost of reclaiming what was rightfully ours is only a fraction of the lives they destroyed."

Kumava stirred.

"Speak," he prompted.

"Is this not revenge?"

"It is a reclaiming."

They sat in silence, meditating together. The storm that Hizrith had summoned swept over them, charging south, rolling thunder and rain across the Mystwood.

"Come," the master said.

They opened a hidden door beside the southern window and stepped onto a narrow balcony that encircled the tower. Above them, the great clock shuddered as it kept time. Rain fell upon their scales and robes.

"Listen to our land," Hizrith said. "For someday, what I received today will be passed to you."

He reached out his claw and tapped the air. The sound of a silver bell *tinged* through the storm.

Down below, at the nearest crossroads, the street rumbled and churned. Stone and dirt lifted into the shape of a great figure, bearded, towering nearly to the height of the balcony. Stone eyes, pulled deep from the ground, turned upward to him.

"I come, as summoned. I am Oxillian. How may I help you, Master?" He spoke in Continental.

Hizrith licked the air. "Ceon'hur," he said, invoking the ancient name for the Guardian of Moth and Kelt Apar. It had been the humans who filled this creature with life using rituals they'd learned from lagharts. "Do you know how to ssspeak in the laghartt language?"

"Yes," came the reply, using their words.

"Then you shall speak it now, and always. And you shall take our form, and appear as a laghart. The humans are your masters no more."

The creature bowed, and his body shifted. His beard retreated, his legs bent, a tail elongated, and a row of spikes emerged along his long spine. A tongue of dirt and pebbles tasted the air.

"No more shall you be the Green Man," Hizrith said, "but a dragon of stone to honor our long-lost ancestors of ages past."

The Stone Dragon bowed his head once more.

"Go now to the south," Hizrith said, "to the Fortress of Sea and Sky. Any human Mystic you encounter anywhere on the island is henceforth an invader. I brand them Unclaimed and sentence them to death. For the one called Pomella AnDone, I strip her of her powers and banish her from this island. Do not let your past friendship to her cloud your ability to fulfill my command. If she resists, or Unveils the Myst, then her life is forfeit. Do you understand?"

"Yes."

"Then go, Stone Dragon, to the fortress."

TWENTY-SEVEN

A SYMPHONY OF STARS

Pomella shuddered with sadness and fear. She wiggled against the oak branches Hizrith had twisted around her, but in her child-sized body she couldn't slip free.

The Creekwaters of her diminutive Mystwalk flowed past her, carrying her sadness like fallen leaves into the darkness beyond the borders of her dimming memory. Slowly but with steady tenacity the water rose toward her. It clawed at the dry bank, one fingertip length at a time. Soon, she realized, it would consume her. She would drown in the sorrow of her own memories.

She sighed, and blew out a strand of loose hair that hung over her face. Mia and the other Mystics she loved were in danger. Now that Hizrith possessed the Mystic name of the island, there was no telling what he could achieve. The lineage of human masters was broken and the loss had come during her time.

In her pride Pomella had believed that she could come into these Mystic Skies and inherit the Mystic name of the island by herself.

But her pride led not only to failure but also to catastrophe.

She wondered whether her body would ever wake up. After the Creekwaters drowned her here, would her body die? Only a decayed corpse would greet Norana when she came for her in the cell.

It no longer mattered. Pomella resolved to accept whatever fate the Myst had in store for her, for the other Mystics, and for all of Moth.

The Creekwaters crept closer, consuming the small patch of land.

Pomella released her struggle against the binding oak branches and let herself hang. Below her, discarded pages from *The Book of Songs* lay upon the ground. Their imagery contained labeled flower diagrams, star charts, recipes, and other minor sketches. The Creekwaters hadn't reached the pages yet, but soon they'd be drowned. In between the meticulously printed text were hand-scrawled musical notation and lyrics. Some of the words to "Into Mystic Skies":

> *The night has gone;*
> *The sun lifts and flies.*
> *Always I'll follow you,*
> *Into Mystic Skies.*

Despite all that was happening, Pomella couldn't help but giggle. Coming from her four-year-old body, it sounded especially ridiculous to her ears. She had *gone* into the Mystic Skies. And here she would remain.

No time passed, or perhaps all the days of all of her long life marched by like the slow and steady procession of the rising Creekwaters.

Pomella neither slept nor remained consciously awake. She hung from the oak branches that she'd created and had turned against her. Her mind detached from her young body, freeing her of physical pain or discomfort, leaving only an abiding sense of timelessness.

Origin and destination, converged.

An endless circle in which every point was a potential beginning and ending. Pomella hung at the fulcrum, the center of the hourglass where time was neither past nor future. She had no staff, no name of the island. Only herself, a rising creek, and the ruined pages of an old book.

And the Myst.

The Myst, the fabric of reality. The foundational, supremely alive essence upon which every person, every experience, every thought, arose and returned. Whole lives and worlds and universes rising and falling, *breathing*.

"Breathe," Pomella whispered, but to her ears it was the voice of her grandmhathir.

"Singing is just breathing, but with emotion, and power."

The oak branches tightened around her wrists and arms. The Creekwaters lapped at the first discarded page of *The Book of Songs*.

"You *are* the music," said Tibron. The same words he'd spoken to her in an early dream-memory. "Sometimes, you just need to remember it."

Pomella's feet touched the ground. She no longer had the body of a four-year-old, but the much taller form of a teenager. She glanced at the branches holding her by the wrists, and flexed, snapping the branch and yanking her arms free.

"Your breath is life," said Yarina from nowhere and everywhere. "And all life comes from the Myst."

Pomella breathed, and tilted her face upward. With a thought, she Unveiled a gown of silver and golden light that settled across her adult form. Her hair caught in the wind of the Unveiling, unfurling behind her.

"Sing, Pomella," Lal said, his voice light and dreamy, like it had been during the warm spring days of her apprenticeship.

She Unveiled the Myst some more, and scattered pages of *The Book of Songs*, some soggy at their edges, arose in front of Pomella, twisting upward on vines of silver-gold strands of Myst. The pages shuffled around one another until they arranged themselves in order once more. The cold Creekwaters encircled Pomella's ankles.

"Sing me a song, Mhathir," Harmona cooed, her voice no older than the four-year-old one Pomella had spoken with.

"Sometimes, the hardest steps to take are ones we've taken a thousand times before," Vivianna said.

The handwritten words to a song illuminated on the book's pages. They glowed with pinkish light, lifting off the page to float in the air.

"Sing," said a chorus of people. "Breathe."

"Find your song," spoke a final voice.

Her own.

In the silence of her deepest memory, Pomella filled the void with song.

> *"In the vast, unknowable Deep,*
> *Where faded memories sleep."*

It had been so long since she'd sung, but when the first words passed her lips a light blossomed within her. *This* was who she was. A girl lost, an apprentice seeking, a Mystic, a mother, a master, now found.

> *"I sailed glorious skies,*
> *Unseen by your eyes.*
> *When all fell apart,*
> *It shattered my heart."*

She could not return from the way she'd come. What was past was gone, and she would leave it behind, cherished, not forgotten, but no longer carried. There was only forward, onward.

The fulcrum of the hourglass.

Pomella looked down at the ground as she sang.

> *"Lifting my sight,*
> *I rose as the light,"*

She'd thought this was the bottom of the abyss, the deepest point of her well of memories. While it might have been those things, Pomella also knew that every ending was also a beginning.

She flared her arm out and the oak that she'd hung from twisted and elongated, forming a staff of silver and gold to match her gown. It shone as the living sun ablaze in her hand, alive with life-affirming energy and warmth. Like the staff, Pomella glowed with the power and stillness of time.

> *"And let my voice soar,*
> *At last, forevermore."*

Bending her knees, she gathered her power and leaped into the air, toes lifting from the ground, body ascending. She spun the memory-world around her, wrapping it like a cloak, then inverted it. The Creekwaters rotated above her head, and the sky descended from her. The creek became rain, and Pomella rose into the falling water.

Forward, onward, not into her past, but returning to her present.

She rose and fell at once, lifting through the abyss that was now a mountain slope. Buffeted by the winds of her rising song, Pomella soared, glowing and streaking with silver and gold.

One last time her family and friends and lovers and enemies sailed past her, stars shining to her across time, riding the winds of their own lives, echoing her song back to her.

Together they harmonized to a symphony of stars and light,

ribboning past their shared experiences. The memory-worlds that Pomella had walked faded away, returning to the chambers of her mind, crumbling the notion that they'd ever been real, and demonstrating to Pomella that with time there was only *now*, only the fulcrum of the hourglass.

The symphony, the song of Pomella, the song of the Myst, sang on.

One by one, the stars-that-were-lives dimmed and faded. Gone Hector, her strength. Gone Lal, her teacher. Gone Harmona, her beloved child. Gone Vivianna, her closest friend. Gone Vlenar, her guide. Gone Tibron, her beloved. Gone Mia, her hope.

Until only a single star remained. It bloomed before her, rushing to meet her at the end of a long, long passage. She knew this star, this familiar warmth upon her face, for it sang the loudest to her, drawing her close.

She found once more that she had a hand, and that it was aged and wrinkled. She reached it toward the light that now filled the entirety of her existence.

Her fingers brushed the star, and the last of the Mystwalk fell apart; the Mystic Skies vanished.

The song had ceased to be sung, but the symphony played on.

TWENTY-EIGHT

LAND, SEA, AND SKY

Pomella awoke to the foggy reality of her cell. Exhaustion like she'd never known crashed over her. She swayed, her body refusing to stay upright, and like a dropped handkerchief she fell.

Yet she never hit the cell's stone floor. Strong arms caught her.

She opened her eyes and saw him.

"Sim," she creaked though parched lips and dry throat.

"I'm here, Pomella."

He was so young, somehow hardly a day older than when she'd last seen him. His blond hair was as thick and unruly as she remembered, his features still strong. Thick stubble grew upon his cheeks, but not a gray hair to be seen. Only his eyes, as blue as a Springrise sky, had changed. Looking into them, Pomella saw a lifetime of wisdom. A thousand lifetimes. With a glance, she could see he was more than Sim, so much more than the boy who'd followed her out of Oakspring, and even more than the hardened ranger he'd become in the mountains of Qin.

Perhaps this was yet another dream, another deeper part of the Mystwalk. But no. Her arm throbbed with a dull ache. Her wrists burned where the iron manacles bound her. This was the real and physical world she knew.

Pomella licked her lips and tried again for words, this time managing to whisper. "I searched for you," she said, "for so long. . . ."

"Then this is where we begin again," Sim said. "Here. There's little time. Drink this; your body's been starved and lacking water for days."

"How . . . long?" she managed.

"From what I've been told, it's been fourteen days since you were arrested," Sim said.

Fourteen days. Which meant she'd been meditating for around ten days without water. Her mind spun, trying to understand how that could be possible. And how was it possible for Sim to appear here, still young and strong? But those thoughts fled quickly, replaced by the memory of the symphony that had raised her through the abyss, into and beyond the Skies, and brought her here.

She wanted to leap to her feet and dance. She wanted to swing Sim around by the arms, letting tears of joy roll down her face as she sang. The Myst hummed in her, infusing every bit of her with its harmonious perfection. Yet in her state she could barely keep her head lifted.

A canteen with warm liquid touched her lips. She sipped, and it was as though she'd tasted water for the first time. She drank again, paused, and again.

"People can't live without water for this long," Sim said, his voice low. "I don't know how you did it. When I entered this cell, I found your hummingbird circling you. She moved with such speed that protective rings sheltered you. Nobody harmed you because of her." He paused a heartbeat before continuing, "You've clearly become something, someone, extraordinary."

She should've been hungrier. Perhaps she should be dead. The symphony remained in her heart, yet it quieted, and retreated, now humming its constant harmonies in the back of her mind.

"I . . . I failed," she murmured. Exhaustion lured her toward sleep. "Sim. The island. Hizrith."

He nodded, though it was unclear to Pomella if he understood.

"Your granddaughter is here," Sim said. He shook his head, and the faintest smile cracked the edges of his lips. "A granddaughter. By the Saints, Pomella, we lead strange lives. Come, let me get these chains off. I'll carry you."

He unsheathed his bladed walking stick and wrested the blades against the iron shackling her wrists. Pain blazed through her arm. She cried out. A glance revealed her wrists were bloody and blackened from days of touching the metal.

The next moment she was in his arms. She had only a moment to look back at the cell she'd been in before they were out the door, descending stone stairs. Had she really sat upon that thin straw for so long without food or water? Had Ena truly protected her that entire time? She could only imagine what the guards had attempted to get past the little bird.

Sim and Pomella left the room, leaving only a slanting beam of sunlight shining in from the high window.

Sim had never been to the Fortress of Sea and Sky, at least, not in this lifetime. He'd seen it from afar twice, once when he'd left Moth with Rochella and once again when he'd returned with Shevia during the days of Crow Tallin.

It had been both a lifetime and a *thousand* lifetimes ago, yet the memory was still fresh and clear. He looked at Pomella, his oldest, dearest friend, cradled in his arms and marveled at what he saw. She was aged and frail and skeletal thin. Carrying her was like holding a sack of air and light. Her dark skin had paled from lack of food. Her once-wavy hair now crinkled like dried twigs. One of her arms rested lightly around his neck while the other was bruised and shriveled. Her eyes drifted closed and her cracked lips moved wordlessly.

The last time he'd seen her had been as she fell away from the window of the Tower of Eternal Starlight during those fateful final moments of Crow Tallin. She'd called to him, and then she vanished and he'd been alone. Alone and trapped within another person's life. Suffering for choices that became his own.

Descending the long spiral stairs with Pomella in his arms, Sim stepped over the unconscious body of an armored Shieldguard. The solider had been one of several he'd had to dispatch in order to reach Pomella's cell.

A streak of light, trailing silver and gold dust behind it, zoomed up the stairwell, buzzing around Sim and Pomella in circles. A wave of surprise and joy filled him. It was either Hector or Ena. Sim had never been able to tell Pomella's hummingbirds apart. He wondered where the other one was.

The hummingbird's presence stirred Pomella back to wakefulness. "Ena," she whispered.

The clanging of armored soldiers rushing up the stairwell caught his attention. His eyes narrowed. Six, by his quick judgment. As long as he held the stair advantage, he could overcome them in these tight confines.

He moved to set Pomella down, seeing no other choice if they wanted to get out of the jail tower.

"No," Pomella said. Putting her hand on his chest. "Walk."

"But the Shieldguards," he protested.

"Walk," she breathed.

His instincts screamed to set Pomella down and engage the fight. She was tired, not fully lucid, and possibly dying.

Yet she might be a High Mystic now, or perhaps something else that he didn't understand.

The hummingbird, Ena, flew ahead, then pulled up to hover and wait for him, clearly indicating he should follow.

Setting his jaw, Sim followed her, carrying Pomella in his arms.

The Shieldguards set upon them, but as they approached, their eyes widened. Sim wondered what it was they saw. He was dressed in an odd mix of his old ranger clothes with bits of Kilpa's clothing added where his old garments had worn out. His trousers, Kilpa's shoes. His vest, and an old gambeson of Kilpa's. And here he was carrying an old woman down the steps like a skeletal bride.

Yet each of the Shieldguards stopped, and watched as he passed, his wary eyes waiting for an attack. None came.

The soldiers set their swords down and the captain removed her helmet. She stared wide-eyed at Pomella. In her eyes Sim could see a flickering halo of light reflected.

Sim's suspicions drained away. His muscles relaxed. Every step he took from there to the exit left peace in its wake.

Mia rocked back and forth on her heels, gripping the laghart bow as though it were a child's comfort blanket. High above, rain clouds gathered, and already a drizzle began to fall. Sim had told her to remain out of sight within the main courtyard of the fortress, but it wasn't easy waiting around. She'd found cover in the stable, which sat across the wide-open courtyard from the prison tower where Amma was being kept.

Ena, her hummingbird, stirred with nervous energy beside Mia. The tiny fay had appeared shortly after Mia had brought Sim and Nabiton into the fortress by merging with Rion. Her brother had only grumbled a little when she'd instructed him to go into the fortress and wait for her to join him.

A sudden commotion startled her. Six Shieldguards, clanging loudly in their armor and weapons, charged toward the prison tower. Sim was inside there, too, and they'd be trapped.

"Go," she told Ena. "Warn them."

The little hummingbird zoomed away, moving faster than Mia's eyes could track.

"Such a remarkable little familiar," Rion said. "You should get one of those."

"*You're* my familiar!" she snapped back.

Nabiton lurked nearby in the shadows. Mia had briefly considered leaving him behind in the foothills for safety, but she knew
he would've hated that. She understood that all too well. Too
many people in her life assumed she was weak because she didn't
speak. Nabiton had a lifetime ahead of people making those same
assumptions about him. She wouldn't be one of them.

More Shieldguards stationed themselves outside the prison
tower, and others set out to patrol the courtyard. Mia figured they
were safe for the moment, but if one of those patrols found them
before Sim returned . . .

The door to the prison tower opened, and out walked Sim,
carrying Amma. Relief flooded Mia as she saw her grandmother
resting her head against Sim's chest. The older woman stirred, but
even from this distance Mia could see how tired she appeared.

"Well, I'll be buggered," Rion said, pushing off the wall he'd
been leaning against. "He has her."

With a glance at Nabiton, Mia stepped closer to Rion before
whispering, "You need to leave."

"I—what?" Rion said, his face aghast.

"We need a way to escape. But you have to leave the fortress first."

"But what about Amma?" Rion said. "She's my grandmother, too!"

"This isn't a request. I'll be fine."

"How will I get past all those Shieldguards?" Rion said.

Mia didn't have time for his games. Grabbing him by the shoulders, she spun him around. Focusing her attention and energy, she
reached into his back, her hand passing right through his well-cut
traveling cloak. He always loved the dramatic, so she'd indulge him.

Rion gasped as Mia rummaged her hand inside his back. She
found what she'd been searching for and drew forth a pair of
glowing wings. The wings unfurled from Rion's back, wider than
twice his arm width. Silver-and-gold smoke wafted off them.

"Ancestors!" Rion said, his eyes wide. "Why didn't you give me these before?"

"Just hurry!" Mia said. Without thinking, she kissed her brother's cheek. "Be safe." She shoved him away.

Cackling with excitement, Rion tested the wings, which billowed dust all around them and stirred Mia's hair. One, two, three pumps of his wings and Rion was airborne, soaring high above the fortress into the rain clouds.

Her brother dealt with, she turned to see the Shieldguards outside the tower laying their weapons onto the ground. One of them dropped to his knees and touched his forehead to the ground.

Mia didn't know what was happening, but she grabbed Nabiton's hand and ran to Sim and her grandmother. Relief and happiness flooded her at knowing Amma was safe. As Mia approached she understood why the soldiers had put aside their weapons. The Myst pulsed from Amma in an unfathomable fashion that Mia had never experienced before. She could see nothing exceptional with her eyes, but a sense of peace radiated from her grandmother as if she were the sun. An overwhelming sense of pride blossomed within Mia. This was her grandmother. Her master. Her Amma.

But the smile vanished from Mia's face when she saw how wasted the older woman was.

"Mia dear," Amma said when Mia reached out a hand to touch her arm. It was like touching a sand sculpture, and Mia feared that with even a little more pressure her grandmother would dust away.

"What's happening?" Nabiton said. "I hear soldiers."

"We need to go to the northern gate," Sim said, nodding in that direction.

Mia tugged his shirt and pointed south.

He shook his head. "Nothing but trouble that way. Follow me."

They hurried across the courtyard, and Mia marveled at how they weren't stopped by Shieldguards. Hope, like the rising sun, rose within Mia. Perhaps they would make it out safely after all.

They just needed to give Rion time to get far enough away from the fortress before they could merge with him and join him in the nearby wilderness.

No sooner had that thought crossed her mind when the entire courtyard exploded.

The jolting explosion woke Pomella from the trance-like sleep she'd been in. Sim carried her still, and he twisted toward the ongoing commotion.

When he'd angled her enough to see, her heart sank.

Oxillian rose from the courtyard, his massive body assembling from the cobbles and dirt that the fortress was made of. But the shape he assumed was unfamiliar to Pomella. Rather than the gentle Green Man she knew, he appeared as a stone terror, with a long tail and protruding spikes along his spine. His face was more laghart than human, and he walked on four legs rather than two.

Stones rolled into place, completing the torso and tail and thick limbs. Thousands of pebbles clustered together to form his snouted face, which had a menacing expression upon it. Brightly polished stones gleamed for eyes and teeth, and a whipcord tongue of dirt and rock snapped out.

He roared and Pomella heard a laghart-like hiss within that terrible scream.

"Put me down, Sim," she said, her breath still wispy.

Sim's scowl told her he didn't think that was the best idea, and Pomella admitted she might be more frail than she realized. But there was little choice at the moment.

"Please," she said, and this time managed to put some strength behind the word.

He complied but kept his hand nearby to steady her. She was glad he did because she wavered and nearly fell once she put her weight on her legs.

"Pomella," he warned.

Mia wore a concerned look on her face, too.

"I'm fine," Pomella declared, and pushed his hand away. She straightened her back, and oh, by the Saints, how she creaked. But despite the storm clouds she could feel the sun shining this day. She breathed in life, breathed in the Myst. Her muscles firmed and her bones hardened. The song from her Mystwalk still echoed in her awareness.

She took a step toward Oxillian, and for a moment she was back in that place beyond the physical world, where time and place dissolved. The fortress became a mountain, a plain, an ocean, a void of ice. It cycled, endlessly, becoming and unbecoming. This place in all its incarnations revealed itself to her as a single, flawless moment. The people around her cycled as well, young and old at once.

Mia, in particular, caught her attention. She shone like Pomella had never seen before, full of untapped energy. Glowing wings surrounded her, and a nimbus of light encircled her head. Pomella's heart burst with love for her granddaughter and the way in which her potential had begun to truly blossom at last.

Pomella brought herself back, not allowing herself to be released from the immediate need of *this* moment. Facing Oxillian, she took another step, then another, and soon she was moving in a way familiar to her aged body.

Wisely, Sim and Mia didn't try to stop her.

Ena hummed beside her, adding to her strength. "Find my staff," she said to the bird.

Ena blazed away, leaving a trail of silver and gold.

"Ox!" Pomella called, but it came out as a hoarse croak. She wet her lips and swallowed to get moisture in her throat, then called again, "Oxillian!"

Only one other time had Pomella seen the Green Man appear in a terrifying stone form. Once, long ago, in the mountain cave at the summit of MagDoon, during her third apprentice Trial, he'd been lured there and trapped. In that conflict he'd taken on the form of the mountain, and impaled a man, letting the victim's blood drain down his stone arms.

Now, as she shuffled forward, missing her Mystic staff more than ever for its steadying presence, Pomella looked up at the Green Man, her lifelong friend, as he turned his terrible attention onto her.

Pomella hoped Ena could find her Mystic staff soon.

Ena.

She is Ena.

Fast, and she is there.

Wait, pause.

Pomella.

"Find my staff."

Ena.

She is Ena. She is fast.

Find the staff.

Fast.

Blur-buzz the world flies.

Sim and Nabiton and Mia and Ox and others.

Fast by they pass.

Wait, pause.

Find the staff.

It hums.

Hums like Pomella.

Close.

Fast, and she is there.

Fast again, and there she is.

Closer.

Long fast. Circle.

Past the walls.

Into the window.

Dodge–dip the guards.
Ena.
She is Ena.
Wait, pause.
A Mystic.
Like Quentin–Kilpa.
But female.
Like Ena.
Not Hector.
Hector is strong.
Hector is gone.
Ena is sad.
Always sad.
Ena.
She is Ena.
Pomella.
Find the staff.
It is there.
Fast and she is there.
Iron!
Iron on the female–Quentin–Kilpa.
Circle.
Swing.
Fast.
Up.
Circle.
Iron is danger.
Iron pushes her away.
Iron makes her slow.
Ena is fast.
Circle.
Slice.
Blood on female–Quentin–Kilpa.

"It's hers! Kill it!"
Hunter now.
Hunter more.
Hunters three.
Iron more.
Ena is fast.
Up.
Iron in many places.
Find the staff.
Risk.
Hector did risk.
Hector is gone.
Ena is sad.
Always sad.
Ena.
Ena risk.
Pomella.
Ena loves Pomella.
Dive.
Fast and there is Iron.
Spin.
Again.
The staff.
It hums like Pomella.
Hector is strong.
Hector holds staff.
Strong, and he is there.
Ena.
Ena is strong.
Ena loves Hector.
Staff is heavy.
Ena is strong.
Strong, and she is capable.

Lift.
Away.
Iron.
Spin.
Up.
Out window.
Fast and she is there.
To Pomella.
Always to her.
Fast, and she is there.

Oxillian loomed over Pomella. She aged before him in every moment, cycling from maiden to mother to master and back, again and again. So it had been when he first arose in Oakspring to invite her to the Trials.

Her heart pulsed, sending vibrations through her foot into the ground. To him.

Every heartbeat, every pulse, from every person on Moth, resonated through him. So it had been from the start when the first High Mystics summoned him. The waves beat eternally at the shores of his awareness, and the sun warmed every leaf upon the forests and trees of his island body.

But here, now, he saw Pomella for what she was: an invader. One who would destroy the lineage that Hizrith had only begun to build.

"It's me, Ox," Pomella-the-invader said. "Do you know me?"

He surged, rolling his awareness through the soil and stone. He focused on the town of Sentry, miles to the north, through the streets, through the wooden tower, to where his master waited. Hizrith lurked in his mind, and when the master spoke Oxillian echoed his will.

"Pomella AnDone," Oxillian intoned. "Your lineage has ended.

Kelt Apar is no longer the domain of humans. By ancient right preceding your lineage, High Mystic Hizrith now claims this domain. All human Mystics are hereby branded Unclaimed and sentenced to death."

Pomella stepped closer to him. "And what about me? Look at me, Ox. I'm your friend."

It was true, he knew. He loved her, as he'd loved the multitude of people who had lived and died in Kelt Apar. From Abingupa, the first human High Mystic who led the ritual of summoning on the first summer solstice after Brigid's Crow Tallin, to Daravant and Kompai and, of course, lovely Serrabeth, who called him Stumpy and once kissed his nose.

But no matter how he loved Pomella, like he had loved all of them, she was an invader now, and High Mystic Hizrith had made his decree.

"You are declared Unclaimed, and your life is forfeit."

A twinkle of light shone from a nearby gate, followed by a streak of light that flew across the courtyard. It came to Pomella, spun once, twice around her, and settled in her hand.

A Mystic staff dropped into her hand and her heartbeat quickened.

"Forgive me," Oxillian said, and slammed his stone claw down upon her.

Sim cried out as the stone Guardian smashed his fist onto Pomella. Although she stood only an arm's length away, he couldn't reach her. The ground heaved, rounding the stones beneath his feet and pushing him back, causing him to tumble.

Oxillian towered over the place Pomella had been standing. His massive stone fist had pulverized the courtyard. Sim's heart wrenched. There was no way somebody could have survived that.

Sheer terror threatened to overcome him. He screamed again and charged toward where Pomella had been, but a wall of stone burst from the ground directly in front of him, blocking his path. He slammed his fist against it, hammering it with all his strength until pain forced him to stop.

"Oxillian!" He spun away from the pillar impeding his path and saw Mia nearby, holding Dauntless. His fingers twitched. Lor Gez's treasure called to him, as it ever had. It was *his*, Brigid's, and if he could unleash its power . . .

More pillars of stone jutted upward around him, striking at random. Oxillian shifted his stance and tried to pull his arms away from the place he'd struck Pomella. Yet his arms remained stuck there. Where his clawed fists had been, the stone glowed red-hot. The color shifting to a seething white causing the stone to melt. Sweat beaded on the side of Sim's face.

Leaping over a Shieldguard who'd been too close to a pillar striking from the ground, Sim ran toward Mia. Her eyes widened in surprise.

But as he reached to grab the bow from the startled young woman, he stopped.

Dauntless had been Brigid's. Not his. And the way Mia held it now, with such familiarity, he couldn't take it from her. The bow had been an instrument of death in Brigid's hands. The lagharts had followed her in large part because she'd claimed the Relic by force from Lor Gez.

He wanted to tell Mia to draw the bow. To *see* the invisible bowstring. To pull it with her mind, drawing its power into focus beneath her fingers. To unleash it in fire, lightning, and death. Even Oxillian might fall beneath its might.

But Mia was not like Brigid. The young woman's ways were more thoughtful, less brash. Brigid was gone. The bow was Mia's now, and who knew if it retained its powers.

"Mia—" he began, but was cut off as the molten stone exploded outward behind him.

Pomella's staff ignited in her hand, surging the Myst around her. Its strength infused her.

As Oxillian's clawed fist rammed down on her, she Unveiled a razor-thin blade that cut an arc upward above her head, then spread as wide as her arms were outstretched.

Enclosed within a bubble of stone, Pomella refocused herself. The timeless vision filled her awareness again, and she saw Oxillian as he had been in all his forms. She saw him as the stone laghart he was now, and the gentle man of flowers he'd been before. He was the island, always had been, without separation.

Now, after a lifetime of training, having breathed and walked the Myst, Pomella experienced what she'd always heard and taught. Just as Oxillian was the island, so she was the Myst. The infinitesimal separation between her and the Myst dissolved, until she was one with it completely.

She exhaled, and the stone around her melted.

With another breath the stone blasted away, leaving her untouched.

She turned her physical eyes again to the present moment—the moment of time perceived by her loved ones, anyway.

Oxillian showed no indication of pain, but surprise played upon his lizard-like face.

"I'm sorry, Ox," Pomella said. "But this needs to be done."

She placed her palm upon the Green Man's stony limb stump, and surged the Myst between them.

Mia pulled Nabiton down with her as stone debris exploded outward from Oxillian. The echoing sound rang all around her.

"What's happening?" Nabiton asked, covering his ears.

Mia wished she knew. Looking up, she could only see the hem of Amma's robes; the rest of her was blocked by Oxillian's stone form.

She took Nabiton's hand and patted it reassuringly.

Sim was nowhere in sight. She had to find him. Rion had nearly arrived at a safe place northwest of Port Morrush. As soon as he was safely outside, she could gather Sim and Amma and they could merge with Rion and escape. She hoped it would be enough distance to at least get a head start before the Shieldguards and whoever else might pursue.

Keeping Nabiton's hand tightly gripped, she hurried them from behind their cover into the open courtyard. But before they'd traveled more than a couple of steps, a group of armed figures emerged from the inner keep. Six Shieldguards surrounded Norana. Another figure, the old Mystic woman with thin metal plates piercing her skin, walked beside the baroness. The Mystic carried a tall iron staff topped by three forked prongs, no thicker than the width of Mia's thumb.

But it was the presence of one other man and his Hunters that captivated most of Mia's attention.

Carn walked behind the baroness's entourage. His leather duster billowed somewhat as he walked. His wide-brimmed hat shaded his eyes.

Mia tried to suppress her rising fear. No matter how many times she tried to put the hateful man out of mind, he haunted her memory and terrified her.

The baroness and her Mystic took in the chaos of the courtyard. Norana spoke a command to her Shieldguards and they tightened their formation around her.

Suddenly Oxillian roared again. His stone arm that had struck Amma had melted off. He arched back, then plunged back into the ground. For a breathless moment, the courtyard lay utterly still. The ground had become restored as if Oxillian had never been there.

Amma stood in the center of the courtyard alone. She leaned heavily on her Mystic staff and labored with her breathing.

From nearby, Sim regained his feet. "Pomella!" he cried, and ran to her.

The ground fountained upward, consuming Amma.

Mia caught sight of Norana, whose face barely contained her fear. The baroness saw Mia. "Arrest her," she said.

The Shieldguards rushed toward Mia.

Through the Myst, Pomella merged with the land, and with Oxillian. He surged against her, trying to overwhelm her completely. She closed her physical eyes and projected her sight beyond her body.

She witnessed herself encased in stone in the middle of the courtyard. Gentle rain slicked the entire fortress. Only Sim stood near her. Mia and others also moved about the courtyard. Shieldguards. Norana. The Iron Mystic. Carn.

Oxillian's physical form was nowhere to be seen, but the ground rippled with his energy and presence. His presence was in her mind; and she, within him.

Pomella had to trust Sim to keep Mia safe. For now, it was all she could manage to keep Oxillian from destroying her. The Green Man—the great ceon'hur, the Guardian of Moth and Kelt Apar—hammered her with his power. The entire might of the island rode within his assault.

"Free yourself, Ox," Pomella said to him. "You need not be bound to anybody."

Oxillian punched the stone beneath her physical feet, trying to crush her.

Pomella Unveiled, and Oxillian's strike dispersed harmlessly before it reached her body.

"I don't believe you want to destroy me," she said. She spoke through her parched physical throat, knowing Ox could hear her.

The ground shook, gathering for another attack. Distantly, Pomella was aware of her body leaning on her Mystic staff.

Oxillian had supreme command of the ground. She could not overcome him alone. She needed strength from elsewhere.

Far below the fortress, down the cliffside that it sat atop, the ocean twinkled, oblivious to the assault raging nearby.

Expanding her awareness again, Pomella reached into the ocean, to the water that resided outside Oxillian's control. She pulled upon it like the moon commands the tides. From the air she pulled wind, gathering and gathering until a gale-force cyclone circled beyond the Port Morrush harbor.

Pomella breathed, and brought the wind and water together, forming a wall that surged skyward, higher than the clifftop upon which the fortress rested.

Back in her body, she raised her free hand, her injured one, palm upward, and lifted her feet off the ground, breaking her body's direct connection to Oxillian.

The wall of wind and water stood poised, ready for her to command.

Opening her physical eyes briefly, she found Sim standing beside her hovering body.

"I'll protect you," Sim said.

Again, all of existence *cycled* before her eyes. The shifting and eroding land. The moving stars. The dying humans who turned to dust, only to rise again in new forms. The land changed. The world changed. But Sim remained as he was now. Forever youthful. A man with many pasts but no future. Timeless in his own way. His song, like one that echoed from the chorus of stars in the inverted abyss of stars, sang in harmony with hers. A low chant, like a *huzzo*. His voice, calling her name. His heart, calling hers.

"Together then," Pomella replied.

The ranger nodded, twirled the walking stick in his hand, and a blade leaped outward.

Closing her eyes, Pomella brought the water and wind to her body. It shaped itself around her, taking on her physical characteristics. Her skin was seawater, flowing beside the currents of her energy. The wind became her hair and gown, shining with light and ocean foam. A water staff appeared in her hand, shaped identically to the physical one she carried. She added a rickety lantern to hang from the serpent's mouth like she'd carried on her Mystwalk.

Ena rushed to her, encircling both her physical body and the new flowing shape laid atop it.

Pomella placed her awareness into this ethereal form and smiled at Ena. Then she leaped skyward away from the fortress, away from her body and those she could bring danger to. She let herself blend with the sky, letting the rain add to this new incarnation. Below her, MagDoon and the Ironlows stretched north to south, their peaks reaching out in silent salute to her.

Ena followed beside her, gold and silver dust streaking behind her.

Pomella set her watery form to the ground somewhere in the mountains, miles to the north of the fortress. The moment her water feet touched the ground, Oxillian erupted beneath her, taking his stone laghart form.

He roared, sweeping claws at her. Free of her aged physical body, Pomella leaped out of the way. Ena circled her, flying faster than a stone spinning on a string.

Growling, Oxillian merged back into the ground but rose again, this time far larger. He stood hundreds of times the height of a person, as tall as a hill, and struck down at her. Pomella let herself disperse, puffed away like a rain cloud on a summer day.

Ena zoomed away, spiraling upward faster than the wind, and hovered just out of Oxillian's great reach. Pomella pulled the moisture and water and air together to reassemble herself. With an amused smile, she took the form of her teenage self, just as Oxillian knew her when they first met.

"I will not harm you, Ox," Pomella said. "And you cannot hurt me. I am beyond you now."

The massive Oxillian submerged again, restoring the land, then rose a third time, pulling the Ironlows with him. He rose higher and higher, made of mountains. Entire swaths of forest tumbled in upon themselves to form his arms. Deep soil folded upon itself, shaping itself into musculature. A tail swung back and forth, covered in trees and mountain peaks. Oxillian, miles long and tall, roared and Pomella was certain the sound carried to the Continent and beyond. Waves of energy quaked outward from the epicenter where Ox had risen. Structures fell and more distant mountains buckled. Dust bloomed across the island like thick fog.

Pomella's heart ached as she thought of the people and animals and fay lost in this transformation. How many mountain villages, dwellings, nests, and burrows had been consumed?

Pomella rose into the air until she hovered in front of his titanic face. Oxillian's chest heaved as though breathing hard. His eyes—made of boulders pulled from the deepest bones of the island—glared at Pomella.

"This has to end," Pomella said.

"I cannot let you live," Oxillian said. River streams fell from the wide pools of his eyes like waterfalls of tears. "Thus am I commanded by High Mystic Hizrith."

With immutable strength, Oxillian spun, his form slow but unstoppable, trampling even more ground and lives. As he gained momentum, his mountain-spiked tail thundered toward Pomella.

"Then I come for your master," Pomella said.

She Unveiled the Myst, pulling its energies across the sky. From the rain clouds she consolidated their moisture and wind. From the distant ocean she pulled unfathomable amounts of water, arcing it high, high over Moth. All who stood upon the island surely witnessed the soaring tidal wave that flew above their heads, twinkling reflected light from the sun.

Like in her Mystwalk, she was the fulcrum. The center of land and sea and sky. She became the water. She became the energy. She became the command she sang out, striking Oxillian with the full force of the elements she'd gathered.

The ocean and sky crashed into Oxillian's mountain, piercing him. Pomella, embodying the Myst itself, pressed harder. Oxillian resisted, but again she pushed. He screamed at her in defiance, quaking the island. Pomella's assault blasted away Oxillian's soil. Blades of wind and water cut through him like the finest sword cuts.

Finally, the mighty ceon'hur tumbled backward, pulverized by the force of Pomella's strikes. But as he crashed, he merged back into the ground, restoring the mountains and rivers and land, just as he had done countless times in his normal way. Where the Green Man walked, he left no damage. So it had always been.

For the rest, Pomella redirected the energy again, sending the remaining water to fall as rain across the island. For once, she mused, she didn't mind a little shower falling on Moth.

With a thought, she dispersed her form and let it blend with the clouds.

Far away, atop the Sentry clock tower, Hizrith watched the events unfold through the eyes of the Stone Dragon. His Mystic staff, which contained fragments of Seer Brigid's, lay across his lap.

He watched in stunned silence as Pomella struck the ceon'hur down. Hizrith's connection to the Stone Dragon snapped away as the great creature fell.

Hizrith stood. "Stone Dragon!" he called. "Rise again!"

The ceon'hur did not answer.

The trees surrounding Sentry began to sway. A blast of wind and a crashing roar swept from the south, thundering across the town. Hizrith flinched as the clock tower windows rattled. The entire tower groaned.

"Master?" Kumava said, coming to stand beside him. She scented of fear.

Sudden rain fell upon the windows. One moment it was a drizzle and the next a torrent, soaking all of Sentry. Muffled cries of confusion from beyond the large window sounded from guards and commoners alike.

The rain gave way to falling fire. A ball of burning rock blazed downward, smashing into the top of the clock tower. The roof above Hizrith exploded.

Hizrith lurched forward, smashing his face upon the window. Pain roared across his entire body. Fire and blazing timber rained around him.

Kumava screamed. She hung over the edge of a destroyed wall, clinging to a beam.

Outside the cracked and bloodied window, the city seemed to spin. Somehow, the ground rushed up. Hizrith's eyes widened. The tower was *falling*.

Hizrith summoned the Myst and blasted out the remainder of the window and leaped. Pain stabbed in his side, ripping open a wound. His body was far from youthful, but in that moment the rush gave him strength.

As he fell, he Unveiled more of the Myst to cushion his landing.

He collapsed onto the ground far enough from the tower to avoid being crushed. Screams from both lagharts and humans filled the town.

But it was not over.

Flaming boulders streaked though the sky. They had come from the Stone Dragon's shattered body, directly toward him in his tower. A portion of his mind marveled at the mastery required to complete such an assault. If this truly was Pomella's doing, from halfway across the island, then her power had become considerably more than he had ever known.

The stones flamed down, pulverizing the clock tower.

"Kumava!" he cried.

Finally, the bombardment ceased. The smell of sulfur filled his nostrils and heat blazed from the burning tower and nearby buildings.

The rain continued to fall, harder than ever, snuffing the flames and sparing neighboring buildings from damage.

He spun to the south, staff in hand, and focused once more on the land. The ceon'hur's vision returned. Shattered though the creature might've been, he could not be destroyed.

Through the Stone Dragon's eyes he saw the courtyard of the fortress. Pomella's physical body hovered above the ground. A young man with yellowish hair stood guard beside her.

Hizrith smiled. "Strike me all you want," he snarled through the ceon'hur, "but I have another tower!"

He pulled the Myst to himself, gathering it in waves, then commanded the Stone Dragon to shift again, and to carry himself and Kumava to the west and south, to a wide clearing where a stone tower with a green conical top awaited.

The ceon'hur obeyed, and engulfed Hizrith and Kumava into the ground, carrying them to Kelt Apar.

TWENTY-NINE

THE MYST

Pomella knew the moment that Hizrith left Sentry. The air he'd been breathing changed. The space his body occupied voided. The rain she'd brought to Moth no longer fell upon his scales.

Awareness of her own body was distant now, or at least no closer than that of every other living being upon Moth. Her mind and heart reeled from the scale of it all. She had only to open her mind a bit more and she knew she'd sense people beyond her island. Distantly, she could already feel Harmona, living her life in Qin, halfway around the world.

The whole world still cycled through its ages. As Pomella breathed, so did all of time. This was where the great masters and Saints went when their lives ended. But a lifetime of studying and meditating on the Myst could not prepare her for the experience of awakening to the realization that she was inseparable from it. Where she had thought of herself as a drop of water her entire life, she'd been the ocean and the rain and their entire united process.

Her heart beat, and every world that had ever been, merged or separated, aged with her. The idea of *Pomella*, a woman from Moth, dissolved and returned. Like the tides endlessly lapping at the shores of time, so, too, her immediate awareness ebbed and rose.

How did this happen? Was she dying?

No. This was something else. Her old body, as weak as it might've been, continued. Rather than dying, she was becoming supremely alive.

The Deep Myst and Saints and all she'd ever loved and cherished called to her. It was there, within her grasp. She could merge with them, forever becoming part of them. She could dissolve her physical body into energy as Lal had once done and become an eternal embodiment of the Myst in a new way.

"Not yet," she whispered to herself. Sim and Mia still needed her. Moth still needed her, but in a different way than she'd previously understood.

She shifted her thoughts and found Hizrith. Rain fell upon him once more. He inhaled air in a new location. He'd gone to Kelt Apar.

Pomella breathed and formed a body of rain and air beside the monument of past masters in the clearing of her lifelong home. Through the timeless eyes of the Myst she saw every master, human and laghart, standing there, waiting and smiling. She walked among them, holding out her hands for them to touch. It was merely the wind and energy passing through her water hands, but still she experienced their warmth and presence and love.

Saint Abingupa, with his reserved smile. Saint Serrabeth, with her radiant eyes. *Zurnta* Mylezka, licking the air with a calm and knowing demeanor.

Lal and Yarina stood at the far edge of the clearing. They bowed to Pomella as she passed. As one, all of the past masters streaked into Pomella's heart.

Her feet-of-rain stepped out onto the wide Kelt Apar lawn and approached the central tower. She focused her vision on the present form that the land presented—the same as it would appear to her physical eyes. The rainstorm fell upon Kelt Apar's burned-out grass and willow tree and ran in long rivulets down the side of the cold tower wall.

Hizrith waited for her in front of the tower.

Mia and Nabiton collapsed behind a crumbling stable, trying to catch their breath.

"I have no idea what's happening," Nabiton said between gulps of air. "Other than you yanking me everywhere and running. Are we safe?"

Mia risked a glance past the pile of wooden debris toward the courtyard. Amma and Sim were outside of her angle of vision, but she also couldn't see the Shieldguards they'd been running from. She squeezed Nabiton's hand to reassure him. Her heart felt as though it would burst from her chest.

Somehow, they'd avoided capture, but every time she thought she saw a way out, there was another cluster of Shieldguards or Hunters.

Rion was clear of the fortress now and waiting for them a safe distance away. She could merge with him, but she had to get Sim and Amma first.

Peering toward them, she couldn't see an easy way to reach them without stumbling into Shieldguards or Hunters. Sim had been a blur, attacking anybody who got too close to Amma. She hovered above the ground, her eyes closed in some sort of trance. If Rion were with her, he'd probably say something about how only their family would be ridiculous enough to have a grandmother who floated above the—

A firm hand yanked her back by the hair. She cried out in pain. Hearing her cry, Nabiton called out, "Mia!"

Warm breath puffed across her face. "Found yah!" Carn snarled, and threw her back into the courtyard.

Mia rolled across the uneven ground. Pain stabbed her ribs and head. She pushed herself up in time to see Nabiton lurch toward Carn, but the older Hunter shoved him out of the way. "I'll deal with yah in a moment, traitor," Carn said.

The Hunter twirled a glaive in his fist as he approached Mia. "I liked you, Mia," he said. "I thought we had something. But I hear yah ruined things for Hizrith, and put the agreement with Norana at risk. You've become more trouble than yer worth."

"Mia!" Nabiton called out. He'd found his feet but stood there with his onkai unsheathed, spinning around, not knowing where she was in all the chaos and sounds filling the courtyard.

Carn towered over her. Rain dripped from his wide-brimmed hat. Mia scrambled to her feet, but Carn kicked her hard in the chest, knocking her back to the ground. He leaped at her, swinging his glaive. Mia rolled out of the way just in time. The glaive chipped the stone where she'd lain.

Far outside the fortress, Mia sensed Rion waiting. All she had to do was close her eyes for a moment and she'd merge with him. She'd be free of Carn and his frenzied attacks.

Carn swung the glaive again. Mia tried to spin out of the way, but the iron grazed her back. She screamed as pain flared from her ribs to her shoulder.

She staggered. Rion waited, but so did her death.

Her sliced back still faced toward Carn. She could see Sim and Amma now that she'd moved past the fallen stonework.

Sim patrolled around Pomella, his onkai raised in defense of anything or anyone that might approach Amma.

Pomella still floated above the ground, her peaceful face tilted upward with eyes closed.

Mia dropped to her knees.

Looking back over her shoulder, she saw Carn approach her like a predator preparing for the final kill.

The laghart master bowed low to Pomella. "You have become something extraordinary," Hizrith said, speaking the laghart language. Within the Myst, languages and all other barriers melted away. "I am humbled to be in your presence."

Beside Hizrith stood another laghart Mystic. Pomella sensed wondrous potential within her. An apprentice, she knew. For a moment time cycled again and she saw them both turn to ash and rise again, over and over.

The wind carried Pomella's voice. "Not humble enough to yield Kelt Apar."

"Surely now, great mistress," Hizrith said, "your experience is beyond the limits of time. Do you not see it? The endless cycle of human and laghart lineages? Turn your gaze to when humans drove us from these lands. How they murdered us. Seer Brigid saw as you do now. She saved us by sending us across the sea to Lavantath and promised we would one day return. My coming is not about conquering. It is about fulfilling the promise of the Myst."

Pomella did see. She witnessed all Hizrith spoke of in its unfiltered truth. The endless cycle of violence between humans and lagharts dated to eons before the Dragon Kings. It all became a part of her.

She snapped back to the present, unwilling yet to dissolve into the eternity of experience.

"That cycle will end, Hizrith."

"My lineage will bring peace that the rest of the world can learn from."

"No," she said. "It won't. You don't have the capacity to lead the world as you envision. Not in this weaving of your journey. Live again. Try again."

Hizrith's tongue snapped out. Angry energy gathered around him. Conflicted confusion swirled around the apprentice standing beside him.

"Do you not understand?" Hizrith snarled. "See it! You defeated my Stone Dragon, but you cannot destroy him when he is everywhere!"

He slammed his staff onto the ground and Oxillian emerged from the ground, towering high like a rising mountain. He took the form of the laghart-like creature, and Pomella understood Hizrith's name for him.

"Ceon'hur!" Hizrith commanded. "Seize her friends. Seize every human. Grasp them!"

Pomella briefly opened her weary physical eyes back at the fortress. The ground rumbled as claws of stone burst forth beneath every person present, gripping them in a stone-tight fist. Mia and Sim struggled and screamed. Nabiton cried out to Mia. Even Carn, who had been stalking toward Mia, cried out in surprise as a fist of stone wrapped itself around him and held fast. His glaive fell to the ground.

She witnessed the same everywhere across Moth. Every child and mhathir. Every person, Touched or Unclaimed or noble, found themselves in Oxillian's fist.

"Yield," Hizrith said. "Leave Moth forever and do not interfere, or I will kill them all now. Every human, regardless of class. You spent your life seeking that equality, and now you will have it."

Pomella's rain body stepped forward. "Hizrith . . ."

"Move again and they die! Decide now!"

Pomella hesitated, and a tiny seed of fear crept into her. Her rain body wavered. She sensed the heart in her physical chest thundering.

But she released that fear one last time. If she could release her daughter, her husband, her friends, her master, and her own desires, then she could do this. Oxillian could and would destroy every human on Moth if Hizrith commanded it. She could strike the laghart master dead, but his dying command would trigger the ceon'hur in the same way.

The present world dissolved, and she became one with the Deep Myst. All life appeared to her as weaves of energy, temporary and short-lived beside the scale of time. What was this petty conflict beside that? What were these lineages they clung to? These labels of caste and name? The squabbles lasting mere decades or centuries? Beside the expanse of all times and places, it was nothing.

In this supremely true experience, there was only the Myst, and she was one with it completely.

"Ceon'hur," Hizrith said, "kill them."

The command spread from the laghart master into the soil of Moth. It spread outward across the island. Oxillian, obedient to his master, heard the command and acted.

Pomella breathed.

Hizrith possessed the name of the island and commanded Oxillian through it. Within Pomella's oldest memory, beside the Creekwaters, he'd learned the Mystic name of the island and recorded it into *The Book of Songs*. But now Pomella knew a deeper name. One that encompassed Moth and more. Through the song of her loved ones, the song of all times and places, she had *become* the name.

She knew the name of the Myst itself.

The name of the Myst, the label that humans and lagharts gave to the primordial force that manifested all phenomena, couldn't truly be spoken. Or known intellectually. It could only be experienced at the deepest, purest form of existence.

"Good-bye, Ox," Pomella whispered.

Looking into herself, into the essential nature of the universe, through the lens of all her experiences, Pomella *changed* the name of the Myst.

A sense of final relief radiated outward from the Green Man. Oxillian's body crumbled.

In the same moment, Pomella's water body splashed to the ground.

The fist of stone clutching Mia crumbled like dust. But rather than merging back into the ground like Oxillian normally did, it simply tumbled into an inert pile of rock and dirt.

She tried to scramble free of the rubble, but her back still blazed with pain. The pouring rain and dirt had already become mud, which further hindered her effort.

Meanwhile, Carn had managed to free himself from the stone that clutched him. Enraged, he screamed and knocked the rocks loose.

Nearby, Nabiton struggled to free himself from the stone.

"Rion," Mia muttered, calling to her brother.

But there was no answer.

An aching hollowness yawned wide within her. More terrifying than the deadly Hunter or the rampaging Green Man was the fact that Mia couldn't sense her brother.

"Rion!" she gasped more loudly, desperately trying to be heard.

Carn swiped rain off his pants and picked up his glaive. His face was a mask of focused anger.

Mia reached out with all her energy and awareness to Rion, trying to merge with him. But nothing happened. The link between them no longer existed. The winds that connected their thoughts and hearts were simply gone.

"Mia!" Nabiton called. "Where are you?"

Carn snarled at Mia, then strode toward Nabiton and lifted the glaive for the killing blow.

Mia had to do something. With Rion nowhere to be found—

"Carn, no!" she shouted.

The Hunter stopped. "So, you do have a voice."

He approached her. His murderous glaive dripped with rainwater.

Mia struggled to free herself one more time.

"Rion!" she called again, trying to be heard by her brother.

Carn's eyes widened. "How do you know that name—"

A bloody onkai blade burst from Carn's chest. Behind him, Nabiton stood in a wide stance, his eyes downcast and arms spread wide. He'd struck out, blind but focused, and found his mark.

Carn tried to turn and see his attacker but could not. He fell to the ground, and Nabiton yanked the onkai free.

The grizzled Hunter collapsed, his dead eyes staring past Mia.

With a grunt of pain, Mia freed herself from the mound of stone holding her and limped to Nabiton.

"Mia," Nabiton said. "My love."

"Nabiton," she whispered for him to hear.

To Hizrith, it was as though a dark cloud passed in front of the sun, muting the beauty of the world. The wind ceased to speak. The land no longer pulsed with life. The trees slumbered once more.

Pomella's water body vanished, and the ceon'hur crumbled.

"Stone Dragon!" Hizrith commanded. "Rise! Obey me!"

Nothing except the rain answered him.

Snarling, Hizrith Unveiled the Myst.

Nothing happened. He reached again for the Myst, but it was as though there was nothing to reach for anymore. A hollow emptiness filled him. He felt exceedingly withered.

"Kumava," Hizrith hissed. He turned to his apprentice. With his aged eyes and the rain, he struggled to see her. The rain dampened her scent, further concealing her from him.

"The Myst," Kumava said. "It's . . . gone."

A profound sense of fear clutched Hizrth's heart. "No," he said, shaking his head. His tongue flicked out, trying desperately, instinctively, to taste the Myst. "No! Hemosavana! Come to me!"

But the mighty bird did not come to him.

He whirled around, his old body lurching with pain at the sudden movement. "What's happened! Where is—"

A dagger rammed into his heart. He looked down, and saw Kumava's pale blue claw holding the weapon. He looked up at her in shock.

"This is no longer your island or world," Kumava said. "The *kanta* will build without you." She slowly pressed the dagger deeper.

The last thing Hizrith saw as his life ended was that his apprentice's pupils were not slitted, but rounded.

Pomella drifted in and out of consciousness. In brief moments her eyes opened to see a courtyard in chaos. Strong arms held her, but before she could see whose they were she drifted into unconsciousness once more. Mia was close, as well, and others she knew.

Oxillian's consciousness dissolved, and for an instant she cradled all his power and awareness before she funneled it back into the ground. A new Guardian would rise again when the time was right.

For now, though, she had to rest. To sleep.

She closed her physical eyes and awoke as the universe itself.

EPILOGUE

TIMELESS

On the island of Moth, under subdued rainy skies, a party of Murk dwellers led by Riccan the hunter-gatherer entered Kelt Apar. Now devoid of its namesake's power, Oxillian's Wall crumbled beneath its own weight, leaving wide expanses where Riccan and his assortment of Touched and Un-claimed individuals could knock down the iron fence behind it.

There they found Kumava, soaking from the rain, with her claw and robes only partially washed clean of her master's blood. In ex-change for their sparing her life, she offered them Hizrith's body and a true accounting of what had occurred. She promised, too, to journey with a human escort to Sentry in order to command the laghart army to stand down.

When Mia arrived three days later, accompanied by Nabiton and Sim, Kambay and the other Mystics awaited them. Already camps had sprung up across the wide dead lawn. The remains of the once-cozy cabins had been claimed, including Amma's old house and its garden. The fay were still present, but they no longer glowed with silver or golden light. They appeared as solid as any-thing else in the world, and did not vanish. They flew and scam-pered around, undaunted by the Murk dwellers who had come to claim the land. It seemed to Mia that perhaps the fay and humans could live in harmony after all.

"The central tower is no longer locked," Kambay said as they approached it. "I preserved what I could inside, but eager scavengers still had their way."

"What of Mistress Vivianna?" Nabiton asked.

Kambay looked from Nabiton to Mia. He shook his head. "We found her body. Her face was as serene as I've ever seen."

As sad as that news was to Mia, a different fear remained with her. She glanced around the grounds, irrationally hoping to see Rion. For three days she'd called to him, searched for him in her mind and dreams. But those dreams were merely the normal experiences of restless slumber. He was gone, taken along with the Myst and her grandmother.

Mia sighed quietly to herself. She doubted she would ever find her brother again. She looked back at the plain covered wagon slowly trudging along behind her. Sim walked beside it. Amma slept inside. Her body still breathed, although faintly, and she was otherwise unresponsive. Nobody had seen Ena since Oxillian's final attack.

"What of Norana?" Nabiton asked.

"She will stand trial by the Murk," said Riccan, the man Kilpa had introduced to Mia nearly a month ago after she'd fled Kelt Apar.

Kambay nodded. "More changes are upon us. What began with Crow Tallin has finally come to fruition."

No, Mia thought to herself with another glance at the wagon. It had begun when her grandmother first came to Kelt Apar.

The rain continued for another four days, although it fell less intensely than the day at the fortress. More people arrived from all across Moth. Word spread quickly that the Mystics were now powerless. Among those who walked through the newly fallen Wall were Higren and Gonlen, who had assisted Mia and Nabiton in Sentry.

No sooner had they arrived than they left again quickly with Riccan and Kambay to return Kumava to the laghart army.

Mia and Nabiton stayed alone in the tower with Sim as he kept vigil over Amma in the uppermost chamber. A handful of brave Murk dwellers attempted to force them out, but one glance from Sim's hardened eyes and they backed down.

Most of the library had been looted and Mia could find nothing in any of the remaining books that hinted at what could have caused the Myst to simply vanish. She meditated often, trying to find her way in the dark to a place where she could sense the rise of energy that heralded the Myst. But in every instance, she found nothing.

Outside the upper chamber's lone window, Mia watched the trials and political debates occur on the muddy Kelt Apar grounds. Although she couldn't hear what was said, she could feel the debates and arguments being shouted back and forth. She wished Rion were there. He would've loved to mill about all those people, noble and common alike, and report back to her what he heard.

Instead, Mia listened alone.

On the ninth day since Mia arrived, the people of the Murk, Touched and Unclaimed alike, with additional representatives from Sentry and Port Morrush and Enttlelund and the northern villages, executed Norana. Elona, the oldest and last remaining ruler on Moth, ceded her power. A governance was formed to determine the shape of Moth's future.

Mia paid scarce attention to it. That night, Amma stopped breathing.

In the deepest hours of the night, when Mia finally slept, Sim approached the bed Pomella lay upon. Mia sat in a cushioned chair beside her, her hand resting beside her grandmhathir's.

Slowly, Sim bent over Pomella and placed the side of his head against her chest. He remained there for a long time, eyes closed, not moving. He waited with the patience of a mountain and finally he heard it. The faintest *thump*, like the falling of a single raindrop upon a pond.

Her heart. Pomella lived.

Easing his arms gently beneath his lifelong friend, Sim lifted Pomella from the bed and carried her out of the room. Mia did not stir. He left Pomella's oaken staff behind.

Nabiton stood near the bottom of the stairway, blocking the tower's lone exit. Sim approached him silently.

Nabiton reached out a hand and touched Sim's shoulder to identify him. He found Pomella, too.

"I expected you would take her eventually," Nabiton said.

"I've left the other onkai for you in the upper chamber," Sim said. "I no longer need it."

Nabiton inclined his head in thanks. He paused a moment, choosing his words. His hands remained on Sim's chest.

"Tell me," the younger man said. "Do you still see the path?"

Sim looked beyond the tower door to the grass beyond. Only the night called to him in a quiet voiceless song.

"No," he said.

Nabiton's face fell. "Then the Myst must truly be gone."

"No," Sim mused. "The Myst is there. But now it's like the path. You have to find it."

"What'll become of the Mystics?" Nabiton asked. "I fear for Mia. She lost something besides her ability to Unveil, though I don't yet understand what it is."

"The Mystics will adapt with time," Sim said. "And so will Mia. I suspect she had a unique method of Unveiling. But things are different now, and that is lost to her. Take care of each other."

Nabiton placed his palm over his heart and bowed.

Sim carried Pomella over the threshold of the central tower for the last time. He carried her across the charred lawn, beyond the remains of the Wall, and into the Mystwood.

He carried Pomella east through the Murk. Nobody witnessed them even though they passed directly through homesteads and busy roads. They traveled as though they were light and wind, leaving a wake of peace in their passing. Countless mounds of earth and rock stood everywhere like cairns marking the place where Oxillian had gripped every human across Moth.

Northward their journey took them, along the foothills of the Irownlows Mountains. Cold, late-autumn winds bit at Sim's skin, but he no longer sensed them. At last, they came to the mountain known as MagDoon. The mountain of legend.

Sitting at ease upon a boulder at the base of the long path winding to the summit was Shevia.

The old woman wore a hooded white cloak, trimmed in dark red. Seeing Sim and Pomella, she stood and removed the hood. The wind caught her silver hair.

"She lives?" Shevia asked.

Sim nodded.

"She changed the name of the Myst," Shevia continued. "I knew the moment it happened."

"Can you still Unveil the Myst?" Sim said.

"No," Shevia said, "a new age is upon us now. It will be a long, long time before somebody discovers the new way."

"How did you know we would come here?" Sim said.

Shevia approached and touched Pomella's cool face. "My friend, Sitting Mother, led me here long ago," she said. She stroked Pomella's hair. "Farewell," she whispered. To Sim she said, "And farewell to you, Guardian."

With a nod of understanding, Sim carried Pomella up the slope of MagDoon.

With every step, time slipped away from Sim. The seasons blended to one. Snow fell, then melted. The sun rose, then fell. The moon eclipsed. Other travelers, human and laghart and fay and the Touched, came and went, passing them on either side of the trail he steadily trudged up. Some wandered as though lost. Some searched deliberately for answers.

But none saw them.

As he crested to the summit's region where a large cave existed, the memory of all his previous lifetimes came to him.

He gazed back across the land, to the distant ocean, and then to the path he'd walked.

No more. This would be his final ascent. As the mountain was timeless, so would he become.

With gentle reverence he laid Pomella down in a hollow in the deepest part of the cave. Countless memories swirled around him.

He kissed her on the forehead. "Together," he whispered, and backed away. A sudden motion caught his attention. Ena, no longer glowing, fluttered into the cave and settled on a rocky outcropping near Pomella. Sim stroked the tiny bird's plumage with a finger, then left the cave.

He emerged and stood at the cavern entrance, eyes up, attentive. His body settled into a comfortable resting stance, and his mind expanded.

The mountain, whose roots went deep to the core of the world and into the heart of existence, welcomed its new Guardian. Mag-Doon covered Sim's legs, his chest, his arms, and his face. Blue eyes became stone.

Time and years passed, and the last ranger lived on as the Guardian to the cave and heir to the might of the former ceon'hur. His body stilled, yet his vision and heart never ceased.

There Sim remained, unyielding and eternal, until the mountain wore away and the world's last memory had long, long faded.

In the years and decades that followed the fall of Kelt Apar, numerous seekers came to MagDoon's summit. Most were turned away by the Guardian, usually with an unseen gentle persuasion, and a few by force. A small handful, the worthiest, found their way past the Guardian and into the depths of the cave.

There came a time, in one particular year, during one particular lifetime, when a woman managed to walk unhindered past the Guardian statue and slip into the cavern on the night of a full moon. Shadows born from the celestial light filled the cave, so the woman lifted her rickety lantern, which hung upon an oaken staff with a snake carved into its top. She pulled back the hood of her patched green cloak revealing curly, short-cropped hair streaked with thin lines of gray. The woman approached the back of the cave and found the person she sought.

Light from the lantern played upon the dusty, hundred-year-old figure sitting upright in the back of the cave. Nearby, a stone hummingbird watched from its perch.

"Beloved grandmother," Mia said, "I've come to see you at last."

Amma's head was bowed as though she slept. Mia slipped to her knees and set the lantern staff on the ground. She bowed and touched her forehead to the ground.

Slowly, Amma tilted her head up. Her eyes remained closed, but a thin silver line emerged across her forehead and spread open, revealing the shining outline of a single eye.

"Ulammia," Amma said. Her voice was as dusty as an empty bowl.

A sense of wonder and power stirred within Mia, a sensation she had not felt for over twenty-two years. She licked her lips.

"Amma, I've come at last."

"Granddaughter," the old woman said. "You warm me."

"Some said you still lived," Mia said, "but I had to see for myself. My children are grown and making their way in the world. I am happy. But I have one question, and if anybody knows, it's you."

"What do you seek?" the old woman asked.

Mia swallowed her fear. "Rion," she said. It was a name she hadn't spoken aloud for years, not even to Nabiton. "When you . . . changed . . . everything, he vanished. Is he gone? Can he be found? And if so, where?"

"He never left you, my beloved," came the reply.

Mia bit her lip to keep the joy and relief from overwhelming her. In all these years, she'd hardly let herself hope that perhaps he could be found again. "I—I made my peace with it," she managed. "But I never said good-bye to him. We never . . . He was just . . . gone."

"He was your way of touching the Myst. Now he lives in a place yet to be found," Amma said. "Release your attachments. Lay claim to nothing and let nothing claim you. Go within yourself. There you will find him."

"Oh, Amma," Mia said, and hugged her.

As her arms wrapped around her grandmother, a surge of peace and love and power raced through her. For a moment she remembered the sensation of Unveiling the Myst, of holding and manipulating the primal forces of the world. For a moment she remembered touching her Amma. To Mia, there was no difference.

When she pulled away, she scrubbed her wet eyes. "But how?" she asked. "I cannot sense the Myst. How can I . . . how can the world find it again?"

"Find your brother within yourself," her grandmother said. "When you do, you will discover something new together. And the world will follow, if you teach them the way."

And so Mia did.

Decades turned to centuries. Centuries to eons. The needle wove lives in and out of a timeless tapestry. The mountain ebbed, its Guardian eroded to little more than a shapeless boulder near a collapsed cave.

And at last, after a thousand thousand lifetimes, when the world had forgotten its own history and cycled anew, a seeker came at last to the cave.

Long had the Saint within the cave waited, residing in stasis while the world outside cycled through the ages. The world had long ago forgotten her name.

The seeker who came carried a bow and a branch, and a cloak of grass. "Beloved Saint," she called, "I am Brigid the Red, Daughter of None but the Woods!"

The seeker reached into her pack and pulled out a branch of fire, which was as long as her foreclaw and bent in two places. She shook it, and it flared to life with a warm, flickering light.

Her fiery orange and red scales glimmered in the torchlight as she approached the Saint sitting in the depths of the cave.

The seeker dropped to her knees, tongue slashing through the darkness to taste the air. "You cannot be dead," the one called Brigid said. "The ceon'hur claimed you livvved!"

The Saint sitting in the cave stirred her awareness. It had only been moments since the last Brigid had come to see her, and moments ago since she herself had been a girl seeking answers in this cave.

"Daughter," said the Saint.

Brigid prostrated herself, her tail swishing behind her. "Beloved Sssaint, I pray for your help. It is sssaid that you are the key to unlocking ancient power."

"Seek the name of the Myst," said the old woman, "and share it."

"But where will I fffind this name you ssspeak of?"

"The Myst lives within all," said the woman. "Leave your bow, cloak, and branch," she commanded. "Revoke your name and quest. Lay claim to nothing and let nothing claim you. Release your attachment. Embrace only the Myst, and all will be found. Now go!"

The woman called Brigid fled, fulfilled her destiny, and returned in the next lifetime.

Again and again.

At the heart of all existence, beyond time, beyond location, where memory and the waking moment overlap, the woman once called Pomella AnDone, the Sitting Mother, the Hummingbird, the Nameless Saint, opened her eyes. Under her gaze the island once known as Moth flourished, drawing to itself more dreamers, more singers, more saints.

She breathed, and all of existence breathed.

She sang, and the chorus of the universe harmonized with her.

ACKNOWLEDGMENTS

Many thanks go to the numerous people who supported me in the writing of this third novel of the Mystic Trilogy.

To Robert Davis, my editor at Tor Books, for actively supporting all my endeavors. Additional thanks to others at Tor, including Tom Doherty, Devi Pillai, Lucille Rettino, Sarah Reidy, Anna Merz, and Rachel Taylor.

Also, to Melissa Frain for her early belief in the series and her ongoing friendship.

Thank you to my agent, Eddie Schneider, as well as to Joshua Bilmes, for their guidance and support.

I'd like to acknowledge the assistance of and offer thanks to Crystal Shelley, who provided services as an authenticity reader for this book.

I'm honored that Mary Robinette Kowal performed the original audiobook narration for the Mystic Trilogy, and I'd like to thank her for her time, talent, and willingness to bring these books to life in a special way.

A special thank-you to my close friend Brad Kane, whose original short story directly inspired "The Snakebite" and "The *Zurnta*" chapters in this book.

As always, the amazing individuals in my writing group helped me get through tough plot holes and other writing challenges. To them, I offer eternal thanks: Laura Sherley, Andrew Wilson, Kevin Dean, Heidi Odell, Nikki Sherley, and DJ Stipe.

Other early readers who provided invaluable feedback on this book include Ruby Petargue, Kris Nedopak, Kris McFunstigate, Brooke Coe, Ryan Coe, Jennifer Johnson, Ellis Johnson, John Monsour, Matthew Showers, Drew McCaffrey, Ellie Raine, Stacey Holditch, Kristina Gruell, Laurie Fox, George Hahn, and the amazing Andrea Stewart, who also provided the cover quote.

I'd like to thank my mother, Joyce, for her unwavering support throughout the years. To my sons, Aidan and Andrew, who were children when I began writing this trilogy and have now grown to become fine young men that I'm immensely proud of. Thank you also to Jennifer Denzel for her longtime encouragement on this grand endeavor.

And a special thank-you to Nicole Stephenson, who stood beside me at every step of this final novel, helping me with everything from line edits to creating space for me to write. Like Tuppleton, you both carried me and sheltered me when I needed it.

At long last, we've come to the end of this tale. Thank you for reading and for being witness to Pomella's journey. Although this book marks a conclusion, I look forward to traveling with you on many adventures yet to come.

Jason Denzel
January 2022